MURDER MOST PUZZLING

Wildcat Publishing Company, Inc.
P.O. Box 366
Greens Farms, Connecticut 06436

First Edition, 1998

Book designed by Irwin Wolf
Cover designed by Gwen Frankfeldt

Library of Congress Cataloging-in-Publications Data
Robinson, Lillian S.
Murder most puzzling: a literary mystery / Lillian S. Robinson
p. cm.
ISBN 0-941968-09-X (hardcover)
I. Title.
PS3568.0312M87   1998
813′.54—dc21   98-4888
CIP

BT 21.45/12.07 8/98

MURDER MOST PUZZLING

A Literary Mystery

LILLIAN S. ROBINSON

WILDCAT PUBLISHING COMPANY, INC.

In Loving Memory
of
Kaela Petrov-Levin
1920–1987
poet, radical, mother, feminist, mentsh

"this body,
like writing, *still standing."*

MURDER MOST PUZZLING

1

＊

SOMEHOW, I MANAGED to suppress the question, *how did I get into this?* until I caught sight of the flimsy plane in which I'd be making the trip to Jaegersville. An electrical storm, the tail-end of a hurricane wreaking considerably more havoc further south, had delayed our takeoff by some hours, and the tarmac in the Philadelphia airport still glistened with rain as I shouldered my carry-on bag for the hike across.

As I edged up the mini-aisle from the entrance in the plane's attenuated tail, I noticed that the seats in the first few rows were turned down.

"Something wrong with these?" I asked redundantly.

"Oh, because of the storm and all [*what all?*] the captain needs your weight near the rear of the aircraft." The flight attendant smiled as if her explanation actually made sense. Reflecting that a truly sensible person would take her weight right off that "aircraft," I chose a more centrally located seat and decided not to think about sinister omens. Once aloft, as they say in Flightspeak, and bouncing along through remnants of rain, I wrenched my mind from contemplation of the term "air pocket," and thought about Becca instead. Not that that provided much comfort.

Three weeks earlier, barely recovered from my Paris-to-San Francisco jet lag, I'd been invited to read my poetry at a feminist arts festival in Pittsburgh the week before Labor Day. To get two honoraria out of the one trip, I'd called my friend Jenny and found she could squeeze me into the schedule of a series she runs in Philadelphia, then called Becca to invite her to one of the readings. Although I asked the switchboard at the college for Professor Parsons' office, a matter-of-fact voice answered "Ebbing Archive."

"Professor Parsons?" I asked again, rather more hesitantly.

"She isn't in today, she's home sick," the voice informed me, and recited another number.

It was Becca who explained that "isn't in today," though literally true, was something of an understatement. She'd been away from her desk for most of the summer, and the diagnosis was now definite. "They give me two to twelve months," she told me. "Yes, I know it sounds like a jail sentence, but I *want* to serve this time. So they start the therapy, the chemo, a week from tomorrow."

While her voice went calmly on, I tried to respond to the announcement with as much grace as she'd put into it and caught myself nodding idiotically into the telephone. I'm supposed to be the punster-in-chief, but little jokes about life sentences and death sentences were beyond me just now. For a moment, it felt as if my voice had gone altogether.

"I want this not to be true," I told her at last. "God, Becca, what can I say?" (*Don't have cancer, Becca. Don't say you'll be dead in a year.*)

"Say? Nothing. Although I must admit *I* said a highly improper word when they told me and shocked the sweet young doctor to the quick. You're right—there's nothing *to* say. But there's something you can do for me."

"What, Becca? Of course."

"You can come to see me."

"You mean when I go back East? Before I come back here to Berkeley?" I had consulted a map of Pennsylvania before I phoned, and my blithe West Coast confidence that "Back East" is all one densely-populated mass had been rudely shaken. I'd assumed that *everywhere* in Pennsylvania had to be close to either Philadelphia or Pittsburgh. Well, Jaegersville is smack in the middle of the state, that is, in the middle of nowhere. A nowhere with mountains.

Becca refrained from adding, "When else, dummy? I just told you I've got stomach cancer," but I could fill that part in for myself. "Well, I'm reading in Pittsburgh on the Monday night and in Philadelphia on Thursday. I guess I could leave a day early and stop off with you in between. Is there—I don't know— a train I could take?"

"A train? What continent do you think you're on, girl? Or do I say Madame la Comtesse?"

"Don't call me that, whatever you do. It's costing a lot of money and anguish for the right to be just Jamie again. And I should have remembered there are no trains in America."

"Not around here, anyway. We do have a commuter plane, though. You could fly here from Philly after your reading—say, Friday or Saturday." I noted how she finessed the idea of taking a bus or renting a car so I could work in the visit between my other two stops. A dying woman could hardly be expected to realize that in the unlikely event that I could *get* a reservation for Labor Day weekend, it would mean missing my cheap fight back to California. "And don't worry about the money," she added clairvoyantly. "The college will pick up the tab."

"What college?"

"Ebbing, the one where I hold the chair of poetry, remember?" Her voice also started sort of winding down, but for the next few minutes she sounded more like a travel agent than a poet, and by the time we hung up, she had me signed, sealed, and as good as delivered. She also did not explain how come her college would foot the bill for my private visit to a friend's deathbed.

Alain, my husband, used to refer to Becca as "your former professor," but the French cognate is one of those "false friends." In the English language, as in the Berkeley English department, she wasn't entitled to be called "Professor." Although I'd taken all her poetry workshops in grad school, Cal had never deigned to promote her above senior lecturer. Literature departments can be snotty about people who actually *make* the stuff those departments study, especially if the writers don't also have advanced degrees. Becca was a woman in her forties with an ailing husband and a couple of young children, then a widow in her fifties with two teenagers. I guess they figured they didn't have to give her the academic status that matched her slowly ripening reputation as a poet. They had her anyway. I remembered how Becca took center-stage at antiwar meetings during my undergraduate years—her birthright Quaker's serene sense of what was right reinforcing the poet's devastating sense of language. As I got to know some of those English faculty better, I could see why they might have hesitated to welcome that particular combination into departmental deliberations. It was also easy to understand why, once her children were on their own, she'd been ready to accept a richly endowed chair from this little college in Pennsylvania.

Becca was not the best teacher I ever had. In a very real sense, she was the *only* teacher I ever had. I'm one of the lucky ones who made it through a Ph.D. with relatively little trouble; I got to study with professors from whom I had something to learn, whom I respected, some of whom even respected me. But Becca's poetry workshop was another part of the forest from all that. When people argue about whether creative writing can be taught, I come down squarely on both sides of the issue at once. Of course, there's a hard, stubborn knot at the center of any writer's being that no amount of teaching can give you if you don't have it. And of course a writer has to be free to take risks and even to blunder in all sorts of unimaginable directions without anyone's butting in and saying it's too big a risk or too foolish a blunder. Nonetheless, in Becca's class I learned to find my voice as a poet and to trust it.

Surveying the landscape from the frangible commuter plane in which I was apparently serving as ballast, I rejoiced in a luminous greenness unknown to Bay Area summers. I tried to block out the other passenger's loudmouthed banter with the attendant and think about why I'd agreed to this trip. I had originally phoned Becca out of a momentary feeling of triumph at arranging those two readings and a deeper sense of my own terrible need. Returning from the debacle of my marriage and my life in France to a set of open questions back in my own country, I had looked to Becca for affirmation and support. Instead, her own need had been greater, and the feeling that now impelled me to her side was the same one that had made me reach out for *her* help in the first place. Maybe that was my first mistake. But I refuse to be caught saying that love, this kind of love, is ever a mistake.

The plane descended rapidly into the squared-off fields. I've seen smaller airports on Greek islands, where the same individual sells you your ticket, takes it from you inside the plane, and then steps into the cockpit as pilot, but never in high-tech America. The four or five private planes poised on the airstrip made the one I was climbing out of look like a 747.

"Dr. Jameson?" The breathless blonde introduced herself as Laurie Messer, from the college, swept the carry-on out of my hand, and led me to a van marked "Ebbing College" in what felt like one smooth gesture. Tired and anxious as I was, this cheerful, competent undergraduate transmitted some of her youth and energy on the ten-minute drive into Jaegersville.

The village street seemed to loom up very suddenly, and we stopped in front of a white clapboard house with green shutters. It looked like a house for the gracious provincial rich, not one I could imagine Rebecca Parsons living—or dying—in. Laurie left me on the porch, and, as I turned back from thanking her, the door was opened by a blonde woman in a white uniform

"Come in," she said. "They're waiting for you in the library."

This information seemed so sinister—*the body in the library* was all I could think of— that I had no room left to wonder who "they" were.

It was a real library, all dark paneling and deep recesses, with bookshelves nearly to the ceiling, and Becca sat there, imperturbable in her bottle-green *robe d'intérieur* ("hostess gown," I corrected myself sternly). As far as I could see from the outside, she looked pretty much as she always had. She was flanked, however, by two rather grave gentlemen, and, after hugging me close for a moment, she turned and told the woman who'd opened the door—and who must, therefore, not be a real nurse at all, but an invalid's home-helper—where to take my suitcase. This left the rest of us to introduce ourselves.

"I'm Dr. Walker," said the older gentleman "and this is Dr. Walters." Walker and Walters didn't sound exactly like an old vaudeville team, I thought, but it wasn't going to be easy to keep them straight. (*Walker: beard, Walters, not.*) Well, perhaps I wouldn't have to address them by name.

"How do you do? I'm Margaret Jameson, invariably known as Jamie."

"If it comes to that," said the younger doctor, who towered over his associate, "I'm Preston Walters, invariably known as Walt."

This coincidence, mild as it was, branched off into several quite satisfactory side streams of nomenclatural small talk, as they resumed their seats and I took the one that was presumably meant for me. Eventually, though, Walker (and now, at least, I needed no mnemonic device to avoid confusing the two names) steered us into a new bypath. "But you're actually *Dr.* Jameson, aren't you?"

"Well, yes, but I'm not your kind of doctor. *(The kind that might give this patient of yours back her life.)* I'm just a Ph.D. in English. We don't . . . " They interrupted in chorus to assure me that that was the very degree *they* both held, Walker being head of the English department at Ebbing, while Walters—now eternally Walt to me—was the dean of faculty. Fortunately, they didn't allow me to finish my sentence about how academics don't use the title "Doctor" very often—except at colleges that feel insecure about their status. No matter how small the talk, it seems, the potential for a full-sized foot in the mouth is never absent.

"You are Doctor," my interlocutor pursued, "but you've never actually taught?"

"Depends on what you call 'actually.' I was a lecturer my last year at Cal."

"Not a T.A.?"

"No. In fact, I was never a teaching assistant. I had a research grant at the Bancroft Library, instead. By the time that particular project was finished, my four years of support had run out, too, and since I wasn't quite finished with my thesis, they appointed me a lecturer."

"That means they thought very highly of her," Becca put in.

"Anyway, I taught undergraduate creative writing and a course in women's literature. Then I got a Fulbright Lectureship to France—that was another year's teaching, come to think of it—and stayed on, so I've never had a regular academic job." *(And now I'm nearly thirty-five, about to start looking for my first one in a buyer's market. . . .)*

"You know," Becca mused, "I'd quite forgotten you had that Fulbright. If anyone had ever asked me, I'd have just said you met Alain during his time at Berkeley and went back to Paris

with him, moving up from 'Doctor' to 'Countess' in the process."
I couldn't figure out what motive she might have for raising the
Countess business again, but her intentions, however opaque,
were obviously good.

"Look, Becca, once and for all: As far as I knew—and as
far as the facts went at the time—I was marrying the French
experimental novelist Alain Fautour. No Comte Lambert de
Fautour in sight."

"He was just a no-a-Count then," Walt muttered unexpectedly. The other two looked at him, Becca in apparently neutral
surprise, Walker quite sharply. I was pleased to remember that,
despite their respective demeanors, the younger man was actually the boss. "I'm sorry," he added. That was in very poor taste.
I understand you're recently divorced."

"Legally separated. The divorce is in process. And, as far
as taste goes, I'm just glad I didn't happen to think, while we
were still together, that I was going down for the Count. Because
I can't resist a pun, either." Walt had engaging eyes behind his
professional horn-rims and, when he grinned, revealed a most
undeanly dimple.

"Many poets love puns, but Jamie's the only one I've ever
known who makes a living from them." Becca was lifting the
veil on yet another obscure corner of my life history, though not
as prickly a one as Alain's title.

"You earn your living as a punster?" Walt sounded as
though he might be open to a mid-career change of his own.

"It's not exactly a living. But I construct the crossword for the
Review of Literature. It's the British kind, all puns and anagrams."

"You mean *you're* Pangloss? But how can that be, when I've
been cursing you every month for my whole adult life!" I figured
that though Walt was a rather boyish type, he had to be eight or
ten years older than I was.

"Well, you haven't actually been cursing *me* all that time.
Pangloss is a kind of corporate name—like Miss Lonelyhearts,

say—for whoever is in charge of the puzzle. I've been the object of your opprobrium for some time, though—even during my years in Europe. Anyway, I bet you *finish* the puzzle every month, dire imprecations and all."

"I do, and I love it."

Walker interrupted again. I was trying to make light conversation with my fellow guests until they decided to leave, but his agenda was apparently to extract an annotated edition of my *curriculum vitae*. Now he wanted to know if crosswords were my sole medium of publication. It sounded as if he took for granted they were.

"Oh, no, she's published lots of poetry, and her dissertation, as well." Becca spoke like my advocate, though I didn't see why I should need one.

"And your dissertation was . . . ?"

"Well, my assistantship was for work on the Hayward family papers—mostly helping with the cataloguing and editing. But in the process, I got interested in Helen Elizabeth Hayward and decided to do a study of her work for my thesis. When my mentors at Cal were ready to publish the critical edition of her poems they made my thesis—a revised version of it, at any rate—volume four in the set."

"And who was Helen Elizabeth Hayward?"

"She was a California poet at the turn of the century. Not a major figure, by any means, and I certainly wasn't trying to exaggerate her achievement, just get a clear sense of it. She was essentially a regional poet, I'd say. But she wrote a lot about the Bay Area, about coming to terms with being a woman and a writer against the particulars of that landscape. Which, of course, was precisely what I was doing myself, so her work had personal meaning for me, too."

"But you didn't go on looking for other—ah—*role models* to devote monographs to?" The trendy phrase was as sour as a lime on Walker's Anglophile tongue.

"No, the role was more important to me than the models, you see. So I kept on with my poems, sending them back to the U.S. for publication, usually, and I didn't publish much else except a few dozen reviews. I never even got the poems together into a book manuscript. Of course, if I'd stayed here and been involved in the 'publish or perish' ethic, it would have been very different." There was what the books call a perceptible chill in response to this. "I'm sorry, now *I'm* in poor taste. I know that's how your world works, and I have nothing against it. It's just that I've been privileged to write only what most engaged me and, from that, publish only what seemed right and ready."

I was interested to observe that, if anything, what I had meant as a candid apology only heightened the chill. Luckily, at that point, the nurse or whatever she was wheeled in a three-tiered cart with drinks and gave us something else to occupy our minds. Becca pointed out the mineral water for my benefit.

"You don't drink?" asked Walt, who seemed to be showing more interest in me as a person than as a marginal member of his profession. He even seemed to approve of an abstemiousness taken so much for granted.

"Well, I'm not a teetotaler—probably no one who's lived in France for eight years could be. I do drink wine with dinner, and the better the wine, the better the dinner, as far as I'm concerned. But otherwise, no."

Becca asked me if there was even a French word for teetotaler, and I explained that there was nothing so catchy. "You could say *abstinente* or I've been called a *buveuse d'eau*, a water drinker, which has a somewhat sneering quality to it, though it's what I'm doing right now, after all." Walt nodded approval again, quite as if it was any of his business.

All that got us through the drinks, and then Walker and Walters—I decided the vaudeville team would have been Walker and Rider—got ready to leave, as I'd been expecting them to do from the moment I understood they weren't a pair of cancer specialists on a holiday housecall. They'd apparently finished their business with Becca before I arrived, and I thought it misplaced courtesy on their part to stay so long after my arrival, when their hostess was growing more haggard every minute. Now I thought I could detect the shadow of illness under the bones of her face.

"Well, Tom?" Walt asked, "Shall we give Rebecca the green light?"

"Er—certainly, certainly," the chairman bubbled, bobbing his bearded chin up and down like a goat looking for its next good graze. "And let us know what she says. Tomorrow." I paid no attention to this for the time being, because I was concerned about Becca and, in any event, it could have nothing to do with me.

Nonetheless, we assured one another of our pleasure at meeting each other, and Walt actually winked at me. (Another first, after the dimple and the puns, in my experience of administrators.) He was really quite attractive, I thought, if you like the type. Unfortunately, when Becca had mentioned my meeting Alain while he was an exchange lecturer at Berkeley, I'd flashed on his old bedroom on Hillegass Street and a certain way he had of leaning back naked against the pillows and waiting for me. It was too soon—about a century too soon, by my reckoning—for some long tweedy American to stir me.

Almost as strange as wondering even for a moment whether I was attracted to the dean of faculty at Ebbing College, though, was my feeling that he and I had something in common. People are always responding "That's not funny!" to remarks I can't seem to suppress. I see the funny side of grim situations, and I find playing on words helps me get through, and Walt clearly picked up on that—because he did it himself.

Once they were gone, Becca turned to me. "I'm not going to apologize," she began, "but I have to get to bed. If that plane of yours had been on time, I'd have explained everything before they came over. Now it'll just have to wait until tomorrow. Mrs. Moyer will serve you dinner—she's a fine Pennsylvania Dutch cook, and since I'm living on instant breakfast drink, these days, she doesn't get much chance to pull all the stops out. So don't be surprised if it's a seven-course meal. Anyway, enjoy. There are books all over the place, and I've given you the prettiest room in the house."

I took in all these arrangements with astonishment. For weeks, in Berkeley and on this Pennsylvania trip, I'd been crashing with people for whom I was an encumbrance, however welcome, and who, themselves, were very much *there*, and now I'd become an exquisitely treated guest with a disappearing hostess. She was almost out the door before I asked, "Becca, do you get *The Nation?*"

"On the shelf behind you. Why?"

"Busperson's holiday: I thought I'd do the puzzle. Thank you for everything. You're a better hostess than I deserve."

"I love you for coming. I'll explain tomorrow why you're here."

By this time, I could think only about small, immediate things, not cryptic generalizations. So I devoted myself to Mrs. Moyer's cuisine—Stoltzfus County's highest art form—did a couple of *Nation* crosswords (regretting, as always, that I never get to work my own tougher ones in the *Review*) and admired my charming blue and white room, complete with a wide four-poster bed.

It wasn't until some hours after a breakfast fit for a whole Dutch haymaking crew that Becca emerged, led me back to the library, and took advantage of that green light she'd been given.

"I didn't mean to make such a mystery," she began. "It's really quite simple: we're hoping you'll take my job for the year."

My initial shocked response was hardly adequate, so I asked, "Who's 'we'?"

"Well, I must admit the idea was mine to start with. I find that all this resting I have to do, when I'm not actually sleeping, has given me a lot more time simply to *think* (concentrates the mind wonderfully, as Dr. Johnson said in a related context), but Walker and the dean agree."

"You mean all that yesterday was a job interview?"

"Yes, and you did remarkably well without coaching. They wouldn't have settled for someone who wasn't qualified just because it's the last minute. But you showed you have the right combination of skills to carry the work for the year."

"I do? If I ask what it involves, will you promise not to interpret it as meaning I'm taking the offer seriously?"

"All right. But you'll see that you'll *have* to take it seriously." Becca's serenity was unshaken by my lack of enthusiasm. It was the way she used to act at those meetings in the sixties when she *knew* she was in the right. "It's a rather long story. Elizabeth Ebbing Brock was a member of the family the college is named for. Coal country money and she was its princess. Ever since the college was founded, with her great-uncle's endowment, people named Ebbing have remembered us in their wills—to a greater or lesser extent, of course—and there's almost always been a family member on the board of trustees.

"When Mrs. Brock died, back in 1931, she was in her eighties. She left us some money for scholarship aid and an annual poetry prize—you know the sort of thing—and she bequeathed her papers to the library. The stipulation was that they not be unsealed for fifty years after her death. At that time, the current professor of poetry was to be asked to prepare the materials for publication, as appropriate. A modest stipend—something like twenty-five hundred dollars in Ebbing Company stock—was allotted to cover editorial costs.

"Well, by the time the papers were ready for release, there was no professor of poetry, hadn't been for years, but Ebbing Coal, which had already diversified into Ebbing Company by the time she died, had subsequently become Ebbing Technology, the stock had split any number of times and then, sometime in the seventies, the company merged with a big multinational, Consolidated General. That modest stipend was now enough to *endow* a chair, and they brought me in to start a creative writing program and, incidentally, to deal with the papers. Elizabeth Brock wrote poems all her life and never published one. And she kept a journal that—well, I hope you'll see it for yourself."

"A coal country Emily Dickinson?"

"No, no, a distinctly regional poet. I liked the way you said that about Hayward, yesterday. But it's her journal that I think you'll really enjoy—the access it gives you to the mind of a woman of her day and class. She tells you, in precisely the same tone, what families they entertained, when they moved from the town house to the country house and back (this was always a big production, apparently), what experiments she was making in free-verse techniques, and how she hated her husband until—at least until—the day of his death. It's an extraordinary document."

Becca went on to describe the job: two writing courses each term, one of them an advanced poetry workshop, plus the work on the archival material. "There's quite a lot of it, but there are no deadlines, and there's money for whatever help you need.

"The college owns this house and it's part of my remuneration—along with an enormous salary." She named a figure that would have taken my breath away if I were the kind of person who gasps at dollar amounts. I claim no particular credit for this. Large sums of money never seem quite real to me; I know them, as with Alain, chiefly by their ill effects.

"I'm taking early retirement as of this month," Becca continued. "The search for a new occupant of the Chair will take at least a year. Meanwhile, the salary is available, and we could share the house. And don't worry, I'll have nurses when it gets to be too much for Mrs. Moyer. I'd like not to have to go into a nursing home or a hospital, but if they hired anyone but you, I'd have to turn over the house, of course."

I was silent when she finished. All the details fit so well, the way they rarely do in life. Maybe that's what happens when a smart person has nothing to do but think. Only my own plans and feelings were missing from Becca's elegant equation.

"You wanted to see me," Becca pursued more slowly. "I gather you called me because you needed a shoulder to cry or lean on, maybe both. And then you agreed to come here because you had an emotional reaction to learning about my illness. You said you wanted to do something. Well, assuming that wasn't just a platitude, it turns out you can really make a difference in these last months. I'm not out of bed and alert that many hours a day. To have someone here for those times who wasn't paid help but a long-time part of my life, someone I really care for . . . ."

"What about your children? Not that either of them could teach or edit the manuscripts. But to be there for you?"

"Jack is married now. He and his wife are on the folk music circuit, traveling mostly around New England, out of Cambridge. And Ellie's in law school at UCLA. I hope they'll come as often as they can, but I can't ask them to disrupt their lives."

"Whereas my life . . . ?"

"Is already disrupted. If you want it put more diplomatically, I've caught you in transition, and I'm offering you the elements to rebuild your life." I must have looked unconvinced, because she went on, "Tell me, Jamie, why did you move back to Berkeley when you broke up with Alain?"

"I'm not entirely sure. It was partly because that was where I left off, eight years ago."

"And do you have a life there?"

"What do you mean?"

"Well, to start with, where have you been living?"

"I've been staying with Matt Steiner and Jeannie Rhodes up in Kensington. But there's a collective house down near Cal where I know most of the people. They expect an opening in the middle of September."

"What about a job?"

"Lou Patterson thinks they can get me onto a new project at the Bancroft. Seems another family of Native Sons with literary ambitions has left their papers to Cal. He was waiting until his codirector from history got back before giving the go-ahead. But he didn't expect any trouble, and Reston, the historian, will be in Berkeley in a week or so. So that should take care of me for the year, and, meanwhile, of course, I'll start looking for an academic job."

"Jamie, this is 1985. The market isn't what it used to be. That's why this temporary job would give you an edge." I said nothing. She continued her inventory of my plans for this year. "Have you got a new man?"

"Not exactly."

"The house and the job were 'not exactlys,' too, but I fail to see. . . . "

"I don't know if you remember Nick Harvey? I went with him for a few months when I was at Cal."

"Was he in the doctoral program, too?"

"No, he's a musician—-a composer—and he plays with the Berkeley Jazz Ensemble. I'm sure you've heard them: they used to do lots of Movement benefits. Anyway, Nick and I broke up fairly amicably, which wasn't so common with me in those days, if you recall, not long before I met Alain. So he looked me up when he came to France early last year and we spent a lot of time together."

"Is that why you left Alain? Because you were having an affair with this Nick?"

"No, it wasn't—because I wasn't. Nick stayed with the two of us down at Fautour, and he and I just talked for hours. But Alain had already begun to change. . . . "

"You'll have to tell me more about those changes. That is, if you want to."

"I do. Or I will. But what's important is that afterwards, as things got worse with Alain, Nick began to seem like the embodiment of everything I respected that I couldn't find anymore in the man I'd married."

"Such as?"

"Such as commitment to his work as an artist. Such as integrity, living according to principle—personal and political. Nick and I didn't even correspond, but by the time I got back to the States, I'd developed a pretty full-blown fantasy about him. Or rather about him and me."

"And?"

"And I called him when I landed but he was on tour. He didn't come back to Berkeley until just before I left on this trip. When we had dinner together, he started right off telling me how he had this wonderful new girlfriend and this beautiful relationship and practically *apologizing* for being caught up in a spell of monogamy. But by the end of the evening he was essentially saying he'd fit me in. Oh, don't look so disapproving. You did ask what 'not exactly' means when it comes to having a man. It means that I was staying on one of those futon couches in Matt and Jeannie's living room and he's living with the new girlfriend, so we went our separate ways that night. He said he'd talk to Rachel—that's her name—and that she was going up to Mendocino the week I'd be coming back. So we'd see."

"See what? What *I'd* like to see is you telling him to take his 'fitting you in' and shove it. And I'm offering you the chance to do that, not to mention a job and a place to live."

"Is that what it means to have a life: a house, a job, an exclusive lover?"

"They're certainly a start. But there are more important things—like real involvement in your work or a political commitment or, if God really loves you, both. And what I've found the most important of all . . . "

"What?"

"Friendship. Loving friendship." She had me, and she knew it. She called the dean and made an appointment for me to see him first thing Tuesday morning.

2

*

BY THE TIME I set off for Dean Walters' office at 9 o'clock Tuesday, the small gridiron that mapped Jaegersville's streets was already familiar territory. On this first walk across campus, however, I was impressed by the general quiet prettiness of the place, although it lacked the spectacular scenic effects you find at Berkeley or Santa Cruz.

Becca had taken a nap on Sunday afternoon, and later I gave her a tape of my Philadelphia reading. As we listened to it together, I heard mostly the weak spots, but my exacting teacher told me I had matured as a writer. "Your voice has authority, now, Jamie. Along with the old intimacy of tone, there's the ring, almost, of—well—prophecy." After that, my solitary confrontation with Mrs. Moyer's chicken pot pie might as well have been the Nobel Prize banquet.

The next day, though, Labor Day, Becca had a setback. She never felt well enough to come downstairs, and my brief visit to her room seemed to tire as much as cheer her. She shooed me out for a walk and, as I paced orderly streets on which I was the only pedestrian, I wondered how many of our days would follow the same pattern, and how long even that would last. Of course, my love went out to Becca in her newly installed hospital bed back at the house, but it occurred to me that I'd signed on for a lonely year at a time when I very much needed not to feel alone.

The Ebbing campus two weeks before the start of classes was not an animated scene, either. It was a relief to turn into the administration building, where people—mostly women, in these outer offices—were pursuing their usual routine. It seemed ironic that any aspect of a college administration could be a relief from my own isolation.

Walt seemed more relaxed without his elder junior around. Rising enthusiastically, if awkwardly, from his desk, he offered me a seat on a long sofa and took the other end himself. He began by asking after Becca. The inquiry and fetching his own coffee and my tea, rather than summoning a secretary to perform the service, won him good marks in my book.

"We're thankful Becca's going to have you with her. A lot of us here have come to care very much for that lady, but you can give her something the rest of us can't, the connection with her own world that she has a *right* to at the end."

"The last rights?" I asked gently, confident he'd understand that a punster in mourning is a punster still.

His sympathetic smile was engaging, and he spent an hour taking me through what I'd need to know about the job. He made it sound almost like fun. At the end of that time his wrist alarm buzzed, and a red-haired secretary put her head into the office at the same moment, as if summoned. "Captain Ehrlich is here," she told him.

"Right on time, too, the sadist. That's the head of campus security, Jamie, and he does have an appointment. What are your immediate plans?"

"I'm taking Becca over to her first chemotherapy session this afternoon, though she made me swear that from now on I'll let Mrs. Moyer or a student chauffeur do it. And tomorrow I'm off to the Coast to wind up everything I set in motion for the year and pack my belongings. I'll be back in ten days." *(I'll close my new bank account, smooth things out with the commune and Lou Patterson, and say good-bye to Nick, when we never quite got around to saying hello.* The other tasks were simply chores, but the thought of Nick made me uncomfortable.)

"What time is Becca's appointment?"

"Four o'clock, at the Hochstetter Clinic."

"It won't take you more than three-quarters of an hour to get there. So if you can stick around until 12:30, we'll have lunch before you go, and I'll see if Tom Walker can join us. Meanwhile, we'll set you up with the archive so you can see what you've gotten yourself into. Just don't get trapped by Gwen Ehrlich going on about procedures." It was the redhead who walked me across campus and introduced me to the librarian, the apparently over-explanatory Gwen Ehrlich. On the way, I planned a diplomatic speech.

"Since the Dean's going to call for me in less than two hours," I told Gwen, "I don't want to start anything that shouldn't be interrupted in the middle. So I think what I'll do is just dip into the papers here and there, start familiarizing myself with the collection—and then ask you for a real orientation when I get back from California next week." She assented with minimal reluctance. Of course, I reminded myself, I was the boss now.

Gwen did fuss as she showed me the files that Becca and her assistants had catalogued: poetry, correspondence, journals. "There are only these two boxes of uncatalogued material left" she pointed out, and left me to it. Somehow, the room itself, which housed the archive and was also to serve as my office, felt almost haunted. I realized that this was the first time I was actually stepping into Becca's place and assumed that any sense of foreboding, any presentiments of death, came from that. So, ignoring—let's face it, *denying*—any sixth sense, I resolutely turned to the papers themselves.

Recalling my training at the Bancroft, I saluted the insight and imagination with which these papers had been filed and cross-indexed. I read some sample poems from different periods of Elizabeth Brock's life, though I had no way of knowing, as yet, how representative they were. Becca was right about their overall quality—decent, if not riveting —though I thought perhaps she underestimated their level of technical innovation. Here, according to the biographical note stapled inside the first folder, was a woman educated in a provincial ladies' seminary just after the Civil War, and living in apparent isolation from the intellectual and artistic ferments of her lifetime, who had nonetheless managed to embrace and experiment with all the most advanced literary forms of her day. And that "day" had taken her at length from rhymed schoolgirl sonnets to the explosions of stylistic daring that marked the early decades of this century.

I wondered if Elizabeth Brock really had kept so aloof from the literary community, and I leafed through the index to her letters looking for hints that she'd met or corresponded with Pound, Stein, Joyce, Amy Lowell, *anyone*. The index just glared back, yielding no answers.

That was why I turned to the two boxes of uncatalogued material. Maybe the elusive link to the modernist world just hadn't been listed yet. The papers here were not in folders; in fact, they weren't filed at all, just piled one on top of the other. Elizabeth Brock's journals, I'd already observed, were handwritten and kept in separate bound volumes, but no one had yet separated the poems in these boxes from letters, old invitations, and receipted bills. I concluded, with frustration though not surprise, that it would take a longer and more systematic effort to answer my questions. Meanwhile, part-way down in one of the boxes, I found a faded grey cardboard folder tied with lavender ribbons.

The manuscript inside was in *her* hand, which I'd begun to

recognize, and its title, in elegant copperplate, was *Helen-Eliza-beth*. Well, as the author of the only existing monograph on a poet named Helen Elizabeth Hayward, I was bound to be intrigued.

It began even more intriguingly. On a page by itself stood the single sentence, "This is the true story my diary could not tell." I began to read. The "true story" was about the developing relationship between Lizzie, Elizabeth Ebbing, and her closest school friend, Helen Breckenridge, known as Nellie. After finishing (or *being* finished) at the seminary, they corresponded, copiously and passionately, about the meaning of life and their feelings for each other. At age 19, their formal education completed, they were both clearly steeped in the patterns and the rhetoric of what historians now call "women's culture." They were one another's truest reality.

The pages chronicled "Lizzie's" stay with Nellie and her family in Philadelphia: their weeks together, the shopping and sewing, the unavoidable round of calls and callers. Yet there were also long hours of discussion in which the two girls, ill-fitted for such an exercise by their families, their schooling, and their religious training, tried to figure out how to make some sense of their lives.

Much talk went on between them of "Nellie's troubles." Having taken to the ritual study of the piano with exceptional enthusiasm and accomplishment, she wanted to refine and develop this gift, attend a conservatory, perhaps study in Europe, attempt composition as well as performance. Her family, it appeared, was shocked and heartbroken. To spend so many hours of each day, so many years of her young womanhood, on such a project was the next thing to sacrilege for these people. To contemplate playing professionally—not that I could tell, from what Lizzie wrote, if that issue was even raised—would have been like today's sweet girl graduate announcing she hoped in time to qualify as a streetwalker. Nothing had been positively forbidden—the family didn't work that way, but operated through loving assumptions that pried, poked, molded, shaped, suffocated, and eventually crushed—but *everything* in the scale of home values was already starting to take precedence over Nellie's practice time.

The question was canvassed between the girls, rehearsed in Lizzie's copperplate recollections, and then reopened in the letters that passed between them, some of which were actually included in this manuscript, when Lizzie went back to her own family's summer place near Jaegersville. (Ebbing College already existed on its present site nearby. It was, of course, for men only. Despite her family name, there was no place here for Lizzie, the fledgling writer.) I was most interested in the recurrent theme of Nellie's musical career and how it was to develop, but the girls devoted at least as much of their correspondence to what I thought of as philosophical—even theological—abstractions. And to their love for each other, which brought into being the complex, single creature they made between them: Helen-Elizabeth; Lizzie-Nell.

All this took on a new dimension—I was now skimming as fast as nineteenth-century penmanship allowed—when Nellie returned Lizzie's visit. Slowly, but with gathering momentum, the shared Victorian bedroom became the scene of mutual erotic discovery of their bodies. Lizzie's prose, less crisp and well-formed than in the later journal entries I'd read, was at once unequal and more than adequate to the love-making this memoir described in hushed detail. She—they—did not know the names of certain parts of the body or the pleasures to which those parts could be incited. Neither of them seemed to have any idea that other girls and women had made the same discoveries, done the same exciting things to one another. And they seemed to make no connection whatever between these ecstatic acts and what goes on—did they know that either?—between men and women. Not only were the clinical words of my own vocabulary entirely alien to their store of information, but so was the discourse of lovers who have some idea what to expect.

What there was instead was a literal and extravagant sensuality. Lizzie felt and described with all five senses before she approached the more localized sensations for which she had no lexicon and no diction. There were pages on the feel of fabrics—linen and piqué dresses, a lawn nightgown—the smell of clothing, hair, and skin—lavender, clean hay, strawberry—the taste of different folds of Nellie's flesh, overt and concealed, the sound of their whispers and sighs. And then the feast of vision, the first time they actually saw each other naked!

There was to be a dance that night. (Would ball dresses have been cut low in the late 1860s? Would these girls know what the décolleté and the sedate waltzing were meant to lead to? How tame—or revolting—would all that courtship ritual have seemed to them!) In preparation for their late night, the two young ladies were sent upstairs to rest between lunch and dinner. They were *made* to be alone in the curtained room by day, *instructed* to lock the door. And how obedient they were, how helpful with one another's layers of encumbering dresses, petticoats, stays, chemises, stockings, drawers (the very underwear seemed to my uninstructed eye to have underwear beneath it), taking down each other's pinned and braided hair, Lizzie's dark, Nellie's blonde, and letting it drape across their own and the other's breasts and shoulders. . . .

On *my* own shoulder, a large, gentle hand came to rest and made me start, so complete was my absorption. If I wasn't exactly panting open-mouthed over the book, I was nonetheless afraid my arousal might be patent, since I was so conscious of my own sensations and my response to the feel of a warm hand on my shoulder.

"You found something you like?" Walt smiled.

"Oh yes. The whole archive is interesting, but this memoir is just—exquisite: the most remarkable bit of nineteenth-century lesbian erotica!"

Professor Walker was unable to join us; I was relieved that I wouldn't have to tell *him* about the manuscript just yet.

"Nineteenth-century lesbian erotica, eh?" Walt savored the words over his Bloody Mary, as we waited to be served lunch at the Campus Inn. He waved to a couple leaving their table and nodded warmly to the woman being seated just behind us, but stayed focused on my provocative description of what I'd been reading.

"That's only if you need a quick label," I told him, fishing the unwanted lime out of my mineral water. "It's also priceless women's history. And literature—finely made literature."

"What do you think should be done with it?"

"Can't say until I read through it *and* the rest of the papers. Maybe—no, I think definitely—*Helen-Elizabeth* should be published separately, but I have to find out first how this story ends and how it fits with the rest of the archive. And I'll need to consult with Becca and with the other faculty whose field this touches."

"Which faculty?"

"Well, for starters, who does nineteenth-century American lit?"

"I do. Or did, before I got kicked upstairs. Now Betsy Robards covers that area And you're in luck: she's the person who's been pushing Walker for courses in women's literature. Betsy and Bill are your neighbors, by the way. They're right next door to Becca. But Betsy won't have a lot of time to work with you on this."

"Just you wait 'til she sees *Helen-Elizabeth* ! Not that I mean to trample on what she's already working on. I just hope she's not at the beginning of a project."

"I don't think you understand, Jamie. Faculty here don't *have* 'fields' and work on 'projects.' We're teachers. And the normal load is four courses a term—Becca's chair involves half that load, of course—so even those of us who started out thinking we were scholars—really excited about our research and writing—eventually learned to channel it all straight into the classroom."

"But how can you keep up the excitement when you're cut off from all the give and take, the discourse in the field?"

"Are you *defending 'publish or perish'?*"

"Well, not as a form of careerism, but as intellectual survival. A scholar who doesn't publish—well doesn't the scholarly part perish?"

"I guess it does. The question is whether it really matters, how much you miss it. People at the big research universities have always seemed so—so—driven to me. It's hard enough just to keep up with a field."

I didn't say that, by definition, spectators don't keep up with a race. The metaphor was too close to rat races, which would support his side of the argument, and, besides, this was a nice man I felt suddenly sorry for. Now, though, I understood the coldness in the air last Saturday when I'd apologized for publishing only one book of criticism, a sheaf of poems, and an unspecified number of reviews. My casually unconventional career must have seemed pretty "driven" to Walt. And Walker must have thought I was nuts or just hopelessly pretentious. Changing the subject, I asked Walt how he'd become a dean, and he explained that the college had desperately needed someone who could advance its mission as a teaching institution. From his point of view, it was a way of extending himself as a teacher, getting his ideas about education to reach more students than he could in his own classroom.

"There's a group of us who joined the faculty in the sixties and thought of ourselves as the Young Turks. Well, now, of course, we've become the Old Goats, but once in a while that lets us do some good things for teaching and learning around here." It occurred to me that there's more than one way of being driven, more than one vision of success or even power. Still, I felt myself responding to something in Walt, an openness and readiness to engage that was precisely the opposite of what I expected from an administrator. (But when had I ever shared a lunch table with one before? What other dean had ever grinned at my puns and volleyed them back every time?)

"I can't help liking the dean," I told Becca as I drove her to Hochstetter, which turned out to be the name of a nearby town as well as its clinic. "But it's so sad."

"About his wife?" she asked.

"What wife? I meant abandoning research and writing once he got involved in teaching at Ebbing."

"They all do, here—or most of them, anyway. That was your one faux pas at the interview. I'd have warned you—"

"I know, if the plane had been on time."

"It's a tricky situation, though," she went on, "because an endowed chair—all that money and what counts around here as a reduced teaching load—calls for someone who's got a reputation in the world outside Ebbing College. And how do you get that except by publishing? Then the chair's in creative writing, and poets do tend to want to publish their work. Even my temporary replacement would have to be published. Anyway, they accepted the facts of life in this case. You and I won't set any kind of precedent, you see."

"But your presence here must have shown them that a person can write and publish and still be a great teacher."

"I'd like to think you're right," agreed Becca, "but, frankly, I think they offered the job to me in the first place because fewer women poets are drunks. Especially Quaker women poets. You know how obnoxious some of those guys can be. In a confined space like Ebbing, it would be even worse than at a big university." She mentioned a few alcohol-sodden names and I saw what she meant.

"It's not a dry campus, though, is it?"

"There are all kinds of Byzantine rules for the students, but faculty parties are rather boozy affairs. Except when the Walterses are there—both of them."

"Why's that?"

"Virginia Walters is an alcoholic. She's in the hospital at the moment—the other wing of Hochstetter, in fact—and it's hardly the first time. At parties, when she's on the wagon, she's very much—very self-righteously—the recovering alcoholic, but she invariably relapses." Now I understood Walt's nod of approval at my sticking to mineral water, along with what I *should* have been pitying him for. All of which made it clear why I was picking up sexual signals from this man who hadn't really been making advances. What I'd sensed was not necessarily his availability, but his essential need.

That thought reminded me of his hand on my shoulder, my response to it, and the manuscript that so stirred me. So I changed the subject abruptly. For the rest of our ride and the time we spent in the waiting room, I told Becca about my find.

On the way back, however, we didn't talk at all. The chemotherapy had sapped her vitality to a terrifying extent. We couldn't know yet what the long-term effects would be, but in the silent car, I felt I was in closer proximity to death than I had ever been.

I felt close to death in a different way when I boarded the commuter plane to Pittsburgh the next afternoon. When I'd accepted the position at Ebbing I had failed to reflect adequately on the fact that, in so doing, I was also accepting these planes as my link with the outside world. My gloom was not lightened by having passed an insomniac night because my bedroom was too hot for comfort. When I'd finally admitted to myself that I couldn't sleep, I padded down to the library to find a book. I picked *Emma* off the shelf, but, recalling Lizzie and Nell, thought for the first time that maybe Jane Austen hadn't told us everything about young ladies who were handsome, clever, and rich.

On the flight from Pittsburgh to the Coast, to banish thoughts of Becca's face after the chemotherapy, I worked on my next Pangloss puzzle, the December one, deadline September 15th. This technique succeeded so well at inducing oblivion that I went on. I like to get a few months ahead, anyway, and the January and February puzzles were finished by the time the plane landed in San Francisco. "They'll need some polishing in phrasing the definitions, is all," I told myself. I'd once tried to break myself of that habit of speaking—even thinking—in substantive clauses, after I read *Butterfield-8*, where John O'Hara says its a verbal tic of native Californians.

I had a week in Berkeley, if you reckon a week as the French do: eight days long. The business part of my visit turned out to be easy. Some of the people in the house I'd planned to move into knew Becca and heartily approved our arrangement. They even invited me over for a spaghetti dinner before I left.

As for Professor Patterson, he approved, too. "If we'd given her a regular tenured position here," he fumed, "she wouldn't be dying in the middle of Pennsylvania."

"Lou, she has cancer of the stomach. It can happen anywhere. And who even knows when it started? She's only been back there for three or four years."

"No, I realize that not even the Berkeley English department is an infallible shield against the ills of the flesh. I mean, if those s.o.b.'s had been willing to regularize her appointment—and God knows a few of us tried—she might be dying anyway, but with hundreds of friends around her: colleagues, peace marchers, poets, ex-students, street people, *everybody*. Well, I'm glad at least you'll be there, Jamie, representing what should have been."

If my days were full of quiet rearrangements, my nights were alive with Nick. It turned out he understood better than anyone why I had to go back to stay with Becca—because he was the only one who insisted that I explain myself. The others, uninvolved, thought it was a "nice" thing I was doing. Nick, who had something to lose, challenged what he saw as a quixotic gesture. Here he'd been ready to announce that he and Rachel had reached a new, nonmonogamous stage in their beautiful relationship. My return from France had been the crisis—the potential crisis—and they'd transformed it into a strength. Or so he maintained.

"She says you sound like a wonderful person, Jamie. She'd really like to meet you when she gets back."

"Not this time around, Nick. I'm not staying in Berkeley, after all." And I told him why. But he kept pressing and pressing, and I got down to the bare bones of it: that someone I loved was coming to terms with mortality and I could actually help her to do it well. Or I could leave her alone to die. Period. By the time I was telling him about Becca's face after the treatment, I was crying so hard I couldn't stop—the first time I'd let this happen—and that was when he finally said he understood.

The way we made love that night and all the remaining nights of my stay had something in it of those tears of mine and something of a fierce assertion of life. It was as if we were trying to dig immortality out of one another. Becca, I knew, would hardly have chosen to be the occasion of this passionate coupling. But it wasn't just that, either. We were saying hello and good-bye at the same time.

Before I left, I tracked down Cathy Ross, who taught courses in lesbian literature at two different colleges in San Francisco. When I told her about my manuscript find, she reminded me that Erin Ni'Connor, to whom she'd introduced me at a conference years ago, was the premier scholar in this field and lived in Philadelphia. "The woman knows everything there is to know about nineteenth-century women in Pennsylvania," she concluded. "Especially lesbians."

Thinking of myself as a penurious Berkeley grad student, I dithered for hours before figuring out that, with my new job, I could afford to change my return ticket to give me half a day in Philadelphia on my way back *(would it ever feel right to say "home"?)* to Jaegersville.

Erin Ni'Connor was as tall, bulky, and red-haired as I remembered. When I staggered up the steps to her West Philly row house apartment, she took one look at me, decidedly unfresh from my cross-country flight, and prepared a pot of Irish Breakfast tea. Not until I was well started on my second cup would she let me tell her about *Helen-Elizabeth.* Naturally, she wanted to hear how the story ended.

"That's precisely what I don't know yet. I can't even tell you if the end is in the manuscript or if that's just pure sexual idyll. Do we have anything else like that from the nineteenth century?"

She shook her head. "Nothing like so early and so—so straightforward, uncoded. Except male pornography *about* lesbians. But from the women's actual point of view, no."

"Anyway, I don't know if the manuscript I've got will tell how the relationship ended, whether they were caught or what. What do you suppose their families would have made of it, anyway? The two girls were incredibly innocent, but it's clear they knew they were doing something forbidden. Would the families have thought they were mostly evil or mostly crazy if they found out?"

"They might not have been into such fine distinctions." Erin was caustic. "There's another category that cuts across those two, anyway: freak of nature." There was a pause, then she asked, "You say your Lizzie got married?"

"To one Alfred Enfield Brock. She seems to have been quite young at the time. At any rate, he died in the late 1890s and she turned their country place, not far from where I'll be living, into a year-round residence."

"For what: *forty* years round?"

"So it seems. She wasn't a recluse or anything. No reputed eccentricities at all, in fact, except for the writing. But she didn't

take advantage of his death to break out—at least geographically. She was in her forties when he died, with plenty of money
from both sides. And she was writing away—just ripe, you'd
think, for contact with the people who were defining modern
literature. And with the international lesbian community. Not
to mention the overlap between the two. I mean, Stein and Toklas
met in Paris around 1907. Lizzie could have gone to New
York—the Village—or to Paris. But it's clear from the archive
that she just stayed in Jaegersville, PA."

"Did she have a lover there?"

"Becca says there's nothing in the journals to suggest that
she did. And the other thing I don't know is what became of
Nellie."

She helped me define the critical issues, figure out what
questions I needed to ask, and told me how to look for answers,
inside and outside the manuscript. And she agreed to come up
to Ebbing as a consultant when I had a better handle on the real
questions. ("At a hundred and fifty dollars a day? Are you kidding?" I was delighted to be able to tell this gifted, unemployed
scholar that I wasn't.)

"If this treasure had to fall into the hands of a straight
woman, Jamie, I'm glad it was you," Erin remarked as I got ready
to leave. "At least you know when Stein met Toklas."

"Thanks—I guess. I hope you realize, though, that 'had to'
has nothing to do with it. The odds were that the professor of
poetry would be a man, and not necessarily a sympathetic one,
even. How could Lizzie have known that, fifty years down the
pike, not only would it be okay to unseal this stuff and there'd
be an audience of women ready and eager for it, but that the
professor of poetry would be—well—*me* and not some macho
jerk?"

"We don't know *what* she knew. But she did the right thing."

Erin had helped me set my soap-opera questions about
"what happened to Lizzie and Nell" into a broader and more

intellectually responsible framework. But on the commuter plane—somewhat less bumpy this time around—I went on wondering about the personal dimension of the story, because it was from the more intimate side that Lizzie's extraordinary little book had grown. What became of Nell, I decided, very likely depended on what happened to the love story I was in the middle of reading. I somehow doubted that it had gradually petered out and given way to nice, "mature" heterosexual attachments. Lizzie's marriage certainly hadn't been that and she hadn't had another man in her life. No, whatever happened, it couldn't have been a happy ending. If there was any connection between Lizzie's affair with Nell and her marriage to Brock, I suspected it was more like the relationship between crime and punishment: a hasty marriage arranged after the discovery of the girls' "guilty connection."

In that case, would Nell have been similarly disposed of: married off posthaste, committed to an asylum, or (a happier thought) packed off to Germany to work on her music? Had she perhaps died suddenly, as people always seemed to be doing in the nineteenth century? Did she kill herself? Or did she become a minor celebrity whose lost compositions a feminist music historian was even now preparing to bring to light?

If their relationship was exposed, which of them was blamed? I was sure one of them would have been considered the seducer, the corrupter, while the other was cast as the injured innocent. From the narrative, it seemed as if Lizzie was the more active partner, sexually, but that might be precisely because it was Lizzie's narrative. Especially given her conceptual limitations, it was easier to write about what she did than what was done to her. And Nellie was the more enterprising one in many ways. After all, it was she who was being thwarted in her yearning for a musical career. Then again, maybe she seemed more ambitious only because her ambition was frustrated, while Lizzie, who wanted just as much to be a writer, had, in her dogged, idiosyncratic way, become one. There were a lot of speculative questions, but at least my meeting with Erin had shown me how to turn them into something that could reasonably be called "research."

So you can imagine my shock when I let myself into the archive Monday afternoon, elated after my first class of the year, to discover that the manuscript was no longer there.

3

∗

I THINK I knew from the first that someone had stolen it. But I kept my cool *(tel quel,* Alain would have commented— such as it is) and went through the proper motions of searching. Since I believe in the law of physics concerning the Demateri- alization and Spontaneous Return of Objects, I kept looking in the only likely places. Only when I admitted to myself that this activity was fruitless did I turn to other people. Gwen Ehrlich, first, who looked as if I was accusing her of malfeasance, when all I did was ask.

"One of the uncatalogued pieces?" she sniffed. "Well then, it can't be in the catalogue, can it? And if it's somewhere in the files, I wish you luck. But it couldn't *get* in the files without someone's following our procedures—of course, you don't know about all that, yet, but it's meant to double-check against just that sort of misplacing of documents. Naturally, you don't know the system," she repeated, amply illuminating the source of her animus against me and my apparently casual handling of archi- val materials.

I guess, from her point of view, I'd marched in, displayed

no interest in or respect for library procedures, and, the next thing we knew, an important document turned up missing. If a new boss is always disruptive of cherished practices and routines, I had rapidly proved myself not only an uncomfortable element but a dangerous one.

"So, of course," she continued, "not knowing how we do things here, you could have filed it—which, of course, would be *mis*filing it—yourself."

"Not inadvertently, I couldn't. I've had a very rigorous training." I wondered if it might help to drop the names of the Special Collections librarians under whom I'd worked at Berkeley. After all, every field has its internal celebrities and I was pretty sure they'd be among the ones in the library world. But I remembered Walt's cautions about the reverse snobbery at the College and decided they applied to this case. "If something is uncatalogued, I know enough to leave it with the uncatalogued materials, even if I haven't mastered the particular filing method. What about the student assistants?"

"There weren't any assigned for the summer session. Professor Parsons was coming in fairly regularly until she got sick, but she was outlining editorial work that undergraduates couldn't be much help on. You'll have a team of assistants again, with the new term, though we haven't got the names yet from Financial Aid."

"Financial Aid?" I asked weakly.

"They're paid with Federal Work-Study funds. That saves the money in the endowment for professional help."

"Well, have any professional helpers been around since that Tuesday I was here, the day after Labor Day?"

"No. You see, they work on specific instructions from the person on the Chair and there haven't been any since Professor Parsons got sick. Besides, they don't have keys. Neither do the students, for that matter. Everyone signs in and out through me."

"I didn't, just now. Becca gave me her key." She frowned

slightly at this laxity. "You did let me in the other time, I remember. Does this mean no one else has a key?"

"I couldn't say. You'll have to check with Security on that, when you call them in."

I was providentially prevented at the last moment from giving my opinion of campus police. The fact that she bore the same last name as the security chief had belatedly registered. "Sadist," Walt had joked when the male Ehrlich showed up on time for his appointment. But it was no laughing matter to anyone who'd been in as many campus demonstrations as I had, much less faced the CRS in the streets of Paris.

This did serve to remind me of Walt, though. "I'll report to the Dean first," I said, trusting my action would be misinterpreted as a proper respect for the chain of command. In fact, I had simply recalled that Walt was with me when I put the manuscript away before we left for lunch. I reached for the campus directory and the phone. "Thanks—ah—Gwen," I added to her perhaps mortally offended back as she shut the door behind her.

"Walt? This is Jamie," I said when the secretary put me through. "I'm over at the archive and that manuscript seems to be missing." (*And why "seems"? Either it's here or it's gone.*)"The one I was looking at when you came by for me the other day."

"You mean, the les-"

"That's the one. You wouldn't have any idea—?"

"I'll be right over, Jamie. Sit tight." Surely, anyone truly concerned about the state of my nerves would advise me to sit *loose*. Instead, while I was sitting tight, I had time to realize that, if it really was a theft I was dealing with, I'd been going about the thing all wrong. Not only had I started babbling about the missing manuscript, but I 'd confided first of all in the two chief suspects. Gwen and Walt both had access to the archive, and I'd even told him, over our friendly lunch, what was in the manuscript. I could just imagine Erin, who'd congratulated me, after all, because "at least" I knew when Stein met Toklas,

patiently explaining to me that no *lesbian* scholar would have
gone running to some straight male administrator to report her
exciting find. Not that I'd exactly gone running. *Worse, you went
out on a date*, I reminded myself mercilessly. *What makes you
think that Mr. White Liberal, with his leather elbow-patches
would be just dying to expose the College's benefactress as a filthy
pervert? Remember, he asked right away what you planned to do
with it. . . ."*

Walt came in, his reassuring bulk dispelling some of my
paranoia. How could I suspect this huge puppy of a man?

"Are you sure it's actually missing, Jamie?"

"*Of course* I'm sure!"

"Well, I remember you were reading it when I came in the
other day. Completely absorbed, I should say. I saw you put the
manuscript in the cover-thing and tie up the ribbons. I mean, I
particularly noticed you retying them. But I can't say I recall
what you did after that."

"I put it back where I found it, in this box."

"How do you know it was this one and not the other one?
They look identical to me."

"In a sense, they are. Each one is a jumble of unsorted
papers. I gather they're the last two whose contents haven't been
catalogued and filed. I put the cardboard folder back in the
nearer box. But it wouldn't make any difference if they'd been
switched around because I've searched through both. There's
nothing in either that's remotely the right size, shape or weight."

"What about the files? There are only the two boxes, but
hundreds of files," he needlessly pointed out. "Many hundreds.
I don't *remember* your doing it, but couldn't you have absent-
mindedly stuck it into one of those drawers?"

"Absent-mindedly? Walt, I am a trained archival re-
searcher. It's about as likely as—as a nurse absent-mindedly
poisoning her patient."

"But you'll check it out?"

"Of course I'll check it out. Myself, because I do know what the thing looks like, with or without its cover."

"Besides" he added, "If someone took the thing, that would be the smartest place to hide it."

"Because they wouldn't have to risk being seen with it, you mean? And yet it would seem impossible to locate?"

"Something like that. And the Purloined Letter touch is always appealing."

"But who would want to do such a thing, Walt?" I had not crossed Walt off my woefully short suspects' list. It does take more than a playful-puppy look in the eyes for me to let down my guard. But I'd figured out that the only investigatory mask that would be at all credible was one of perfect candor. I remained convinced, however, that this most likely suspect was— well—highly *un*likely. Walt and I left the archive together, and I double-locked the door, nodding to show Gwen, at the desk, how perfectly under control everything was. On the way out, I had the momentary thought that *this* was the source of my foreboding that first day in the archive.

Becca was on the chaise longue in the living room when I let myself into the house fifteen minutes later. "You got mail," she told me. "Virginia Woolf."

"Nonsense, Becca. They found her body on April 18, 1941. And what would she be writing to me about, anyway?"

"Don't be silly: I didn't say she had. It's a postcard, one of those women writers series. Besides, you're a pedant. No poet should be *allowed* to get a Ph.D. and litter her mind with useless dates like that."

"Considering how you encouraged me to get credentials *they'd* respect, not to mention how you always said the poet was above all a noticer of material facts—Hey, you must be feeling better?"

"Yes, actually, I am. Too bad I've got the chemo again tomorrow. I was even going through some of my poems from the past few years and wondering if you'd be interested in helping me put a new manuscript together."

"Interested? Oh yes, Becca, yes!"

"And you ought to be compiling a manuscript of your own, you know. I'll do what I can—"

"No, you mustn't take any time from your own work."

"I mean do what I can with Richardsons—to urge them to publish it." Two more gifts I didn't deserve.

My postcard, dated the morning I left Berkeley, was from Cathy Ross, who'd put me on to Erin as an advisor on the *Helen-Elizabeth* project. "P.S.," it began incongruously, "I just want to make sure you keep me up to date on Lizzie and Nell, as the story comes clearer. Remember, they belong to *us*, too."

What if Cathy knew that "finders keepers," editorially speaking, had just turned into "losers weepers!" Instead, she was reminding me that *Helen-Elizabeth* belonged to a community that extended well beyond the borders of Ebbing College. I turned the card over. Virginia Woolf (1882-1941) looked at me with her beautiful, knowing eyes. She told me in no uncertain terms that I'd failed to live up to expectations.

"Becca," I announced, "I am a disgrace to the cause of women's literature."

"Cause? I thought it was an effect."

"You really *are* better today!" She was even well enough to hear my tale of woe and make several intelligent suggestions. After all, no one else knew the archive as well as she did.

Only after Becca had gone up to bed did I consider the sinister implications of that knowledge. Becca belonged on my list, too—ahead of Gwen, in fact, because I'd actually told *her* what was in the manuscript. Now I felt even more like a traitor. Becca, who was indeed familiar with the archive and the nature of *Helen-Elizabeth*, but who had just offered me a chance to serve contemporary poetry by helping with her last volume! Becca, who had said she'd encourage her own publisher to bring out

my first book of poems! Becca, who was prostrated half the time
I was away and who, even on her best days, wasn't so great at
the mechanics of standing and walking!

Why didn't I list myself while I was at it? It was about as
probable. *So there it is. Suspects List: Preston Walters, Rebecca
Parsons, Gwen (-dolen?) Ehrlich, Person or Persons Unknown.
I'd better get to know some more Persons around here, is all I can
say. This list is absurd.*

And that was how it came about that my first months at Ebbing,
when I should have been meeting my students and colleagues in
the same spirit of amicable interest they displayed toward me, were
actually spent gauging all these new faces as possible candidates
for the vital fourth slot on the list of possible abductors of *Helen-
Elizabeth.* I immediately instituted an excruciating one-by-one
comparison of the catalogue to the actual contents of the entire
archive. Everything in the files was what the catalogue said it was.
I found no lesbian erotica stuck into or between random folders. I
met the three student assistants, whom I reluctantly entered on the
suspects' list, since they'd been part of the project last year, as well,
and presumably knew their way around the archive. Provisionally
eliminating the other 1200 hundred students, I was left with Ann
Capobianco, Mike Freund, and Laurie Messer.

No one could have an alibi, since I didn't know when the
document had disappeared. I'd last seen it, of course, the day
after Labor Day, when there were very few students around, at
least officially. But Laurie had been on campus then, as I had
reason to know, one or both of the others might have been, and
anyone who was supposed to be elsewhere might have come and
gone. At the other end of the period in question, the theft was
discovered on the first day of classes, when all of them were
legitimately around both campus and library.

Thus, although it would have been easier to establish their
movements or alleged movements, I was left with the tougher
job of ascertaining their probable attitudes toward schol-

arship, library collections, disappearing evidence, the Ebbing family, women writers, women's rights, lesbianism, and anything else that might constitute the nucleus of a motive. This meant that I tended to seek out more opportunities for individual contact than might otherwise have arisen in the course of the work.

It turned out that getting to know the three assistants as suspects (what a word!) also served as an orientation to both America and American students in the '80s. I learned all sorts of interesting things, which added up to zilch as far as my investigation was concerned. Laurie was majoring in English, Mike and Ann in History. (You had to be doing one or the other to work on the project.) One afternoon, I overheard them talking about the ever-present issue of majors and their relation to future careers. Although I guess the point is that they *weren't* ever-present, at least as a pair, when I was their age. And I realized with a much-belated start of recognition that, if they were representative students and I was sitting in for the professor of poetry, then I no longer had any claim on the identity I'd left the country with eight years before, that of radical Berkeley student.

Anyway, Mike was complaining that he was "practically the only mule not majoring in some kind of business subject: Finance or Marketing or whatever." It made perfect sense to me that the dumb animals would make that choice until I recalled his fraternity pin: Mu Upsilon Lambda. "Well, a few of them are pre-something—"

"Like professional?"

"Yeah, but that's not what I want, either."

"Aren't all you history types supposed to be heading for law school?" This was Laurie, who was taking my advanced poetry workshop and developing a style that captured her breathless manner of speaking. "I mean, look at Ann."

"Yeah, but that's not what being a lawyer means to those guys."

"What's not?"

"What Ann wants to do—like women's rights cases and so on."

"It so happens," put in the future feminist attorney (who, like her peers, was leery of that particular F-word) "that even doing gender issues and women's constitutional rights, I'll be earning a lot more than my dad did at the steel mill, even when it was operating." An embarrassed pause ensued. Although all three of them were, by definition, on financial aid—that's who gets Work-Study, after all—Ann, whose father was an unemployed Pittsburgh steelworker, had a *full* scholarship. "But that doesn't mean," she added lamely, "that I think it's the same as mergers and acquisitions or something."

"Well, that's where the serious money is."

"So why aren't you heading that way, Mike, like the rest of your boozin' buddies?" It was Laurie and Ann who'd clued me in on MUL's hard-drinking reputation.

"Well, that's what I'm talking about. I'd really like to keep on doing history, but there are no jobs for Ph.Ds and who wants to live on a professor's salary, anyway?" I thought fleetingly about Ann's father again, then returned to a comparison of their views with those of my own generation. Not only had it never occurred to me to consider the state of the job market before I signed up in a doctoral program, it hadn't even seemed *relevant*. Real life for me was going to be learning and teaching about women's literary voices, while adding my own poems to the pool. And, of course, making the revolution.

"I don't think you should necessarily expect to make a good living doing what you love best," Laurie added. "I'm going to keep writing poems—" *That's my girl,* I began internally and prematurely, as she continued, "and meanwhile my uncle's offered to create a place for me in his ad agency until I get the experience to go out as a copywriter anywhere on Madison Avenue."

In my day (*and if that was fifteen years ago, who am I now?*), we'd have prodded Ann none too gently about her plans to work strictly within the system, while Mike's and Laurie's assumptions about success, money, and meaning would have been totally outside our ken. Yet I knew from the media that, in the eyes of the *Zeitgeist* (I pictured them looking like the ones on a potato), the problem was that these kids were not materialistic *enough*, insufficiently committed as they were to their destiny as yuppies.

Sometime in those early weeks, I became aware that Mike had what we used to call a crush on Laurie, who appeared oblivious to this development. She dated a succession of beefy specimens before settling down in that disquietingly domestic way college kids often seem to, these days, with a young man who rather resembled a frog and devoted *his* assistantship to running Psych department rats through mazes. This was better, I assured myself, than doing lab work with frogs while resembling a rat, but on more than one occasion I caught myself on the verge of pointing out Mike's sterling qualities to Laurie—one of them, as far as I was concerned, being that he had *not* made a clear and virile career choice. I had no idea, at any rate, what impact all this might have on Mike's attitude toward women, lesbians, or library property.

Need I add that—despite all my startled recognitions— all three were nice kids? None of them seemed crazy, malicious, or even unduly playful. None of them had the shadow of a reason for stealing that manuscript. And, as far as my subtle probing could ascertain, none of them knew of its existence. If it were not for my consternation at the short list that remained once they were eliminated, I'd have crossed them off as suspects by October. After mid-November, when all three stood vigil with me outside the Trustees' meeting on South Africa divestment, I was even less likely to suspect them of the theft.

Meanwhile, I was getting to know my colleagues in different settings and at a different, more rapid rate. The first weekend of the school year, I was invited to a party next door. Betsy and Bill Robards, both in the English department, looked like their names, which is to say, like pastel illustrations for a child's reader. In place of the expected dog named Spot, however, it was the Dean I saw tussling on the living room floor with a laughing four-year-old.

"Come in, come in," urged Betsy. "I can't tell you how happy I am to have you here!"

"You sound like the witch in *Hansel and Gretel*," Bill told her, as he took my coat, although nothing less haglike than this slim blonde creature could be imagined.

"But I wasn't saying I'm glad you could come to our party— though of course I *am* —but to Ebbing. Walt tells me you do women's literature. I've been trying for years to persuade Tom Walker that we need courses like that, but he's not convinced they're respectable. You're up on all the French feminist stuff, and maybe that will impress him."

"Oh, but I'm not up on it. It's true I've just come back from France, but I was only at a university for the first year I lived there. I was mainly doing my own writing, and the feminists I worked with weren't into theory."

"I thought all French feminists were into theory."

"An understandable impression—and one carefully nurtured on this side of the Atlantic by the folks who want to make theory the only politics. Actually, the women's group I worked in was setting up a birth control, abortion, and sexuality clinic in a town near our country place. Our big theoretical issue was how to get *crédits*—municipal funding—but keep feminist control. Otherwise, women's interests would become a political football between the Socialists and the Communists and maybe one of the far left parties, as well." (By that last year, when it had threatened to do so, Alain was telling me to keep out of what was clearly over my head and none of my business. I failed to see how women's bodies were either.)

"You mean, your group was more into city council meetings than Writing with the Body or the struggle against—what is it?—phallogocentrism?"

"Watch out, or you'll get me on my hobbyhorse about the difference between phallogocentrism and phallocracy—which has to do with whether you think women are oppressed by a symbolic system, on the one hand, or a social one, on the other."

"And you're saying that the French women's movement—"

"Betsy," Bill interrupted. "Isn't it about time you took Walt up to bed?" I was shocked to my Parisian core by this revelation of college-town sexual mores. Considering the enormity of my error, they were pretty quick on the uptake.

"Walt's our little boy," Betsy giggled. "He's Preston Walters Robards and the dean's his godfather. It does get confusing at times, but there's no nickname for Preston and I refuse to live with a child named Wally. Anyway, why can't you put him to bed, Bill?"

I'd been wondering the same thing, myself, but then, childless feminists are often puzzled by other women's domestic compromises.

"I've got those canapé things in the oven," Bill explained, "and they're taking longer than the recipe says. I want to keep an eye on them." It was what you might call an extenuating circumstance.

Walt took Betsy's place next to me, bearing a full bottle of fizzy mineral water and an extra glass with a couple of ice cubes. "No lime," he pointed out. "Though why I should do anything for you after this week—Labour Day, indeed!"

"What?"

"Well, it was really 'our American cousins' that threw me, because that was the play at Ford's Theater the night Lincoln was shot."

"Walters, *what* are you talking about?" Bill was entirely baffled, though of course I'd figured it out, relieved that it had nothing to do with the missing manuscript.

"Pangloss. It took me all week to finish the puzzle in the September *Review,* because of that stupid clue about the pink tea. I still know it by heart: 'A pink but veddy British tea party for an American holiday.'"

"Well, I usually do throw in something seasonal, you know. So I wanted a reference to Labor Day and thought I'd put a little twist on it by spelling it the British way. The clue started out something like 'A British party—Labour, you see—for an American holiday.' That would have been too easy, so, instead, I characterized the party's politics—pink—stressing that it was English by mentioning tea (see: it wasn't the *tea* that was pink) and then got in the American holiday through the hands-across-the-sea kind of thing. Lincoln couldn't have been further from my mind."

"Yes," said Walt, as Bill drifted off to the kitchen and his dilatory canapés. "All very simple. At least, if we have to have a mystery on our hands, it's a good thing we've got a cryptographer on the faculty to solve it."

"Sorry, my thing is verbal puzzles. I don't even read mystery novels very much, because I can never figure out who done it."

"Speaking of your archive—as we were, indirectly—there's someone you ought to meet." He caught the eye of a dark-haired woman with one of those map-of-Ireland faces. Presumably, that was what made her look so familiar. "Jamie, this is Sharon Reilly, from History. She's the official historian of the Ebbing family and the most diligent scholar on our faculty."

"Then you're just the person I need to talk to. And luckily, what I need is mostly gossip, not real history, so I won't be poaching on your preserve."

"I'm not sure I have a preserve—I mean, there's not really an *official* historian. But I'm related to the Ebbings on my mother's side, so this all started as researching my own family history. But I guess I do know a lot of the gossip, as long as it's somewhere in the records."

She certainly did. I couldn't judge how good Sharon was at seeing forests, but she was definitely up on the details of all the trees. While consuming an impressive quantity of Scotch, she talked about dead Ebbings, Brocks, Burchards, and Muellers (these last two being collateral relations of the family in whom I had not the slightest interest so far) as if they were likely to join the party later that evening. The members of Lizzie's family had been essentially literary characters to me, but Sharon gave them another dimension. People left us alone for nearly an hour as conversation groups formed and re-formed around us. At the end of that time, I asked if there was any evidence that there'd been "talk" when Lizzie married Alfred Brock.

"It did happen awfully fast—no time for a formal wedding back home, for instance. And their first child was born less than ten months later. I've always wondered about it, myself."

I wondered too, but not about that. "Nine-plus months doesn't argue for a shotgun affair," I pointed out.

"She may have been lucky and carried beyond her due date. But what I suspect is that she wasn't pregnant when they got married, but he *had* already seduced her. He was a widower, you know, a dashing, experienced man and twice her age, so even in those days—anyway, that would explain the quick marriage, and then, of course, she would have gotten legitimately pregnant on the honeymoon."

I'd seen a portrait of this fascinating older gentleman. He turned *me* off, and I'm certifiably heterosexual. Even without the evidence of aversion in Lizzie's long-time journal and the further story of *Helen-Elizabeth*, Sharon's theory seemed improbable. Wedding-night rape was more likely. I said nothing about my suspicions, however, and asked her instead what she was doing with the material. "Are you working on a book—or a bunch of local-history articles?"

"Oh, nothing like that." She stiffened and looked wildly about her. "I'm just getting the material together." I couldn't tell if she meant she was still at an early stage of the research—which it certainly didn't sound like—or if she had some reason for never going public with what she'd amassed, however extensive. Mumbling another half-sentence, she moved away before I could ask.

"She's a real scholar, isn't she?" Walt was back at my elbow.

"She sure is! But what does she mean about just getting the material together? Does she feel it's not ready to publish or what?"

"I don't know." The matter was clearly of little interest to him. "She just doesn't publish it. Doesn't seem to want to."

"Dr. Jameson," we were interrupted by a woman who looked like a piece of ripe fruit, glowing with life, and plump, too. "I'm Lola Santiago from Spanish. We were just talking about setting up the language tables at lunch for the term. Would you be willing to join the French Table?"

"Do I have to sign up to do it on a regular basis?" I asked her.

"Well, we prefer it, of course. But we understand you might get weary of hearing undergraduates butcher (she pronounced it bootcher) a beautiful language. I feel the same way about Spanish, of course, but it's my job to teach them. And at least I get to hear good Spanish at home." As I used to hear good French in *my* home. Before I could wax sentimental about the fact, I remembered Becca's explaining that the Santiagos were Chilean exiles and that her husband had spent some time in a concentration camp after the military coup in '73. My nostalgia for the language I was used to hearing around me seemed, by comparison, a voluntary self-indulgence. I agreed to be a drop-in at the French Table.

Sharon had moved back into the group, and Lola invited her

to participate in the program, as well; there was great need for German and Italian speakers. "Oh no," Sharon demurred, "I don't speak any foreign language well enough, and I don't know a word of Italian."

"Another thing we wanted to ask you," Betsy said to me, making room beside her. "A lot of us want to do something for Becca—visit, entertain her, run errands, take her little gifts, whatever—but we never know when it's okay to go over and when it'd be more of a hindrance than a help. Mrs. Moyer is so protective, I always feel more like an intruder than a concerned neighbor. Is there some time that's usually safe to venture in?"

"Well, Mrs. Moyer goes off on Sunday after breakfast, and, even in those weeks when Becca has her chemotherapy on Tuesday, she's better by then."

"The thing is, we all want her to feel free to say she can't see anyone, or to get up and leave when it starts being too much for her."

Thus it was that the bunch of us sitting around the Robards' coffee table planned the regular Sunday open-houses. Like Alice B. Toklas, I cooked on the help's night out, usually big pots of things that could serve an indeterminate number, and our guests would bring a salad, a bottle of wine, a dessert. More important, they brought a range of interests and personalities into our quiet house. Once, we read a one-act play aloud, and once Bill Robards' string trio played chamber music. But some of the pleasantest times were when nothing in particular had been organized. After the first evening, which turned out to be rather too big a party for Becca to handle, the number of guests would vary from two or three to maybe eight. The *dramatis personae* varied, too, though Betsy was almost always there and Walt never missed a Sunday. Each week, as I came to know him better, it seemed increasingly unlikely that he had ripped off *Helen-Elizabeth*. The process of elimination is not supposed to work to eliminate everyone, but that was certainly how it seemed to be going.

On one of those Sunday evenings—it must have been late October or early November—I came back from stowing leftover chili in the refrigerator to hear Betsy expounding to a group, all women that particular evening, about a key difference between male and female students at Ebbing.

"The guys think their professors are failures. Not because we don't teach at a more prestigious institution or have long lists of publications—because, in that sense, I might agree—but simply because we're academics at all. Even our top salaries are so low by their standards, how could they think well of anyone who's willing to work for that little? But the women in our classes think of us as successful professionals. It makes for a whole different approach."

"It's true," Amy Garber, the only woman in the Math department, nodded. "I had a girl tell me the other day that I was a role model for her. I didn't know how to explain I'm not such a great model, and, in any event, I don't want the responsibility."

"She'd better not let Tom Walker hear her call you that," I told her, "or he'll bounce her back into remedial English. In his mouth it has the force of an obscenity."

"Well, whatever you want to call it, *you're* certainly a role model for the aspiring women writers on campus." Camille Morris, the campus psychologist, who also played the cello in the trio, addressed this remark to me. "Unfortunately, they can't always tell a role model from a fashion model. At least, some of them now seem to believe that every woman writer lives in elegant sports clothes."

"Only if she's been married to a rich Frenchman. But I really have nothing else to wear. I thought no one would notice, as long as it was just shirts and sweaters and pants, anyway."

"Silk shirts and cashmere sweaters and beautifully cut slacks—but who's counting?"

"It seemed like an empty gesture to leave them behind. So I arrived back in this country after nearly eight years of marriage with practically no cash to my name and all this nice clothing. I thought if things really got desperate—if I couldn't find a job—I could sell my Chanel suits."

"Suits, plural?" Apparently, Amy was counting.

"I have two. I plan to wear one at the MLA conference when I give my paper on Helen Hayward and the early conservationists. Then if anyone wants to interview me for a job, I can look as if I don't need their mere vulgar *money!*"

"Did you ever tell me where MLA is meeting this year?" Becca asked.

"Chicago. I can't say I look forward to it. If I have to spend the week between Christmas and New Year's at a convention of ten thousand professors of literature, it seems redundantly infernal to hold it in Chicago!" That was when Walt came in, bringing a great sheaf of chrysanthemums, and no one mentioned designer suits again that evening.

The invitations I received and the open houses I hosted were not the only way I got to know my colleagues, of course. There were also faculty meetings. At first I kept quiet, because I didn't know the background to most of the issues that arose. In October, though, Carlos Santiago got up just before the end of the meeting and asked that the question of the College's investments in South Africa be put on the next month's agenda.

He was a tall, gaunt man, handsome the way a hawk is handsome. "If the matter goes on the agenda," he stated, "I plan to introduce a faculty resolution calling on the trustees to divest."

There was an uneasy silence, and the chair was clearly about to announce that he'd heard no second to the motion, so I seconded it. On the way out of the meeting, a couple of people told me almost shyly that they were glad the issue was coming up. I also heard a few nasty murmurs about Santiago's probable motives in raising it. Only one objection was addressed directly to me, however.

"Dr. Jameson," said Professor Charles Rowland with nervous formality, smoothing back a lock of already over-disciplined blond hair, "I have a great deal of respect for you. After all, you've published more than almost anyone on the faculty." I thought this was an odd reason for respect, since he hadn't read the stuff. "But *as* a scholar, don't you think we should avoid making decisions on matters outside our competence, where we can't judge for ourselves?"

"Well, you're a historian. Don't you make judgments all the time about events where you weren't present and persons you haven't met? You've learned what constitutes historical evidence and how to evaluate it."

"I'm sure you mean well," he began condescendingly.

"And *I'm* sure that if you'd been to South Africa as I have you'd want to see to it our trustees don't shut their eyes to the evidence." I wish I could say he slunk away, but in fact he sort of scurried, as I'd seen him do before.

"I didn't know you'd actually been to South Africa, Jamie," Sharon Reilly commented.

"I've been all over Africa. My husband's last novel takes place in a mythical postcolonial combination of Togo, Mali, and Cameroon, so he had to check out those places, and a bunch of others that turned out not to make it into the book. But your colleague Rowland is insufferable. Did you catch the bit about why he respects me?"

"Well, he's always scribbling away at articles and reviews, himself. I think he wants to write his way out of this backwater, as he calls it. And I wish to goodness he would, even if it meant wishing him onto some other university in the process. I feel so guilty about him."

"Whatever did you do to him?"

"It's what I did to Ebbing. I hired him, you see. After all, he's young, urban, a Columbia Ph.D., and his thesis—which at that time he claimed he'd be publishing, though nothing seems to have come of that—was on Afro-American history. The person Rowland was supposed to be replacing—he was retiring because of poor health—actually died in the middle of the search and he was the only one who'd actually read any of this famous thesis. So I took over, and how was I to know it was one of those 'slavery wasn't as black as it's painted' numbers? I actually thought he'd be a breath of fresh air around here. And now no one else will hire him because he comes from Ebbing and, besides, all that writing he does isn't really very good."

"So he can't actually do it—write his way to a better job?"

"With the market in history the way it is, my cat Herodotus has as good a chance!"

One of the incidental responsibilities associated with the chair of poetry was to run the series of monthly readings by visiting writers. Becca had organized the year's schedule the previous spring, so all I had to do was to introduce the poet and take care of what I came to think of as the ground arrangements. Regina Wells, October's guest poet, had already come and gone ('that lady is *in*sane," one of my students remarked, I think with admiration), when I got a call from Martin Miles, or rather, his wife.

"Marty broke his hip. He's still in the hospital. He should be out by the fifteenth of November—God, he'd better be!—but not in any condition to go around giving readings. Tell Becca he sends his love. In fact, it's the first message he's sent without a single curse word in it."

When I conveyed this message to Becca, along with the news that Miles had fallen off his horse, she suggested that I take his place. "I've been thinking what a shame it was that you're coordinating this whole series and not getting a chance to read, yourself. Besides, I'd love to hear you in public one more time."

"You really think you'll be able to make it?"

"If I'm counting right, that's a week when I don't have the chemo. At any rate, this second series of treatments doesn't seem to weaken me as much as the first." Becca's two-month minimum sentence was just about over, and the doctors no longer seemed to think that she might go any day. Even I was less haunted by visions of coming home to find she'd stopped breathing. Conversely, I was falling into the dangerous pattern of expecting her to go on dying indefinitely. At any rate, I ordered a new poster for the fifteenth with my own name on it. The print shop did me proud, with wonderful peacock blue paper.

At the November faculty meeting, a few days before my reading, Santiago submitted his motion on divestment. I seconded that one, too. There was more favorable comment than we expected, and no one exactly wanted to go on record as supporting apartheid. They just questioned whether Ebbing's giving up its holdings in companies that do business in South Africa might not be either too trivial to be noticed or actually "hurt the very people we mean to help." (Much of this commentary was sincere, but some of them disingenuously offered both arguments at once.) Charles Rowland also wondered—with all the conventional "due respect"—whether Professor Santiago who was not, after all, a U.S. citizen, was the proper person to make expert recommendations to American investors.

Santiago's voice seemed free of emotion as he rose to respond, but his accent was slipping badly. "Professor Rowland, with all *my* respect, on this I am an expert: I know what is fascism. I know what is preventive detention. I know what is mass arrest. I know what is torture. I may even make claim to know what is a sin against our common humanity."

The scientist (Carlos is in the Bio department at Ebbing) had carried the day's poetic weight. So I just read the faculty a short, highly statistical flyer listing human rights abuses and their relation to big-dollar investments. Charles Rowland scurried away before the vote, although I was sure he thought he was stalking out. There were a few abstentions, but no one voted against the motion—which, of course, had only moral force behind it.

The next day, Laurie and Ann cornered me in the archive and told me that some of the students were planning a vigil outside the trustees' meeting. "Actually, we're going to start the night before and stay there all the way through the meeting. We hope you'll come, since you cosponsored the faculty resolution."

It delighted me that Ebbing students were suddenly talking my language. So I replied, "Sure, what's the date?"

"We start on the evening of the fifteenth."

"But that's when I give my poetry reading!"

"That's okay, you can join us later. I plan to slip away and hear you, myself."

There was a gratifying turnout at the reading, and I felt a real rapport with the audience. A lot of writers are showoffs, but even they share with the rest of us a temperament, a kind of inwardness and isolation, that's almost the precise opposite of the actor's. Yet, at least in this country at the present time, if our isolated condition gives rise to some words that people respond to on the page, we are then expected to go out and perform. With no training and a "script" produced by our entirely unaided selves. It always amazes and moves me, therefore, when it works, when my words, uttered by my own voice, have the power to capture someone's attention, not to mention their emotions. When I finished that night, after they started clapping, some people tentatively stood up, and then the rest rose too. (I hate feeling pressured to do that when I'm in an audience, myself, but I'd never realized before how positively exalting it feels on the receiving end.) I announced that after the reception I was joining the vigil across the Green, and invited everyone to come on over.

There was a lot of hugging and kissing at the reception, another thing that seems to happen when the reciprocal emotion at a reading works. Walt got to me first, though, and just looked solemnly down at me, without indulging in any physical displays. "You're *good*," he informed me portentously.

"You sound surprised. After that introduction you gave me, too!"

"I still didn't expect—" He didn't seem to know how to finish, and there were enthusiastic huggers waiting to take his place. I drank a few cups of disgusting dining service punch and left for the vigil.

Walt was on the steps of the humanities building as we went out. "Look," he said to me, "I meant to ask: are you free for Thanksgiving?"

"The day itself? Yes, I guess so. Becca's kids will be here for the weekend."

"Then please let me take you to the Savage Inn for dinner."

"Sounds wild—sure. Coming to the vigil?"

"You know I can't, Jamie. I'm supposed to be above all factions."

"In that case, would you take Becca home? She's looking pretty worn out." He agreed at once, but when we announced this intelligent arrangement to the woman herself, she had other plans.

"Oh, no, you don't. I'm going to the vigil."

"But Becca, you can hardly stand."

"It won't be my first sit-in. And it may be my last. What are you afraid of, Jamie: that I'll catch my death?"

So I spent the long night in front of a hand-painted banner that had quite recently been an Ebbing College bed sheet, arm in arm with my student Laurie and my teacher, Becca. For the first time since coming to Pennsylvania, I felt I was absolutely where I belonged.

In the aftermath of that night:

Becca showed no lasting ill effects. She spent two full days in bed, but then she often had to do that anyway. "I always insisted on living in my own way," she reminded me. "That goes for dying, too." I was forced to agree with her. The Trustees did not dismiss the movement for divestment, nor did they vote to divest. Instead, they appointed a committee to look into the matter. "They could always switch on the TV and look into *it*," Laurie suggested scornfully. I told her victory doesn't come at the first attempt and counseled patience. As someone who started college in 1968, I had the grace to wonder who I was to give such advice. The manuscript was as lost as ever. I had a date for Thanksgiving dinner with the Dean.

4

*

IT IS A truth universally acknowledged, nowadays, that the traditional family-oriented holidays are hard on single and divorced people. Let me tell you, they're not much fun for the non-monogamous, either. Quite early in the semester, I had checked a calendar and realized that, by rescheduling my Monday workshop following Thanksgiving, I could have nine free days for a trip to the Coast. My relationship with Nick was "on hold"—barely begun and with no chance of developing for the rest of my time at Ebbing—but that needn't have prevented our spending the vacation together. It was his commitment to Rachel and the awkwardness of my arriving during a family-type holiday that put a visit to California in the Not a Good Move category.

Not going to Berkeley by no means entailed staying in Jaegersville, however. In fact, I was hesitating between Philadelphia and Pittsburgh friends when Becca told me she hoped to have a formal meeting about her "arrangements" while her children were in town. She seemed to think it was important that I be present. "We could do it on the Friday or, better still, the Saturday of that weekend, so if you want to have Thanksgiving dinner elsewhere, that won't get in the way. Of course, I'd be delighted to have you to dinner with us, but nobody will be insulted if you make other plans." Considering that Becca wasn't exactly *eating* dinner, these days, that meant a lengthy and lugubrious meal with a couple of young people I'd last seen seven or eight years ago when they were at Berkeley High and the unknown folk singer-wife of one of them, while all were busy assimilating their mother's condition. Walt's invitation to the Savage Inn "fell," as the French say, most conveniently.

"It's a very nice place," Becca assured me. "A restored eighteenth-century stone tavern up in the mountains. They get a lot of the weekend yuppie trade from Pittsburgh. First-rate food—not the kind you call pretentious, either—and wonderful antiques."

"Why 'Savage'?"

"It's the name of the village and, I suppose, its founder. Most of these old Pennsylvania towns have something that was a hotel or inn at one time, and a lot of them are still places of public accommodation. They range, though, from very basic country bars to family restaurants to what amounts in this case to an elegant little hotel."

"They've resurrected a lot of authentic Colonial recipes," Walt explained on the long drive up to the Inn, "and they rotate them, especially since so many use seasonal ingredients. Thanksgiving and Christmas are their big numbers, though, with Thanksgiving having the edge, because it's so solidly American."

"Then it's ideal for me. I haven't even celebrated Thanksgiving for eight years, and anyway, in California, what we actually experienced in terms of the landscape and the weather was nothing like all those Pilgrim-Fathers illustrations."

"Is this landscape closer?"

"Well, growing up, I had a picture book of the 'Over the river and through the trees' poem and it always amazed me, because there was *snow* on the ground—of course, there would have to be, for them to be traveling by sleigh—but it looked so exotic! And now I'm disappointed: here I am Back East at Thanksgiving and no snow."

"It's too cold. We may get some yet, though. If I'd realized it would gratify your childhood wish, I'd have done like the skiers and 'thought snow' instead of hoping it would hold off so our day wouldn't be spoiled."

The Inn itself was not a disappointment. "Oh, wow!" I exclaimed inarticulately. "In California, you know, only the Missions are this old, not real houses or hotels. France is a different story, of course—history at every turn—but our Paris apartment happened to be in a Second Empire building, and even down at Fautour the chateau was rebuilt in the 1820s." *After the restoration of the Bourbons.* I shuddered.

"You really lived in a castle, Jamie? That's a hard act to follow."

"It's just a big sprawling country house, sort of rose-colored brick, in the middle of a park. 'Castle' is something of a mistranslation. To me, it always suggests moats and fortifications—another children's-book image, I guess." I didn't ask why the chateau, castle or not, should constitute any kind of act for him to follow.

The holiday had me remembering my own childhood, but it seemed to remind Walt chiefly of his parenthood. Over a meal that even the fake eighteenth-century menu, larded with references to "sallets" and "pyes," could not cheapen, he talked to me about his children. The two sons in college, the boy and girl in boarding school, were all with their mother's parents in western Massachusetts. "It's ski country," he added, "so I don't have to feel personally rejected."

"Would you, otherwise?"

"You know, I think so. I was basically a single parent to those kids for a lot of years before it was fashionable. It's hard to have all of them away from home most of the year, and even harder that they don't consider seeing me the highest priority—in fact, the only priority—for their vacations. They're all a little distrustful of their mother, in their different ways. There's been some point for each of them when she's let them down with a bang. But they do trust me, and they love me, too, I think, so I only go on about rejection when something like this comes up." He paused. "I've got no reason to feel sorry for myself, anyway, since their so-called rejection has left me free to be drinking champagne with a lovely lady."

"I wish you wouldn't say things like that, Walt."

"What would you prefer?"

" 'Woman,' first of all, whatever the adjectives. And how about ones that are at least true: like 'smart,' 'funny,' 'strong'? I'd love to have someone agree that I'm a strong person."

" 'Drinking champagne with a strong woman.' It wasn't exactly what I had in mind, but I like it."

"Well, it's very decent champagne."

After dessert, while Walt was in the men's room, I got into conversation with the two women who ran the Inn. I was interested in the sources of the recipes and how they'd been adapted to modern ingredients and equipment. "The results are terrific," I told them, "absolutely honest and regionally authentic, but *haute cuisine*, too. Have you ever considered doing a cookbook?"

"Well, you know, we have, sometimes," said Marge, the older and rounder of the two, who was in charge of the kitchen. "You're not the first one to suggest it. But neither of us has a clue about how to write a book, and of course the Inn keeps us pretty busy."

"If you decided to do it, this is just the lay—woman to advise you," Walt told them, as he rejoined me at the table. "She writes books and she's a terrific cook, herself."

"That would be great! I wish you'd consider it."

"It'd certainly be a delightful vacation," I laughed, "since I'd have to come up here to stay for awhile. But whether or not I actually get involved, I have a title for you. To cash in on the vogue for the 'new American cuisine,' so-called, your book should be *The Old American Cuisine.*"

"You see?" said Walt. "She really does have the flair. Could you serve our coffee in the library, Sally?"

As the two went off, presumably to get coffee and library ready, I asked Walt why he wanted to move us from this delightful, low-ceilinged dining room.

"The library's special," he promised. "Besides, I want to talk to you alone."

I was his guest, so I refrained from adding that we were sitting at a table for two and there was hardly anyone else left in the dining room, anyway. Besides, the library—Turkey carpet, thick red draperies, and a collection made up entirely of the past eighty years' worth of bedside reading—was worth it. The coffee service was on a low table in front of the fire. Walt filled our two cups and drew aside a curtain. I caught my breath at the sight of snow on the ground and the bare branches.

"At least your wish is granted. I don't know how long this has been going on, but I took a good look from the end of the porch when I went out, and it shows no signs of stopping. The trouble is, these crazy mountain roads just aren't safe in the snow, especially after dark, and it's like this most of the way back to Jaegersville. That's probably why the dining room started clearing out fairly early, and it never was entirely full, which means they probably had cancellations from the western part of the state."

"That's true: Becca told me Thanksgiving dinner here is always booked up well in advance."

"I imagine some of the expected overnights have canceled, too. At any rate, you made such a hit with Marge and Sally, I'm sure if need be they'd turn out of their own bed or beds—

"I wondered about that, too," I admitted.

"But what about us: do we ask for one bed or two? I've been hoping you'd come back home with me for the night, but I don't want anything to happen just because we got snowed in together. You deserve more than a cliché, Jamie." His hand clenched on the curtain where he was still holding it back for me to see the snow. "God, I want to make love to you!"

His contained excitement woke an echo in myself. "Okay," I agreed unromantically. "I'll go talk to Sally when I've finished my coffee, and then—" I felt for an absurd moment like a Victorian bride, "and then we can go for a walk in the snow. At least, if those pretty French boots of yours can stand the exposure."

"They're Italian, and I wouldn't miss a walk in the snow at night if I had to go barefoot!"

Alone in the library, I felt some surprise at what I'd just consented to. Walt wasn't the first man to talk his way into bed with me, but I couldn't recall anyone else who'd managed it without a single touch or kiss. Why was I doing this, anyway? There was no grand passion on my part, surely, whether at first sight or as the culmination of long, solitary fantasy. Sure, Walt was an attractive man, but I'd always acknowledged the fact, as it were, objectively, feeling myself rather indifferent to his brand of lanky good looks. Furthermore, although I was trying hard not to slot people into pigeonholes, his being the dean underlined the real difference between us. *He wouldn't even go to the vigil, remember? You're about to make it with a man who feels he can't "take sides" about South Africa, for crying out loud! And besides, who stole that manuscript, anyway?*

Walt came back with his coat on and dropped my cape onto my shoulders, letting his hands rest there for a long moment. "All set," he grinned and looked conspiratorial. After all, he couldn't know the treacherous direction of my thoughts. We walked in the snowy woods with a flashlight to guide our steps. When we came back, we refused the Colonial hot posset Marge pressed on us and asked for a bottle of champagne to take up-stairs. "Well, you're the customers. And Sally's given you the room with the biggest bed—custom-made for Marcus Savage himself."

I wondered, surprised, if she was making a jocular reference to our prospective exertions on the big bed, but it turned out that Marcus Savage had been unusually tall for his day, maybe six-foot four or five, like this Walt with whom I was now committed to commit pleasure.

And pleasure it was, though different for each of us. It's another universally acknowledged truth that men who have been deprived of sex for some time are very quick to arouse and be satisfied, whereas, for women who've been forced to repress their desires, it takes much longer to rekindle. So there was a sense in which, although the act was technically complete, Walt and I reached out for one another and missed. Yet I found it undeniably pleasant to pull the thick eiderdown up over our naked bodies and fall asleep with a man's big arm around me. It was more than pleasant—it fed a deep and unacknowledged need for human connection.

And, after all, it was better in the morning, at first light, when we seemed to have all the time there is and took as much as we needed. As I drifted back to sleep afterwards I caught myself thinking, "If you can't get what you want, maybe you'll get what you need." (*So now you're relying on Mick Jagger for sexual insights, Jameson? And grossly misquoted to boot!*)

When I woke again, it was just after nine. In sleep, the big man beside me evoked even more images of little boys and puppy dogs. It was six A.M. in California. Nick and Rachel would be side by side, asleep, or perhaps stirring each other to wake and make love as we had, enjoying the freedom of Thanksgiving Friday. I found I could contemplate this with equanimity. In the other direction, it would be three in the afternoon in Paris. Maybe Alain was getting up from his desk and leaving to keep an

appointment with his current—*one would have to say "mistress,"*
I guess. (Though for all I knew it could be "fiancée" by now.) This
picture was unexpectedly painful, even though it was Nick, not
Alain, with whom I envisaged a future. Maybe for just that reason: Nick and what we might work out between us represented
success, however qualified; Alain failure, however justified.

At the edges of the silvery blue curtains, narrow slivers
of sunlight gave broad hints that the weather had cleared. I
edged out of bed and went to the window to look. Under an
almost suspiciously blue sky, the snow was already on its
way to slush. It had lost last night's magical quality, but there
were delightful patterns of light and shadow, even on the
sodden patches.

"What a beautiful sight to wake up to," came Walt's voice
from the bed. "A nude woman in the winter sunlight!"

"Strong sun, too," I told him, pulling away the curtain. "It's
already ankle-deep in slush out there. The roads back to town
should be completely clear well before dark."

"Are you in that much of a hurry to get back?"

"No. It's just that we stayed here because of the snow, so—"

Walt unexpectedly quoted Donne: "'Why should we rise
because tis light? Did we lie downe because 'twas night?' We
don't have to go back just because the roads are open."

"Well, I certainly have no appointments in Jaegersville until
tomorrow afternoon—you know, when Becca's set that meeting
with me and her kids."

"I have to spend the afternoon at the hospital, tomorrow,
with Virginia. But why don't we stay up here today and tonight?
Unless they're predicting another batch of snow."

"Okay, but let's make sure about the weather forecast.
Meanwhile, you can use the shower first. No, no, don't be gallant. I hate having to rush my bath because I know someone's
waiting their turn."

When I emerged, wrapped in a thick white towel, Walt was

back with an armload of motley offerings from our hostesses. "Marge and Sally couldn't agree what size you were likely to wear, so they sent up an assortment of ski pants for you to try. One pair's more funky than the next, if you ask me, but they thought you'd rather slosh through the woods in them than what they called 'that skirt.' "

"In tones of deep contempt, I take it? It's not exactly sloshing gear."

"Actually, the tone was more like reverence. What is that anyway: suede?"

"Uh-huh. Are the hiking boots for me, too?"

"Yes, but if they don't fit, they say come down and try the others. There's a limit to how large a selection I could take upstairs, especially with this pea jacket thing they added to the pile. I told them you could try it on down there, after all, but they insisted."

"Pea-jacket, thanks! I was blocking the English word—it's *vareuse* in French—I'm really bothered at all the common words I've mislaid in my own language. It's mostly those little household objects that you never learn how to say when you're *studying* a foreign language but have to pick up when you actually live in a country. And then they slip my mind in English. Well, someone whose business is words simply cannot afford to be ransacking her mind all the time looking for 'ball bearing' or 'carbon paper' or 'panty hose.' Oh—these dark blue pants fit fine. And I think they go okay with my sweater."

"Looks like blurred genres to me. What do you call that color: wine?"

"In conversation, you could. A fashion magazine would call it Burgundy in English and Bordeaux in French, speaking of blurs. How come they didn't lend *you* anything downstairs?"

"They did—this electric razor. Frankly, it looks like *it* was used by Marcus Savage, too, but we'll end up about equally presentable."

What with a morning walk in the woods, an afternoon slosh through the marshy fields, and four authentic-to-the-quick regional meals (for there was tea in the library after the slosh), there was plenty to keep us busy all day. Besides, we'd always found it easy to talk to one another. A night together, with some not-so-great sex and some quite good sex, had brought us that much nearer to intimacy. On our damp meadow walk, Walt told me more about his wife.

"We met my first year in graduate school—*our* first year, I should say—and we got serious about each other very fast. This was in 1962, but that's not what people mean when they say 'the Sixties.' Culturally speaking, if you ask me, it was just the Fifties with a higher number. So we got married when we finished our M.A.'s—because I think we were both too insecure not to. Neither of us had gone out with a lot of other people before, and never with anyone who was interested in the same books and ideas that we were. We met in Carl Werber's seminar—did I tell you?—a year or so before he died."

"Was she—was Virginia—already drinking?"

"No more than anyone else. I think it all might have worked out if she'd been able to stay in the doctoral program. But they cut her fellowship once she was a married woman—poor risk, you know, professionally speaking—and we were considering whether we'd both go part-time the next year or take turns going full-time for awhile, when Ginnie found out she was pregnant. Her family lent us money so we could take care of the baby while I finished my course work and prelims."

"If she hadn't had the baby, would they have lent money to replace the fellowship that got cut?"

"They had some of the same attitudes to married professional women that the university had. Anyway, Virginia didn't want to ask them. I think partly because it wasn't their kind of thing—they're very well off, but essentially philistines, from her point of view. And partly because she suspected they wouldn't let us pay them back. That's the kind of 'loan' it turned out to be when Craig was on the way."

"So you felt you had to be the one to stay in grad school so you'd be able to support a family?"

"Something like that. At least so Virginia's father—or his trust funds—wouldn't have to. I got the job here as soon as I passed my exams, and I wrote my thesis while I was starting out as a teacher. It probably took me twice as long as it should have, which I guess is when the joy went out of the research business for me, especially since the teaching load here is so demanding and the kids kept on coming."

"'Kept on coming' sounds like they marched in of their own accord or by their mother's sole invitation. I mean, you had something to do with it, too, didn't you?"

"It certainly wasn't my idea to have four of them that close together. Virginia's very—I guess you'd have to say—single-minded: when she stopped being a promising graduate student she threw herself into motherhood. When she was pregnant the first time, I think we expected that once I got my degree things would ease off so she could go back."

"That was going to be my next question."

"But it didn't work out that way. I took the job here because I wanted to be independent of my in-laws as soon as possible. Virginia was into being a full-time mother, but she found it made incredible demands—though I think she made most of them on herself—that she just couldn't meet. Anyway, there's no Ph.D. program in English near enough to commute and nothing much else for an Ebbing faculty wife to do. At least, Virginia's not the real estate or petite boutique type—"

"But the town librarian's a faculty wife, too, and the director of the community arts center, and Becca's accountant, if it comes to that."

"That's now, this was twenty years ago. Anyway, Virginia had started two things, and from her point of view—which is not just single-minded, but perfectionist—she'd failed at both of them. And the kids were still too small for her to think of learning some new profession she could practice in Jaegersville, even if that had seemed like an attractive option. So she drank instead."

"How long has she been—ah—drying out down at Hochstetter this time around?"

"It's not just drying out, anymore. By now, it's a more complex psychiatric problem. One of the crowning ironies is that her illness has meant my salary, even as dean, can't make us independent of her family. They pay for a lot of her treatment that doesn't come under Ebbing's health insurance, plus the prep school tuition. Luckily, Ebbing does help out once the kids get to college. But I guess you could consider the boarding schools fringe costs of Virginia's condition. Jaegersville High is pretty mediocre, but that's probably what we would have settled for if they had had two parents at home."

On the way back to the Inn, I offered an unsolicited feminist slant on Walt's story. Virginia had obviously been a victim of the constricting social expectations imposed on women. It was the feminine mystique syndrome and she had been unable either to embrace or resist it.

"That strikes me as rather facile," Walt commented when I finished. "You can't just reduce individual lives to what was happening in history."

"Well, you reduce them to a matter of personal idiosyncrasies. Virginia 'happens' to have this kind of personality or temperament, so she does this or that. Individuals do live in history."

There was a painful silence between us as we entered the Inn, and it lasted through the teamaking ritual in the library. It was Walt who broke through it first. "I'm sorry, Jamie. This stuff is so close to me it's hard to see how it fits together with the way the times were and how they've changed. Even when I talk about the culture of the Fifties or say things like 'that's now, this was then,' I can't take it all so—so—politically. In a sense, it's easier for me just to see it as Virginia's sick *response* to the conditions. After all, lots of other women met the same obstacles and overcame them. Or at least didn't turn into chronic alcoholics."

"Well, maybe there are social explanations for the individual reactions. But I was going to apologize to you, too. It's easy for me to be objective and make glib historical judgments when it's not my life. Walt, I'm so *sorry* for you both!"

"But remember what I said twenty-four hours ago: I'm hardly an object of anyone's pity while I'm sitting opposite a strong woman drinking—well, now it's tea. Particularly when that woman has just become my lover!"

Which was all very well, but I felt uneasy about what had happened to Virginia's life—and his own—and what role I'd be playing in their story. I changed the subject: "After tea, would you like to see how I construct a Pangloss puzzle? The outline for the March one is in my purse, and maybe I could even get a start on April."

"How about after dinner, instead? What I was thinking about for right now is going upstairs and peeling those dumb ski pants off you."

"Well, that sounds like a friendly amendment. Though I can undress myself, if you don't mind." I'd never been to bed with a man in his forties before, but this was not what the tales of declining sexual powers had led me to expect. The circumstances, to be sure, were atypical.

So we made love and had dinner and constructed the puzzles and went back to bed for a chaste night and an affectionate morning. Then we had to get out so he could drop me in Jaegersville on the way to the Hochstetter Clinic and his wife. I didn't feel I was exactly taking anything from Virginia Walters, but I didn't like to think of her waiting for him, either. At least, I found I was feeling less judgmental than I'd been before of this woman who'd sought refuge in the bottle. As if all the judgments were mine to make, anyway.

Back at the house, I found that time had worked its customary miracle on the Parsons kids, turning them from ungracious adolescents into sensible young people with a conscience. Becca was solemn as she explained how she'd disposed of her estate.

"You know, the last problem I ever thought I'd have to face at the end of my life was anything you'd call an 'estate.' (Well I guess it is the last, isn't it?) But I sold the Berkeley house four years ago, which is to say, some time after the real estate market out there started going haywire."

"Haywire how?" asked Patsy, Jack's wife.

"Further and further up," he explained. "It's crazy: no one *we* know could afford to buy a house there now, much less a big one like we had."

"I cleared a very large sum on the house," Becca continued inexorably, "and put it in the hands of one of those socially responsible investment firms: no South Africa, no war contractors or nuclear power, and so on. They do very nicely for me." She was almost smug about it. "I could easily live on the interest alone, but I haven't had to, so it's gone to the American Friends Service Committee. But I've still been able to add to the principal each year I've been here, what with the size of the endowment and the free housing.

"Then I started thinking about what you kids' different needs would be and got all confused: Jack's a man, Ellie's a woman, but he's the one with the marginal-income profession; then again, I don't want to encourage Ellie to feel she *has* to do the sort of law that brings in big bucks."

"Don't worry," her daughter put in, "big bucks and I are just not meant for each other."

"Eventually, I went back to first principles: the money's split evenly three ways, Jack, Ellie, and the Friends' Service

Committee. There's a twisted genius of a lawyer working out the most advantageous tax situation. But before the division, a sum is going to be taken off the top for my literary executor to take care of the unpublished poems and other papers. That seems especially important now that I've begun writing again, instead of getting my last volume together, as Jamie and I once planned."

"Do you *have* a literary executor, Becca?" I asked.

"Why do you think I invited you today? Who else do I know who's equipped to take it on?"

"Does it mean I'd have to stay here?"

"Not necessarily. It's up to you to decide what to do with the papers—even what library to donate them to—and there'll be a little bit of money to cover the costs of that end of things, along with an editorial fee for you. But I'm afraid I can't rival Lizzie Brock in generosity."

"You *know* it's a job I'd do for nothing. Though I'd still rather have you around than a bunch of—of 'clever financial arrangements.' " The young people, less accustomed to continual talk about Becca's death, caught what seemed like a single breath among them. I felt I'd trampled on feelings they hadn't had time to grow used to and shifted the focus slightly. "Your mother, among her other forms of wisdom, has done this money thing right, too. You'll each have enough to keep you from having to sell out, without its being so much that just having it means you've sold out. I've lived in close proximity to inherited wealth, and the things it does are not pretty."

"Speaking of Alain," Becca broke in, "Ellie, may I let Jamie in on what you told the rest of us the other day?"

"Well, it's awfully embarrassing, but maybe it'll make it easier for me to ask her some other questions, so okay. Actually, I'll tell you myself, Jamie: it's just that when I was fourteen and fifteen I had the world's biggest crush on Alain."

"But you didn't even know him," I objected.

"Do girls that age usually know the rock stars or whatever that they're in love with? Actually, I knew Alain better than that. He came by for you a few times after classes at the house, and you brought him to dinner once, before you went off to France. I used to fantasize that he'd Discover me, and carry *me* off instead."

"Part of me wishes it had happened just that way. But, believe me, Ellie, you're better off."

"That's what I wanted to ask you. Not if I'm better off, I mean, but—well—what *happened* to Alain? How did the idol of my youth turn out to have feet of clay?"

"I think it comes with the territory of being an idol."

"But about Alain—if you feel you can talk about it?"

"Oh, it's probably an object lesson in something or other. Well, you knew Alain as he was those two years in Berkeley."

"A suave, handsome Frenchman?" asked Patsy.

"Not really handsome and definitely not suave. But incredibly vital. He had twice as much sheer energy as anyone else."

"And sexy," put in Ellie, imitating her adolescent self. "In my fantasies, he always deflowered me up at Strawberry."

"Sexy is part of it," I agreed, recalling inwardly that I'd been the one to introduce *him* to Strawberry Canyon and its various pleasures. "But *wild*, too. Did you ever read any of his novels? He was making the French language do things no one knew it could. Just being with him, listening to him, even reading him was like being drunk on life. Or is that a cliché nowadays? Anyway, to me, he was radicalism personified—his whole being was the spirit of May '68, a really daring imagination applied to all received truths, social relations, politics, literary forms, everything. He was—or he seemed to be—a born rebel.

"But he was also a born aristocrat—literally. That class in France doesn't seem to produce many rebels. It's not like England, where you can meet all sorts of eccentrics in the peerage, including some whose eccentricity it is to be artists or leftists or even both. They provide them with certain safety valves in France, but they also keep the lid on tighter. And it works, from their point of view.

"So Alain was an anomaly, and of course in revolt against his family, as well as the system, because his family *was* the system. Marrying me was a part of that, I think. Having someone like me for a mistress would have seemed absolutely normal to them; it was the marriage that was shocking. He had one elderly aunt who was upset that, on top of my being a non-Catholic, an American, a bohemian writer, and a Berkeley radical, I was 'not born.'"

"What did she think: you were hatched or something?"

"It just means not a member of European nobility. It didn't even bother them so much that my family was working-class American. Practically no Americans are 'born' as far as they're concerned, though they'd have welcomed some American bucks, God knows. Anyway, Alain was thumbing his nose at his background by marrying me, but we really were a well-matched couple—at least, as he was then. So we had nearly six good years together. More than seven, counting Berkeley.

"Then the unthinkable happened: his father and both older brothers were killed in the same car crash. It was on their way back from Fautour at the end of a long weekend. Alain inherited the title and the estates and the responsibility. And he accepted them, with all their implications. It started—slowly, at first—to look as though he was trying to turn into his father. And eventually—though it took a couple of years—I realized he'd succeeded. All that energy got directed into becoming what he would now say he always was or was meant to be: a correct, uptight conservative on his way to being a reactionary. And essentially—well—corrupt. When I left, one of the right-wing parties was talking about running him for the Assembly. You'd have gotten out, too, Ellie."

"And your position is that inheriting money did all that?" Patsy asked.

"Not just money, but class—and, of course, the family trauma didn't help, either. I don't know: maybe that trauma, the deaths of all three older males in the patriarchal line, did free him to become what he really was."

"You had no children? Because it would be so hard—"

"It would, and I wish I could feel I was lucky not to. I had two miscarriages before all this happened, and we were strongly advised not to try again. Now he'll be able to beget an heir, after all—with a suitable dam, this time."

"I've never heard you sound so bitter about it," Becca commented.

"Well, my first priority has been to keep myself going. But I've had occasion to think a lot, this weekend, about unfulfilled potential and coming up against dead ends in life. I guess there's more than one kind, is all. And that reminds me, Becca, why did you make such a point of my having been a French countess that first day, when Walt and Walker were here?"

"I just wanted Tom Walker to know that you could handle the Pennsylvania aristocracy aspect of the archive. He's a terrible snob, and I thought that would help you get the job. Whereas, from his perspective, I'm sorry, but it just doesn't do any good to know your grandparents were dust-bowl migrants, even though that went into making you who you really are. I figured you might as well get *some* mileage out of that title."

"I did—however many miles there are between here and Paris."

"Speaking of that first interview, is Walt coming by tomorrow evening?"

"He didn't say. If he doesn't, it would be the first Sunday he's missed."

But he didn't miss. Becca and I were rather subdued after Patsy and Jack set off for Cambridge in their weathered van, with Ellie aboard as far as the Philadelphia airport. Becca could never know, now, which farewell would be the last one. So the

Sunday visitors were welcome and, since it was a holiday weekend, Walt was the only friend who came over. He and Becca
talked about coming to terms with your children's growing up.
It occurred to me that, by the standards Alain now endorsed, my
trouble was failure to accept my husband's growing up. The
thought left me as gloomy as the other two.

So it was good that Walt was there for me at bedtime. I may
have stumbled into this thing, I thought, but perhaps it was a
fortunate fall.

5

*

"WOULD YOU LIKE to see Brockland?" Walt asked me the following Friday.

"Lizzie's house? Sure, can we really just go out there?"

"Well, the estate belongs to the college now, you know. As dean, I can get hold of the keys pretty easily. And I'm inviting you, so, yes, we can just go out there. It's not a very long drive." As we made plans for the next morning, I was glad the conversation was taking place by phone, so Walt couldn't see my expression at this reminder that I'd become the dean's girlfriend. I am usually someone who insists on facing facts, but I still found it hard to confront this one head-on.

I might not like the label, I reflected that Saturday, or approve of administrators as a group, but it was certainly nice to have a man in my life who thought up things I'd enjoy doing and put a friendly arm across my shoulders on the way out to his car. Of course, I could get along without such a relationship, but who was I to deny myself the sheer comfort of it?

"Brockland was the husband's house, is that right?" Walt asked as he negotiated the mountain curves.

"As the name indicates. The Ebbings and the Brocks both had summer places—big estates, it sounds like—in this part of the world. That's how they got to know each other, although there may have been some prior connection between the money from both sides, as well."

"Then your lesbian manuscript has no connection with this house?"

"Well, I don't know where the story in there ended. As far as I'd read before it disappeared, all the sexual stuff happened at Greenlawns, her own family's place."

"Then why did she choose to stay at Brockland after her husband died? I've had this picture of her moving back to the family summer place year-round, but of course I realized Brockland wasn't it—as you say, the name alone should have clued me in—and it didn't have particularly pleasant association for her, either. So why stay there?"

"*My* question is why stay in the middle of Pennsylvania, when she could have gone anywhere in the world? But if you mean why keep her husband's place, which was far from a honeymoon paradise for her, that's easy. Under a patriarchal inheritance system, anyway. Her own family's home, the one with the delightful girlhood memories, naturally went to her brother. You know, Manley Burchard Ebbing. His portrait is in my office."

"I think I know: the one who looks like a walrus?"

"Walt, they all look a little like walruses. Haven't you noticed? Let me tell you, it makes for some creepy hours, when I'm working alone in the archive."

"Maybe we should unspook it, make love up there sometime, under all their shocked walrus noses!"

"It's not clear they'd raise so much as a walrus eyebrow. The Ebbings were a pretty horny bunch, from what the archives suggest and Sharon Reilly confirms, and as for old Brock, well, of course, *I* think of him as no better than a rapist, but Sharon sees him as an 'experienced older man' who seduced our Lizzie before he made an honest woman of her."

"Speaking of Sharon, have you done something to hurt her feelings lately?"

"No, I thought we got on quite well, in fact. We've had a couple of good talks about what she always calls The Family. Why do you ask?"

"We had a committee meeting the other day, to talk about honorary degrees for next spring's Commencement. We're proposing Becca for a Doctorate of Humane Letters, by the way, if—"

"If."

"Anyway, we also have this custom of awarding M.A.'s *ad eundem.*"

" 'To those' who what?"

"Who are senior members of the faculty and aren't graduates of the college. The idea is that this way all the faculty become alumni, too."

"Very cozy. But what does it have to do with Sharon's feelings about me?"

"Your name was on the list of new senior faculty, and she pointed out right away that it didn't belong there, because 'senior' is normally interpreted as meaning tenured and permanent, whereas you don't have a continuing appointment."

"True enough, though perhaps a tad officious."

"But then someone said that, although you don't automatically get the degree, we could vote to award it as a nice gesture, for stepping in at the last minute and making yourself so much a part of college life."

"Makes me sound like an old fraternity tradition or something."

"You know what I mean. So then Sharon started to talk about how you didn't fit in all that well, harping on what she called your fancy degrees and all your publications."

"What's so fancy? Doesn't she have a Ph.D. herself?"

"Not from a place like Berkeley. She had to go where she was offered the most financial aid."

"Well, so did I."

"We're not talking about facts, Jamie, but Sharon's interpretation of them. At the meeting, it looked as if she would have kept on in that vein, except that it became clear, even to her, that some people were choosing to interpret 'doesn't fit in here' as a reference to the South Africa business. So Sharon had the grace to shut up, and the committee voted to recommend the degree. But I wondered why this flare-up about what she called your 'snob appeal' When I tried asking her, afterwards, she just sort of shrugged it off."

"I can't imagine what's bothering her. We've been on the same side about divestment, and I don't think we've ever discussed anything else, except her dislike of Charles Rowland— which I heartily second—and the Ebbing family skeletons. Mostly that. And it even turns out she's a whiz at cryptic crosswords—does Pangloss every month in about twenty minutes."

I'd seen many photographs of Brockland in the archive, but none of them had shown the locked wrought-iron entrance gate, well away from the house itself. Walt opened it and drove through. "Why has the college held onto this huge empty place all these years?" I asked him as we swept up a driveway that amounted to another country road.

"We haven't. It wasn't Lizzie who left it to us, but her grandson, just a couple of years ago. There has been some thought of our renting it out as a conference center or something, as well as a lot more thoughts about selling it. Meanwhile, we use it for occasional faculty retreats and so on. This year's college Christmas party is here, too—a dinner dance. You'll be getting your own invitation from the president this week, I imagine, but I wanted to ask if you'd be my date for it."

"Walt, I keep expecting you to tell me we have to be discreet.

I was even preparing to resent it and tell you that I don't live like that. And instead you don't seem to mind if people do suspect. If it comes to that, Marge and Sally, up at the Inn, and Mrs. Moyer at my place, don't just suspect, they know. And now you're talking about our advertising ourselves as a couple at a College function."

"It's not as risky as all that: Marge and Sally are in the business of being discreet about their customers, and Sylvia Moyer wishes me well and definitely won't gossip about my love life. She worked for us, once, during one of Virginia's bad spells, and Ginnie was—well—abusive to her. As for the party, maybe I'm kidding myself, but it isn't exactly like wearing a scarlet A on our chests; I escorted Becca a couple of years ago, in fact. Everyone who works for the college is invited, and people sign up to sit at dinner with their own group of friends. So you'd probably be dancing with Bill Robards and Santiago and whoever else is at our table, not just with me. And, frankly, the people I'm closest to will think it's wonderful that I have somebody."

"I just hope there were quotation marks around those last two words."

"Well, that's the way they would put it. But I'm so tired of being an object of pity—'Poor Walt with his Crazy Wife'— I'd almost prefer to offend the ones who would *be* offended. And the others will envy me, for a change!" It was a point of view, though based on reasoning that was fundamentally alien to me. But then I found this whole social scene a little strange. Dinner dances for heterosexual couples in formal clothes are not how Berkeley characteristically entertains itself, and I'd left Alain rather than be drawn into the French version of such a life. The thing is, I wouldn't have dreamed of accepting the invitation to the Christmas party if it weren't for Walt. Which came right back to the contradiction of being the dean's girlfriend.

I got out of the car under the porte-cochère and Walt opened the heavy outer door. "This is a great house for a party, anyway," I observed, in response to my own thoughts, as we walked through the drawing room and the ballroom. "The last thing it looks like, though, is a writer's house. Do you know where she did her work?"

"The library down here was just for show." He opened a door and I saw an elegant, soulless room whose walls were lined with handsomely bound sets of classics that might have been ordered by the yard. "I get the impression that real life was lived upstairs. Lizzie had a study up there and also a very serviceable writing table in her bedroom."

We took the front stairs, a grand expanse of polished oak. Lizzie's bedroom was a corner one, with windows facing in two directions, but, in the Pennsylvania December light, that still lent an air of austerity—not to say bleakness—to the rather stiff furniture and hangings. "Serviceable" was a term that suited more than the writing table.

"The other corner room was apparently Brock's bedroom. When he died and she moved here permanently, she made it her study." Walt led the way across the hall.

"If nothing else, it was a good way of getting rid of his things," I pointed out. "And marking off space for her writing right where he used to dominate the scene might seem like getting her own back in more ways than one." This room got the morning sun and looked more welcoming than the other. The books here were clearly well read and well loved, the desk arranged to suit a real person's tastes and habits. "But it's more than a revenge place," I went on. "It was clearly meant for her most joyful and productive hours. Doesn't it give you the feeling that she could walk in, sit down at her desk, and start writing again?" We stood there in silence for a moment, our arms brushing against one another, invoking the presence, if not precisely the ghost, of Lizzie Brock.

"That's not just the decor. Someone's added to the effect by leaving a writing folder out. It's even the kind we know she used, like your lost manuscript was in."

"Yes, it—" I strode over to the desk, picked up the folder, and untied the ribbons. "Walt, this *is* the manuscript! This is *Helen-Elizabeth!*" If he let out any sort of exclamation, I didn't hear him, because I was paging through the sheets of ladylike penmanship I'd given up hope of ever seeing again. "It's not a second copy, either. See? Here's the marker I left in it when you came to take me to lunch that day."

"The Purloined Letter," Walt said slowly. "I thought that would mean stealing it and leaving it there in the archive. Instead, it's right out on the author's own writing desk for anyone to see—except that there's no one here to see it most of the time."

"And you—you—?" I couldn't finish my question and ask if he really hadn't known it was there when he led me to it. Led me right up to it.

"What do we do now, Jamie? You can't just stand there clutching it to your bosom."

"The first thing is to make sure no one can ever get hold of the only copy again. And the second thing is to try to find out who took it and left it up here."

"Number one is easy, thanks to the copy machine. We'll make a copy—"

"More than one," I interjected.

"Right away. But how do we catch the thief?"

"We set a trap, of course."

"Fine: what sort of trap?"

"I don't know."

"Jamie, you said that with such brisk authority, I expected to hear 'This is what we do next.'"

"Well, I don't have a clue about how to set traps and things. I told you once I don't read mystery novels. But it's obvious we do have the bait: the original manuscript. Ralph Ehrlich made a great point of letting me know, at the time of the theft, that it has no intrinsic value. Actually, that's not quite true—he just doesn't know that particular market, which is pretty specialized. But its greatest value *is* as a literary document, a text, and once we've got the copies, we've got that. For it to work as bait, though, the thief has to keep thinking this one's still the only copy. Which means nobody's to know we've found it."

"Easy enough. Practically nobody knows it was lost, do they?"

"The two of us, Becca, and both Ehrlichs, the sister and brother, though back in September I assumed they were husband and wife. (Either way, it's funny, because they had such different attitudes to the loss of an archival document.) And of course the person who took it knows, too."

"Anyway, nobody's to know we have it. So how do we get it away to copy?"

"We'll have to do it right now. And one of us should stay behind in case the thief comes by. Not that I know how likely that is, because it's not clear how long the manuscript has been here at Brockland. I'm assuming since sometime in early September."

"In fact, we had the freshman picnic out here the weekend before classes started, on the Friday. You must have still been out of town."

"Incoming students are the least likely suspects, but who else comes to that picnic? Anybody who would also have been on campus the week before?"

"The President and his wife are there, and I am, and the dean of students, and Ehrlich—Ralph, not Gwen—because Security is always around when there's a crowd. Plus all the faculty who are freshman advisors, as many as can make it, anyway. and the upper-class big brothers and sisters—again, as many of *them* as can make it—though most of them were still off campus the previous week. But we don't know, do we? The thing could have been stolen *during* freshman orientation week, a day or so before the picnic."

"So it doesn't eliminate anyone. Who would even notice an extra faculty member who wasn't a freshman advisor? Or a student who wasn't a big sibling this particular year? Not to mention all the people who were here legitimately because they are advisors or siblings. The main thing is: I gather the gate was left open, and it's usually locked."

"That's right. So the person either brought the manuscript that day, which was not long after the theft, or has a key and can come at any time."

"And that's why we can't both go now and make the copies. If the person has a key, they could come back, so one of us has to be here to keep the thief from going up to the study."

"I should be the one to stay," Walt offered, "because my presence is more intimidating: I'm a lot bigger than you, and I'm the dean. Besides, I don't like the idea of your waiting alone here, especially with the car gone."

I let this heavy chivalry pass, because it was the outcome I had in mind. There was no way that manuscript was going out of my sight until the copies were made. And, far from eliminating himself from the suspects' list now that it was expanded, Walt had awakened the gravest suspicions by bringing me here at all.

"I can lock the gate behind me," I offered, "so the person wouldn't know anyone was around until they open the door and there you are—"

"Doing what?"

"Well, there are lots of old books to read. Or didn't I see the December *Review* in the car?"

"The mail came just as I was leaving the house this morning."

"Well, you can do Pangloss. It's one of the puzzles I put together on the plane to California the day after I discovered the manuscript. Maybe it was being stolen at that very minute."

"So the thief creeps into a locked and supposedly deserted mansion and finds—ta da!—the dean in here doing a crossword puzzle? Talk about anticlimaxes! What I meant was, what am I *supposed* to be doing here?"

"Waiting for me, of course, which has the virtue of being true. You took me up to show me Elizabeth Brock's home—since I've got the Brock Poetry Chair and am working on her papers— and I borrowed your car to do an errand."

"What kind of errand and why are you doing it once we're already here?"

"Doesn't matter. I'm just giving you your motivation as an actor. You don't have to explain anything. It's the other person who should be on the defensive. In any case, the person probably won't come today. I mean, there's no reason to. Of course, I can't figure out what reason there was for taking the manuscript up here in the first place."

"So, assuming no one does come, what do we do once we've got a couple of copies?"

"The original becomes bait. I can't think of a trap for when we're not here—and we can hardly move in for the duration or set a guard—but we will be around the next time the house is officially open to the college community."

"The Christmas dance!"

"Right! And now at least this date business makes some sense." I'd forgotten Walt didn't understand how exotic his world was to me, as if we'd been living in parallel cultures that never touched. Downstairs, as I fastened my cape and Walt got the *Review of Literature* out of his car, I realized that he was assuming I'd take the manuscript back to Ebbing to copy. "The machine in my office would be best, but it'd be hard to explain what you're doing there, and creepy for you, anyway, on a Saturday morning. I guess the safest place is where there are the most people."

I made no comment, because I had no intention of going anywhere near the college at all until the copies were made and the original was back in Lizzie's study. And I also found I didn't want Walt to know where I was heading. Only after I locked the big gate from the outside and got back into the car did I make that decision.

According to the map in the glove compartment, we were only a little less than halfway between Jaegersville and Flissburg, which I knew was a university town. In the nineteenth century, it was the home of Flissburg Normal School, which became a State Teachers College early in the twentieth. Nowadays, all such institutions in the Pennsylvania system had become comprehensive universities, each bearing the name of its location. There were some twelve thousand students at Flissburg, which argued for many coin-operated copiers on campus, perhaps an attended one at the library, and maybe even, if I'd been living right (though fat chance, if it depended on that) a commercial photocopy shop off campus.

As I drove, I asked myself why it still seemed so important to identify the thief. After all, I had the manuscript back, which was certainly all I had cared about when I compiled the original suspects' list, probed around among the student assistants, and so forth. Never for one moment had it occurred to me that the thief might have destroyed the manuscript, so finding out who had it always meant getting it back. And I'd assumed that getting it back would mean learning who'd taken it. But I'd also never thought of pursuing the thief—legally, for instance—once *Helen-Elizabeth* was restored to me. I realized that the reason I wanted to identify the culprit was so that I could exonerate Walt in the only quarter where a suspicion of him existed, my own mind.

"If I weren't sleeping with this man," I mused, "I wouldn't care if he'd stolen the thing—at least, *now* I wouldn't care. All that would matter is that I can read the rest and make it available to other women. But then, if I weren't sleeping with him, I wouldn't have gotten it back. That's true whether or not he knew it was at Brockland when he took me there."

I recalled my moment of hesitation in the library of the Savage Inn after I'd consented to spend the night with Walt. It was a more political concern that had moved me then—you don't get into bed with the enemy, and someone whose position prevents him from acting on conscience comes dangerously close to that—but even then I'd remembered my suspects' list. Nonetheless, I'd put my reservations aside and gone ahead along the path of least (sexual) resistance.

And what? Walt had proved a kind and ardent lover. It was comforting, if not wildly exciting, to go to bed with him. If that comfort was to continue, what was needed was a clear and un-ambiguous "not guilty" for Walt in the matter of the manuscript.

Flissburg turned out to have a main street with student-oriented shops, including the copy center I needed. Since it wasn't yet high term paper season, they promised me my copies within the hour.

"Good," I agreed, "I've got to have them before the Post Office closes. And can you tell me where to find a Notary Public in town?"

"Two doors down, at the insurance agency." I wrote out a formal attestation that this document was a photocopy of a holograph manuscript by Elizabeth Ebbing Brock (1849-1931), signed it, and got it notarized. In case of my unexpected demise, even the copies would have a pedigree. As for the unexpected demise, I didn't anticipate that a cleverly cornered thief might murder me to avoid exposure, but I lived so close to the planning for a death, these days, that some of it simply had to rub off.

Across the street, I noticed the kind of college-town restaurant that evokes warm memories of Berkeley: a sign with a big yellow sunflower on it advertised home-baked, whole-grain breads and homemade soups. But the visceral comfort I craved went back even further, to my childhood, so I sought out a classic luncheonette and ordered a bacon, lettuce, and tomato sandwich and a chocolate malted. I do love French cooking, but I swear, if they had BLTs and authentic malteds in Paris, I'd have weathered my marital crisis with far less psychic damage.

They were finishing my copies of the manuscript when I went back, and I made it inside the post office just before they locked the door. By eleven minutes after noon, when they let me out of the Flissburg Post Office, padded mailers containing the manuscript and the notarized declaration, were on their way, registered and insured, to Cathy Ross in San Francisco and Erin Ni'Connor in Philadelphia. Now, whatever might happen to me or the original, I'd placed *Helen-Elizabeth* back in the community it belonged to.

Before heading back, I stopped at a hardware store and copied Walt's keys to Brockland—for whatever it was worth.

When I let myself in to the big, brooding house, Walt told me that no one had disturbed his morning's labors over Pangloss and that he felt my "wassail" clue was unfair.

"What about 'ride a common carrier under the mistletoe'?"

"Oh, 'buss'—at least that one was easier than usual. But I can see that this is going to be a strain on our relationship, Jamie." I hoped it would be the biggest one.

"Well, to make up for that and your unadventurous morning," I told him, "I'll buy you lunch at that little place I passed up the road. Their sign says 'Platters,' though not platters of what."

"What are you going to do with these two copies?" Walt asked me after we'd ordered what in my case was a redundant meal.

"One's for you—for your files, actually—and one's for the archive. I plan to catalogue it but make a completely opaque catalogue entry, so, if the thief is someone with access there—and we know he or she did get into the archive that one time, at least—it won't be recognizable." We left the original on Lizzie's desk, exactly as we had found it.

It was late afternoon when we drove onto campus. "I'll just

stop at the archive," I told Walt, "and meet you back at your office in a few minutes." Ignoring the enhanced creepiness of an early-December Saturday, I made a bland entry for the manuscript, cross-indexed it, and then, on an impulse, instead of filing the copy, signed it out to myself.

"I don't call that filing a document," Walt observed, noting the folder under my arm as he let me into the administration building,

"I thought I'd read it tonight."

"*I* thought you were coming back to my place."

"They're not incompatible plans. After dinner, I'll curl up and read about Lizzie and Nell, while you finish Pangloss."

"Come into my office, and I'll show you where the other copy is. This file cabinet is kept locked when not in use, and I rarely need to consult anything in it. That portrait over it is Hiram T. Wolper, who was president of the college between certain nineteenth-century dates you'll find on the little metal tag."

"I'll remember: the cross-eyed one in the academic robes." I paused and looked around. "But Walt, they're all somewhat cross-eyed and they're all wearing black gowns. Why are my portraits—the ones in my office—walruses and yours cross-eyed?"

"Yours are almost all blood relatives, of course. The subjects, I mean. But there's a rational explanation for this resemblance, too. The portraits of all the past presidents used to be displayed in the library, in that big conference room where committees sometimes meet. Back in the sixties, though, we hired an art professor who went crazy in a rather drastic and public way and cut all the eyes out of the presidential portraits with his Xacto knife. They were restored, of course, but I don't know whether the job went to the lowest bidder or whether eyes in paintings always look like that if they're put in separately. That's why they're hung in the offices of senior administrators now, so no one can get at them again."

"But that means that you all have to do your work under their cross-eyed gaze, which is a strain on the senior administrators."

"True, but I have an idea for straightening them out. Actually, it's the same idea I had for your walruses, but these fellows *would* be shocked." He drew me over to the long sofa. "Besides, it's what I wanted to do the first time we sat here together."

"You concealed it admirably. Well, pretty admirably," I amended, remembering the vibes I'd picked up. "But you didn't do anything about it."

"We have some pretty tough sexual harassment procedures, you know. Betsy wrote them, modeled on the ones at—I forget where—but some university where life is clearly a lot more exciting than around here. Anyway, what would you have thought if the dean who'd just hired you had made a move like this?"

"Mm. I see your point. I doubt whether I'd have thought well of you. Much less taken an active part . . . ." The cross-eyed portraits certainly got their money's worth. And we made another good picture to enhance his future administrative routine.

In comparison, the evening at Walt's house passed quite decorously. He grilled a couple of steaks for us, serving them with the garlic bread that is apparently *de rigeur* in American middle-class entertaining, as well as a very nice Nuits-St.-Georges and a big salad. There was cheese and fruit for dessert.

"Wonderful! I'd forgotten, before I came back, that there isn't usually a cheese course in this country."

"Would it have been enough to keep you in France, if you'd remembered?"

"Not quite."

For a while after dinner, Walt and I worked separately in front of a big fire in his living room. He solved the Pangloss puzzle, and I, if you could call that working, read about the transports of Lizzie and Nell, looking for the first time on one another's nakedness and finding it good. More than good.

It was only after Walt had turned out the light in his bedroom and fallen quickly asleep that, lying beside him, I rehashed some of the contradictions in our relationship. I had enjoyed our time in his office, had given myself to it without reserve or second thoughts. Yet we had gone there in the first place to file what he thought was one of only two copies of the reclaimed manuscript. I'd taken additional precautions that he knew nothing about, just in case he had done something that, *if* he had, should keep me forever out of his bed. Precautions that, if he were the thief, would protect a priceless piece of women's literature. And history. As I thought about which women's tradition it *most* belonged to, a more obvious irony struck me, and I fell asleep over that one, curled against the back of my male lover, whose innocence I earnestly hoped to demonstrate.

6

"BUT IF WALT had anything to do with the theft," Becca asked me the next day, "why would he let you find the manuscript all of a sudden?"

"That's a problem," I admitted.

"Let's go back a step: why would he steal it in the first place?"

"To protect the college from association with a lesbian, especially one whose memoir is an uninhibited celebration of what lesbians do together."

"It was clear to him that you took some kind of publication for granted?"

"Absolutely. At lunch that first day, I was only talking about how, not whether."

"So, according to this scenario, he would feel he had to move quickly, while you were away. But then why change his mind?"

"One: he could have decided it wasn't such a big deal about perversion in the Ebbing family tree."

"Homophobia isn't cured that easily. If he had that attitude—though I must say I've seen no evidence of it—but *if*, then he'd be unlikely to see the light so fast."

"Well, this one's sort of mawkish, but reason number two is that, now that we're lovers, he wants to do something to please me."

"So he'll give you back the manuscript and the hell with smearing Ebbing College? You know, Walt is very serious about this place and his job, so that one sounds rather thin to me."

I forbore recounting the scene in his office yesterday afternoon. Besides, a man could be dedicated to his job—even if it was a job I couldn't imagine wanting—and still enjoy acting out a sexual fantasy he's had at work. "Unless he thinks that because we're lovers now he can make sure I don't publish it."

"How would he do that? Or think he could?"

"Affection, manipulation, coercion, I don't know. But that way he could have it both ways. He would be doing a nice thing for me at the start of our intimate relationship, and he would still be protecting the college's good name, because the book wouldn't make it into print. *Helen-Elizabeth* would be like a little erotic Christmas gift, our private turn-on, courtesy of a pair of long-dead lesbians. Well, if he thinks I'd prostitute my professional integrity or my politics that way—"

"Remember, he probably *doesn't* think so. But I can see why you'd like to pin it definitively on someone else." She paused. "Jamie, if you think it's even possible Walt returned the manuscript to please you—however unlikely we've decided that is—does that mean you feel he's—ah—serious about you?"

"I doubt it. It's mostly that we've both been without anyone for so long—"

"I'm not sure about him, but 'long' is measured in months, in your case," she put in acidly. It occurred to me that Becca's widowhood had lasted nearly ten years, now, and that Stephen Parsons had been ill for some time before that.

"Long enough, believe me. Anyway, here we both are. Well, you've noticed the Noah's Ark quality of this faculty: everyone paired off two by two?"

"I came here single, female, older than almost all of them, and earning twice as much money. Yes, I've noticed it."

"And you've made a place for yourself here. But you have to admit that most of these people aren't—aren't—"

"They're not. They're tame. That's what we have in common, you and I: that we're not. It's the writing, you know. It demands a certain courage, and for some that carries over into the rest of life."

"At least, I have you, here, while you had nobody, at first."

"To get back to Walt, though: you don't think he's one of us trapped in the destiny of one of them?"

"No—I just meant that he is trapped. No one expects him to live like a monk or anything, but he can't lead a swinging bachelor existence, either—not that there's anyone around to lead it *with*. Anyway, he says he—ah—was attracted to me from the beginning. That sounds mostly like sex, if you ask me— along with certain other natural desires that go along with it, desires for companionship, intimacy, a little fun."

"And that's what drew you to him?"

"No, *he* drew me to him. It's the first time in my life I've been involved with a man I never even considered in advance as a 'possible.' He did all the work. But, sure, I need sex and companionship and the rest of it, too. Things are very intense between us on one level, but what it amounts to, in the long run, is that I love him only just enough to make the sex and the intimacy and so on work."

"What do you mean?"

"I don't have sex without some strong feeling there. I can't. It may look pretty casual to you, but there has to be *something* there for me. On the purely physical level, I could never just walk into a singles bar, pick up a man—even a very attractive one—and go to bed with him. I mean, I could do it, of course, but I couldn't relax enough to make it worthwhile for myself— sexually, that is. I've even had sex with men the first time I met them, but that pull was there, even though—no, because—we'd met in some context that wasn't just about meeting a sexual partner. Anyway, I *like* Walt. That's why I don't want to believe he took that manuscript. But I could never love him without reservations."

"What are your reservations?"

"Well, he does belong to this place, which means he's accepted everything too readily: a marriage and a career that both went nowhere. And he accepts the limitations of his dean's job the same way. It's as if he thinks someone else will do the right thing about South Africa, just as someone else will produce the scholarly books he could have written. So it's okay that he's tied up with other stuff, even if the other stuff is comparatively trivial."

"But he does care about decent education, which is hardly trivial. He was reputed to be the best teacher they had around here. And, because of that, he's been a good and imaginative administrator."

"Becca, you're not trying to sell me on him?"

"No, no, I love Walt dearly, but I can see he's not the man for you."

"Good, because I hadn't got to the worst part: he's a product of the Fifties, as far as the sexes are concerned. The liberal Fifties, to be sure. But the women's movement is an interesting rumor to him, not a personal revelation. And even the superficial things he's aware of—that more of his colleagues' wives now have careers, for instance—haven't really touched him personally. I think he assumes they couldn't help his own wife at this point, and there's a level where I feel he wouldn't really want that, because it means he would have to take more responsibility for what happened to her. No, he's not the man for me. He isn't what Alain used to be, what Nick still is."

"One-half of Nick." Becca was clearly surprised and troubled that the man was still on my mind. "Or one-third, the next time he happens to meet—"

"All right, if you believe that love is divisible that way. Whatever fraction of Nick is available is a more authentic part of my life than all of Walt. And remember, I don't get all of Walt, either."

"I suppose not. At any rate, this is getting *us* nowhere. The thing is, if even this limited relationship with Walt, whom you love only just enough, is to continue, you need to be certain he's not a thief and a liar."

"It sounds awfully crude, put that way."

"I am not noted for the crudity of my discourse. In any event, you're hoping that, *a*, the real thief will be invited to the Christmas dance—which is inevitable unless it's a student—that *b*, he or she will accept the invitation, and, that, *c*, once out at Brockland, will be unable to resist going up to the study to gloat over the manuscript. Or at least check that it's still in place. Then what?"

"Then, *d*, I leap out and say 'Aha!' like Pooh-Bear—or I don't, as the case may be—but at least I *know* and I can go on with my life here."

"Then I wish you the very best of luck!"

The night of the dance was cold, but the raw dampness of Thanksgiving had given way to a chill clarity. As we drove out to Brockland, more and more stars appeared as we got away from the artificial lights of the town. It was probably because we were both tense about the evening—appearing together as a couple, however well camouflaged, and hoping to trap a thief, as well—that Walt picked a quarrel with me. Or I with him, I don't know.

"My kids will be home a week from today," he remarked. "At least, the two youngsters will. Craig and Russ may take a day or two longer, but they'll be back before Christmas Eve, too."

"You're really looking forward to it, aren't you?"

"I am. You know, since Thanksgiving weekend, I've meant to say something more about that: I told you I never wanted four children so close together, and I certainly didn't opt for what it all did to Virginia. But once the kids were on the scene—and particularly since I've had to take so much responsibility for them—they've been what gave meaning to my life."

"I did understand that," I said softly. "After all, I remember how you felt about their not coming home for Thanksgiving."

"I hope you remember all of it. Because I also realize that if it weren't for their not coming home, I wouldn't have you."

"The converse is that, once your kids get here, we won't see much of each other. I won't be around for a lot of the vacation, anyway, and this coming week I have to work on my MLA paper, because Becca's gang shows up a week from today, too, and I need to be finished by then."

"But I thought that with classes over and no exams to grade, you'd be free to spend more time with me, maybe even take off for a couple of days at the Inn, say Wednesday and Thursday."

"I don't see how I can, Walt. I'll have the evenings free, of course. But remember, on the 28th, I've got to stand up in front of anywhere from 30 to 300 people and talk rationally about Helen Elizabeth Hayward and the conservation movement. It's been a while since I've worked on that material, and I don't want to make a fool of myself."

"You'd never do that. Can't you just—"

"Just what?"

"Rehash what's in your book. That's what most of this so-called scholarly productivity is about, anyhow."

"Not mine! I finished my thesis more than seven years ago, and the book's been out for nearly five. I have lots of stuff on parallels between Hayward's poetry and the writing of John Muir that isn't even in there. It's all new and exciting."

"Funny: I was under the impression that our relationship was new and exciting, too." I let him have the last word, because I didn't want to get dragged into the futility of saying, "It is, but this is different." *As* a last word, his remained in the air for a long time, while we drove silently on to what seemed a less and less gala destination every minute. Finally, not far from the gates to Brockland, Walt pulled into the parking lot of the roadhouse that advertised "Platters." He stared straight ahead out the windshield.

"I guess we'll never agree about this stuff," he said at last. "I used to be a scholar, too, and I remember the way a new idea can grip you. Sometimes, when I listen to you, I don't know if I feel I've lost something or outgrown it. And the thought of the Savage Inn, going up when we *know* what we're going to do when we get there—"

"It is a nice idea, just not for this week. But we can have other kinds of fun."

"We sure can." He pulled me into an uncomfortable embrace. One of the difficulties of kissing someone in a small car with bucket seats while wearing a cape is that you rarely get the use of both arms. But at least when Walt started the engine up he was in a less resentful mood.

Brockland lit up for a big party was nothing like the dim grey mansion I'd been remembering. The word "luster" kept revolving in my mind as I took in the gleaming lights, the flowers, even my colleagues in their unaccustomed finery. Walt was the youngest man wearing a dinner jacket—deanship *oblige*, he'd warned me—but even the men in dark suits, including those who wore a coat and tie to class every day, looked different—better cared for. The real difference was with the women, though. In my sleeveless white silk blouse and long black velvet skirt, I was in the middle of the spectrum. Most of the faculty wives and the women professors wore what used to be called cocktail dresses, vivid colors, rich fabrics, low necklines, but street-length hems. The secretaries, cafeteria workers, and maintenance crew, however, shone in full evening regalia, long dresses, elaborate hairdos, rhinestone jewelry.

Dinner went on too long and too heavily; the presidential

toasts afterwards created the bizarre impression that we were at a wedding where the bridal couple had neglected to show up and they'd gone ahead with the reception anyway. Eventually, though, the waiters got the signal to clear the floor for dancing, and they did so with impressive speed and grace. I felt less graceful myself as I stepped out with my escort. Creature of the Sixties that I am, I never learned classic ballroom dancing at the right age. And, needless to say, I'm not so great at what they call following. I got through it without disgracing myself, however, and we worked out a plan for keeping an eye on the stairs to the second floor, as well as the reflected lights from the study window. We'd take turns going upstairs to patrol, but we had to leave the way apparently clear or our quarry wouldn't take the bait.

After the first dance, it went pretty much as Walt had predicted. I danced with Bill Robards, who told me how pleased he and Betsy were that Walt and I were "together," and with Frank Garber, an engineer who'd been to one or two of the open houses, who told me how delighted he and Amy were that Walt "had somebody."

Then Carlos Santiago asked me to dance, and he was so good he made me feel like a competent—even an exquisite—dancer. We didn't talk much, so unconsciously I formed echoes in my head of the words to the song that was playing familiar lines about moonlight and kissing and holding. Carlos danced me out the French windows onto a terrace. The fresh air felt delightful for a few moments, then far too cold. "Here, take my jacket," he said, pulling it off and draping it over my shoulders. It felt warm from his body.

"Won't you be cold?"

"Oh, no," he explained illogically, "in Chile, it is summer now."

"This is like the old movies I used to see as a child. In scenes of elegant parties, there was always a terrace handy to dance out onto."

"I have seen those films, too, as an adolescent. Only the couple would have kept on dancing out here, then stopped and kissed. This troubled my boyhood very much: that they would kiss and kiss and never go any further. It was like the torment of my own dreams, all that North American kissing!"

"At the risk of spoiling what sounds almost like a line from Neruda, I should point out that it was symbolic sex."

"Which is no way to make love," he said with Latin literalness. A pause ensued, somewhat longer than it should have been, and then he added, unnecessarily precise, "I am not kissing you." There was no right answer to that, so I said nothing. "I am not kissing you," he repeated. "But perhaps it is my revolutionary duty to kiss you. Lola and I are very well together and we are agreed to have no outside adventures. But I feel I owe it to the struggle—"

I burst out in an unromantic giggle. "Carlos, if you had kissed me a few minutes ago, I would have liked it very much— probably more than would have been good for either of us. But why you should conceive it as a solemn duty—"

"It is not funny, Jamie. I want to save you from that lout you are with. You are too valuable to get mixed up with all that bourgeois nonsense."

"I'm *not* mixed up with it. What nonsense, anyway?"

"Over and over in my country, I have seen it," he went on, as if I hadn't spoken, "the *compañeros* who went with women who had no political consciousness. And the men were content to leave it that way, not to share their ideas, even after marriage. The revolutionary *women*, though, if they fell for a man who was not in the movement, he took them out of action. Most did not— they found men with similar ideas—but those who didn't, well, they sold out to the love of respectability and the power of the male in society."

"Carlos, none of that has anything to do with Walt and me."

"Bah! I put my arm around you, that is not for love making,

but only it *is* a little cold. Listen, Jamie, your husband, he was a Frenchman, no?"

"Yes."

"At least not one of these WASPs—all buzz and no sting. And he was a revolutionary?"

"Was is right. When he stopped being one, I left him."

"Then why settle for this big, well-meaning boob? I like Walt—"

"Then I'd hate to hear what you say about someone you felt contempt for."

"I like Walt, as I say, but a man who refuses the lessons of history, as this one does, he is *criminally* innocent."

"Santiago, believe me, I have not 'settled,' as you say. I do like Walt, but my seeing him changes nothing I believe in and work for. That's why—" I realized suddenly that I could make out Carlos's sculpted features a lot more clearly. A light in the room overhead—Lizzie's study—must have been switched on. "I'm sorry, I've got to go now," I said, pulling away from him as I slipped out of his jacket, feeling like an unrehearsed Cinderella.

"Thank you," I called back over my shoulder, though if anyone had asked me what for, I would have been hard put to it to explain. For his concern and for thinking I was "valuable" enough to rescue, whether I needed rescue or not. For a new twist on the old *machismo*.

At the top of the stairs, I stopped and, quite literally, got my act together, then marched down the hall. I could hear voices in the study, low, familiar, but not quite identifiable. *Walt's the one who should be doing this. He knows them all better.* But how could we have imagined there would be more than one? The words I could make out were only those I was expecting and maybe projecting: "memoir," "publish," "lesbian."

I pushed open the door brusquely.

"Oh!" I pretended to gasp. Feigned surprise was rapidly

overtaken by the real thing. Sharon Reilly stood with her back against the writing desk (I noticed she shifted slightly to conceal the manuscript from me) and Charles Rowland was advancing toward her. I pretended to think I'd interrupted a lovers' tryst rather than an argument about a document of whose presence I was supposed to be unaware.

I leered. It is by no means easy to leer at will, especially with such an improbable couple as its object. Sharon, reasonably smart in her usual tailored clothes, looked dowdy and waistless tonight in a misguided ecru lace number. And Rowland, ten years her junior, had fair, pasty skin and a premature paunch that Betsy always claimed was a "smugness belly," where others might have one from beer or age. Whatever tension there was between them, desire had nothing to do with it. Their own for each other, anyway. "Sorry," I cooed, as suggestively as I could. "I was just looking for a place to lie down—lousy champagne. (*So bad I didn't drink any, in fact.*) Well, maybe you two were looking for the same thing? But this is obviously not the right place for any of our purposes."

As I left, I was already wondering why I hadn't confronted them. But I had been unprepared for two suspects, and, knowing Sharon's feelings about Rowland, especially unprepared for these two. I had no idea how to force an unraveling of the story that would expose the original culprit. With Walt now in the clear and the contents of the manuscript safe, the matter seemed, quite literally, academic.

Carlos stared at me when I came down as though I actually had left him holding a glass slipper. I smiled in what I hoped was a reassuring fashion and looked for Walt. A man that size is easy to spot in a crowd: all you have to do is look up, instead of around. It's less easy to catch his eye, however, unless you're well over 6 feet, yourself. It turned out he'd been on the lookout for me, too, though.

"Lights on in the study, eh?" he muttered in my ear as we whirled awkwardly into the dance.

"Yes." Brevity was essential on my end, since the ear-muttering could not be reciprocal. "Sharon and Rowland. Together."

"They didn't do it together, surely?" I shook my head. "Then which of them—?"

"No idea."

"Well, you seem unreasonably elated, then. I don't see how you're going to find out, if you didn't cross-examine them then and there, as I gather you didn't." Another shake. I could hardly explain that I was so elated—unreasonably, as he observed—by finding him not guilty of a crime he had not committed, had never contemplated, and had apparently never imagined being suspected of. But I felt that a weight had been lifted. Not one of the big weights I carried about with me: Becca's illness, the collapse of my marriage, my essential isolation. Compared to these things, maybe this other hadn't been a weight, but merely an obstacle. Now it had been removed, though, and I could take my comfort where I found it. And I found it in Walt, whatever Carlos Santiago might happen to think of my doing so.

"Walt?" I asked, as we stood by the punch bowl, our backs to the room.

"Yes, Dr. Pangloss?"

"Do you want to stay really late?"

"Well, no, in fact. I'd like to get you home while we're still awake enough to enjoy it."

"Then I'm ready to go as soon as we figure out a way to make the substitution—I brought a copy of the manuscript along—and get the original out of here."

"Easy, if you don't put your cape on until we get into the car."

"I see what you mean." And so I did the bait-and-switch (or at least the switch of bait), stowing the manuscript in the car of a man I now knew would help me take care of it, then pulled the cape that had been draped so casually over my arm onto my shoulders. "Home, Preston. And now I've found a use for your real first name, after all."

"Your place or mine?" he responded. "I've finally found a use for that question."

"Well, which of us would look sillier going home in the morning in these clothes? I think I would. Besides, there's a wall safe in our library." And so the manuscript of *Helen-Elizabeth* came to rest in that safe. I poured Walt a cognac to cleanse his palate of the grotesque drink proffered at an official college party, and I got myself a San Pellegrino. After a brief, happy interlude in the four-poster, my lover and I came to rest, as well.

After that, the Christmas vacation was an appropriate reward for conscientious effort. Mine was organized into three parts, geographically determined: ten days in Jaegersville, four in Chicago, and another eight in California.

As I'd warned Walt, my paper on Helen Hayward and the founding of the Sierra Club took me the better part of a week to whip into shape. Nonetheless, as I'd also foretold, we spent a number of pleasant evenings together, though he never seemed entirely reconciled to my absorption in my daytime labors. He was not even as entranced as I'd hoped by the tale every California schoolchild learns of how John Muir got Teddy Roosevelt to camp out with him in what was to be Yosemite, to assure the preservation of that wilderness site. And he was even less interested in the connections between all this conservationist folklore and Hayward's own poetry.

By the time Ellie and Jack Parsons and Patsy Maynard-Parsons arrived, I was ready to devote my time to helping them deal with what was happening to their mother. Nonetheless, their joint reaction to how Becca's condition had deteriorated since Thanksgiving forced me to admit that, even as the treatments were restoring some of her lost energy and appetite, the disease was still doing its unspeakable work. The four of us hugged a lot and even cried together, but we also did our best to make it a rich and cheerful holiday.

On Christmas Day, having assured Mrs. Moyer more times than I cared to enumerate that it was all right for her to go to her daughter's house over in Hochstetter, I prepared the dinner, roasting a goose in the Alsatian fashion. I also used some of last summer's home-canned prunes and invented a dessert that was a cross between an English plum pudding and a French *tarte aux quetsches*. It was surprisingly good. Becca even ate a little bit of each course. I saved some of the dessert for Walt, who phoned to ask if he might drop by for a few minutes. He brought his four kids, which I hadn't expected, and they all politely said they couldn't have eaten another mouthful anyway. I was nervous for a few minutes about meeting them for the first time. But I reminded myself that they didn't know they were meeting their father's—whatever I was. They certainly didn't act as if they thought of me as a special person in his life or theirs. A good-mannered reserve, in fact, was the keynote of their behavior, making them seem younger than they actually were. Their attention, anyway, was focused on Becca, whom they'd known ever since her arrival in Jaegersville. Her present state made them tongue-tied and uncomfortable. In the circumstances, if I had suggested that we all sing Christmas carols—a highly unlikely proposal—the idea would have fallen very flat indeed. But Jack and Patsy were in the business of getting people to sing in groups; they got us all going and made it feel like the most natural thing in the world.

Walt and I left them to it and slipped out to the kitchen. He was very taken with my attempt to lighten the heaviest of British culinary classics, but also interested in how much body contact could be achieved standing up in a kitchen in two minutes. Not enough, we unsurprisingly concluded. "It's been nearly five days," he groaned. "And you're going away tomorrow!" I forbore to mention that the second stage of my trip promised a break in my own celibacy.

"That," I admonished him instead, "in no way increases what we can realistically expect to do on the stepladder, the dishwasher, or even the butcher block while the combined youth choir out there goes on about French hens and gold rings and the rest of it. We're supposed to be adults and adults invented repression. Anyway, I've got a Christmas present for you."

"I have one for you, too. Actually, this is for your office. In some ways, it's a coal to Newcastle, but it'll be something of your own there, at least." The "coal" was a heavy brass walrus, intricately modeled, which closely resembled several of the Ebbing family portraits. I had gone to some trouble over Walt's gift, but I hadn't thought to incorporate any of our private jokes into it.

"*Their Wedding Journey*," he read, unwrapping the book I'd chosen. "Well, I guess we're still honeymooning, after all." On the other hand, if you want to see an intimate reference, you can find one anywhere. "How did you find a Howells first edition in Jaegersville, of all places? I know you haven't been anywhere in months. I also happen to know you frown on robbing library collections."

"It's fresh from Shattuck Avenue, Berkeley. An old classmate of mine, a casualty of the academic job market, deals in Americana. So I called Peter and told him I wanted a present for someone who did his thesis on Howells. He couldn't talk me into the autographed first edition of *A Hazard of New Fortunes*; at his asking price, resistance came very easy. But he made me promise to come in and pay for this one in person—the well-tested idea being that I am constitutionally incapable of walking out of a bookshop empty-handed. He also made a big point of the extremely good condition this copy was in. Which, of course, probably means no one's ever read it."

"I'll reread it while you're away. And think of you the whole time." Late the next afternoon, I left for Chicago, where I joined thousands of my fellow MLA conventioneers. My paper went well—I was even invited to submit it for a special journal issue on literature and ecology. My job interviews were dead ends. And then I went on to California. Yes, I saw Nick while I was in the Bay Area, and yes, "seeing" is a euphemism. On the whole, it was good for me to be with a man I loved without reservation, but that doesn't mean it was easy. The brevity of my stay and the presence of Rachel in his life made sure of that. On the way home I spent another few hours in Philadelphia, poring over the manuscript with Erin Ni'Connor.

7

*

"SO IT TURNED out the brother was the villain of the piece," Erin began, once she'd supplied me with tea—Earl Grey, this time. Her copy of *Helen-Elizabeth* was open to the last page. "And what a name for him," she added. "Manley Ebbing: it's what they call over-determined."

"Well, whatever his name was, he started out doing no more than countless boys have done in repressive societies: peep at his sister because hers was the nearest female body *to* peep at."

"You're defending him, Jameson?"

"Hardly," I protested. "I'm just saying it's not surprising, is all. We've both met women who've been through a lot worse in their own families, and that's in these times. Anyway, young Manley-the-Walrus."

"The what?"

"I'll explain later. Anyway, he appears to have developed some kind of a crush on Nellie. Or maybe that's too innocent a word. An obsession's more like it. Whatever you call it, his peeping must have increased as her visit wore on. The rooms adjoined and there was a connecting door with, we must assume, a keyhole of some sort. At any rate, it's clear that he eventually saw more than he bargained for."

"And kept on watching. I wish we knew for how long."

"It's too bad Lizzie doesn't say."

"But we're lucky it doesn't seem to have occurred to Lizzie to revise her descriptions of what had gone on once she realized there might have been an audience the whole time. Or maybe there wasn't—depends how soon Manley acted."

"That is, confronted the two of them with blackmail, sexual blackmail, on his slimy little mind. At least, that's how I read it."

"There's no other interpretation," I agreed, "even though Lizzie doesn't make it clear exactly what he wanted Nellie to do for him in return for his silence. I guess anything we can think of would have horrified the girls about equally."

"So of course they told him he was a disgusting little beast, and he knew enough to realize that in the eyes of their society they were the beastly ones. In fact, 'beast' would have been the least of it. He went to his parents. I mean, of course, to his father."

"What words would he use to describe it?" I wondered.

"He found a way, don't worry—man to man."

"Do you suppose the girls told him what *Manley* had tried to pull?"

"What difference would it have made? Unless they could prove their own 'innocence,' *his* offense wouldn't annul theirs. And to the patriarchy, even in Victorian times, what Manley wanted would have seemed natural—just a bit premature. So Nellie was sent home in disgrace."

"I wonder how they told *her* family."

"They got their vicious point across somehow, never fear."

"And we know that Lizzie married Brock soon after. But that's not in the manuscript. It ends on a note of—would you even say defiance? It's more confident than that. She says,

'I know that Nellie and I will be together always.' Period."

"So what happened to Nellie? Jamie, you've got to find out."

"I will," I assured her. "*We* will. I couldn't really start the research last fall because the manuscript turned up missing—"

"I gather that's why this copy arrived on my doorstep a few weeks back, accompanied by cryptic notes about what to do in case of unspecified emergencies, and stamped with every patriarchal seal you could dig up."

I gave Erin a summary of my adventures: my discovery of the theft, abortive search for a suspect, recovery of the manuscript and efforts to protect it, and the puzzling implication of Sharon Reilly and Charles Rowland in the affair.

"But now you've got the thing back, and you've spent the semester researching Lizzie's other writing, haven't you? So you can go full speed ahead. Where do you start?"

"Well, that's where the 'we' comes in. As soon as the semester is under way, in two or three weeks, say, I hope you'll come up for that consultantship. You're the nearest scholar who knows anything about nineteenth-century women, gay and straight—and it sounds like you know everything."

"There's no lesbian scholar at your college?"

"I don't even think there are any lesbians. Ironically enough, if I'd had to name one candidate, I'd have said Sharon Reilly."

"The one who—"

"Uh-huh."

"And she's the expert on Lizzie's family, too? It'll be interesting to see how she reacts when you bring her great-granny—"

"Not quite."

"—out of the closet."

"Yes," I agreed. "Interesting."

Erin's arrival on campus the last week in January was like the advent of a beneficent tempest. "What is this 'knee' business?" Becca had asked when I told her I was expecting a house guest named Ni'Connor.

"The feminine of the 'O' or 'Mc' so many Irish names start with. I guess it's still a patronymic, but at least it means 'daughter of,' not 'son.' You find it in the literature and some Irish-American feminists have taken it up."

Hoping Erin would charm Sharon Reilly—even winning her Irish half back onto my side would be nice—I invited her to bring the history majors' seminar to Erin's public presentation on networks in the lives of women. She did bring them, but sat rather as if she were a parent accompanying a boring grade school field trip, and left before the question period. Erin had not only failed to charm her but seemed to pose some sort of challenge—or maybe threat.

Charles Rowland, on the other hand, homed in on Erin's remarks about women's networks. Trimmed of the false obsequiousness and the genuine contempt, his question was essentially what possible use it was to study such relationships.

"Some historians," she explained quietly, strategically making it sound as if she didn't realize he was one, himself, "make much of the distinction between political or institutional history and what's called the new social history. I believe, myself, that there are fundamental concepts that link the two visions of history's proper purview, concepts like 'social relations,' 'culture,' and 'dominance,' for example. From this perspective, the study of women's lives—the way they themselves experienced these forces, their capacity for resistance—is as much a part of history as the evolution of constitutional government." I wanted to stand up and cheer. This husky, no-nonsense woman with the short red hair, who'd never been able to get a regular academic job, not only knew what she was talking about, but possessed the enviable ancestral gift of gab.

"What about sex?" Rowland pursued. "What if you find out that some of these women's networks were more than just sewing circles—if your research exposes them as something more sordid?"

"You mean, if there were lesbians among them?"

"Well, yes."

"Then, using those same key words, I'd try to understand what it was that enabled them to resist the *social relations* of *dominance* in their *culture* and create an alternative for their own survival. It's an approach we could use to learn more about cultures of resistance in general. Perhaps it's like that famous story of what Lincoln is supposed to have said when someone complained that General Ulysses S. Grant was a drunk: 'Then send a barrel of whatever he's drinking to the rest of my generals.' "

I wasn't sure how many in the audience could even follow that, but Ann Capobianco clapped her hands twice, then stopped in embarrassment, since no one else was applauding. At the workshop that Erin gave the next day for my student assistants, it was Ann who asked the most and the sharpest questions.

"I wish I could take a course on women's history," she told Erin and me over coffee afterwards. "As it is, I try to do my papers on feminist topics, but that doesn't always fit the courses, and even where they do—"

"Yes?"

"Well, like the seminar with Dr. Reilly this term is about Pennsylvania history. I wanted to do my project on Italian women in South Philly, but she said no. When she says 'Pennsylvania,' she means 'Mens-sylvania,' and the other side of the tracks from what I mean, anyway."

"A Reilly?" asked Erin, incredulous.

"Remember, she's only part Irish," I explained. "On her mother's side, she's related, quite distantly, to the Ebbing family, the people who founded this college."

"One of whom wrote the lesbian memoir."

Erin had no way of knowing, of course, that I had not gone public with the contents of *Helen-Elizabeth*, even to my assistants. Remembering Ann's applause the day before, I decided she was safe and told her about it. Then, as I watched her expression and Erin's face seeing that expression, I made an offer. "If you're interested, Ann, you can work with me on the background to the manuscript. It won't be like a course, but you'll certainly learn a lot about women's history."

"Can Laurie do that, too?" She was like a child asking to include her friend in a proffered treat.

"Sure, I guess so. That means you'll both get the interdisciplinary background: you'll learn to read the document as a literary text, and she'll learn to place it in history. But I warn you: it's harder work than the cataloguing and so forth you've been doing."

Most of Erin's week in Jaegersville was spent showing me how to follow up the women's-history aspect of the archive, particularly in its Pennsylvania setting. She also gave me some leads on how to go about uncovering what happened to Nellie Breckenridge. "I'm amazed I don't even recognize her name. Which may mean one of your more dramatic guesses was true, that they packed her off somewhere: Europe or an asylum. At least you know she didn't die that year or shortly thereafter." The records were clear enough about that. "So the only problem is where, how, and how long she lived."

"Some 'only'!"

"Well, now you've got assistants working on this particular manuscript. Is the other one—Laurie, is it?—a lesbian, too?"

"Oh, no. And I wouldn't say 'too' so confidently. I don't think Ann knows *what* she is. She was brought up a strict Catholic, and it's all pretty heavy for her."

"Well, haven't you seen that book about the lesbian nuns?"

"All I'm saying is that coming out at her age, with that background, in this environment—well, it takes time. Especially since I suspect it would be a very pure kind of coming out: no actual lover on the scene."

"Not Laurie—you're sure?"

"Laurie's the one who looks like a cheerleader. She's a feminist and would be in the movement, if there were one around to be in—she and Ann did organize our South Africa vigil—but she's got a boyfriend."

"Then Ann will have to find herself by herself, without Laurie."

"I think so. That's another reason I'm glad you're here: in your being, as well as what you came to lecture on, you say something about relationships between women."

"She has a model of that right in front of her."

"She does?"

"You and Becca. She can see that the love between women is not only for when you're young and hale but carries right on through. And that it isn't only for lesbians."

Not long after Erin's visit, my other personal relationship at Ebbing hit a sandbar. Walt had, of course, been unimpressed by the invitation to publish my MLA paper, especially since the tight deadline, coinciding with the opening of a new term, meant I had to work on a couple of evenings that we might otherwise have spent together. "But this is important," I tried to explain, sensing in advance the futility of my effort. "It's not just that I get my work noticed, but also that otherwise Will Fellowes will have a whole issue on American environmental literature without a single piece about women."

"Well, what difference does it make? How many people are likely to read that issue of some scholarly journal, with or without a woman in it?"

"Not a great many, perhaps. But it can have on influence on the way those people—college teachers—think about the question and how they present it to students. And it goes into all the bibliographies. Don't you see? When I publish something like this I'm teaching teachers." He didn't see. I ran into him in the Jaegersville post office as I was addressing a manila envelope for the completed article. He was sending off a package.

"My daughter left behind some underwear that was still in the dryer," he explained.

"Well, I'm sending off an undertaking of my own, though no undergarments." I showed him the first page of my piece. He made some ungracious remark about how maybe I'd have some free time for a change, now that it was done, and we made a date for the weekend. Maybe I should say, *"Nevertheless,* we made a date for the weekend."

There was steak for dinner again, with salad, garlic bread, and a good Burgundy. "Actually, I don't know how to fix much else that's fit for company," Walt confessed. I knew cooking wasn't a skill men of his generation were encouraged to acquire, although he'd certainly had a couple of decades for remedial work. But I remembered the last time we'd shared this same basic meal, the day we found the manuscript at Brockland and then came back to campus and made love in his office. One shadow had fallen across my comfort, that night, my doubts about his possible role in the theft. With that problem solved, I felt too much at home here in front of the fireplace to challenge his culinary deficiencies.

"Surely, I'm not 'company,' " I offered suggestively.

"Well, I certainly feel you belong right here." He put his arm around me and stroked my shoulder through my satin shirt. "Which reminds me." He wasn't going to ask me to move in, was he? There are limits to the tolerance of any small town, any denominational campus, and I was certain that bringing his girlfriend to live in the house while his wife was hospitalized would violate those limits. Besides, I was here in the first place because of Becca, and sharing her house was a big part of my role. I tried to tune in on what Walt was in fact proposing. "You haven't got anything set up for next year—no interviews on other campuses?"

"No, I told you MLA didn't work out for me this time around. Once the new books are out—the scholarly edition of Lizzie's memoir and my book of poems—plus the book I've already published, I imagine I'll be more salable."

"Well, in the meantime, we can try to get you another year here."

"I thought there was a search committee looking for a permanent occupant of Becca's chair."

"So there is. I'm on it, in fact—as dean of faculty and as a member of the English Department. And that's the point. We've been kind of slow getting started, and it wouldn't take much for me to slow it down further, make it impossible to arrive at a decision this Spring, so we'd have to keep you on."

"But—but I'm here mainly for Becca."

"And?"

"And there's very little chance she'll be around for any part of the next academic year. Jaegersville and Ebbing would feel really empty without her. I don't think I could face it. "

"What about me?"

"Walt, you know our relationship is—"

"What? A matter of expediency?" he put in bitterly.

"No. A lucky encounter. Very lucky. For both of us, I think. But we aren't really part of one another's lives. Not in the long run." I ran my thumb over the top of his hand. "You know it's true. I don't exactly belong here at Ebbing, and you have Virginia. In the long run," I repeated the phrase deliberately, "well, even I have someone who fits into my life better."

"That Frenchman, your husband?"

"No, no," I said, with some regret. "Alain doesn't fit into my present *or* my future. But there is someone in Berkeley I'm seeing, someone from the past who's come back into my life." I told him Nick's name.

"He's some hot shot at your dear old alma mater?"

"Berkeley the town, not Cal, the university, " Berkeley the People's Republic, as its detractors like to say, Berzerkeley, weird hippie capital of the West. Afraid of tilting the narrative too much the other way, I mentioned Nick's band and the award they'd won for their first album.

"He's single?"

"Not exactly." Remembering Becca's response to that equivocal phrase, back when she decided to remake my life for me, I smiled ruefully. "He's living with someone, but it's a nonmonogamous relationship. Obviously, since he's seeing me, too."

" 'Seeing,' present participle. You're seeing this guy now, meaning sleeping with him?"

"Well, not *right* now. We live on opposite sides of the country, and my situation here—with Becca and the job, I mean—plus Nick's being on the road so much—but just on the West Coast—and his involvement with Rachel, it all rules out even what you could call a commuting relationship."

"So you're stuck with me. Thanks a lot. Anyway, you finessed my question. You do sleep with him—or you have more recently than ten years ago?"

"What is this, a cross-examination?"

"Don't you think I have the right?"

"No. In fact, the phrase I would have chosen is 'none of your business.' But yes, if you must know, I slept with him back in September, when I went to get my stuff. And again when I was there over Christmas."

"Over *Christmas*? But you've been 'seeing'—sleeping with—me since Thanksgiving." He obviously was really hurt, and I had no desire to cause further pain, but I had to get this straight. "Look, Walt, you seem to think I betrayed some understanding that I wasn't aware we had."

"Whereas I wasn't aware it had to be spelled out. When two people start sleeping together, they drop their other relationships."

"Unless, of course, one of them is married."

"You know I have no sexual relationship with Virginia."

"That wasn't what I meant. I wanted to know your etiquette for adulterous affairs."

"Well, the people I know don't really do a lot of cheating, except as a sort of—transition to divorce and remarriage."

"So monogamy is the rule, and 'cheating,' as you call it, is okay, in your theory, if it's part of *serial* monogamy. The only thing you object to is honest nonmonogamy. Is that it?"

"Jamie, I don't have any theory. All I know is, I don't want to share my lover with every Tom, Dick, and Harry that comes down the pike."

"You make it sound like I'm promiscuous. It so happens I only go to bed with men I care for. But the main point is that what you call 'your lover' is a separate person, who makes her own sexual decisions. It's not up to you to 'share' or not to 'share.' It's not about a—a commodity on the market."

"It certainly isn't. You *give* it away."

"Don't you see, there isn't any 'it'? Any *thing*? All there is is a quality, an experience. It does have to do with how you apportion your time. That's the problem with Nick and Rachel and me. So I understood that when you were jealous before, it's been about work that kept me from spending time with you."

"You sound as if you think it's the same thing."

"It is, in a sense, because you have the same attitude about both: grudging. In fact, I felt the same way about mentioning the article I just finished, because I knew you wouldn't be impressed or proud—"

"What a grievance! So now it's my fault you sleep with this Nick character, because I don't appreciate you?"

"I'm about to bring out my first 'I didn't *say* that' of this argument. All I meant was that I already knew your attitude to my—ah—professional achievements."

"That's really what it's about, isn't it, Jamie? Ebbing College isn't good enough for you, because we don't value those 'professional achievements.' And I'm not good enough because

I haven't got any achievements that you recognize. I don't publish, so I haven't attained the success you look for in a man!"

"Success? *Nick?*"

"He just won a Grammy—"

"Not—"

"Oh, whatever prize you just told me about. And look at your husband, too."

"Hardly the big time and the glitter, either one."

"In their own frame of reference, Jamie. And in ours, publication is."

"It's too much: my friends would probably argue about whether I've been going with you because I've sold out to respectability or to status or the patriarchy. And now you, the object of this hostile speculation, come along and tell me I've sold *you* out because I worship success, of all things! Why can't people believe I'm making honest choices and honest mistakes?"

"Mistakes?" he asked—hopefully, I later realized.

"Yes, by getting involved with you this way. I'm sorry, Walt, I guess I always knew we were looking for different things, but I deluded myself we could find them together, anyway."

"That's what you're sorry for?"

"Do you expect me to apologize for going to bed with Nick? That would be like saying I'm sorry I have brown eyes."

"It's that natural, you mean?" This was definitely more in sorrow.

"Well, not quite as natural as that, I guess. It's more of a choice, like saying I'm sorry I put on this purple shirt today, because you don't like the way it fits me."

"You just said that so I'd look at the way it clings to your body. Because you know I do like how it fits you."

"Walt, can you really think I want to seduce you so you'll stop being angry? I think we have what they call an irreconcilable difference, here. And I'm sorry for it, because I really like what we—" I couldn't decide on the verb tense, so I left the sentence unfinished.

"But not enough to change your other habits?"

"No, because I couldn't change how I feel. And you?"

"No." His tone left no room for ambiguity, as it was. Then he added, "I'm not so hard up I have to take other men's leavings."

The tone had been quiet up until then. More in sorrow, as I say. But now I lost my temper. "Okay. But remember: you said your days in that office of yours would be 'permanently transformed' by what we did there the afternoon we found the manuscript. So go on remembering that day, Dr. Walters. It's the curse I leave you with." And I marched out. At least, I hope I marched.

Thus ended my illusory grab for comfort. Considering how small the campus and the town both were, Walt and I managed to avoid one another quite successfully in the ensuing weeks. He didn't stop coming to the open houses, though. For Becca's sake, I was glad, and he knew that was why I was. Even the first Sunday, however, he showed up with a date, someone who had never come to any of them on her own. So I was supposed to understand from this that Sharon Reilly had taken my place in his life.

8

*

SHARON REILLY, SHARON REILLY, did I really spend so much time in those weeks of February and March wondering what made you tick? I certainly marshaled and re-marshaled the available information: When we met in September, you looked familiar. Did I suspect already that you would come to loom large in my life? At that first meeting, you talked to me for ages about the Ebbing family and its ramifications, but you shied away when I asked about your plans for publication. Later, you took the right stand on South Africa and, in connection with that, on Charles Rowland. And you were friendly to me. We even joked together about some of my "Pangloss" clues.

Then it all changed: Walt told me the day we visited Brockland that you'd said nasty things about me at a committee meeting—petty, unjustified things. And you seemed to avoid further contact with me. So the tension was already there the night of the Christmas Dance, when I caught you and your supposed enemy quarreling over the manuscript. Which neither of you could have known about unless you'd taken it—right? But how could you, with your respect for archival integrity and family history, have stolen a family manuscript from a library? And if you did, why take it to Brockland, to Lizzie's own study? On the other hand, if it was you who'd caught Rowland out, why not just tell me so?

Why were you hostile—and maybe even frightened—when Erin Ni'Connor visited? Why did you refuse to let Ann work on the term project she chose? Why did you tell her this women's stuff wasn't really history? And why have you started showing up at my house in the company of my own former lover? Why do you look so triumphant about it, when you're not even sleeping with him? Because you aren't, Sharon, are you? I can read Walt that well, even if you remain a mystery to me.

I went over this one-sided catechism a lot more often than I rehashed my history with Walt. There simply was not as much *there* to think about. Walt had been an intimate part of my life for a couple of months. We'd broken up in an unpleasant way, but the unpleasantness was tied up with why the break had had to come. I missed him. More precisely, I missed what I'd enjoyed with him. And that did make me feel ashamed, that I could regret being without a lover, a relationship, more than the particular man.

As often happens at such phases in one's life, I got a great deal of work done, both on *Helen-Elizabeth* and my own writing. I spent more time with the other friends I'd made in Jaegersville, too. The Robards, though lamenting what they found a baffling turn of events, were as supportive as the Santiagos, who openly congratulated me on the break. I also took up running, a pantywaist's half mile at first, then a mile. This activity did not serve the traditional purposes of the cold shower. In fact, it made me acutely conscious of all my body's needs. It did, however, help me get into shape for whatever was coming, even if all I could be sure was coming was that one day the weather would warm up enough to get me off the indoor track and onto a dirt road in the country.

But winter was taking a long time to bring itself to an end. March had come roaring in all leonine and was showing no signs of assuming a more ovine disposition before it went out. That afternoon not long after the Ides that I went over to the library at the end of my creative writing workshop was as chill and gloomy as its predecessors. Mike Freund was waiting for me outside the door to the archive.

"I couldn't get in," he explained. "You were late—"

"Sorry, my class ran over."

"And Miss Ehrlich doesn't seem to be around. My hours were supposed to start at four." Mike was very conscientious about details.

"Don't worry. It's not even a quarter past." I groped for my key, but, although it fit the lock as usual, it wouldn't turn. Mike saw me put down the pile of student work I was carrying and shook his head. "No, using both hands won't help. When it jams like this it means the door's locked from the inside. Whoever was in there last went out through the back, the door to the stacks, and forgot to unlock this one first."

"Then how do we get it open?"

"You have to call Security. They have a special key to go in through the stacks."

While we waited, I talked to Mike about Lizzie Brock's later poetry. If I had to, I could probably recite every word of that conversation today. At length, we heard someone enter the archive by the door from the stacks, but nobody opened the outer one to us. Instead, a voice spoke unintelligibly into what, after a moment's confusion, I realized was probably a walkie-talkie. I knocked again and got no response.

It must have been only two or three minutes, although it seemed a lot longer, before Ralph Ehrlich, the head of Security, and several of his uniformed men joined us outside the archive. Ehrlich rapped, calling out, "Jack!" and the guard inside opened the door at once. Before they could keep me out, I stepped in with the police and saw the body. I wasn't quick enough to keep Mike from seeing it, too—though why I had this impulse to protect a young male of 20 from what I was seeing myself, I couldn't have said. Some elevated idea of a teacher's responsibility, I think.

"It's Dr. Reilly!" Mike exclaimed. "Is she—?"

"She's dead." There was no other explanation for the way she was simultaneously the focus of all activity and entirely marginal to it. The room had a weird, feral smell; Sharon's arms and head lay on the library table in a mockery of rest, as the wound to her skull and the thick, ugly patch of blood testified definitively. I felt dizzy and reached out for Mike's arm.

"Someone killed Dr. Reilly." My assistant was still assimilating the basics. "Here in the archive." In a moment he would come to the other salient fact, one that was making me sick to my stomach. "They—they hit her in the head with your little statue, the walrus."

When Ehrlich officiously cleared the room, I made a deliberately ambiguous gesture to Mike, left the library, and ran across the Green, straight to Walt's office, gulping air as the wind made my cape billow grotesquely around me. The dean had no one with him, but the reception he accorded me was so cold as to have been rehearsed with an audience in mind. "Dr. Jameson, you hardly have the right any longer—" As if I'd been in the habit, when we were lovers, of barging into his office too flushed and breathless to speak.

"Walt, look, it's Sharon—"

"I certainly have no intention of discussing my—"

This posturing was especially irrelevant just now, but, considering what was coming, I hesitated to interrupt with as much irritation as I felt. "Please listen," I said deliberately. "Sharon is dead. Someone attacked her in my office—with the little brass walrus. I came to you because—" Because, for whatever hopeless knot of reasons, I felt he had to know first.

I told him Security was already on the scene and had summoned the state authorities. Walt pushed his chair away from the desk and rose, looking down at me for a long, shocked moment, and then we left together to go back to the archive. No one had missed me, but Ralph Ehrlich seemed to have acquired a few more men, and the State Police arrived with a redundant ambulance a few minutes later. The archive had been sealed off with yellow tape labeling it what it had just become: the scene of a crime.

A uniformed trooper took my statement and told me a detective would be around to speak with me in the next day or so. Meanwhile, I was free to go home. I waited outside, however, until they took Sharon away, nearly two hours later. Something of the same impulse that had sent me to Walt's office held me in place until the unexpected guest had left mine. Stunned as I was, I felt I owed her this courtesy. I don't recall how long Walt stayed, since he carefully avoided the part of the library corridor where I stood.

Mrs. Moyer was serving Becca dinner when I came in. Betsy Robards, grief-stricken, had already stopped in to tell them about Sharon, so I added my bit to the domestic tranquillity by taking a deep breath and collapsing in a faint on the dining room floor. People dream when they faint—at least, I do—and the images this time involved Sharon trying to tell me something. But it was too confused and fleeting to grasp. When I came to, Mrs. Moyer was hovering over me with the solicitude I'd seen her display only toward Becca, all other invalids and almost all other *persons* appearing to her in the light of an interference with her fundamental duties.

"It's the shock," she explained unnecessarily, helping me to the chaise longue. "I'll make you some of that herb tea you like, and when you feel a little stronger, you can have your supper on a tray in here." This was really what I'd come to Jaegersville for, all right. Becca could sit up to the dining room table, and I was to eat off a tray!

Becca and I talked quietly about the murder for the rest of the evening, and I explained my instant suspicion that the place of death was connected to the motive for it. Yet even though Sharon was so closely associated in my mind with the loss and recovery of the manuscript, it was hard to see what that could possibly have to do with her limp, sad body in the library, months later. I couldn't think why she had come to my office. Like all her other motives, the one for this last action remained obscure.

I had no classes the next day, and my office was perforce inaccessible, but I went over to the gym to run, as usual, slipping out at a moment when Mrs. Moyer was preoccupied with Becca's bath. My assumption was that if I kept to my normal routine, I'd also hear the latest about the investigation. On campus, college business seemed to be proceeding according to routine, but there was a new, grim note, as well. It made me feel exceedingly ill-at-ease in my sweat suit, as if I were wearing it and not one of the Chanel numbers at Sharon's actual funeral. It was rather like one of those naked-in-public dreams, and made it hard to engage anyone in the information-sharing process. So it was not until quite late in the afternoon that information came to me, in the unprepossessing form of Detective Captain Hal Endlich of the state police.

"Captain Endlich?" I inquired, when Mrs. Moyer ushered a grey-haired fiftyish man into the living room. Apparently no one had ever told him that crewcuts were out of style. Long out. "Finally."

"You expected me sooner? Why is that?"

"Oh no, I was just translating your name: Endlich. And our campus police chief is called 'Ehrlich.' " I was clearly babbling so as to delay—but he might think evade—the canonical "few questions" he said he had for me. The whole point was that I had fewer and shorter answers for him.

"What is your full name, please?"

"Margaret Leigh Jameson. Everyone calls me Jamie, though."

"Miss or Mrs.?" was the uncompromising reply to this.

"Neither."

"What?"

"Ms., or around here they say 'Doctor.'"

"Just around here?" More than a trace of the Pennsylvania Dutch made the word "chust."

I thought I'd be tactful about a local institution. "Well, some colleges seem to use the doctoral title more than others."

"But you're entitled?"

"I'm entitled."

"Your address, Doctor?"

I gave him this one. On learning, however, that I had been in Jaegersville only six months and would be leaving soon, he wanted to know my permanent domicile. "I haven't got one." We established that I hadn't voted or paid U.S. taxes in some years.

"Then I need your previous address." Transformed by his tone into a vagabond, I was rapidly reminded how the facts of anyone's life can be made to sound suspicious, once there's a reason for suspicion. Not, of course, that there was, in my particular case. What there was, though, undeniably, was a body, and it had been in my office, dispatched with the funny little statue Walt gave me for Christmas.

"Okay, but it's in France: 142, rue de la-Tour-d'Auvergne, 75009 Paris." I had to backtrack and spell it for him word by word before we could proceed through a series of laborious questions ascertaining my date of birth ("Then you're thirty-five *yizzold*," he concluded, accent on the "yizz"), that I was by occupation a poet and a temporary professor at the college over the way. In his repetition of the two simple syllables, "poet" also sounded like "gypsy," and not a cheerful, adventurous gypsy, but a wild and murderous one. Endlich also dragged me through what I had hitherto considered the sparse details of the discovery of the body.

"You were late coming back from class, then?"

"A few minutes."

"A three-hour class, and it still runs over?" More grounds for suspicion, apparently.

"Yes." How to explain that the students were there because they were really committed to their writing and that aspiring writers will take all the time you're willing to give them and then some? Besides, no classes were scheduled for the following hour, so they didn't have to run off, and there wasn't another group waiting in the hall for that room to be vacated.

"So you ran 20 minutes over?"

"All together."

"When you arrived at the archive, you encountered this— ah—Michael David Freund. Is that right?"

"Well, just outside the archive. Students don't have keys, so he had to wait for someone to let him in." No, I hadn't been late for an *appointment* with Mike, though I usually did try to get to the archive around four. Gwen normally let the assistants in when I wasn't around, but this time *she* hadn't been around.

"Did you form any impression as to her whereabouts?"

"No." Actually, I think I assumed she was in the ladies' room, which I wouldn't, myself, have characterized as anything so ponderous as "forming an impression." For that matter, I didn't think of the library's small staff lounge as "whereabouts," either.

"Otherwise—" In his accent it came out "otterwise." I pictured myself lying athwart a sleek sea mammal, otterwise, as it were. "You noticed nothing unusual before the door was opened and you saw the body?" My little otter swam regretfully away.

"No. Except that we had to get Security to open the door. Since, as I'm sure you know, the door into the library stacks functions as another exit, but not normally another entrance.

Someone using the archive can go from there into the library stacks, but unless they leave the door propped open, which we're *not* supposed to do, it snap locks and no one can get into the archive that way." "You recognized the corpse right away?" he pursued.

"I think so, but, in any case, Mike Freund said her name out loud while I was still trying to take it all in."

"You recognized the weapon, as well?"

"Oh yes. It's a little statue that belongs to me."

"You admit it's your property?" He paused, then asked as if it were highly significant, "Is there anything in the office that's your own property besides the murder weapon?"

"My property? Well, I never thought of it that way, but I guess the tea-making apparatus is my own. I mean, I went out and bought an electric kettle, a teapot, and a set of mugs for the office. Plus the tea, of course. Otherwise, the room is furnished by the college, even down to the paintings on the walls." The original walruses.

"But the weapon is something you brought to the office?"

"Yes. I mean, not *as* a weapon, of course."

"You've had it long?"

"A few months."

"In fact, we understand that the dean—this would be Preston Endicott Walters of Crabtree Lane in this township?—gave it to you for Christmas."

"Yes." Although I hadn't known about the "Endicott." It certainly over-determined the use of a nickname.

"The dean gave you the murder weapon as a Christmas gift?"

"Well, naturally he didn't know it would turn out to be a weapon." Was I repeating myself? It certainly felt that way. "It was a kind of a joke." *Great, now he has me saying that Walt and I think giving me a murder weapon was a joke!* "I imagine he thought of it as a work of art."

"And is he in the habit of giving expensive works of art to

the young lady professors?" "Expensive" was clearly synonymous with "art" to him.

I ignored "young lady professors." It contained too many
errors to tackle and keep anywhere near the point. So I replied
tersely, "I wouldn't know, but this wasn't an especially valuable
piece, just a cute little statue."

"At the time then, at Christmas, you were close to Dean
Walters. You were—going out together?"

I could think of worse characterizations, even though we
tended, more often than not, to stay in together. "Yes, we
were."

"And you stopped seeing each other since then?"

"Yes."

"When was this?" From the surreptitious glance he gave his
notes, I realized he already knew, as he'd known about the gift
of the walrus.

"The end of January. I could probably figure out the exact
date, if I took a look at my calendar."

"That's close enough. Whose idea was it to break up, yours
or his?"

"It wasn't that kind of thing. We found we disagreed about
something quite fundamental—and then I guess we agreed to
disagree." True enough. In principle, I could never have a relationship with a man who refused to "share" me, but I'd have
been willing to keep on with Walt if only he hadn't *said* so. On
the other hand, his saying so was a measure of *his* unwillingness
to keep going on those terms. Or had he simply expected me to
dissolve in apologetic tears so he could be generous and take
me back? This was a new thought and came close to diverting
me from the interrogation at hand.

"So you say it was mute-chill. You have someone else now?"

"Not—" To anyone else, I'd have said, "Not here in Jaegersville." But it was clear that, for Endlich, Jaegersville, PA, was
the entire universe or close to it, and, in any event, I saw no

point in bringing Nick's name into it. "Not at the moment."

"What about Dr. Walters: has he been keeping company with anyone?"

"He went places with—with the deceased, with Sharon Reilly." I stumbled over one of my French idioms but I could hardly call poor Sharon "the defunct," could I? "But it wasn't a real—I mean it was a different sort of thing."

"Different how?"

"Well, they were old friends who sometimes did things together socially, is all. They had no—intimate relationship."

"Maybe that's why you were jealous?" The "ch" at the beginning of that last word combined with the absurdity of the suggestion to make it literally incomprehensible for a moment. But we proceeded. At length.

"And it turns out," I explained to Becca after he left and I'd poured myself a stiff San Pellegrino, "that I'm this guy's number one suspect. He didn't get here until past four in the afternoon because he was busy trying to break my alibi."

"Couldn't he?" she asked curiously.

"The doctor says Sharon was killed somewhere between noon and 3 or 3:30 at the outside. Well, in the morning—too early, but in case their estimate is off—I went running in the gym, and a gratifying number of people saw me there. I mean, I wouldn't normally be gratified, the way I look when I run, but it comes in handy. Then I showered and changed, all still on the other end of campus from the library, and went over to a committee meeting."

"You're on a committee? They never expected *me* to do that."

"It's the search committee for the new professor of poetry. Of course I'm not a member, but they're about to cut their list and they asked for my professional advice. Which I doubt they're planning to take. I think it was by way of being a courtesy. But it means a number of senior faculty and administrators—including Tom Walker and Walt, of course—had their eyes on me until about a quarter to twelve, when I left to meet Laurie and Ann to discuss their research over lunch."

"Mightn't you have done the murder on your way?" As if she were seeing if I could have fit in a little errand.

"I had the two of them meet me—providentially, in the event—outside the conference room, and we walked over to the Campus Inn together. Anyway, the relevant time, if the doctor is right, begins at the very moment we were seated at our table. Then, as it happens, Laurie is *in* my one o'clock class, so we were together going back to the Green, as well. We went right past the library and even stopped in the ladies' room at the same time. Then I was in class from one until after four. That's what took Endlich all afternoon, tracking down sixteen students who swear I didn't leave them for a moment."

"You didn't have them do a writing exercise?"

"No, thank God. Because I sometimes do go out and come back, in that case. But we were discussing a short story Pete Borza brought in. You remember Pete, don't you? Well, he takes so long to get to the point in his prose that it's not always easy to get to the point in critiquing it. So I was there, visible and audible, the whole time, and later as I made appointments for conferences. Eager as he is to nail me and, I think, essentially distrustful of the young, even Endlich found it hard to believe all of them were my dupes or my accomplices. He did say they were 'very loyal'—which, believe me, is no compliment in his book—but that seems to mean that most of them also took the opportunity to tell him I'm a great poet and a wonderful teacher. In addition to having been in Seminar Room B every minute from one to four yesterday."

"Well, that's good, anyway. Your students' praise lasts. Police inquiries don't."

"Murder ones do."

"But why should he be so eager to, as you say, 'nail' you?"

"Because he's constructed a hypothetical narrative where I'm the only person he can find with what he thinks is an acceptable motive."

"Acceptable?"

"Credible, anyway. In his frame of reference."

"Okay: I give up. What is this motive of yours?"

"Jealousy. Woman-scorned division."

"Over Walt?"

"Uh-huh. Once I'd implied that I didn't think Walt and Sharon were even sleeping together, which to my mind made it not quite real as a man-woman thing—"

"Sexist reasoning. But do go on."

"Anyway, to me, that meant Sharon hadn't *replaced* me in Walt's life. I don't know if he brought her here on Sundays to show me that he could find someone new right away or because he felt he'd been burned in an intensely sexual liaison—ours— and wanted something—cooler, for awhile. Anyway, his thing with Sharon was even less complete than his relationship with me. I'm sure of it."

"Endlich, I take it, is of a different opinion."

"Him! He's worse than Walt! If Walt comes out of the Fifties, this one's from the Dark Ages! His idea was that Walt chose Sharon over me precisely because he'd already gotten what he could from me—sexually, that is—whereas Sharon didn't put out, so she was a nice girl he could respect. And even marry. I guess that's really from the Fifties, too, just another neck of the woods. So I was jealous that he'd thrown me over, and I either killed Sharon in a rage when she came to tell me something about her and Walt—they found a letter she started to write to me—or I planned the whole thing, premeditated it, as they say, and lured her to my office."

"Did you point out—?"

"That we're all a little long in the tooth for such antics? I mean, Sharon was about Walt's age—mid-forties, anyway—and

I'm no spring chicken, myself, when it comes to stories about virgins versus bad girls and boyfriends who refuse to buy the cow once they've had the milk for free. Becca, he actually *said* that—about the cow, I mean."

"But *I* meant, did you point out that Walt is not in a position to marry anyone?"

"Of course I did. Not that that's irreversible. I even threw in the fact that I'm not free to marry at the moment, myself, since he was clearly not convinced by my assurances that I don't want to marry the dean."

"Was he impressed by these legalities?"

"Who knows? But he seemed to have taken the point that a countess is higher up than a dean-ess, and that I left the count anyway. So maybe it'll mean Alain will get a discreet visit from the Sureté or Interpol or someone. Only if they ask *him* if I'm likely to fly into a murderous rage over some woman who'd played her cards right by keeping her legs crossed—well, I can't even guess what he'll think is the funniest answer to give!"

"Didn't you tell me Alain had lost his sense of humor?"

"Yes, but what a thing to have to depend on!"

"Well, no matter what conflicting views they get of your character—someone came to question Mrs. Moyer, too, by the way—you've got a perfect alibi. So there's nothing to worry about."

"Oh, no? As long as they can't think of anyone else with a motive, I bet they're not going to *look* very closely at anyone else. Which means I have a shadow over me, poor Sharon's murderer gets away with it, and, incidentally, there's a killer somewhere on the Ebbing campus."

"You mean a psychopath?"

"Not an indiscriminate one. I don't think he'll strike again or anything. But anyone who would do that is a psychopath, which just means a crazy person, after all. And that *fool* who believes Victorian sex manuals won't be following up the real clues. It just makes me mad, is all! Anyway, tell me about Mrs. Moyer's interview with the cops."

"First you have to tell me about the letter they have. You just sort of threw that in as part of your supposed motive. What letter?"

"Well, we know that Sharon came up to the archive. No one seems to know how she got in, but either she came to see me or she chose a time when she knew I definitely wouldn't be there. And she started to write a note to leave for me. She began with an apology of some sort—Endlich was only paraphrasing—and she didn't get much further. So *he* sees it as a candid apology for taking my man away from me—an apology I violently refused to accept—and *I* assume it had something to do with either the manuscript business or maybe why she changed her attitude toward me. They may boil down to the same thing. In either case, it would have nothing to do with Walt."

"I wouldn't be so sure," Becca drawled cryptically.

"Well, I would. She said I was an academic elitist and so on at a public committee meeting before anyone knew about Walt and me. Anyone but you, that is. And I don't exactly see you running to Sharon Reilly with this juicy tidbit of gossip."

"But I did. Not run, I mean; I do have my limitations. But Thanksgiving weekend, on the Friday, Betsy Robards called to invite you over to supper. She said Bill had made something 'distinctly edible'—I recall the phrase—out of their leftover turkey, and she was asking a bunch of people to come help eat it so they'd be shut of the damn bird. Anyway, I told her you weren't coming back until the next day, because you and Walt were still up in Savage. It was obvious to us both that you might have been snowed in the night before, but if you were staying on, it was because you were having a good time—together. Betsy and I even had a matronly—well, whatever the opposite is of commiseration—"

"Congratulation?"

"Anyway, we rejoiced together for a moment or two, in a decorous sort of way, before she hung up."

"And you think that if Sharon came to that supper, Betsy might have told her?"

"Didn't I say? Sharon was already *over* there. I'm sure Betsy got off the phone and told both Bill and Sharon what she thought was lovely news about their dear friend—*all* of their dear friend—Walt. You have no idea how people here go around bewailing the fact that that good, kind man has no woman to screw. It's well meant, I'm sure, but it borders on the obscene!"

"I do know. I got the converse of it once the same people knew we were a couple: so pleased he 'had' somebody. But, Becca, why didn't you tell me that Sharon knew about Walt and me? At least, when she said that stuff to the Honorary Degrees Committee the very next week?"

"Because you didn't tell me she'd done that. So I'll send the question right back: why didn't you mention it if it hurt your feelings?"

"I don't know. Yes, I do. In fact, three reasons: one, it was so petty, two, Walt told me about it the same day we found the manuscript, so I had much bigger news by the time I got home, and three, your own honorary degree was still supposed to be a secret, so I didn't even want to mention that committee to you. Over-determined is what it is."

"But now we're assuming that it was Sharon who was jealous of *you* over a man. Which would mean she was interested in Walt, herself, that early on."

"Well, there isn't a big selection around here, you know."

"However, what you don't know is that Sharon was very close with Virginia Walters. They even drank together, before Sharon understood that with Virginia it wasn't a hearty overindulgence but a real illness."

"Then could she have resented me on Virginia's behalf? I

mean, here's everyone else congratulating each other on good old Walt's having finally found himself some sexual outlet—"

"They do mean well."

"I'm sure. But no one seems to waste a thought on poor Virginia. Of course, I didn't either. At least, not as a barrier to going to bed with her husband. But if I were her *friend*—"

"Though Sharon did start dating him after you and he broke up."

"That's the whole point. *They* weren't sleeping together. Though I suspect that was his idea. I'm ready to swear he didn't have that kind of feeling for Sharon. So she can—could—tell herself it was all right just to go out with him. And if any of that jealousy of me did happen to be on her own account—well—she could sublimate it all very nicely. *She* wasn't betraying Virginia the way Walt and I did."

"I wonder if Virginia would recognize the distinction."

"Virginia?"

"I imagine she might feel worse about his dating a friend of hers—and how can she be sure there's no sex?—than going with a stranger who is conveniently slated to leave in a few months."

"Becca, are you thinking that *Virginia* could have killed Sharon?"

"Weren't you just saying it had to be a crazy person? Well, Virginia Walters is the only *certified* crazy person with any connection to this business."

"It'd probably be easy enough to check. Her movements, I mean. But Virginia—I just can't imagine—"

"Mrs. Moyer could. Which brings us back to her conversation with the police, as reported by herself. Apparently, she had a low opinion of the deceased, based at least partly on the fact that she drank too much and used to do it in company with Virginia. And her judgment of Virginia is none too kindly. After all, she's seen things that none of the rest of us really have—participated, not just witnessed them, if it comes to that. So she told the police that Virginia was a monster, her friend Sharon not much better, and, as a girlfriend, would be cold comfort to that nice, patient, saintly man who'd unaccountably loused things up with the sweet, warm, loving girl he really deserved."

"Ah: me?"

"You. After what you told me, I see that Endlich must have tried to get her on his side on the morals issue. In fact, he probably just assumed a church-going Dutchwoman of his own generation would be eager to join in condemning the Scarlet Woman."

"Me, again?"

"Yes. But she wouldn't play. As far as her own life is concerned, she may be the pillar of righteousness he took her for. But her job has given her a broader point of view. From what I gather *she's* gathered nursing at a hundred death beds, what she values most is the readiness to give to others, and you have that in abundance, Jamie: loving and giving."

"If only Walt saw it that way instead of talking about giving 'it' away, we wouldn't be in this fix! Anyway, thank heaven for Mrs. Moyer. She may have succeeded in insinuating Virginia Walters onto their list of suspects. Not that I like the first-Mrs.-Rochester touch and all these tales of female jealousy."

"But do you have a male candidate to propose?"

"No, not seriously. You know something else weird, Becca? Endlich kept asking me if I knew anything about some Florida connection in Sharon's life. He even mentioned Disney World once. And he clearly didn't believe me when I said I didn't know what he meant. What on earth do you think that was about?" Becca shook her head in perplexity.

SHARON'S FUNERAL WAS held in the College chapel with as much grandeur as the simple setting could muster. Classes were canceled, and a surprising number of students and

faculty actually went to the service, along with several repre-
sentatives of the Ebbing family. I was unfortunately beyond
noticing whether they resembled the murder weapon. A Catholic
priest and the college president who was, after all, an ordained
clergyman, shared the pulpit. But despite—maybe because
of—two more visits from the police, I had the feeling that the
fact of Sharon's death had already come to be seen as a part of
history. It was almost a shock that we still had to go through the
rituals of burial and mourning.

I tried to remember good things I knew about Sharon: She
was a loyal friend *to* her friends and a meticulous scholar. She
had a nice sense of humor. She loved animals. *"My cat, Herodotus, has as good a chance in this job market."* As good a chance
as Charles Rowland, on whom funeral clothes looked surprisingly appropriate. Back in the fall, she'd told me that Herodotus,
now altered, had been given that name so he could sire a kitten
named History. "Because Herodotus was the Father of History,
you know." I resolved to find out who'd taken charge of Herodotus.

In the vestibule, Walt came up to me with a patently conciliatory expression on his face. Once again, I was irresistibly
reminded of dogs—puppies, not those in mangers.

"Do you have a ride to the cemetery, Jamie?"

"I wasn't planning to go, so I just walked over from the
house."

"I wish you'd come. With me."

"Well, that will give Captain Endlich something to ponder,
all right. Though what even he thinks we could get up to in a
funeral cortege—" Walt guided me to his car as if I were his
maiden great-aunt, a very fragile one. "Why aren't you a pall-
bearer, by the way?" I asked as he unlocked the door on my
side.

"Someone decided it wouldn't be appropriate."

"Whyever not?"

"Because the police have shown too healthy and too sustained an interest in my movements that afternoon. They like my motive or what they conceive to be my motive, though I was at an official lunch after the committee meeting you came to and then two more committees, thank God, because nothing could convince Endlich, otherwise, that I didn't want to kill Sharon, had no reason to, and would have been incapable of it."

"Have you noticed the way Endlich always says 'otterwise'?"

"Yeah, the wise old otter."

I giggled. It was pleasant to be back on this kind of basis with Walt, even lined up behind a hearse that had not yet started its grim progress.

"Jamie, I asked you to come with me so I could apologize for the way I spoke when you came to my office. It wasn't an easy thing to do, and I made it harder on you, but I'm—I'm grateful that you did."

"Even if Endlich misinterprets it? Although I must say, his explanation of *my* motive wouldn't hold much water if we were in this thing together." I told him why I was supposed to be jealous of Sharon.

"The only grain of truth in that mishmash is that I wasn't sleeping with her. We'd been colleagues—old pals—too long, and she was a close friend of Ginnie's. I just couldn't think of her that way."

"Do you know how *she* thought of it, Walt?" I asked quietly.

"No. There would have been only one way to find out, and I wasn't about to open that can of worms. Which, I suppose, means, yes, I suspected it might not be as mutually platonic as all that."

"But Walt, if Endlich has *you* on his list, too, what's your motive supposed to be?"

"Motives, plural, take your pick, but all based on my having been—however briefly—the official boyfriend. So, as I say, you can choose: either I was enraged because she rejected me sexually—"

"Enraged enough to kill her instead of just seducing an undergraduate, *comme tout le monde?*"

"It's not funny, Jamie."

"It wouldn't be if you *had*. But it's all so far-fetched. This is, as my students ceaselessly remind me, the 1980s. Which to me signifies we're going down the tubes fast, but to them means it's the Present Enlightened Age. Anyway, what are your other motives?"

"Also sexual: they suggested I really was sleeping with her and she was pregnant."

"Surely the autopsy—"

"—made it clear she wasn't. So then they got more Byzantine and decided she'd lied and *told* me she was pregnant."

"But you've had a vasectomy!" The car was stopped at a red light, and Walt's look forcefully reminded me how I'd come to know that. "And Sharon was 43 or 44, and you hadn't been together much more than maybe six or eight weeks—"

"They tend to dismiss the little details. I must admit, though, that they seem to prefer scenarios where Sharon remains the unsullied virgin. That's why I'm only the number two choice, after you."

"Personally, what I'd like is to pin it on Charles Rowland. He's a better choice than either of us."

"I know you don't care for him. Neither did Sharon, come to think of it. But what possible motive or, more important, evidence could you come up with?"

"I don't know, but it'd have to have something to do with the manuscript."

"Jamie, no one would kill over a thing like that. I think you're a little obsessed with the manuscript business. And playing Girl Detective could be dangerous."

I didn't tell Walt I'd rather trap Charles Rowland than be-

lieve his own wife had crept out of Hochstetter, done the fell
deed, and returned before she was missed.

"What's become of Herodotus?" I asked instead.

"A neighbor's feeding him for the time being. Why?"

"Maybe I should take him. It would be a gesture, anyway.
If Becca didn't mind."

Our time at the cemetery was brief, efficient, and depressing. However mixed my feelings about Sharon may have been,
I felt a heavy anger at whoever had forced us all into this confrontation with death. For the first time since my waves of nausea
on the day of the murder, I experienced the situation as more
than a game whose object was getting the cops off my own back.

"Do you want to go back to the president's house?" Walt
asked, once we were in his car again. "He and his wife are
standing in for the family, since the funeral was here."

"Should I?"

"Not called for. In fact, it's just as well if you don't, and I'll
drop you at home on my way. By the same logic, I really ought
to be there."

"We're talking like a pair of conspirators. As if we did do it."

"Because we've both had a big taste, this week, of having
our most innocent actions scrutinized and misunderstood."

"Innocent?"

"Well, normal. Anyway, I have two things I wanted to ask
you. One's business and the other—isn't."

"Go ahead. On the business one. This is not the moment for
the other." Surely even a man with what I suspected he had on
his mind could see that.

"Well, the Personnel Committee had a quick conference
about Sharon's courses for the rest of the term. I suggested that
your friend Erin Ni'Connor might be willing to come up and
pinch hit. It's two sections of Western Civ, the majors' seminar
in Pennsylvania history, and senior thesis supervision. We'd
prorate the salary—"

"So for the remaining third of the semester, at adjunct scale, that's one-third of a pittance times four courses. Very generous: comes to a pittance and a third."

"No, we'd offer her the rest of Sharon's salary. I checked and Sharon had opted for the twelve-month pay cycle, so there are still five months of checks coming to—whoever. At full professor's rates. You might tell Erin she could take over Sharon's apartment, furnished, since the building belongs to the college."

"Are you—ah—authorizing me to make the offer? The whole thing's a great idea. And boy, will Charles Rowland hate it! I'll call right away." We had pulled up in front of my house. I got out of the car thinking about all the unresolved old questions between us and several new ones with names like Endlich, a possibly murderous Virginia, Sharon herself, even that remark about my playing Girl Detective.

"You got a telegram." Mrs. Moyer had been on the lookout for me. I was regretting that Walt's "nonbusiness" matter had made me leave the car without so much as a friendly kiss. It was a situation in which there are no friendly kisses. I also remembered belatedly that I'd meant to find out if Walt had any idea why Endlich kept asking about Florida. "Actually," she went on, "it was a cable. From France. They tried to read it over the phone, but I couldn't make head nor tail of it, so I told them to deliver it."

I tore it open and read: *"Faut tenir le coup. Lettre suit. Fautour."*

"It's just my husband," I said. "He says to hang in there. And that he'll be writing."

9

✳

ERIN ACCEPTED THE offer from Ebbing with alacrity and gratitude. Even Sharon's apartment harbored no ghosts for her. "I only met the woman once," she reminded me, "and she was afraid to shake my hand."

"Afraid: you saw that, too?"

"No big mystery. Straight women who are unsure either of themselves or what other people will think don't like dealing with 'out' lesbians."

"Are you sure? About the description, I mean. Because, remember, when I first got to know Sharon, I sort of wondered if she herself wasn't—"

"That's just the point: people wonder or the woman herself wonders. No, trust me on this one, Jamie. Anyway, this is Monday. I can be there day after tomorrow and start teaching Thursday, if that's okay. Shall I call your Dean in the morning?"

"No, don't bother, I'll— On second thought, go ahead and make it official." Perhaps it would be better not to multiply my contacts with Walt tomorrow. Especially considering what I planned for the afternoon.

As soon as I got off the telephone, I sought out Mrs. Moyer to start putting my idea into operation. "I want to take Becca over to Hochstetter for her chemo, tomorrow. Could you make up a reason why you can't go?"

"Sure I could. But why don't you just tell her you'd like to do it, this once?"

"It's kind of complicated. What I really want to do is see Virginia Walters, and I know it's easier to get to her once I have a legitimate reason to be inside the gates, even in the other wing."

"See Mrs. Walters? Well, sooner you than me, with that one."

"But you'll make it seem natural?"

"Put your mind at rest. I'll think up a wonderful lie for you."

Thus I became an unofficial visitor to the psychiatric pavilion at Hochstetter. Although it was Becca who'd first planted suspicions of Virginia in my mind, she was nonetheless likely to object to any attempt to follow them up. She was particularly apt to take a dim view of my evading the outer and most difficult level of guards and receptionists by *in*vading the hospital's underground passages, and I didn't want her to worry over what might, indeed, prove a foolhardy project.

From summer jobs as a ward clerk and volunteer experience, while my women's group in France was researching gynecological care, I knew something about how hospitals work, and they're not all that different from one another. In fact, I allowed time for more than the two wrong turns and one dead end that I encountered in the subterranean connection between the two wings of Hochstetter. I carried a clipboard, but did nothing else to impersonate a staff member; the suggestion that I belonged there was all Method acting on my part. At the time, I was more frightened that this fragile camouflage would be penetrated than that I might meet a violent lunatic or two on my way to the women's quarters.

Only later did I start dreaming that I'd taken a permanent wrong turn.

The lounge where I found Virginia—by the simple expedient of asking where she was—had a glassed-in sun porch, where she sat reading, as far away as she could get from the TV game show blaring at the other end of the room. The price, for Virginia, was definitely not right. I watched her for a moment before going over to her, and the word that came to mind was "tranquil." *Tranquilized*, I amended, as I saw grey eyes empty of expression in the puffy, fine-boned face.

Virginia wore a washed-out chambray dress of the sort that upper-class New England women affect in the heat of summer. They've always reminded me of prison uniforms. It would have been wildly inappropriate for the weather outside, but was entirely suitable for the tropically heated hospital solarium. It was my tweeds that were out of place. Under them, my back was already damp and sticking to my shirt.

"You're Virginia?" I asked. As irritation sparked for a moment in those lifeless eyes, I quickly added, the way I would to anyone else, "Excuse me, I'm sorry to interrupt. What are you reading?"

She showed me the spine of her book: Jane Austen, Modern Library edition. "*Persuasion*. It's lucky all six novels are in one volume, because they don't let me have too many books. I'm supposed to give more of my time to those craft things: occupational therapy." An infinite scorn was in those last two words, though her essential calm remained untroubled.

"If you think about it," I surprised myself by observing, "all the unmarried women in those books do occupational therapy, only they called it 'accomplishments.' It was the prescribed treatment for their sex and class."

"But *she* didn't—Austen herself. Those novels were *real* fancy work."

At that moment, I was sure Virginia could not have killed

Sharon Reilly, certainly not with the motive and method I'd ascribed to her. But, distrusting my own respect for an adroit play on words, I pursued my investigation. "My name's Jamie," I told her. "I'm teaching at Ebbing College this year."

"Oh, the poet. Walt told me a lot about you when you first came. Then he stopped. Did he fall in love with you?" The question was polite, clearly of less interest than, say, Frederick Wentworth's flirtation with Louisa Musgrove. It seemed that her own pain at my answer would be less than her sympathy for Anne Elliot looking on, helplessly, hopelessly, at that misdirected courtship.

"I wouldn't say 'fell in love.' Just 'got interested,' perhaps." I'd always avoided thinking about whether Walt's feelings went deeper than my own.

"Well, don't let him get you pregnant. He does that, you know." It was as if she was reporting an irritating masculine habit, like snoring, but one in which she had no personal investment.

"He won't get the chance." Not only my own resolutions, but his vasectomy—which, surely, she'd known about at one time—made this patently true.

"And Sharon wouldn't let him, either. An affair wouldn't get her what she wanted."

"Which was?"

"Marriage, the official status. Austen would call it 'an establishment' of her own. Besides," we switched abruptly back into the twentieth century, "she had to have a hysterectomy a few years back."

Didn't those cops know *anything*? I recalled the elaborate scenarios they'd devised to torment Walt, all, it transpired, about the putative impregnation of a sterilized woman by a sterilized man. In the stifling heat, I felt like throwing up. "You're sure he didn't sleep with Sharon?" I persisted, fighting back the nausea with some difficulty.

"He told me he was taking her out sometimes. And she still sent me her regards and all." Whereas he'd stopped mentioning *me* once there was something between us to speak of. *I may be crazy, but I'm not stupid,* as the old punch-line runs.

"You know Sharon's dead?"

"Oh, yes. Walt phoned the hospital and Dr. Krieger called me in to tell me. I'd already seen him for my one-thirty that day and he called me back in." This extraordinary therapeutic attention seemed to loom as large, for her, as the announcement that occasioned it. "They didn't want me to hear it on the nightly news." She *was* pleased with all that thoughtfulness. And she had an alibi for the crucial time, to boot—had brought it out and flaunted it at me.

"How do you feel about her death?" I ventured.

"Very sad, of course," she replied mechanically, adding, after a pause, "Poor Sharon." It was polite, perfunctory. "I wish I could feel more."

Another piece fell into place, as I remembered my friend Jenny Metz's story about the drugs they'd filled *her* with: *"I was waiting to cross the street, but a kid, a teenager, didn't stop for the light. The driver who knocked him down didn't stop, either. But I waited on the curb until the sign flashed 'Walk,' and then I crossed, stepping neatly over the body. The thing is, Jamie, I tended to get too upset over things, so they put me on these capsules so I was incapable of getting upset even where I should have."*

"You mean the pills, Virginia? They keep you from feeling more?"

"You're smart about things. I like you." Despite the way she put it, it was not a child's declaration, but came, like much of our conversation, from a place where there are no social rules and no censors. For someone on my side of the line, it was a terrifying and exhilarating way to talk.

"Look, Virginia, I have a friend who got herself off of pills like that, a poet in Philadelphia. She writes a lot, now, and coordinates a series of readings—I was on one of her programs, myself, just before I came here for the first time. You can fight it off, if you have something to fight *for.*"

There was no answering intensity, but Virginia smiled at me. "That's interesting. You know," she went on, gesturing at the Austen volume on her lap, "there's somebody in most of these novels who's crazier than I am, if believing your own delusions is any measure."

"Virginia," I asked, as I stood to leave. "Have you ever thought of writing these things down? Your ideas about Jane Austen?"

"But first I have to get well for my husband and children." It sounded like a well-memorized lesson.

"No, you don't. You have to get well for yourself. I understand when you were in graduate school you were the star of Carl Werber's seminar—"

"Oh, no, Walt was."

"Not the way he tells it. Get well so you can do an article about the line between eccentricity and madness in Jane Austen's universe. Or the 'work' of marriageable girls—the occupational therapy." I said good-bye and thanked her, making my way to the underground passage with more assurance this time.

Unfortunately, this gave me leisure to think as I went, and my thoughts were anything but pleasant. Walt had called her a perfectionist who made demands on herself that no one could meet. And between the drink and the drugs she might not be able to write a coherent paragraph anymore, much less a sustained piece of literary criticism. Perhaps it was less than wise—and even less than kind—of me to walk in, size up the situation in five minutes, and tell her to do something she was bound to fail at. My own censor, cut off for more than half an hour from her usual silent but effective function in my head, was taking full revenge.

Becca was wheeled out just after I got back to the waiting room. This time, however, my thoughts on the drive home were divided between the concern for her that had become the bedrock of my days here and a strange comparison of myself and Virginia Walters.

Walt had been her first lover—as far as he knew, her only one. And he had begotten four children on that slender body, before it had acquired its artificial, pill-induced thickness. Her lightly freckled skin under the pale blue fabric had once looked as nakedly at him as her blank, candid eyes had looked at me today. She had been open to him in a way I never had, and her intact marriage had shattered her, whereas my shattered one had left me damaged but intact. Somehow, after talking to her, I was sure I could never let her husband touch me again. Before, it had been a combination of principle and prudence that made me say no to a resumption of our relations. Now it was visceral. "Good-bye, Walt," I mumbled.

"What?" asked Becca.

"Nothing, sorry," I said quickly, and continued to address him internally. *If your crazy wife takes up your scholarly career where you let it fall, you won't even know whom to thank. But with her it may truly be publish or perish.* Another creepy thought.

"Spring is coming," Becca commented, as I helped her out of the car, "if you notice details. I'm ready to write about dying."

Erin arrived the next day and plunged enthusiastically into her responsibilities at Ebbing. She asked if she could keep Herodotus, and I decided her need was greater than mine. Not that I had anyone warm and cuddly in my bed, either, but I found I wanted to make a small sacrifice. If Socrates, at the end of his life, owed a cock to Aesculapius, I thought I should allocate considerably more than one altered tomcat to whatever goddess was in charge of my well-being.

On Thursday afternoon, Erin and I met with Ann Capobianco and Mike Freund, the two history majors who were also assistants on the archive. "Is there any way their work here might fit in with the Pennsylvania history seminar?" she asked me. "It might be useful for all concerned."

"Sure. Ann's already working on the memoir. What if she made it her seminar project to find out what happened to Nellie Breckenridge?"

"She won't have—" Erin began, but Mike Freund spoke at the same moment.

"Breckenridge?" he asked. "Would that have anything to do with the Breckenridge Fire?"

"The what?" I replied stupidly.

"In Philly, up in Germantown. It was a big fire that destroyed an entire square block back in the fall of—"

"Don't tell me: 1868."

"You mean, you do know?"

"Never heard of it. Should I have, like Mrs. O'Leary's cow or something?"

"Well, it never caught the popular imagination like the Chicago Fire, and I guess it wasn't as extensive. But, for awhile, the name Breckenridge meant sort of the same thing in local circles. You see, the fire started at the home of Mr. Thomas Breckenridge—"

"The father," I put in.

"And there were several other Breckenridge households in the block. Along with a lot of other rich people. One of the newspapers said something about how it 'altered the destiny of some of Philadelphia's finest families.' But the only fatalities were in the house where it began."

"Fatalities?" Erin asked. I was temporarily beyond speech, and even she raised the question rather faintly.

"Everyone in the house was killed."

"Can we find out all the names?" I asked. "Maybe Ann should take a field trip to consult the old newspapers."

"Jameson, anyone would think you lived in the nineteenth century instead of just studying it. If the Goddess had meant us to travel to libraries at the drop of a question, she wouldn't have given us databases. A front-page event where we have the exact dates and location is a piece of cake for this computer!"

While I contemplated this mixed metaphor, which struck me as considerably crazier than anything I had heard from Virginia Walters in the locked wing of Hochstetter, Erin had ascertained the exact date of the fire from Mike (who, I was relieved to see, did have to consult his notebook), and was punching symbols into the computer terminal in the corner.

"Mike, how on earth do you happen to know all this?"

"I'm researching public services in Pennsylvania, how the idea developed of what things community members should provide for themselves and what should come out of taxes. Did you know that lots of towns in this state still have volunteer fire companies?"

"Sure, we have one right here."

"A place the size of Jaegersville would, almost anywhere. But, like Reading, I think, with a population of 80,000—and it used to be a lot more—has volunteers, not a city fire department."

"Supported by pancake breakfasts and bazaars, the way it is in a village?"

"Well, I don't know the finances for Reading yet, but maybe."

"Philly has a municipal department, though?"

"Yes, and the Breckenridge Fire is part of how it grew."

"I thought Benjamin Franklin—"

"We'll have a printout in a couple of minutes," Erin broke in from the computer corner. "But I just realized you're expecting Nellie's name to be on it."

"Isn't that the point?"

"Well, I got so involved in the details, between Mike's fire—

and it sounds as if you should keep right on with that project, kid—between that and exhibiting the wonders of high-tech research, I sort of *lost* the point. What I was going to tell you when you said Ann should work on this is that she doesn't have to start from scratch. I know now where Nellie was that fall, and it wasn't with her folks."

"It wasn't?" I was back to dull echoes.

"No, I can give you chapter and verse—at least, address and dates—for where she was, instead."

"Go on."

"Well, as you know, I checked the records of the likely hospitals and asylums for you when I went back to Philly in January. Those are in the database, too, as you must have seen from the summary I sent you—what?—six weeks ago. It was all negative, anyway."

"Frankly, I wondered how far to trust that evidence," I told her. "Look at the computerized hospital bills you get today!"

"At any rate, I kept your Nellie in mind, and when I was going through the Medical Institute archives—they've just opened the papers of Dr. Smedley Harris—there she was."

"Where she was? I mean, where was she?"

"In his diary. He would take a couple of private patients at a time into his home—he had a big house in Germantown—for treatment. The diary describes her case, Nellie's, in incredibly prurient terms: lots of language about pollution and self-abuse and her accomplice in filthy carnal knowledge. Along with diagnoses of hysteria and nymphomania, of course. He said she'd been in a state of utter frenzy when the family had committed her to his care, a few weeks after her return from the site of her guilty—"

"A few *weeks* after?"

"Apparently, she was just silent and passive at first—'tractable,' they all felt—and only broke out into what they considered madness—'great agitation,' *he* says—when her marriage was arranged."

"What marriage?"

"Engagement, actually. Dr. Harris says her parents had completed negotiations with the other family to marry her off to the brother of her—ah—partner in sin."

I said something unprintable. Fortunately, I said it in Italian. Unfortunately, Ann understood me and giggled. "Manley?" I asked.

"Him again."

"But he was only fifteen or sixteen."

"They'd presumably have waited until he was of age. Long engagements were pretty much the rule, anyway."

"They certainly were for Manley. Far from marrying Nellie as soon as he was old enough— When did he and Ethel Horseface finally tie the knot, Ann?"

"1890-something. Uh—'96. And I guess you know it was Ethel Horsely he married."

"I do, and he was no bargain himself. Aside from what we know of his character from *Helen-Elizabeth*, that's him up there." I showed Erin the portrait. The printer was noisily outputting historical data, but we ignored it.

"He looked like—a—a walrus!" she exclaimed. All of us stared down involuntarily at the library table around which we were sitting.

"It isn't the same table," I explained hurriedly. "They took it away, I don't know where to, and brought in this other one." But I was at one of the short ends, as Sharon had been, with my back to the door. Our mysteries were coming too close together for there *not* to be some overlap.

"Nellie hated Manley," I went on, "and he revolted her sexually. The idea of marriage at all—much less to him—well, no wonder she was agitated. So then they incarcerated her *chez* Smedley Harris? Did he calm her down?"

"No, thank God."

"What do you mean?"

"She wasn't one of his case histories. Which means he didn't get to do his famous Procedure on her."

"His procedure?"

" 'Pacification,' he called it. Sound familiar?"

"Only from Vietnam."

"Close enough. But you really don't know about Dr. Smedley Harris?"

"Remember how far out of my field I am, here, not to say my depth. But the name is perfect for any villainy you choose to father on him."

"I didn't choose this one, he did himself. Smedley Harris's private patients became the subjects of experiments in pacification: chloroform anesthesia followed by clitoridectomy!"

"What?" This was Mike. Ann explained in a low and remarkably unembarrassed voice what Dr. Harris did.

"Removed the clitoris?" he broke in. "Why would Manley want to marry her after that?"

"Mike," I said, "you are a sweet boy, and you belong to your times. Manley was a nasty boy who belonged to his. So you're saying that *you* wouldn't want to marry her that way, but this jerk wouldn't have noticed the difference—or cared. Erin, you're sure it didn't actually happen in Nellie's case?"

"Oh, yes. Most of the diary is devoted to long descriptions of the cases he followed through on. But Nellie just gets a few pages. I copied those for you—it was going to be my moving-in present. But I didn't think you'd care to read the whole diary."

"Or you'd have copied that, of course?"

"Microfilmed it. We can still do it—"

"Spare me. Unless we need it for negative corroboration. Meanwhile, let's see what *this* machine has wrought." The list of casualties in the Breckenridge Fire was reported in newspaper articles for days after the event. It sounded like the biggest thing to hit Philly since the Continental Congress. "My God! Both her parents, her sister and brothers, and assorted uncles,

aunts, and cousins who were staying with them—the Breckenridges were big on family visits—all killed in their sleep! Some
of the servants, too; they just get less prominence. 'Tragic
Fire'—'Mysterious Origins . . . ." Erin and I looked at each other
for a long moment.

"Well, Ann," said Erin, finally, "there's your project: whatever you can find about the Breckenridge Fire and our Nell. Did
Nellie inherit? And where did she go?"

"What if I can't find out before the end of the term?"

"You won't flunk. It's a course on research methods, after
all."

"But you *will* flunk dinner," Mike urged, "if you don't come
right now. They close the dining hall in exactly four minutes."

"It's almost worth it," she said, looking longingly at the
papers in front of us.

"No, we'll be leaving shortly ourselves." We shooed her out
with assurances that the work would be waiting there tomorrow
morning. When we were alone, Erin and I looked at each other
again in silent understanding. "Arson?" I finally asked.

"Nellie?" she replied.

"Are we saying she murdered her whole family in their
beds? And, unlike the redoubtable Bertha Mason, got out alive
herself?"

"Bertha Mason?"

"The first Mrs. Rochester." It was the second time that name
had been evoked in the past few days.

"Well, wasn't she crazy, too? The original madwoman in the
attic?"

"What do you mean 'too,' Erin? Nellie wasn't crazy, she was
just a girl who got caught with her lesbian lover. Don't you see
what you're saying?"

"I'm saying they did what they could to make her crazy. She
starts out with a bit of lesbian exploring—"

"You've read that manuscript, Erin, it's more than a little."

"Okay, she does some sexual exploring—heavy sexual exploring, if you insist. They catch her, separate her from her lover, lock her up, eventually get her engaged to the kid brother."

"And remember: Manley's the one who caught Nellie and his sister together. And only reported them when they refused to submit to his blackmail. He wanted sex from Nellie."

"So now he was going to get it. For life. And then, to make sure they provide him with a bride worthy of his attentions, they send her off to Smedley Harris for a swift clip of the clitoris. Who wouldn't be a little crazy?"

"But crazy people—whatever that means—don't necessarily commit crimes of violence." I remembered Virginia's quiet face bending over *Persuasion* as I left her on Tuesday.

"Of course not. Somebody presumably set that fire, though, Jamie. And Nellie had the most to gain from it. In that sense, it wasn't crazy at all."

"We don't know yet what she gained, Erin. That's part of Ann's assignment."

"But we know she didn't undergo the Pacification Procedure. That's a gain right there."

"I guess I'd *better* see that microfilm."

"We'll order it tomorrow. But let me tell you, Smedley Harris was a pioneer, years ahead of his time. Clitoridectomy didn't really come into its own until the end of the century. Of course, it's not clear that his patients had the short-term survival rate or the long-term life-expectancy one might wish for. To say nothing of the lives the 'successful' ones led thereafter."

"It makes me want to—to—"

"Be my guest, Jamie, you want to faint? Vomit?"

"Kill."

"You see? But Smedley Harris is long dead, himself. In one sense, whatever happened, Nellie survived him, because we've got *that.*" She gestured at the manuscript." Look, do you want to come back to my place? I can give you a rudimentary dinner and we'll baptize my new pad in California wine."

"Sounds fine, except for the baptism. My palate still belongs to France. And we can reread some parts of the memoir aloud. I want to see if we could we have missed something about Nellie and that doctor and the fire. Just let me phone home first and see if Becca's okay."

Mrs. Moyer told me Becca had spent the day in bed. "But she sat up and wrote some this afternoon," she added.

"That's wonderful. No, really." I could feel her skepticism across the wire. "If she can write, it means she felt pretty well. Not just for sitting and holding the pen, but *thinking, remembering, saying.*"

"And what if she exhausts herself even worse?"

"Writing doesn't kill people. Not writing does."

"If you say so. There's a lot of them writing to *you* today. You got a bunch of letters waiting for you—two from France."

"That'll be the one my husband mentioned in the telegram: 'Letter follows.' I must admit I sort of forgot about it."

"Too busy sneaking around visiting crazy women to find out who murdered a drunk old maid."

"Mrs. Moyer, please: a little Christian charity."

"Where it's due," she said with a note of finality. "I can't spare any from my patient—from the both of yizz."

I apologized to Erin as I hung up, "And I used to think Mrs. M. was taciturn on the telephone: Becca's condition, any messages, and off."

Erin's place—Sharon's place—reminded me of an upscale motel room. "Sure you don't want a drink?"

"Nothing to drink, thanks." But my exchange with Mrs. Moyer lingered. "By the way, Erin, did you find a lot of alcohol here in the apartment? I'm not sure what things of Sharon's were moved out."

"They cleared her clothes and personal effects, but left me

the books and kitchen supplies. And, yes, that included the booze. The woman did herself well: Irish whiskey—Jamesons, should be your brand—by the case."

"Oh, wow!"

"Remember, Jamie, this is Pennsylvania. She may have brought it in from somewhere else because there's not much of a selection at the State Store."

"Which is, in any event, a good ten miles away. I know Sharon drank, I've even watched her do it. So I guess having a lot around doesn't really tell us anything new."

"One mystery at a time. We've got the Breckenridge arson on our hands, as well as a local murder, and besides, Sharon was a victim, not a suspect."

"Except in the larceny case. And then *I* became a suspect once she was the victim." Now I had to explain to Erin about my relationship with Walt, our break-up, and its aftermath. "You certainly lead a varied life," she commented at the end. "So for a while you were going with the dean who at one time you also suspected. Is this the dean I had lunch with today: tall guy, Walters?"

"Yes, didn't you meet him when you were here before?"

"Probably. I think he came to my lecture."

"I know he did."

"That's right, he'd have still been your boyfriend then. And he became Sharon's?"

"*Toute proportion gardée*, he did. He took me to lunch, too, the day *I* was hired."

"Well, I trust he doesn't expect me—"

"Don't worry," I laughed. "He's not a *satyr*." It had, after all, been Walt's idea to offer Erin the job, and he knew her inclinations lay elsewhere. And then another idea pushed Walt—at least, Walt as anyone's lover—completely aside.

"Wait a second, Erin. I'm remembering something. He took you to the Campus Inn, right? Which is where he took me that first day. I'd forgotten all about that."

"You see?"

"I'm sure he has no designs on your virtue. There's just nowhere else on campus that's reasonably quiet. But I'm trying to recall exactly what happened last September. He came to the library and I'd just discovered the manuscript. In fact, I was up to one of the sexiest parts. So over lunch I told him all about *Helen-Elizabeth* and how it would probably be best to publish it separately from the other materials in the archive and so on. That was why I was suspicious of him when the manuscript disappeared. I thought maybe he was trying to protect the College's good name from this nineteenth-century scandal—a lesbian benefactress."

"Which may be worse than anyone knew, if it turns out we've also got a lesbian *arsonist* on our hands."

"Lesbian arsonist mass murderess, you mean," I added hysterically. "Erin, she couldn't have! But if we figure out she did, could we? Publish it, I mean."

"We'll cross that morass when we come to it. Anyway, why are you suddenly so hung up on your first lunch with Walters? You must have gone over that same conversation a hundred times, in your mind, after the manuscript was stolen."

"But I never got a clear picture of the scene before, the little table for two and so on. I've always been back there in groups, as it happens, at the larger tables on the other side of the room or in the back."

"So?"

"So now I can envision it clearly. I was facing Walt. And at the next table, behind him, I mean, so he might not have seen *her*—although he did greet several people, come to think of it— was a woman sitting alone. Over a couple of drinks. Which is probably what prompted the memory, our discussion about her supplies of booze."

"Whose, Sharon's supplies?"

"Yes. Because the woman at the next table *was* Sharon. She

must have heard everything I told him about the manuscript, the erotic descriptions, and my plans to publish it."

"And we know she did get mixed up in the theft, somehow. But why didn't you recognize her?"

"Because I didn't know anybody yet. And Walt waved and smiled at people, but made it pretty clear he didn't expect them to come over to our table."

"He was coming on to you?"

"No, explaining why Ebbing faculty don't publish— Oh!"

"What now?"

"Just: that was Sharon's big hang-up. She did do scholarly research, more than the rest of them put together. But she was practically *pathological* about not publishing it."

"Oh God, the plot thickens. Just what we needed."

"Poor Sharon. Not that I can see what it has to do with her murder. But she did look familiar when I met her at the Robards'."

"When was that?"

"A couple of weeks later. I thought it was because she had this very typical Irish face: you know, broad and florid, with a turned-up nose."

"Typical be damned. That amounts to an ethnic slur. But I know what you're trying to say: it was a familiar enough sort of face that you didn't realize you'd *actually* seen it before. Though in that case I don't see how you can suddenly recall it all these months later. You must be mistaken."

"No, I'm almost sure. So now I have what feels like another piece of the puzzle, but I can't see where it fits. It's like every time I start a process of elimination: I end by eliminating everyone." My meeting with Virginia had started a new cycle of that depressing process, this time for a far graver crime. "But I don't want to keep you up. All this has taken a lot longer than we expected."

"But I thought we were going to read some of the manuscript

aloud, now that we know a little more about where Nellie was in the Fall of '68. Why don't we do that—I drink while you read the manuscript to me? You'll know where to skip and you have a beautiful voice."

"That's a nice idea. I love to read aloud and very few people will sit still for it—unless it's an actual poetry reading."

So Erin sat in a deep chair with Herodotus on her lap, while I began to read the slowly developing story. Trying not to make it a "show-me-the-good-parts" type reading, I left in a great deal of the background material, but just compressing the repetitive passages made the love scenes stand out more vividly.

"Oh God," Erin sighed, when I got to the end of the last love scene before Manley made his ugly proposition; Nell was still stifling screams of pleasure into moans meant for Lizzie's ear only. "Tell me, Jamie: how do you respond to all this?"

"You mean, does it turn me on?" Erin nodded. "It excites me most as writing, but, yes, it moves me as erotica, too. The thing is, it makes me want to be *them*. Does that make any sense to you, Erin?"

"Sure: it's complicated, but it makes sense."

"Maybe I should finish up quickly." I summarized the scenes of blackmail and discovery, then read her the last page, marked by Lizzie's firm statement, her absolute certainty that she and Nellie would be together always.

"Not much of an always. And nothing beyond that summer. What the *hell* became of that woman, Jamie?"

"That's what we're going to find out," I informed her. And went home, sexually aroused and mentally overloaded. Though overloaded, I informed myself sternly, was a bit of an exaggeration. Only two new cans of worms had been opened today—the Breckenridge Fire and Sharon's possible presence at the Campus Inn the Tuesday after Labor Day—with all their respective implications.

Even thus reduced, it was still quite enough for one day.

As I made my way home through the quiet streets, I realized Becca was right, the earth was coming back to life. And she was writing again.

The day wasn't quite over, though. On the hall table lay the four letters Mrs. Moyer had mentioned: one from Richardsons, Becca's publisher, one postmarked Hochstetter, no sender's name or return address, one from Martine DeClaux, my Paris attorney, and a thick one from Alain, down at Fautour. I held them all for a moment, as if it mattered which one I opened first. And decided to start with the bare envelope from Hochstetter, which was carefully addressed to "Ms. Jameson," with no first name and a street number that was off by four digits. It was Virginia, apologizing in her first sentence for not knowing a name I used only in print. *(She realized we're next door to the Robards and how could she know which way the numbers run on Grove Street? Crazy, but not stupid.)* And she could certainly write coherent prose, though her second sentence told me she'd skipped one pill in order to make sure of it. The handwriting was painstakingly clear, with the connected-print look and the Greek *es* affected by preppy girls' schools. She continued:

> It was very good of you to come to see me. None of the others ever did. And I enjoyed our conversation. I'm not sure where this will fit in your own scale of values, but you really know how to talk to a crazy person. Most of the people around Jaegersville have trouble knowing what to say to me when I'm *out* of the hospital.
>
> I have been thinking seriously about what you said about writing, and this letter is the first result. Not that I have decided to revive the epistolary novel, but I want to ask your further advice. If I can actually write something about Jane Austen, would you be willing to read it and let me know what you think?

You will understand, I am sure, why I don't wish to approach the only other English professor I know well enough, and besides he (Walt) says you're the expert on women's literature. Sharon used to say there wasn't any such thing as women's history, but even if she was right, I know that's not true about literature.

Fond as I was of her, Sharon was wrong about many things. You were one of them. When Walt first told me about you—Becca's former student who writes poetry and drinks only mineral water—I asked him if you were good-looking. He said 'No,' but I think with a mental reservation to the effect that he found you attractive anyway. Then, months later, on one of Sharon's visits, she complained that you put on airs, speaking French with the students and bragging about all your publications. So I asked her the same question. She said you had beautiful skin and beautiful clothes, but otherwise no. In my opinion, they were both wrong: at least when you talk about Jane Austen, you are the loveliest woman I have ever seen.

> Sincerely,
> Virginia

Looking up from this letter into the gilt-framed hall mirror, I saw a narrow face with nothing left to give anyone, surrounded by too much messy hair. You'd have to be crazy to call that lovely.

I resolved to send her some stamped manila envelopes in the morning. Upstairs, I stripped off my clothes and bent forward from the waist to brush my hair two hundred strokes.

Then, I opened the letter from Richardsons. Their first reader, they told me, had high praise for my manuscript of poems. If the second reader, who had it now, agreed, they'd send me a contract and try to have the book out by Christmas. The letter itself was brief, but charming—and I would have taken *insults* from anyone prepared to publish a whole book of my poems. When I could look up from this missive, which moved me like a declaration of love, the long-haired figure in the mirror didn't look half bad, even to me. I decided to quit while I was ahead and left my other letters for the morning.

10

*

FOR A SECOND TIME, I dreamed about the underground passages at Hochstetter. It was extraordinarily realistic: the ceiling just a foot above my head and lined with heating pipes, the grey-enameled walls with their incongruous maroon stripe at waist level, the dim electric bulbs. But the sense of panic, of something lying in wait for me beyond the next turning, expressed all the fear I'd been too dumb or too single-minded to feel last Tuesday. It was easier, I realized as I woke, to cross the line between those defined as normal and those defined as mad than it was to come back untouched by the experience.

I lay in bed, and phrases from Virginia's letter returned to me. The letter had some of the spontaneous quality of our brief conversation, though the very act of setting her thoughts down on paper—or maybe skipping her tranquilizer—had brought the censor partway into the act. I hoped that Virginia's critical writing would prove as interesting as her correspondence. It would be dreadful to have to tell her it wasn't worth publishing. Though God knows why she should be held to such a standard. Surely, the occupational therapist—the official one—didn't expect her patients' macramé or whatever to be exhibition-quality. But *my* proposed regimen corresponded to Virginia's own deepest interests, and it called forth the criteria she'd set herself. Therein lay both its value and its danger.

I also found myself going over her implication, in both the letter and our conversation, that Walt had had other women, enough for there to be a recognizable pattern in his behavior toward herself whenever he got involved with one. I found this thought unpleasant, even though I had never assumed that he'd been saving himself for *my* arrival. Yet his friends at Ebbing, cheering our relationship on, had certainly considered him a man in need of feminine solace. Had Walt actually had love affairs from time to time—perhaps with women less closely connected to the College than I was? If Virginia's ideas about his repeated unfaithfulness were a delusion, might she, after all, be capable of a jealous murder?

Two other phrases rankled. Sharon had said I bragged about all my publications. I couldn't remember even mentioning them, except that, at my reading, I'd indicated the group of poems that had just appeared in print. Sharon also apparently considered it snobbish to talk French with the students, yet she had been right there, dammit, when I was invited to join the French table.

That reminded me: I'd left a couple of exercises in French unread. I groped for them on my night table, scanned both, and, hastily tying my blue velvet robe around my body, went in search of Becca. This was too much to keep to myself.

Becca was sitting up in bed reading a typescript, a position that made her look exceptionally vulnerable, but she said she was feeling stronger. "Do you think it's okay for us to start our open houses again, this Sunday?" she asked me.

"Why not? It seems pointless to abandon them because of Sharon, even though we didn't have one last week. Well, the evening before her funeral—no one felt much like a party."

"Good, because I do like to see people. And I want to say I

appreciate your going on with them these past weeks, when Walt was bringing Sharon along to provoke you."

"I get no credit for that. The provocation didn't work. In a sense, it'd have been harder to have him here every week without a date, just gazing reproachfully at me—or longingly."

"Which is what you're in for now, you realize."

"I know. It seems to be my month for unwarranted reproaches and unwanted reconciliations. Just take a look at this letter from Alain. It's a masterpiece—of what, I find it hard to say." I handed her the thin airmail pages and sat at the foot of her bed, tucking my feet under me.

"I've forgotten most of the French I knew, and I certainly can't manage foreign handwriting. Why don't you just read it to me—in translation, if you please?"

"Okay, but *le style c'est l'homme*. The flavor may not come across, this way. And the whole point of writing in his native language when his English is so good was so he could keep control of the different levels of style. But here goes: 'Dear Jamie, This morning I sustained a visit from one of the prefect's upper underlings—' "

"He says things like 'upper underlings?' " Becca interrupted.

"*Sous-prefets supérieurs*. Anyway, 'Paris had forwarded a series of questions concerning you that required immediate answers. Since I am spending some weeks here at Fautour, the individual who interrogated me—admittedly with kid gloves— was not well informed about the situation in which you are embroiled. However, my conversation with him helped crystallize some of my own ideas, which are the real object of this letter.

'All that the functionary this morning could tell me was that you have got yourself mixed up—' But in French," I interrupted my reading to tell her, "there's no 'got' construction, so it sounds rather more deliberate on my part—

'in a messy business—' "

"Messy business?" Becca asked.

" '*Sale affaire*,' my translation may be soft-pedaling somewhat. '—in a messy business. You are apparently suspected of murdering a middle-aged spinster, your rival for the affections of the rector of a provincial secondary school."

"Where'd he get that idea?"

"Well, *collège* does mean high school in France, usually a private one. Of course, Alain knows an American college is something different, but, remember, he's getting a third- or fourth-hand version of the story. 'Most of the information requested of me was factual, involving dates and places of your residence in France and the legal status of our marriage. My opinion of your character was also informally solicited, however. They wanted to know whether I believed you might have committed such a murder. For whatever it is worth, I said categorically not. Although I might be able to imagine circumstances in which you would kill, there is no way you could delude yourself that the murder of some desiccated American virgin—'"

"The Latin male!"

" '—might serve your vision of universal justice. And that is what is required before you could kill. *Un point c'est tout*.' "

"What?"

"It means 'Period.' Where was I? 'I trust, therefore, that you will be able to disentangle yourself—' He says *te débrouiller*, as if I just have to cut some red tape or something— 'from this affair without further damage to your own well-being, your reputation, or my name, which, although you refuse to bear it, I see you are not averse to invoking when needed. Do not hesitate to call on me for any financial or moral support you may require—' oh dear!"

"What now?" Becca asked.

"It's just that one of the radical papers used to run classified ads from prisoners, and that's what they said they wanted from friends outside: *une aide financière et morale*." I shuddered.

"Let's see, 'Assuming that you get clear of this mess, I hope you will give consideration to my proposal. I gather from the situation in which you find yourself that, contrary to your announced plans when you left, you did not settle in Berkeley. It seems strange to me that someone with your qualifications should end up at so obscure an institution, but academic positions must be even scarcer than we had been given to understand.'"

"You never wrote to tell him where you were, Jamie? Or why you came here?"

"Not to Alain. I wrote the lawyer who's handling the divorce. *My* lawyer, that is. So he must have found the garbled version even more mystifying. In fact, he goes on to say:

'The story of the rector and the old maid is beyond me, but must follow from your situation. I say nothing, therefore, about the dubious judgment you seem to have exercised. But it occurs to me that you must be very close to the end of your rope. Certainly, your misguided attempt to establish economic and sexual independence has failed miserably.

'I myself have failed, and this same ill-advised separation is apparently and astonishingly responsible. Despite the general success of our side—' (He means *his* side, the right wing) 'I lost the election to the Socialist candidate, Madeleine Bontemps, whom you always used to complain about after city council meetings.' What I complained about was that she was too cautious, especially about supporting other women. 'Since losing the run-off, I had come increasingly to suspect that it was your absence that tipped the scales away from me. Oddly enough, the—*rond de cuir*' (it means seat-cushion in an office, Becca, let's say bureaucrat) 'who questioned me this morning confirmed this impression. He commiserated with me on my recent defeat, indicating that he had voted for me himself, but that his three married daughters, all clients of your family planning clinic, had not. He had strong suspicions, moreover, that his louts of sons-in-law (I quote him) also voted their wives' loyalty

to the clinic and to "Madame Jamie," and he is not absolutely
sure about his own wife. Although I had observed that the local
feminists were active on Madeleine's behalf, it was not the 15
or 20 of them but the clientele of that damned clinic, who did
me in. At the same time, my patent lack of popularity with these
people was insufficient to endear me to the female stalwarts of
my own sort, who quite openly disapproved of my separation
from "Madame la Comtesse."

'One of my initial responses, I confess, was to curse you for
not getting involved in your murder a couple of weeks earlier.
A nice *fait divers*—' "

"Nice what?"

"Sensational news item. '—I considered, might have shaken
some of this loyalty to you and cost Madeleine some votes—even
if they hadn't gone to me. Since your timing was so wretched,
the alternative is for us to face the next election as a team. I have
spoken to both attorneys, although that *pute* who represents you
was reluctant even to give me your address.' *Pute* means whore,
but here I think he intends a general bad word. 'As matters stand,
it is still possible to stop the divorce action and wind up the legal
separation. I suggest that we do so and that you return here as my
wife. The advantages to you should be obvious, especially after the
experiments' —or maybe he just means experiences, it's the same
word—'of these past few months. It will make a diverting story, of
course, but it cannot be very pretty to be living through. For my
part, I find that I rather miss having someone around me who gets
mixed up in such adventures—not that even you have been accused
of murder before—and that, as I say, the separation has damaged
my political and social standing. So our reconciliation would be of
mutual benefit.'

'If you prefer to see it in this light, it is a job I am offering
you, a far more attractive one than you have been able to find
for yourself. But it must be clearly understood between us that
I am not offering you a *mariage blanc*.' "

"What isn't he offering you?"

"A marriage in name only, without sex. 'In order for this reconciliation to be to my advantage with either the feminist constituency or the prudes, it must look authentic. Neither of us could be known to have a lover, and it is a situation where the best way to avoid unpleasant revelations is to have nothing to conceal. I would have to give up Monique—' "

"Who's Monique?"

"Who do you think? '—and you would form no attachments for an agreed-on period. Now, especially with no other outlet, you and I are absolutely incapable of leading a celibate existence side by side. Not only would a true marriage be healthier for us both, but it might also make it possible to reconsider the matter of a child.'"

"Son of a bitch!" This, amazingly, was Becca.

" 'The advances in technology, especially in the United States, might give us new reason to hope. Perhaps you could ascertain if this is so in your particular case.

'While awaiting your reply to my proposal, and in anticipation of soon being able to go considerably further, I kiss your hands.' "

"What an ending! Is it as sexy an allusion as it sounds?"

"Well, it's his version of the complimentary closings in French business letters, and may also be a reference to *Les liaisons dangereuses*. You wouldn't happen to have a copy—?"

"No, I wouldn't. Anyway, I still think the substance is more interesting than the form. What's your reaction to all this, Jamie?"

"I'm not sure if I think it's more awful than you do, understanding all the nuances, or if I'm slightly less horrified."

"I must admit he's honest. He doesn't claim to be a changed man who still loves you passionately."

"He knows that wouldn't work, so he suggests an ongoing intimacy in other ways. And you have to understand that, from his point of view, he's doing me a favor. He knows I'm in hot water over Sharon—in fact, it sounds as if he thinks my arrest is imminent, though, of course, I'll eventually wriggle out of it. I'm not the one living in a fool's paradise, am I? I mean, my arrest *isn't* imminent, is it, Becca?"

"Of course not. No one told him you've got an ironclad alibi. You haven't even seen your friend Endlich for a while, have you?"

"I guess not since the funeral nearly a week ago. Anyway, Alain thinks I'm in serious trouble, and he also thinks I'm on the brink of destitution—or what would I be doing at a place like Ebbing College? The triangle with Walt and Sharon, at least the way it was reported to him, also has a kind of bottom-of-the-barrel sound to it. He's just missed certain crucial facts that would put it all in a different light. Even so, he doesn't pretend to be galloping up on his white horse to rescue me from this degradation just because I'm his wife and he loves me."

"He certainly doesn't. He needs a wife, and to please both the women's groups and the right-wing ladies, it has to be the same wife that he had before."

"He doesn't even remember—or maybe he never understood—that I used to criticize Mady, the woman who beat him in the election, from the left! On the other hand, though I know this won't win him points in your book, he's also admirably up-front about the sexual thing."

"You're right. As my children used to say, 'It grosses me out.' But he's honest."

"And monogamous. You should like that."

"What he's proposing is a parody—a mockery—of monogamy, Jamie, and you know it."

"Well, I won't argue the point, but I'm not sure I see any difference. What's horrifying to me is that this is Alain, who was once the truest lover I ever had. Or could even imagine."

"I take it you're not tempted by his offer to beget an heir on you, after all?"

"You might be surprised. He knows how much I— And even that has its generous side, too. I mean, he's talking about lifting me from what he conceives as the gutter to a share in a really immense fortune. Which my child would then stand to inherit."

"You mean, you're taking it seriously?"

"No. You see, Alain's misperception has shown me the extent to which I *haven't* screwed up since I left him. He thinks I have a marginal job when, thanks to you, I have a fancy one— more than twice the pay my qualifications would entitle me to, plus free room and board. I'm writing and publishing, I'm successful as a teacher, and my sex life—whatever it may sound like to the prefect's understrapper—has had some decency and warmth to it. He doesn't know about Nick, and even the thing with Walt wasn't what he pictures. But most of all he doesn't know I came to Ebbing because of you. So he doesn't realize that my life here has *meaning*."

"Is that what—?"

"*Yes*."

"What are you going to do when I'm gone, Jamie? Have you thought about it?"

"Only in generalities. I don't have a teaching job for next year, as you know. Perhaps that's just as well. But I've got articles coming out now—oh, and Richardsons wrote to say they got a favorable first reading on my poems, so I may have that book, as well, by the time I start looking again. And when *Helen-Elizabeth* comes out—no pun intended—I'm going to get a lot of attention as the person who discovered the manuscript and did the edition. So let's hope Nellie wasn't really a mass murderer."

"What are you talking about?"

I summarized yesterday's revelations and surmises about the Breckenridge Fire and the Pacification Procedure.

"Alain is right about one thing," she remarked at the end. "Things do happen when you're around, Jamie."

"Yeah, theft and murder in the archives over a manuscript that may be connected to mayhem, arson, and murder in the last century."

"That's what I mean: the man is obviously bored without you. And you haven't yet told me your plans for next year, only that you think you'll have a better chance at an academic job for the year after. What will you live on meanwhile?"

"What I've saved this year—plus what I get from the Pangloss puzzles and the occasional poetry reading—could almost support me. But to make up the difference—"

"You'll have the editorial fee from my estate."

"Becca, how can you think I was counting that in? In fact, I forgot all about it."

"Well, if I get this new series of poems done, you'll have your hands full with my posthumous papers."

"Just keep on writing, then, and don't *be* posthumous for awhile, okay? What I was going to say is that I was thinking of following up the idea of doing a cookbook with Marge and Sally from the Savage Inn."

"You should take that to Mac Richardson, too, if you end up doing it. You know, Jessica Richardson, his wife, was a food editor, herself, and did a book for them some years ago. And you're one of their authors, now."

"Not quite."

"But you've signed on as the editor of my stuff, whatever happens to your own poetry. Though I must say that sounds very promising!"

"Anyway, I thought of going up to the Inn for spring break, to get an idea if the cookbook project would work out. And I've just decided to take you and Mrs. Moyer with me. No, don't say you can't. It's not one of your chemo weeks—I counted. And it'll be beautiful in early April, even from a chair on the porch."

"I wasn't going to refuse. It sounds wonderful. But I thought you'd be heading out to Berkeley to see Nick."

"Who'll be touring in various parts of Oregon and Washington, it turns out. And, really, Becca, I'd rather do this with you."

"For me."

"No, with. I'll call Sally later. When I come back from running." I had realized that, in contrast with the way I'd felt on awakening, I was now eager to get over to the gym.

Still, I was in no mood, once I had run, showered, and dressed, to encounter Detective Captain Hal Endlich just outside the women's locker room, clearly waiting for me. "They told me you were here working out," he explained.

"Running, actually." I hated to volunteer information, even of an apparently innocuous sort, but I also shrank from whatever erroneous conclusions Endlich might jump to if he continued to believe I practiced lifting weights, say—conclusions leading back, however irrationally, to a compact but heavy brass walrus. "You were looking for me, Captain?"

"Yes. Can't we sit down somewhere?"

"Won't these benches do?" They were rather clammy, and, although this was not prime time for the gym, our provisional privacy was by no means secure. I just wanted to get it over with and not have to take Endlich somewhere else.

"I want you to cast your mind back to the day of the murder. You were present when Security discovered the body, isn't that right?"

"Actually, the officer got in through the stacks and radioed. The rest of us came in together when he unlocked the door from inside."

"Why were you so anxious to shove in as soon as possible?"

"Because it was my office, for heaven's sake, and I wanted to know what was going on."

"But then you disappeared. It *just* dawned on them to tell me. So where did you go?"

"Does it really matter?"

"Since we're wondering what you might have altered or re-moved at the scene of the crime, yes, it matters where you might have taken whatever it was."

"Really, Captain! There were five or six Security officers in the room, as well as an extremely observant undergraduate."

"All of them looking at the body. Which seems to have been not so interesting to you—like you already knew it was there, maybe?"

"How could I have—no, don't bother telling me again."

"So what errand was more important to you than Miss Reilly's body?"

"An errand of mercy." Perhaps this could not be misinter-preted, after all. "It seemed to me that Walt—Dean Walters—had a right to hear the news—and not from official quarters."

"You thought, assuming you weren't in it together—that you'd break it to him more gently?"

"Something like that."

"And then you went back to the archive, accompanied by Dr. Walters?"

"I did."

"You made your statements to the same trooper? So you were sure after your talk together that you'd have your stories straight?"

"Look, I don't even know from my own observation that Dr. Walters made a statement at that point. I just made my own—"

"And the trooper said you could leave. But you preferred to hang around the scene of the crime. Maybe to see what infor-mation the police were picking up, or make sure there was some they overlooked."

"No. I stayed outside the room. And only until the body was removed."

"The dean was with you?"

"No."

"No, what? He left earlier? Later? He was on the other side of the hall?"

"I don't know. I didn't notice."

"All this concern about telling him and you didn't notice how he was taking it or when he went away?"

"That's right."

"But then you were all buddy-buddy again"—the *b* had a slightly unvoiced quality, almost a *p*—"at the funeral, weren't you?"

"I wouldn't have put it that way." *For one thing, I've never called any two people puddy-puddy in my life.*

"How would you put it?"

"He offered me a ride to the cemetery. I didn't have my car." *No need to explain that Walt had also talked me into going to the interment.*

"What did you talk about?"

You, you jerk, I very much wanted to say. *You and your cruel delusions about this murder.* I recalled one thing that seemed acceptable and might make less of a mystery of why I hadn't observed much about Walt at the library the day of the murder. "He—he felt he'd been rude when I showed up at his office, and he wanted to apologize."

"That was all?"

"We also talked about your investigation." *Surely that was a neutral enough description of a natural enough topic of conversa-tion.* "Oh, and on the way back, we talked about Dr. Reilly's replacement for the rest of the year. He authorized me," *it was nice to have this quintessentially bureaucratic term handy,* "to call the person who has, in fact, taken over those classes."

"And was that all you talked about?"

"Yes." *A damn good thing, too, that I don't have to tell you what Walt hoped we would talk about.*

"Is that all you want to tell me?"

"All there is *to* tell you."

"Tell me, Dr. Jameson, how do you like working in a room where a murder was committed?"

"Not much." It was easy to be straightforward about that.

"Let us know," he added, "When you're ready to tell us about Florida."

I waited to give him time to go away, so I was still in the lobby of the gym when Laurie and Ann came in.

"How'd you tear this one away from the archive?" I asked Laurie.

"It wasn't easy, but we have a meeting in a few minutes. Maybe you'd like to stay for it. It's to set up our women's self-defense class."

"Why are you doing that just now?"

"Because there's been a *murder* on campus! The police obviously don't have a clue. Captain Endlich was outside when we came in, and that dork couldn't catch a goldfish in a bowl. So a lot of women are kind of scared."

"Well, far be it from me to say a word against self-defense. I took a course like that once. I guess I was about your age, and the women's movement was just getting organized around Berkeley. But I'm pretty sure we're not dealing with a maniac, here. The murderer isn't just going around killing randomly; he had some reason for attacking Sharon Reilly. And if it *were* a mad killer, how would a few karate moves have helped someone in Dr. Reilly's position?"

"This is the first time women around here are getting together for anything and you're putting it down?" Ann seemed puzzled and hurt.

"I'm not putting it down. I just think all illusions are dangerous for women. Look: I'll even be faculty advisor if you need one. Don't expect me to give up my morning run in favor of the martial arts, is all." There was a slight thaw. "You're both taking the course?"

"Oh no, Laurie's teaching it. Didn't you know she's a Brown Belt?"

On Sunday, as Becca and I had planned, our open houses

resumed. At first people talked about Sharon—not about the mystery of her murder, but the woman herself: little acts of kindness they recalled, her feeling for the underdog—and for that Over-cat, Herodotus. It was a warmer, more human ritual than the funeral service or the meaningless words at the graveside.

It wasn't only Sharon's death that was mysterious to me, but her life, so I listened attentively. Even her closest associates, however, offered no clues to the puzzle. The questions that baffled me about the dead woman—her heavy drinking, her refusal to publish her research, even her feelings about her sexuality— were known to these people, but they proffered no explanations. All that was "just Sharon," the way she was. So I learned nothing that would help me broach the mystery of which they were unaware, her involvement with the manuscript. As to the murder, no one even put forward a theory. Nobody could believe it was a member of the Ebbing College community, and nobody wanted to hear that there was no way it could have been anyone else.

Gradually, though still with a certain decorum, the discussion moved away from Sharon. I slipped into the kitchen to make another pot of coffee, and Walt followed. I have rarely seen a man look so woebegone. Before he could refer to the reasons— any of them—for his unhappiness, I took matters into my own hands. It was natural to continue the conversation about Sharon. Not only was it the topic least likely to lead to an unwanted overture, but there were things I really wanted to know.

I began with the biggest turnoff I could think of. "Walt, has Endlich still got you on his suspects list?"

"I'm not sure. I think he's leaning more toward you. Though you were right about one thing: he was nosing around the day before yesterday trying to make something out of our joint trip to the cemetery."

"He also sees no reason—no non-incriminating one—why I

should rush over to tell you that Sharon was dead. In fact, I gather he thinks I was either disposing of evidence or letting my accomplice know that the next stage of our venture in crime had begun."

"Why *did* you come, Jamie?"

"It was an impulse, I guess. What lay behind it was that you were Sharon's friend—and had been mine."

"It wasn't the same."

"I know, you told me that."

"No, I don't mean just that we never went to bed together, but I wasn't even with her as much as you seem to think. Our steady date every week was for these open houses. I took her to a concert on campus, once, and once to the Film Classics series."

"I know: *Potemkin.* Half a dozen people must have told me about that in the next 24 hours."

"Poor Jamie, who couldn't have cared less. But Sharon also had me to dinner at her place once. It was kind of awkward. She wasn't much of a cook, and it was a studio apartment that looked like the Holiday Inn—"

"Yeah, I was there the other night. Now that it's Erin's."

"The thing is, I wasn't sure whether she wanted me to make a pass at her or was afraid that I might. The food, as I say, was lousy, but the drink was good and plentiful, so I had much more of that."

"But one thing didn't lead to another?"

"I told you I wasn't interested, Jamie, and I'm not even sure Sharon was. What I wanted was—"

"Walt," I interrupted, "did Sharon know about your other women?"

"She certainly knew about you."

"I mean from before."

"There wasn't really a whole lot to know. If I did fool around, Virginia would find out—"

"Sitting there in the hospital?" I asked, although I knew she had her ways.

"Or when she was home and going through a bad spell. Then she'd either be wildly jealous—you know, throwing things and trying to attack me physically, even though I'm twice her size— or else unnaturally tolerant, almost encouraging. Either way, she could wipe out something that didn't already have a lot going for it."

I refrained from asking the obvious next question, why our relationship had been different. Instead, as I filled the coffee server, I asked if Sharon had ever said anything to him that whole time about the manuscript, about *Helen-Elizabeth*.

"Never."

There was a pause, longer than any that had intervened thus far. Walt took a deliberate breath. I grabbed the coffee tray and almost ran back into the library. Afterward, however, I did notice that even this intentionally limited conversation had lifted his spirits somewhat. If our talk had contributed to the sense of permanent complicity that's the aftermath of the right sort of breakup, then it was most valuable. As a source of information, though, it was a washout.

In the week that remained before spring break, I tried alternately to make some sense of my two mysteries. If Sharon had heard me telling Walt about the manuscript over lunch my first day, she had known about it in time to have stolen it. But why? Well, to prevent me from, as Erin had put it, "bringing her great granny out of the closet." And thus, if Erin was reading her correctly, from raising some pointed questions about her own sexual orientation. As a motive, it still seemed rather slender. But then, too, Sharon had a phobia about publishing. If I understood that, maybe I'd be closer to the reason for the theft.

As for phobias about publication, I was on the verge of developing one myself. The edited text of *Helen-Elizabeth* was nearly ready to see the light. What was needed was a literary and historical introduction, written by me. But what if we never found out what became of Nell Breckenridge? How much prominence should I give to the various speculations about the fire and her role in it? And, no matter how intelligently interpretive my prose, how much would this story overshadow the manuscript itself? Or would the erotic scenes carry the day—for all the wrong reasons?

What were my responsibilities as a cultural critic, a historian of women, and a woman still fighting for our right to own our sexuality? *Write the truth*, the only ethic I acknowledged as scholar *or* poet, turned out to be an extremely limited guide. For I was unsure not only of the facts (one definition of truth) but of how to arrive at them (another definition) or what their real meaning was (surely the final definition). *We'll cross that morass when we come to it*, Erin had said. Well, I was coming uncomfortably closer every day, and we still hadn't discussed it.

When the galley proofs arrived for my article on Helen Hayward as feminist and ecologist, I corrected them in an hour and sent them back to the journal. It did just occur to me to wonder why I had not stuck to scholarship of this sort: interesting, useful, even political, but remarkably free of ethical morasses. There were no murders anywhere within the Hayward papers, and certainly no one would kill over anything connected with them. It also entered my mind, in this period, that I had perhaps recommended a highly dubious medicine for Virginia Walters. Was the study of women's literature necessarily a healthier addiction, after all, than alcohol or mood-altering drugs?

11

＊

AUTUMN MAY BE the best-looking season in the mountains of central Pennsylvania, but spring is the best-smelling. As we drove up to Savage the last weekend in March, it was apparent that the earth had stirred to life in the days since Sharon's death. The more I learned about my murdered colleague, the greater and the more baffled was my sense of her unfulfilled possibilities—personal, professional, and sexual. Sharon might have chosen, even embraced, these limitations, but that made the finality of her death no less moving. If anything, it left all that was unrealized or unresolved in her life definitively unfinished.

On the land, however, the things that grow and the climate that fosters their growth never really stop at those last weeks in winter when you feel that *this* time spring really won't come. Early or late, the budding and blossoming, the first yellowing-green of leaves do make their appearance—far more dramatically in this part of the world than in the Bay Area, which was still my most familiar American landscape. Until this year, in fact, true spring had been a strictly European phenomenon to me. Driving through the central Pennsylvania hills, I found that I responded most readily to what was most familiar from the Ile de France and the Burgundian countryside: the tentative green of the hills, the early blossoms, and, perhaps most striking, though the product of human art and labor, not nature, the rough stone barns and farm buildings.

On an impulse, I had invited Erin to come up to the Inn for the week as my guest, along with Becca and Mrs. Moyer. We saw her chiefly in the mornings and evenings, so eager was she to try every trail through the reawakening woods.

I established my own routine quickly, too: a morning run and a mid-afternoon walk brought me outdoors, myself, for several hours a day. I was also free to spend a more peaceful kind of time with Becca than we'd found possible of late. For the Inn as an institution, the season was not only an agricultural or meteorological event, but a culinary one, with roots and habits in this region, and I'd set myself to understand and write them. Every afternoon, when Becca went up to rest, I would spend some hours in the kitchen with Marge and Sally and their recipes, lending a hand with dinner preparations and trying to formulate how best to present this traditional cookery for contemporary tastes and equipment. I was beginning to believe, in any event, that it could be done and done by me.

The days resembled each other enough that I wouldn't have been able to say for sure which day it was when the shower in my bathroom gave out in mid-spray. "I prefer baths, anyway," I assured Sally. "Except after my run, and even then I can always—"

"No, that's okay. This is one of Jem's days, I think. So it'll be working before you need it again." Such sublime confidence in a plumber or handyman is rare and, when encountered, must not be recklessly challenged.

That afternoon, I was alone in the kitchen, peeling potatoes, when someone came in the back door. "Hi, I've got your order.

If you can just—oh, sorry: Where's Marge?" The man was about my own age, with a slender, loose-limbed body and a lock of light brown hair that fell into astonishingly green eyes. His stock clearly "bred true," for the boy beside him was his living image, down to the faded jeans and hiking boots, though *his* eyes were an extraordinary hazel color, thanks to a green rim around the brown iris.

"What are you delivering?" I asked.

"Well, if you work here, I guess it's all right to say: I bake breads and pies for the Inn. Whole-grain breads and the flakiest pie crusts in the state."

"Which are not whole-grain, thank heaven! I may be a Berkeley person, but I know where to draw the line. And your stuff is very good, by any standards."

"Berkeley? Then you're not the new kitchen help?" His face showed some consternation.

"No, in fact, the woman they hired never showed up for work." I found myself mildly regretting I wasn't who this remarkably sexy baker took me for.

"Oh, I know: you must be the cookbook lady."

"I guess so." In the Jaegersville post office, once, I overheard the clerk tell her next customer that I was the "new poetry lady up at the college." So now I was the cookbook lady, too, though in these very precincts I had informed Walt that I wasn't a lady at all. "But it's still a pretty fragile identity. My name is Jamie, Margaret Jameson." I held out my hand.

"How do you do? Jeremy Morgan—Jem." He took my hand and shook it for a bit longer than was strictly necessary. "And this is Sam."

"Tell me: why isn't it okay for people to know you do some of the Inn's baking?"

"Because Marge and Sally promote their stuff as 'home-baked,' which is true, but it's *my* home."

"Where's that?"

"Straight down hill from here. First place it's flat enough to farm."

"So you grow things, too?"

"That's *mostly* what I do: herbs, especially medicinals. The place has been called the Medicine Farm for generations, it seems. There's nothing to harvest just now, of course, but it *is* planting time, and once Marge and Sally get someone in here for the season, I'll be giving up my sideline. Which we'd better start unloading. Do you know how to handle the paperwork on an order, Jamie?"

"No, I'm just a cookbook lady around here."

"Then Sam had better go find Marge, while we get the stuff in."

"I think she's in the still-room," I told the child.

"Try there first," Jem added, "but if not—"

"If not, *compa'* I'll check her bower."

"*What* did he say?" I asked his father as he ran out.

"Bower. He's been reading the Arthurian romances and, as far as Sam's concerned, if ladies had bowers then, they must have them now."

"Well, after all," I laughed, "Marge and Sally are the only people I've ever known who have a still-room. They're hardly the bower type, though."

"You can't prove it by Sam. He knows there's a line between fiction and reality, but he puts it in a different place from where you and I might."

"How old is he, anyway?"

"Turned eight last month. He could tell you in years, months, weeks, days, and maybe hours, himself."

"Isn't the Round Table kind of advanced for a kid his age?"

"Don't let him hear you say that. Sam reads everything he can get his hands on. Especially if you tell him it's over his head."

"But what does he make of it all, do you know?"

"Well, he did ask me why the whole system fell apart—in the aftermath of Lancelot and Guinevere, you know—and I said it was an overly rigid value structure, about sexual politics, among other things."

"That's true. It really wasn't until Ariosto wrote the *Orlando Furioso*, say the Fifteen-teens, when you got a good modern mind looking at that chivalric material with some irony—" Sam came back with Marge, interrupting my pedantic lecture to, I reminded myself, a guy who grew herbs and baked bread for a living. Though, after all, I was not the one who'd said "overly rigid value structure about sexual politics" to a child of eight.

"I see you two have met, though you haven't gone so far as to unload the van," Marge pronounced. "I'll tell you what, Jem: Jamie and I can do that while you take a look at her shower. It's not working right." She told him which room was mine, while he went out with us to get a tool box.

"What's up, Sam?" Marge asked the boy, who stood stock-still on our path after his father had gone back inside.

"I'm trying to decide whether it would be more interesting to help you or my dad. Him, I *think*. Plumbing is fun, and I want to see what kinds of things Jamie has in her room."

"Don't worry," Marge told me as he disappeared. "He won't take anything. It's just that Sam is fascinated by women your age—mommy age to him. "

"Hasn't he got a mother?"

"She left when he was a baby. They moved here to get away from it all and then, big surprise, she found it was too isolated."

"What 'all' were they getting away from?"

"The way Jem tells it, he was running from what MIT trained him to be: a killer.

"What?"

"Well, he was a student there in the '60s and early '70s, when their research labs were designing a lot of weapons for Vietnam. He loved technical stuff, but that wasn't what he wanted to do with it. So he came up here sometime in the '70s to see if he could make things live, instead."

"And could he?"

"Well, he's stuck it out for nearly ten years now, and the farm is showing a profit. There's nothing he can't do with his hands: farming, baking, fixing any kind of machinery." Then he was back in the engaging flesh. I noticed he had beautiful hands.

"I understand you're an escapee from MIT. Did you know Chomsky?"

"He was my inspiration. He—well, you don't want to hear the whole saga of my—ah— conversion to peaceful uses."

"But I'd like to."

"But not while Marge is glaring at us. Maybe you could come down to our place for dinner sometime while you're here?"

"Not dinner," Marge said firmly. "At meal times, this is a working author."

"But some other time of day," I put in hastily. "After dinner, say; I'd like that."

"Maybe toward the end of the week, then. Okay *compa'*," he added to Sam. "Let's haul it."

"Why do you call each other that?"

"Short for *compañero—or compañera*, it's unisex. We picked it up in Nicaragua last year. Sam and I were consultants on what they call sustainable agriculture—organic farming, to you."

"How did *that* work out?"

"Well, considering I know zip about tropical plants or tropical pests, not too badly. It was the principles they were interested in, and besides, they're very polite people. Meanwhile, Sam did a few weeks of second grade in a school where each kid is allotted one pencil for the entire year."

Hung up as I am on adequate writing materials, that really got to me. Apparently, it had gotten to Sam, too. On his return, he'd tried to organize his school to contribute to the Books and

Pencils for Nicaragua campaign. "You can imagine how that went over in the Savage-Underhill Combined School District." And man and boy went out to their van.

It occurred to me, as I turned to help Marge with the next stage of dinner, that it had been a long time since I'd met an attractive single man. And that, though my preference and desires were decidedly heterosexual, I had elected to spend this vacation in the company of three lesbians and two middle-aged widows.

At dinner that night, we got onto the subject of the Breckenridge Fire. Between my resolve to take a vacation from *Helen-Elizabeth* and Erin's day-long pursuit of the forest paths, we'd managed to keep off the topic for the entire time we'd been at the Inn.

"Do you realize," she asked me, "that we know practically nothing about Nell?"

"Of course, that's just the point."

"I mean, until she turned up in Smedley Harris's diary, I was beginning to wonder if she wasn't fictitious. Lizzie was a *writer*, after all."

"I've been talking about the manuscript as a literary text since September, but I never thought of it as anything but a true account, no more fictionalized than any other memoir. You mean, there was actually a time when you thought Nellie might be a figment of Lizzie's imagination? That'd make her the most inventive, if not the greatest, lesbian novelist of all time."

"But wouldn't a great novelist give us more access to her character, to Nell herself?"

"So we'd have some basis for speculating, now, about whether she was capable of setting that fire? And under what sort of provocation."

"Exactly. All we know now is that she did exist, she had long blonde braids and a good ear for music, and she gave Lizzie a very good time."

"For what it's worth, there's also all their philosophizing

about the meaning of life in the earlier sections of the manuscript."

"That reminds me," Becca put in. "What was Nell's religion?"

"Episcopal, I imagine."

"Are you sure?" she pursued.

"Well, the Ebbing family certainly was—witness the college's church connection. And the girls met at an Episcopal boarding school at a time when people took these denominational divisions very seriously."

"Some still do," Mrs. Moyer remarked sourly.

"But why did you ask about Nell's religion, Becca?"

"I thought it might be a way into her mentality. And besides, I was rather afraid the Breckenridges might turn out to be Quakers. Fine Philadelphia family and all that."

"No fear," said Erin. "*Those* names are all well known. And can you see a Quaker family packing their daughter off to some quack for a quick clitoridectomy?"

"Well, *I* can't see anyone who calls themselves Christians doing such a thing," sniffed Mrs. Moyer.

The next day, I didn't go running until midmorning because I'd awakened with a poem in mind and wanted to sketch it out, first. Then, without so much as washing, I put on my grey sweat suit and my running shoes, pinned up my hair, and went out the side door of the Inn. I noticed a red Maserati pulling up to the main entrance—because a car like that is clearly asking to be noticed—and as promptly forgot it.

The first days of April were making up for the endless March chill with unseasonable heat; it was not the time of day for a comfortable run, so I took longer to do the mile and a half to which I'd recently promoted myself.

"There's a gentleman to see you," Sally informed me, as I let myself back in. "I'm surprised you didn't pass him as you left."

"What's his name?"

"Didn't say. He talks with an accent, though." Endlich, I concluded, with something on his mind important enough to make him venture all the way up here. "I told him Ms. Parsons was on the verandah, and he went out there—must be half an hour or more. Sylvia Moyer came inside right away." Of course she would. She resented the detective's attempts to put words in her mouth and, unlike me, was in a position to get up and leave the room before the insinuations started.

"I'd better make sure he isn't hassling Becca," I said as, without stopping to repin the lock of hair falling on my sticky and probably flushed cheek, I headed for the French windows on the far side of the Inn's long drawing room. Becca was talking with unusual animation, but her interlocutor was on the lookout and stood up as he caught sight of me. I should have realized that, to Sally's ear, Endlich didn't speak with an accent, *I* did, and so, of course, did my visitor, the Comte Lambert de Fautour.

"Alain!"

With perfect *sang-froid*, a quality he hadn't possessed when I fell in love with him, he took my tentatively outstretched hand and kissed it. I wondered if it tasted sweaty and if he remembered what he'd said in his letter about kissing my hand as a prelude. "What are you doing here?" The question was inane, but inevitable.

"You never answered my letter." I hadn't, but there had hardly been time for him to know that for a certainty. "And I had to go to New York on business—*you* know—so I thought I'd drop in. Two Wall Street lawyers assured me Pennsylvania was just an hour and a half away, so I rented a little car—"

"The Maserati outside?"

"Of course. And I made my way—for much more than an hour and a half, I may say—to Jaegersville."

"Only to find that we weren't there at the moment."

"So your neighbor informed me—the charming blonde?"

"Betsy."

"That was the name. She told me how to get here—and one or two other things as well. I decided not to chance the mountain roads in the dark, though, so I came on this morning." I was beyond even imagining Betsy's one or two pieces of information, and suddenly very much aware of what I must look like.

"But I mustn't keep you here asking the obvious questions," Alain went on, surveying my outfit with amusement. "I'm sure you're eager to change out of your *training* before we talk. I'll stay here with Becca—if she'll bear with me a little longer?"

"There's no way I can refuse," she informed him crisply, and I went upstairs feeling rather like a child who had been *sent*. If any encounter with Alain was a duel, as it was bound at this stage to be, I had come off decidedly second best. Yet he had said nothing that was not scrupulously polite and even friendly. There was only his unannounced arrival and then the one ironic look at my getup—and that I could understand, if not entirely forgive.

After a quick shower, I stood naked in the middle of my room unable to decide what to wear. It was a state of mind I could not recall ever having been in before, certainly not to the point of being literally unable to dress. Tactically, especially after that sweat suit living abundantly up to its name, I needed to be well turned out, yet I was reluctant to meet Alain wearing clothing he had paid for. But I had very little that was new, and my American clothes were more rough and ready than anything I'd brought from France.

Eventually, I settled on an international compromise: my blue denim wraparound skirt clearly proclaimed its American origins, and the thin brown wool shirt could only have been made in Paris. I knotted a darker brown sweater (born in the USA) around my neck, French fashion, and chose beautiful English walking shoes no Frenchwoman would have been caught dead in. Then I decided the single braid down my back made me look too young, so I undid it and brushed my hair up into a more sophisticated negotiating posture, the chignon that only Americans call a French twist. Determining that this was too formal, I undid it and gathered my hair into a ballet-dancer's knot at the base of my skull.

I was getting tired of the whole business of costume as the basis for effective role playing, especially since it was not an occupation or a lifestyle I hoped to simulate by my outfit, but a state of being. I needed to impersonate a woman in control of her life. And I resented Alain for forcing me to think this way. Without his mocking, judgmental eye on me, I had gone about the business of simply *living* my life, unconcerned about what impression of myself that life conveyed. Which was, of course, why I had so much trouble communicating with Captain Endlich.

Downstairs, Alain was still sitting with Becca, but plans had nonetheless been made and preparations executed. He and I were to take a walk, and Marge had fixed us one of the Inn's famous box lunches. Alain had also been provided, I observed, with a canvas tote bag that contained a long pocket for a bottle of wine. And the pocket, in turn, had been provided with a bottle.

I had the panicky feeling, once again, that adults were making plans behind my back. But surely Becca wouldn't conspire with Alain, even in what she imagined were my best interests—not after hearing the proposal he'd sent me. Alain came close to apologizing for that letter as we set out across the pasture where now, at least, as the one who knew the way, I was regaining a minimal sense of authority.

"It would seem," he began, "that I have made an ass of myself. I offered to rescue you from an intolerable plight, and I learn that you are doing very well for yourself." The story of his disabusement beguiled our walk. He had seen Ebbing College, first of all, and, if it was not Harvard or even Berkeley, neither was it the "provincial secondary school" of French police discourse. In fact, I suspected that the grounds of the vacationing campus, with its lawns already green and the blossoms, down there, several weeks advanced over these mountain ones, had given him a distinctly favorable impression of the institution and its status.

He'd also seen the house, which had itself seen service as the President's mansion and the college guest lodge before being converted to the use of the Brock Professor of Poetry. Most important of all, Betsy had explained that it was Becca who held the chair, and why I had agreed to fill in for her. So he now understood some essential related facts: that I had not "ended up" in Jaegersville, as on some academic skid row, but had chosen it so as to be close to a friend with a terminal illness. And that I was being richly compensated for my labors.

I gathered, as well, that Betsy had told him enough about Walt to put that history in a truer light. Betsy, who had named her child for the dean, must at least have been able to make the man himself sound like a worthy lover for me. She also seemed to have helped Alain get the dates clear, so he no longer imagined I'd been part of a sordid little triangle eventuating in a nasty crime of passion.

His conversation with Becca had been more general, but she had managed to slip in a somewhat inflated version of my professional successes. Apparently, she'd also mentioned that this week at the elegant Inn was my party, without specifying that I myself was a guest of the house, and that I was getting heavy friend-of-the establishment discounts for my three guests.

When we came to the orchard, Alain agreed that it was the ideal picnic spot, and we spread the little mat that Marge had provided. I wondered whether the box lunches, too, were authentic Colonial-style masterpieces, but I was sure Marge and Sally had nothing like this wine in their cellars.

"Oh, no, I brought it with me," explained Alain. "I was going to have it uncorked at whatever intimate little restaurant I took you to in town last night."

"Part of your campaign to dazzle Cinderella?"

He smiled ruefully. "I'm afraid so. Besides, I thought I was entitled to something fit to drink while I was doing the dazzling."

I smiled myself—at the idea that, just as renting some wheels meant a Maserati, "something fit to drink" bore a label that had made me gasp. But then, I was *supposed* to be impressed by all this vulgar consumption. Well, I had the Inn itself as a background, the Inn's luncheon as ballast, and the Inn's lovely apple orchard as my immediate setting, so I wasn't doing so badly, myself. And the wine was incomparable.

"But now that my erroneous impressions have been corrected," he added, saying nothing of the arrogant assumptions that had followed from them, "there remains this business of a murder, which also cannot be as it was described to me. You must tell me all about it."

"Well, actually, it begins with a theft—" I wove through our long lunch the story of *Helen-Elizabeth* lost and found and Sharon dead in my office. Walt—suspect in the theft, companion in discovery of the manuscript, accomplice in the Christmas Dance detective-caper, frequent escort of the murder victim, and donor of the weapon—naturally came into it a good deal, and that was all right with me. I also told Alain about the manuscript's historical mystery, though I said nothing of my own ethical dilemmas about how to present it, because they entailed questions of strategic import to contemporary feminists. As long as we stuck to the general issues—women's freedom from forced marriage and genital mutilation, their right to a creative career, maybe even the right to love another woman—Alain and I were still on the same side. Closer to home and to our own day, feminism had become an obstacle to be overcome or contained, and his idea of how to do that was to reestablish a feminist as his wife.

In its own terms, however, the story of Lizzie and Nell, both what was in the manuscript and what our historical research had yielded, was compelling. I realized that Alain was the first person to whom I'd recounted that much of it at once. The writer in him made a good audience, listening appreciatively and putting the occasional sharp question as he refilled my plastic wine glass rather more often than necessary.

"Scheherazade," he said, when I finished. "Does anyone tell as many stories as you do? Or have such wonderful things happen to her?"

"Wonderful! A dead body in my office, her head smashed in with my own—ah—*presse-papiers*, myself the favorite suspect, despite the manifest impossibility of my having done the job, and you tell me it's wonderful?"

"I meant 'to wonder at.' You know what happens to one's vocabulary in any language, if it doesn't get used. You just did the same thing with paperweight, yourself. Anyway, it makes for a most entertaining story. Keep going."

"That's all. Besides, my head is spinning; I'm not used to wine in the middle of the day, anymore, or wine like that one at any time. I just want to be quiet for awhile and watch the sky through the apple boughs."

"Here." He folded his impeccable blue blazer into a cushion for my head.

"What a concession: your exquisite jacket!"

"So it belongs under your exquisite body." I noticed we had switched imperceptibly into French. "It's so hot, I certainly don't need the jacket or even my shirt right now." He'd also undone a few buttons on *that* impeccable garment.

"Ten days, even a week ago, it was still bitter cold, at least down in the valley. I still tend to dress for that weather, we had it so long."

"Well, your shirt could be unbuttoned, too," he said, putting his hand out toward me and then stopping. "But no: you don't like to have the man undress you." I don't. I don't like being passive or feeling like a child. But I did wonder how Alain had become, in that sense and so confidently, "the man."

I soon learned, as he slid down beside me and we began making love. It felt like a continuation of entertaining each other with delightful stories. All the years we'd been together made this one a deeply familiar tale, though our separation assured unexpected excitement. "Mixing memory and desire," I thought early on, when I could still quote, "and that was about April, too." The cruelest month, perhaps, but the act was the sweetest thing in nature.

"I've been trying to think," I said to Alain afterwards, "what you might enjoy doing." He looked down at me with eloquently raised eyebrows. "I mean for the rest of the afternoon. It's market day in Underhill, and we could take the truck and go on down. The Inn has a standing order with certain produce dealers and one of the butchers. It all has to be called for, and there's always a certain amount to be selected."

"A market in America? A real farmers' market?"

"So I understand: fruit, vegetables, meat, fish, poultry, eggs and cheese, plus a live-animal auction and a flea market. All very American. You'll see."

There was an undeniable warmth between us as we returned to the Inn and got Marge's list from her, along with thanks for saving her the trip. "Who gets the keys to the pickup?" she asked, dangling them in front of us.

"I do. I'm not going down these roads in a truck with any Frenchman who's been tooling around in a Maserati!" My husband—amazingly—accepted that.

In eight years together, Alain and I had roamed hand-in-hand through markets all over Europe and Africa. From practical French provisioning—almost daily in Paris, weekly at Fautour—to clamorous, sunlit cloth-and-fruit exchanges in West Africa and equally noisy, exotically-scented Algerian souks, this was another thing we were used to doing—and enjoying—together. We spoke only once of that shared past, when we pulled into the parking area and Alain reminded me of the remarkably similar facility on the outskirts of a village market on Crete—except that one was for donkeys only. Otherwise, this adventure felt picturesque and new. Alain was fully in the spirit, helping to choose the best fruits for the Inn and having to be restrained from irrational purchases at the flea market.

"You'd never get that mirror home in one piece," I told him. "And, unless you've made tremendous changes, neither Fautour nor the apartment is much of a setting for high kitsch, anyway."

"I've made no changes," he said, suddenly serious. "Jamie, can't we find a café and talk before we go back to your ménage up there?"

"Sure, but we have to see that everything gets loaded on the truck, first."

Meanwhile, I mentally translated "café" into "bar," and we found one on the main street of Underhill, its neon beer sign lit up despite the late afternoon sunlight.

"Country bar in the daytime," I mused. "Sounds like a country song." Then, as the bartender approached our table, I quickly appraised my surroundings. "Have you got any—club soda?"

"Sure. Or I could get you a Pellegrino." Like most Americans, he seemed to think the S stood for a first name. What? Steve or Sylvester instead of 'San'?"

"Two," said Alain. "No twist." Then, as the man left, he asked me, "By the way, should we pick up a couple of bottles of wine somewhere to take back to the Inn? I've only got one more like what we had with lunch, and you have quite a party."

"Believe me, Alain, Marge's supplies are a lot better than anything the State of Pennsylvania purveys. But I wasn't sure you were planning to stay for dinner."

"If you'll have me. And for the night—if you'll have me again." The double entendre was playful only for a moment, as he added, "But what I'm really here for, you know, is to ask if you'll have me permanently." At which ill-chosen moment, our drinks were served. If we were a couple on the brink of engagement, it would make an amusing story for our children. As it was, we were an estranged couple who had been unable to have any children.

"Alain," I told him as soon as the barman left us alone again. "We were once really married. How could we pretend to be married?"

"What does it mean, this real and pretend?"

"For one thing, I used to be able to say anything to you that was on my mind."

"And? We haven't exactly been staring at each other in silence all day."

"No, but I've been censoring every remark, thinking first what would be safe and polite. And I don't *want* to be polite with you, I want to fight everything you believe in. What kind of marriage is it—for either of us, Alain—if my ideas are ones you feel you've outgrown?"

"There might be—compensations. I know in my letter I talked about a sexual relationship as part of the contract, but, let's face it, what we have means a lot more than that."

"You also said monogamy was part of the deal, and you would expect me to settle for that."

"You settled for it once—if eight years is a 'once!' Okay, we both had our freedom in principle, but how much use did either of us really make of it?"

"Well, I admit I've been to bed with more men in one month this year than in all the time we were married." I neglected to mention that the total was still only two, that the month in question would have to be carefully calculated from late December to late January, and that, since then, there had been no one at all, until a couple of hours ago. "But that doesn't mean I wasn't 'making use of my freedom' while we were together. I *chose* not to have other relationships, because I didn't need what they offered. I loved you so much, why would I settle for anything less with someone else? I do believe it's possible to love more than one person at a time, but that kind of love is hard to find, and then the third party so rarely understands—"

"I think you're taking a very utopian position. Speaking realistically, isn't it more likely that we were rarely tempted to stray—"

"How I hate that conception of things!"

"—because we met each other's needs?"

"But do we still?"

"You tell me: didn't you like that, before?"

"You know I did. You wouldn't believe me if I said no, anyway. But years of that wouldn't be enough without love."

"And you don't—?"

"I can't, Alain. There's too much that divides us."

"Are those things so important?"

"How could our differences not matter, when you want me back as the female half of some right-wing Dynamic Duo?"

"But you despise my political competitor Madeleine Bontemps. Aren't you at all tempted by the idea of doing her in?"

"You don't get it. What I wish for Mady is not that she be done in from the right, but that she be forced to secure her constituency on the left, especially the women. You see, Alain, you talk about the 'female constituency' as if it's something you can win over by repackaging yourself with a feminist wife—"

"One particular feminist wife."

"But I think you've misjudged the situation. If I may say so," I added, belatedly recalling my manners in a foreign language.

"But I tell you, the clients—"

"That's just it: they appreciate the clinic, and I'm closely identified with the clinic. But not because I'm some charismatic figure. What they appreciate about the clinic is that it meets concrete needs *and* is client-controlled. At least, as far as we could make it. What a candidate has to do to capture that vote is help create more self-managed institutions, not some illusion of a feminist couple. And nothing like that is exactly on your agenda anymore."

"But if you're right, why did they vote for Madeleine?"

"Because she came closer than you did to supporting those goals. Though not very close, unless she's had a change of heart."

"Or an attack of expediency."

"As you say. But what *I'm* saying, Alain, is that there's no way that our getting back together would serve your political ends. It would be a contradiction in terms."

"You know nothing about electoral politics. You always turned up your nose at the idea of a candidate's image."

"So did you, once. And now you're obsessed, not just with electoral politics, but with getting yourself elected."

"You think so?

"Don't you—honestly? Alain, why on earth do you want to be in the Assembly, anyway?"

"It's an important step up."

"To things that I'd ask the same question about: why do you care about that sort of power?"

"You've just answered your own question. Besides, it would be very good for Lambert Fils."

"Isn't the firm doing all right as it is?"

"But I want to leave my own contribution. And, to be frank, the business is nowhere near as interesting, even as little involved in it as I am."

"Maybe you should reduce your involvement still further and go back to your own métier then."

"What do you mean?"

"You're a writer, remember? It's when you stopped writing that—"

"That what?"

"That it all fell apart."

"You mean you'd come back if I were a novelist again?"

"No, just that your giving it up was a symptom of what I'm talking about."

"You're sure? Because it would be almost worth it. Besides, if it's literary recognition you want for me—" This was the second time a man had accused me of looking for that in a lover; a few more times, and I might start believing it myself. "If it's success, it so happens *Macamogo* has just won a literary prize, the Prix Corret."

"Well, congratulations. I never would have thought they'd go for a fantasy about postcolonial Africa. But you aren't working on anything else?"

"That's not who I am anymore, Jamie. If I did write another novel, it will be quite different."

"Or you could just follow your new political tack and end up with all the other stuffed shirts—in the Academy." We looked regretfully at one another and left for the drive back up to the Inn.

When we came into the lobby, Sally asked him whether he would be there for dinner. "Yes, and for the night, too."

"I'm sorry, sir: we don't have a room," she replied. "Jamie's party has four of our five rooms, and there's a couple from Scranton arriving at dinnertime."

"Oh, that's all right," he said, his tone bitter when it should have been airy. "I'll be staying with my wife." We left Sally open-mouthed at the desk.

Dinner went surprisingly well—probably the wine helped—considering our ill-assorted group and, more particularly, the unanswered questions circulating around the table. We dispersed fairly early, nonetheless, with Alain explaining that he had a meeting in Washington the next afternoon. I had a feeling I didn't want to know what sort of meeting. But I turned back to whisper, "Don't worry, everything's okay," to Becca, Erin, and Mrs. Moyer, before I followed him upstairs.

I was pleased now that, on my arrival the other day, some notion of tact had led Sally to put me in a different room from the one I'd shared with Walt. But there really were only five guest rooms. At this rate, once I moved in here for full-time work on the cookbook, every one of them would soon have bittersweet memories.

As if overhearing part of this train of thought, Alain asked, "You're planning to move up here to stay, once Becca—no longer needs you?"

"That's right." It was more than seven months since the diagnosis and, in all that time, I'd never heard one person say the taboo words: *when Becca dies.* "I'd have to be here for a few months straight, anyway, and then come back at different seasons. Which is certainly no hardship—the Inn is so lovely."

"If I thought you wanted an *inn*, I'd buy you one."

"All I want is to write this book about an inn, so no one has to buy me anything."

He made one of those European noises we inadequately spell "Bah," and went off to the shower, returning a moment later to ask, "Is that Erin your lover? She certainly doesn't like *me* very much."

"No, this year has only confirmed my hetero tendencies. Erin's got a perfectly good lover of her own, anyway, an anthropologist spending this year in the field, in Africa."

"I take it," Alain asked astringently as I came out of the bathroom myself, later on, "that you are not attracted by the idea of having a child, either."

"Well, I am, but I don't need any cynical contracts to do it. I'm not sure if technology could enable me to carry a baby to term, but I know it could help me conceive one."

He made that European sound again, but asked politely, "Then you want me to retire?"

"Retire? From what: from politics? Oh: *withdraw!* No, that's okay, I've got a diaphragm in."

"But you weren't wearing this diaphragm," he pronounced the g, like all French people, "this afternoon, were you?"

"No, and you didn't offer any early retirement, either."

"Because I still hoped that you'd agree to come to France, instead of back here, when Becca—" He had a new thought, "You understand, I didn't mean for you to *leave* her?"

"I know that, Alain," I said, more gently, this time. "It's still no. Come to bed, anyway." Without the seductions of the best French wine, the apple blossoms, and the slanting sunlight, I had to confront head-on the fact that I really wanted this. For tonight, at any rate.

It made me feel pretty corrupt in the morning, though. So I thought I would confirm the feeling with a small self-inflicted wound.

"Alain," I said, as he packed his beautiful overnight case. "I'll tell you what I will do, if you like: I'll tell Martine to hold off on the divorce action, and you can let it be known all over the place that I'm doing that. So, for public purposes, you'll still have a wife, the same wife. Maybe the response will show you how crazy your proposal is, even from your own point of view."

"Thank you, Jamie. I'll be in touch with your precious Martine as soon as I get back to Paris. She's very competent for someone who's made her career defending terrorists."

"Alain, you know very well that none of those people was ever convicted."

"Which just proves my point: she's an excellent criminal lawyer. And you may be needing one yet."

"Listen: think about it, first. There are disadvantages to this offer. As long as we're only legally separated, neither of us can remarry. Which is fine with me, for now and maybe for good. But you may want—"

He came over and put his hands on my shoulders. "I don't

think I could ever tie myself to a Frenchwoman, sexually. They don't have your sense of—of openness."

I could think of dozens of French feminists who shared my approach to sexuality. Not that any of them would get into bed with a member of Alain's party. There was no point in even raising it. "What about Monique?" I asked instead, knowing it was the wrong question.

"Monique does everything I want," he replied tartly.

"So?"

"So I have no idea what she wants."

"But all this is just why you should support that clinic you keep cursing. The sexuality counseling, anyway. They could be training a whole army of Frenchwomen worthy of your attention."

"That's not funny, Jamie." He shut his suitcase and left for Washington. But he kissed me good-bye, first.

12

✳

ALAIN HAD LEFT his imprint, all right. Until yesterday, that phrase was just a metaphor. Now it had become a physical reality, one I urgently needed to eradicate. The bed linen and my own body had taken on something of his scent, and I felt that my sexual parts had molded themselves to the contours of his. Had the night left me less ambivalent, I might have cherished these reminders. As it was, all they evoked was shame.

At lunch, Becca, reminding me of my expressions of principle, pointed out that I had actually been quite strong. Still, when I went out for my afternoon walk, I continued to agonize over why I had not simply told Alain once and for all: "You want to appeal to women voters in a campaign opposed to their real interests, and you want me to help you do it. It wouldn't work, it deserves not to, and the very proposal is an insult to me." Instead, I'd tried to reason with him as if he were a reasonable person, a friend, because someone with his name, his face, and his body had been my *best* friend for so long. It was an explanation, if not an excuse.

On my way back to the Inn, I sat for awhile at the edge of

a meadow that was beginning to show tufts of green. Although still composing eloquent speeches in my head, I was at least able to drop down somewhere on the Inn's grounds without immediately translating the setting to the apple orchard and rehearsing what had happened there.

"They told me I might find you up here." It was Jeremy Morgan, the farmer-baker-handyman-revolutionary. With all that had happened in the 48 hours since we'd met, I'd forgotten his very existence. I had taken my showers under the spray he'd repaired, had eaten his baked goods—indeed, broken his bread with an ambassador of the patriarchy—and taken his turnovers on our conciliatory picnic, without giving a thought to the man whose practical skills lay behind these comforts.

So I said, "Hello, Jem," and made room on my patch of grass.

"I came to see you yesterday," he offered bluntly.

"I'm sorry: Marge and Sally didn't mention it."

"It was that nurse—Mrs. Moyer?—I saw. She told me you were out. With your husband." The deep green eyes looked betrayed, which was hardly reasonable, in the circumstances. "She also said the Maserati outside was his."

"Well, rented," I temporized.

"Somehow, I didn't think that'd be your kind of thing, foreign noblemen with custom sports cars!"

"It isn't."

"Well, don't tell me you didn't go to bed with him, after he came all the way from Europe for it."

"He didn't come over for 'it,' as you so gracefully put it. It so happens he had to go to New York to visit his money—I mean, see to some investments in this country. Anyway, the main reason he came to see me wasn't exactly personal. He wants me to go back to him, because he has some crazy idea that he didn't get elected to their Congress because I'd walked out on him."

"And that's not the real reason?"

"Not only does it make no sense in political terms, but it's even more unlikely with their new electoral system. I find it hard to believe he takes it seriously himself."

"But he did drop in—"

"Between his New York and Washington meetings."

"—to pop the question. And sleep with his wife at the same time."

"I might ask—I should have asked some time back—what business it is of yours."

"But you didn't—because you know the answer."

"I guess I do." There was nothing more to say, so we were both silent for several minutes, in a stillness as intimate as a touch.

"Then will you come down to the farm tomorrow night?"

"I don't know, Jem. I'm too mixed up. Look: you're the most attractive person I've met in months, and I really wanted to—get to know you better. Then Alain showed up and the whole thing got so complicated that I just sort of forgot meeting you that day. I mean, I don't forget whole people that way!" All of a sudden, I was crying noisily.

Jem held me the way he might have held Sam and told me that it was okay and would be okay.

"No, it's a lot worse than you know," I sobbed. "That's why I went to bed with Alain, because of everything else."

But how could I explain the rest? *My friend is dying, and I'm suspected of a murder in my office at the college, and a crazy woman needs me to read her article because I was the one who told her to write it. She's the wife of my ex-lover who was dating the woman who got killed in my office. And I'm responsible for a manuscript that a lot of women really need to read, but I may not be able to publish it without its truths getting distorted.*

Another pause. "You're not leaving until Sunday, are you?"

"Are you hoping everything will be all hunky-dory by Saturday night? Because—"

"No, I just wanted to invite you to come see the farm,

anyway, tomorrow or Saturday. With Sam present the whole time, if you like."

"Okay. And Jem?"

"What?"

"You know I'm coming back here to stay, when—when things are resolved down there? And when I do, I *will* want—"

"A friend?" he asked. I just nodded.

On the drive back to Jaegersville Sunday afternoon I told my companions about my visit to Jem's farm. "I don't know why, but I pictured something completely different, an isolated, re- mote, single-father-and-his-kid retreat from the world."

"And it's not like that?" Becca asked.

"Well, for one thing, there are two houses on the farm—have been since the last century, when the original family expanded. So there are acres and acres of land—fields, pasture, and woods—but right next to Jem's eighteenth-century stone house is a brick Victorian with a whole family living in it, friends that Jem and his—I guess wife, Sam's mother, I mean—moved up there with, in a sort of collective arrangement. Jem took me around the field. They grow mostly medicinal herbs, stuff like foxglove for digitalis. He's got regular contracts to supply phar- maceutical firms. And he showed me the kitchen facilities— sparkling clean, by the way."

"Frankly, I've been kind of wondering about that," Erin put in, "ever since you told me I've been eating baked stuff made on an organic farm by the manure-handler himself."

"Well, it so happens I've never seen a more pristine kitchen. Yours is as spotless, Mrs. Moyer, but no better. So you can all relax and enjoy—retroactively."

We dropped off Becca and Mrs. Moyer, and I took Erin home. "You really like that dirt farmer of yours, don't you?" she asked, once we were alone.

"I think so. If everything else weren't impinging on me, I'd probably be falling in love."

"Everything else?"

"Like Becca. And who killed Sharon. And what I should do about Nellie. And whether I'm helping Virginia get better or setting her up to get worse—"

"And Nick?"

"Nick never impinges."

"But you're supposed to love Nick. Some people might feel this was a slight impediment to falling in love with Jem."

"I know that. It's the norm, after all. But I don't believe exclusive love is the only real thing. Loving Nick just raises my standards, is all."

"Well, as I told you once before, you lead a very varied life. So you and Jem have come to an understanding—for when you move back to the Inn?"

"That's just what we haven't done. The one time in the afternoon we were alone—Jem was making some herbal tea for me, home grown, and Sam ran out to play with the kids from the other house I told you about—I really blew it. He came over and kissed me, and I said something like, 'You'll wait for me, won't you, Jem?' And of course he said 'No!'"

"Excuse the dense question, but why 'of course'?"

"Because, on the one hand, he is there. It's his place in the world and naturally he'll be there when I go back. On the other hand, it's not right to transform that fact into something called 'waiting for Jamie,' as if he owed me something."

"Well, it's all too esoteric for me. Maybe that's the real reason I'm a one-woman woman."

"I'll remind you of that, should the need arise. Meanwhile, when is Lee due back from Africa?"

"This summer—sometime. She's been awfully vague about it."

Although we'd pulled into the parking lot behind Erin's house to finish this conversation, I refused her invitation to come upstairs for a cup of tea. I needed to get home fast and put some kind of end to the vacation and its various confusions. Nonetheless, Mrs. Moyer was already patrolling the front hall when I arrived.

"I want to get her up to bed," she whispered. It was all too obvious whom she meant. "But she said she'd entertain that Mrs. Robards until you got here."

Remembering how our Sunday evenings had originated in Mrs. Moyer's inability to distinguish between a guest and an intruder, I left my unopened mail on the hall table and went straight to the library to relieve Becca of what I suspected was a pleasant chat with Betsy.

"I took delivery on all these flowers for you," Betsy explained, gesturing towards a daunting number of vases crammed with yellow roses, "and brought them over when I saw Becca come in. But I admit I stuck around out of unbridled curiosity. What does his note say, Jamie?"

"Whose note?"

"Alain's," said Becca, "assuming he's the source of all these, as well as this modest little orchid plant *I* got."

"Modest? Do you have any idea what that must have set him back?" Betsy was into house plants, herself. "And he sent me one, too."

"It's just Becca's famous irony," I explained. "She also knows—or should—that French people send flowers for any eventuality."

"A hundred yellow roses? I mean, I counted, Jamie."

"Well, that's basically the floral equivalent of the Maserati. Anyway, you know what Blake says: 'The road of excess leads to the palace of wisdom.' Maybe he's trying to learn something this way."

"But what does he say? After baby-sitting these beauties half the day—"

"Not to mention spoon-feeding Alain himself when he came nosing around for information. Whence your own orchid."

"Well, he was so disappointed to have missed you—and so charming. At any rate, you must know I wouldn't say anything to your discredit."

"I do know. I'm just not used to the 'idiocy of rural life,' yet. And that one's from Karl Marx. Anyway, I'm afraid his note's untranslatable. It's a sort of prose-poem."

"You used to say nothing is untranslatable," Becca reminded me.

"I was wrong. This is full of—pornographic puns. Probably the most creative thing he's written all year, more's the pity."

"Well, I think I'll take my own eminently respectable card to my room, along with the orchid. It was nice of him to think of me, anyway."

"It'll still look like a funeral down here," Mrs. Moyer grumbled.

"In a sense, it is one—for my last illusions," I said to Betsy, as the door closed. "All year, I've been having dreams about Alain—as he used to be. In fact, in the dreams, I managed to blot out his inheritance and everything that happened afterwards. So I'll dream something terribly banal: I'm down at Fautour weeding in the garden or in the Paris apartment cutting up vegetables for a ratatouille. And I'm talking to the old Alain. Then I'll wake up and not only am I in central Pennsylvania, but the most commonplace little scene is completely unattainable. And now I'm awake for good."

"So you're not going back to him?"

"No, because the life I had, the man I had, don't really exist anymore."

"But you did—" Betsy and I had never had an intimate conversation before and we had no vocabulary for one. Our usual discourse had hitherto done just fine, even while I was sleeping with her friend the dean. "You did let him stay with you at Savage?"

"I did. And that's what haunts me." Betsy nodded understandingly, though I had trouble imagining her or anyone ever being haunted by Bill Robards. He was, at the very least, too *considerate* to hang around a body or a psyche where he wasn't welcome. "Anyway, Alain's visit had one useful outcome."

"I'm glad of that, anyway." Betsy was clearly wondering whether to regret her own candor with him. "You mean, showing you that this is your real life?"

"No, it's less global than that. I told him all about what happened to Sharon, and he asked some very good questions. Good, I mean, because they forced me to clarify where I could and showed me what areas really are murky. For instance, he asked about Sharon's letter, exactly what she'd said and the tone—"

"What letter?"

"The one she was writing in my office when the murderer— stopped her. Anyway, as a writer himself, Alain focused on that. I realized I couldn't answer his questions because I'd never actually seen it or even had it quoted to me verbatim. So that's the first thing on tomorrow's agenda: call Endlich and see if he's willing to show it to me."

By Monday morning, however, another bureaucratic task took precedence over even that one. After Betsy went home, late Sunday afternoon, I turned my attention to the week's accumulation of mail. Prominent in the pile was a manila envelope addressed in my own hand. Like any experienced writer, I assumed it was one of my pieces being returned by some shortsighted editor and, in no mood to cope equably with rejection, I left that one for last. It proved, however, to be Virginia Walters' draft of an article on Jane Austen. I plunged into the manuscript right away, took copious notes and, relieved at what I found, surfaced too late to make contact with the Hochstetter Clinic that night. Which is why *that* was what I had to try first thing in the morning. But, when I asked for Virginia, I met unexpected resistance.

"That is disallowed."

Ignoring the temptation to expatiate on a vocabulary more suited to the Internal Revenue Service than a therapeutic community, and unwilling to bandy words with anyone who, herself, bandied "disallowed" so freely, I asked to speak to the supervisor of the voice I was addressing.

"I am the supervisor, madam. It is disallowed to telephone patients in that sector."

"In that case, would you please take a message for her?" I thought telegraphically. "Please tell her, without fail, that Professor Jameson will come to see her tomorrow and that my news is excellent. It will really help her state of mind to hear that." She assured me of compliance, though I still felt irrationally guilty that I couldn't manage the trip out there and back, with a reassuring conversation squeezed in, before my one o'clock workshop that afternoon. I told Becca that I'd be driving her out to Hochstetter again.

Endlich, now my second call of the morning, was truculent, as anticipated, and certainly would have said "disallowed" if he'd thought of it. However, he was too busy talking about Evidence in a Murder Case to do so. I got through to him, I think, by patiently repeating the question, "what harm can it do?" He told me he had an appointment with the dean of students later that day and would come by my office afterward. Although he did not refer to the site of our prospective meeting as the scene of the crime, the implied words slid flat and heavy through the telephone wires.

He appeared with a photocopy, perhaps suspecting I planned to tamper right under his nose with fingerprints or other incriminating marks on the original. Sharon had used a sheet of Ebbing College stationery, one she might have brought with her or taken from my own carelessly husbanded supplies, there was no way of telling, and had written only a few lines when her murderer stepped in to make sure she'd have no chance to finish it. Not that there was even a hint, as far as she'd gotten, whether it was the letter the murderer had wanted to curtail or Sharon's more general intentions, whatever they were. After all, it had been left for the cops to find. I stared at the puzzling lines before me:

> Dear Jamie,
> I'm so scared of its going to <u>Orlando</u> that I am writing, first of all, to apologize to you and also to ask for

It was opaque, but strangely moving.

"What do you suppose she was going to ask for?" I wondered aloud, forgetting that Endlich's speculations and my own ran along quite different channels.

"What about 'ask forgiveness?'?" he replied in his most irritating ace-up-the-sleeve fashion.

"She'd already done that, in her 'first of all' clause. She says she's *also* going to ask for something. Asking forgiveness wouldn't rate an 'also.'"

"Depends how upset she was when she wrote. What else would she have to ask you for, anyway?"

"My help, my understanding, I don't know. But that r of 'for' looks quite finished to me."

"You a handwriting expert, too?" he asked unhelpfully.

"Well, now you see it, you see there's no point in holding out about Florida."

"Florida?"

"Disney World, Orlando. What was going to go there that she wanted to stop?"

"I tell you, I have no idea."

"Come on. She doesn't explain. She expects you to know. She even underlines it, to show you it's the clue."

"Well, I don't. You do see that her tone toward me is not aggressive."

220 / LILLIAN S. ROBINSON

"Well, *she* didn't come in and bash *you* in the head while you were writing."

"As you happen to know was physically impossible for me to have done to her."

"I guess so," he responded glumly.

"I take it you're pursuing your investigation?"

"You take right. Did you know Dr. Reilly was a relative of the Ebbing family?"

It took me a moment to make the connection. Apparently, if it had been *my* corpse, he'd have been under less pressure to make an arrest—unless perhaps my in-laws had chosen to create an international incident. Alain's hundred flowers, now insouciantly rearing their lovely heads in every room of my house, came to mind, and I wondered, suddenly, if they were a reference to the Cultural Revolution: was he perhaps trying to tell me something about letting a hundred flowers bloom? But then, his note, written, I gathered, just before catching the Concorde back to Paris, was so inconsequential. . . . All of which took me much too far from Captain Endlich and his question. "Did you?" he repeated.

"Did I what? Oh, realize Sharon was related to the Ebbings? Yes, I did. She took it all pretty seriously, you know. That's why—"

"Why—?"

Why I connected her involvement with family history to the loss of the manuscript and assumed that both were somehow mixed up in her murder. There was no useful way of explaining this, however, so I settled for, "That's why I knew—because it was so important to her. She did a lot of research about the family. Anyway, am I also right in assuming you're investigating our students now?"

"What makes you think so?"

"Your visit to Han Solo. I mean the dean of students." Henry Solow, who must have chosen the macho nickname "Hank" as a teenager, had been readily rebaptized by the undergraduates when *Star Wars* came out. Those kids were now pushing thirty, and some of the current generation of mid-1980s students might have missed the reference, but the sobriquet had clung, nonetheless.

"Well, I did think of the student angle. But Dean Solow says there aren't any real troublemakers on campus right now."

I kept my own counsel about Han Solo's probable views on which students to label troublemakers. And the interview ended on our usual note of thinly-veiled mutual contempt.

Endlich had left me the photocopy of Sharon's letter, and I pondered what the police called the Florida connection. "Orlando" didn't mean Florida to me, much less Disney World, it meant "Roland." Particularly underlined liked that. They're the Italian and French versions of the same name, so the character in *Orlando Furioso* is the same guy who's the hero of the French *Song of Roland*, Charlemagne's nephew. *Wasn't I just talking about the Furioso with somebody? Oh right, Jem Morgan, when we first met, at Savage. That must be why it's on my mind.* It occurred to me that if Sharon had known Italian, this word might be a message that she was scared of Charles Rowland, especially in his relation to the manuscript. But she didn't know Italian. She made a big point the night we met about how she didn't know any languages well—she even mentioned Italian as one she didn't know at all—and then, when she turned against me, my speaking French became part of her grievance. *Besides, this is no game, much less one of word play. The woman was about to be murdered, and here I am wondering whether she was sending me a bilingual message fingering Orlando-Rowland!*

I had just settled down to some work with the manuscript when Laurie and Ann burst into the archive. (Actually, of course, they had to knock for me to let them in, but the overall effect was distinctly one of bursting.)

"Guess what?" This was clearly rhetorical, since they went

on, practically in chorus, "Remember the Circular File Committee, the Garbage Pail Kids?"

"The what?"

"You know, the committee the trustees formed last fall to look into the South Africa question and report. We all thought it'd be just 'file and forget,' so we called it that. Anyway, believe it or not, they're actually going to make some recommendations about divestment."

"What sort of recommendations? You mean *for* divestment?"

"Nobody knows. The report will be out next Monday, a week from today. But we can't exactly plan a response unless we can figure out what they're going to say."

"Why not have a rally or something, anyway? Then you can declare a victory or build for future actions, depending which way the report goes. But I must say it looks pretty hopeful, the fact that they're reporting at all and that they've announced the date in advance."

"Of course, that could be just to put us off the track."

"Frankly, Laurie, I don't think they're smart enough."

"You may be right. So we'll zap them with a rally either way." They left as my telephone rang.

It was Frances Wager, the poet who was scheduled to read at Ebbing on Thursday. Frances Wager with the flu. "Everyone else had the flu in January or February. Early March at the latest," I reminded her caustically.

"So I'm a late bloomer. Is there any chance I could switch with whoever you've got for May?"

"Nope. It's Sean Fergus, and he chose that date because he won't be back from picking shamrocks or whatever in Ireland until then. We can probably schedule you for next fall, though. I'll get back to you. Until then, get some rest and take plenty of vitamins."

Although the flu had missed me this year, I'd seen its ravages among my students and colleagues, and it was a scourge I wouldn't have wished on Frances even if she hadn't been a nice person and a good poet. But I was fumbling for my address book before we even hung up. The opening she'd left was just what the doctor ordered—and I was the doctor!

Jenny Metz was still in her office at her arts center in Philadelphia and, when I told her what the honorarium would be, found that she'd certainly be free to give a reading Thursday night. "Besides," she added, "that's getting known as a prestige series you run up there."

"Anyway, Jenny, there's one other thing—"

"I might have known, for that money."

"No, it's our standard honorarium, with ten percent tacked on because you're coming on such short notice. The catch, if you choose to see it that way, is a visit to the local mental hospital."

"I know some poets do workshops in psychiatric wards," she brought out doubtfully, "the way others do them in schools or prisons. But, with my history, I'm not sure—"

"It's not a workshop, though it's precisely because of your history that you're needed. There's a woman I'd like to have meet you. To talk about your experiences with those pills they had you on. I want her to see someone who stopped taking them."

"You mean, I'm a role model for someone? Is she trying to get free of them?"

"Well, I'd like her to."

"You'd like it? Sounds like practicing medicine without a license, if you ask me."

"I am asking you. Wanna help out?"

"Sure, but no brain surgery before breakfast."

Becca was skeptical about my choice of a substitute poet, because she didn't think as highly of Jenny's writing as I did. "I'm just not sure all that stuff about the mental hospital and the adolescent suicide attempt is what the students need to hear," she opined. "Which reminds me: what are they doing about the next professor of poetry? Is there any news from the search committee?"

"You can search me. Frankly, I think things sort of ground to a halt after Sharon died. Not that she had anything to do with that committee or its mandate, but people are still sort of shell-shocked—all the more so for not admitting it. The college seems to be functioning okay in its day-to-day routine, but tasks that require some special effort just aren't getting it."

"What about replacing Sharon, come to think of it?"

"Same problem: I don't think they've done a thing. Which may mean they'll offer the job to Erin for next year, by default."

"That would be nice."

"Except that her lover is coming back from Africa, and Erin may prefer to be in Philly." I had no idea then that the matter would become an issue.

That night, I dreamed about Sharon—nothing helpful and definite, just Sharon present and trying to speak to me. "You had your chance," I told her when I woke up. But I knew she hadn't, really. She had tried to reach me and had been brutally interrupted. And now she certainly wasn't sending me dream messages about the *Chanson de Roland.*

The next day, Becca and I left a little early for Hochstetter, in order to take back roads and rejoice in the blossoming trees.

"My last spring," she said quietly. "I'm not ready to leave this planet, but sometimes I think I'm more reconciled to it than you are."

"You're probably right. I always did have trouble taking no for an answer."

"So does your husband, it would seem." Becca had clearly come as close as she wanted to the great topic between us and was now backing away from it.

"You mean those roses? They're just a thank-you gift."

"Thank-you for what? Oh! Well, that's rather gallant of him!"

"And you're the one who was grossed out by his original proposal! Believe me, I'd rather have my pride intact and buy my own damn flowers."

"You know, all this makes it a little hard for your other guests to thank you properly for our week at the Inn. I know it didn't exactly work out the way you intended, but it was really lovely for me."

"In the long run, that'll be all that matters for me, too, the time with you. Alain was only a—a distraction."

The abundance of spring did not cease abruptly at the gates of Hochstetter. From her sun porch, Virginia could see the same extravagant display that had so moved us on the trip up. "The great thing," she told me, "is that the pear tree over there won't start getting blossoms for another month or so, when all the others have lost theirs. It was good of you to come, Jamie."

My phone message had not been delivered. "I was afraid you'd be worried—because I was away for nearly a week after your manuscript must have arrived."

"Well, I was, but then I took a pill and remembered that if Walt was on vacation, you must be, too. Did you go out to California?"

"No, the Savage Inn. It's—" I paused in confusion, recalling my own introduction to the place. I found I had no desire to know if she'd been there with Walt, too, or if she suspected him of taking all his women there. "I'm researching a cookbook. I took Becca and her nurse with me, and Erin, the woman who's replacing Sharon in History."

"Sounds lovely—just women." I started with several minutes of unstinting praise of Virginia's article, then told her what I thought remained to be done. That had chiefly to do with identifying which audience, of the several that might want to read about illusion and delusion in the novels of Jane Austen, she wanted to address this article to, and then writing to that audience.

Some animation broke through the chemically-induced calm. "I wish Sharon could hear you," she began unexpectedly, just as I was expecting her to say something like, "You really think it'll be publishable?"

"Sharon? How come?" Presumably, a close friend would wish Sharon could still hear anything, but why single out these rather commonplace remarks of mine?

"Well, I guess you know, she was always kind of funny about publication. She kept her research to herself, and she never seems to have thought about its being a way of telling real people something they might need to know."

"What was the point, then?"

"I'm not sure. I do know this issue was the place where the two sides of her background sent the same message, instead of being in conflict."

"What do you mean?"

"The nuns and the upper-class WASPs didn't agree very often, but they both told her over and over, 'Don't put yourself forward.' "

"You think Sharon believed public expression was primarily about putting yourself forward? She didn't think it had any content or value in itself?"

"I guess not. She used to go on and on about 'academic snobs,' when she was a snob herself—a closet one—about family. And that's just an accident of birth, not based on anything you do. I used to think she chose me for a friend for all the wrong reasons—not that there was anyone else choosing me at all."

"What wrong reasons?"

"That I might have gone to a fancy college and graduate school, but I dropped out after the M.A. Whereas my *family*—"

"I see."

"Anyway, I wish Sharon could hear your ideas about the value of publication. I always suspected there was something wrong with what she used to say, but I just assumed I didn't know enough about it. And Walt was so cynical about 'productive scholars,' too."

"I know, I've heard him. But do you think these ideas about defining the audience will help you revise your piece?"

"Absolutely, and I work fast, too." My face must have reflected my questions, because she added, "I wrote this draft very quickly, on practically no medication. Then, when I didn't hear from you, I started the pills again. I kept on with them even after I realized it must be Spring break. I didn't think you were slighting me, but I needed to get through the time. That's the important thing, killing time."

"Listen, Virginia, will you see my friend Jenny if she comes out here at the end of the week? She's the one who used to take drugs like that, too. I mean, every case is different, but she's a role—" I eschewed the cant phrase, "she's an inspiration. Anyway, she's a lot of fun."

"Sure. But getting this article in some sort of shape will be the best medicine."

"I'm supposed to be saying that to you."

"You have, Jamie. And thanks."

This time, the quiet drive back to Jaegersville was punctuated by questions that yielded no answers, but only further questions. Could anyone who had completed a Ph.D. really feel the contempt for scholarly activity that Virginia attributed to Sharon? Well, as she'd reminded me herself, *Walt* certainly had trouble seeing such work as anything but a self-aggrandizing and ultimately meretricious process. But Sharon did do research—careful, thorough research. I had sometimes wondered whether she grasped larger concepts and principles as well as she did the details. But then, look at Erin, who knew all of the women whose lives *she* studied on that intimate sort of basis and yet never lost sight of the historical forces moving them. So why not assume that Sharon, too, really knew her stuff? Well, because—it came down to that—she didn't publish it.

Could Virginia be right about Sharon's reasons, too? It seemed very thin, somehow, unsatisfying. But that was because I had no way, no credible *subjective* way, at least, of evaluating the need to feel virtuous through self-effacement. Just as I had trouble understanding the lure of strong drink—Sharon's actual weakness—I failed to understand how anyone could resist the appeal of writing, which was my own addiction. So maybe it *was* enough for Sharon, that onanistic accumulation of unshared knowledge. More important: was her resistance to publication strong enough to make her commit larceny to keep a family document from being published? Once more, it seemed the answer *had* to be in the negative, but the facts seemed to point the other way. Aided, to be sure, by the sensitive nature of this particular document and its possible implications for her own peace of mind or her sense of herself. But—and this was the big unanswerable on top of the already shaky house of cards I'd constructed so far—why would any of this lead someone to kill her? If it had.

At home, there was a message to call Erin as soon as possible.

"That microfilm's come: Smedley Harris's diary. You'll have to go over it with a fine-tooth comb to see when and how Nellie left his clinic. All I ever found was her admission record and no case history for the Procedure. But somewhere in there he may have noted her departure. So it's your baby."

"I know, I know."

"And a rich baby, too. Ann got hold of those records, at least. Nellie inherited the lot. There was no one else left, you see."

"Well, don't the legal papers have to give her address? 'Residual legatee: Miss Helen Breckenridge, spinster, of 232 Walnut Street ' or whatever?"

"Sure, but the address, at least on everything Ann's dug up so far, is the same."

"The same?"

"That burned-out shell in Germantown."

13

✳

EVEN THE BURNED-OUT SHELL, I reflected next morning, sifting through the papers Ann had left at the archive, was located on a prime slice of Philadelphia real estate. And the other, undamaged assets had sufficed to support a large family in substantial comfort, without requiring any of them, for some generations past, to disturb the invested peace of their capital. By 1868, to be sure, new fortunes were being made, from railroads, manufacturing, and—somewhere in Pennsylvania, come to think of it—the first oil strikes. Even without additional speculation, though, Nellie's inheritance would have been more than adequate to her most extravagant needs.

She wanted to attend the conservatory? Not only was there no one left to prevent her, but she could afford to *found* a moderate-sized music school or lavishly endow the established academy of her choice. ("Check records Curtis, Juilliard, etc." I scribbled on my growing list of what I feared were probably blind alleys.) With a fortune at her disposal, however, and a musical career in her dreams, Europe seemed the increasingly probable choice. Especially if it was the scene of her own crime she was leaving behind, and with Lizzie duly married to the contemptible Brock. This theory would explain why Nellie's trail went cold in the Philadelphia records after she inherited, and might also provide a rationale for Lizzie's decision to stay put, herself, once she was widowed. If Europe meant Nellie to her, she might be eager to opt out on the possibility of a disturbing encounter.

I pictured Nellie settling into a charming house in Germany or Austria with a beautiful piano, and the best teachers money could buy. But after the student years? Concert tours all over the continent? Or a more retired but still musical existence? And, in either case, perhaps, a woman lover to replace the conventionally if far from happily married Lizzie.

Was it right, though, to characterize any aspect of Elizabeth Ebbing Brock as conventional? There was a stolidity to her journal's descriptions of family life in the late nineteenth century that gave them the feel of parody—intentional parody. Her poems, moreover, made it clear that her mind as a whole was far from conventional. Such freedom of spirit would not necessarily preclude her wishing to eradicate her single shameful lapse, but it might militate against her *regarding* it as shameful. Besides, she had put the manuscript of *Helen-Elizabeth* together *after* the events it recounted, deliberately concluding it with the unqualified statement that she and Nellie would be together forever. She had held onto the memoir, moreover, until her death some sixty-three years later, when she had left it to the College, and she'd apparently been willing to let it be published, once the archive was unsealed.

From the text itself, as well as the mass of other documentation filed all around me, I had a fairly clear sense of Lizzie Brock's character. She was strong-willed, even stubborn, deeply sensual, and adventurous. Nellie—at least filtered through her lover's prose—had a gentler and sweeter nature. But these facts gave no reliable clues to what happened to her after their love affair reached its abrupt and traumatic conclusion. Whether her inheritance had been the windfall benefit of a family tragedy or the profits of her own insanely desperate act in bringing that tragedy about, what had she done once it was in her hands?

Nellie had last been "spotted"—to the extent that historical research has its detective dimension—at Dr. Smedley Harris's private clinic, from which she had apparently emerged with her sex organs and her fortune intact. Diligent scrutiny of the microfilm in the yellow box on my desk might at least yield an answer as to when she had gone. Reluctantly, I threaded the spools into the reader—does anyone actually enjoy using this eye-tormenting equipment?—and began my woman-hunt.

By the weekend, however, I had come up with nothing except that I hated Dr. Smedley Harris, which I already knew. On Saturday, Becca raised a pertinent question. "Why is it so important to find out when Nellie left the clinic?"

"Because, if I can prove—to my own satisfaction, at least—that she was still locked up at the time of the fire, then I needn't so much as raise the possibility of her being the arsonist. I can even mention that she was hospitalized half a mile away without dwelling on whether she somehow got out, set the house ablaze, and got back, unseen by a soul the whole time." Just the way, it occurred to me, I'd once imagined Virginia slipping out of Hochstetter to murder Sharon.

"And if she was released earlier?"

"Then I can't escape the implications. If I include this whole line of reasoning at all."

"You mean, you'd suppress it?"

"I mean I don't know. 'Suppress' is a little extreme, in any event. First of all, it would still be only speculation, and secondly, it's mostly a matter of emphasis—how closely I choose to relate the narrative in the manuscript to what happened to the historical Nell Breckenridge."

"But you do feel it would be suppressing historical truth, don't you?"

"I *think* I do."

Walt came as usual to the open house. In our only private conversation of the evening, he asked me whether I thought Erin would be interested in staying on next year. As I'd suspected, no one had it sufficiently together to conduct a full-scale search for Sharon's replacement in the remaining weeks of the semester.

"Well," I told him, "Naturally, the college would be lucky to get her. I imagine she'd be willing to keep the job for another year, but she's the one you have to ask."

"I will, of course, once I'm in a position to make a proper offer."

"Which means?"

"After I've consulted with History and brought their recommendation to the College Personnel Committee. It's all pro forma, but we do have to go through the motions, even for a one-year replacement."

Erin herself arrived late and seemed rather tense. "Can I speak to you alone?" she asked quietly, as I cut her some coffee cake.

"Tonight, you mean?" She nodded. "Okay, just stick around after the others leave."

Once we had the library to ourselves, Erin got herself a drink and began her story. "You may have noticed how late I got here?" I nodded. "What happened was, just as I was leaving my apartment to come over, Ann showed up."

"Ann Capobianco?"

"Uh-huh. She was very keyed up—maybe she'd been drinking some, but mostly she'd been crying, and then, she said, walking around and around trying to get up her courage to approach me."

"Approach you—why? Her work's been terrific, hasn't it?

And well ahead of schedule thus far. So what's she upset about?"

"Remember the conversation we had about her, when I was here back in January?"

"No, I don't think— oh, about her coming out as a lesbian?"

"Well, we were both right. I was certain that was how it would end and you tried to tell me some of the special problems she'd face coming out here at Ebbing. Neither of us pictured her coming to *me*, though."

"But I think it's great that you're here for her, now. When I talked about how hard it would be in this environment, that was one of the things I meant: that there wasn't any *grown up* lesbian for her to talk to."

"Unfortunately, talking is not what Ann had in mind."

"Oh, no! She—?"

"She wanted me to—to initiate her. She was very—insistent. With a lot about how much she loved me and how I'm the greatest teacher she's ever had and the greatest historian she's ever known."

"You've probably had higher compliments than that last one. But go on."

"Well, I realized, of course, that part of the problem is she's so isolated. She's had these feelings for a long time and it was as if she thought she was the only one."

"In *1986*, Erin?"

"You're the one who said how hard it would be. So I started by telling her that there's a whole lesbian community out there that could offer her support, and where she could find a lover who'd be more—ah—suitable."

"Did you tell her about Lee?"

"I tried to, but her position was basically, 'out of sight, out of mind.' You know, there's a sense in which our lives never seem quite real to students, anyway."

"I know what you mean. The hormones are going full blast,

in their own lives, but they miss a lot of other things that are right under their noses. When I was going with Walt, I was grateful for that smoke screen. Anyway, about Ann—?"

"Nothing I said seemed to have much effect. I'm not even sure she took it all in. And then, while I turned my back to make her some tea in the kitchenette, she—stripped off all her clothes and sort of threw herself at me."

"Oh, Lord! What did you do then?"

"What do you think I did? No, really, Jamie, if you can even ask—"

"I think you thanked the Goddess that She hadn't made you a man."

"What?"

"Because a man might have had a lot more trouble resisting. Just physically, I mean. Ann's an attractive kid."

"But you have no doubt that I did resist?"

"Oh, no. When I said 'what did you do then?' I wasn't casting aspersions on your self-control or whatever it took, but quite literally—as in how did you get her dressed and calmed down and out of there?"

"Well, I just held her and told her that I wasn't rejecting her because there was anything *to* reject, just that I have priorities of my own that don't—that can't—include her. And I told her about the lovely, decent, happy life she is going to have—"

"She is? I mean, you did?"

"Why not? She does have her whole life ahead of her—to coin a phrase. Anyway, eventually, I was sure she wasn't really going to do herself any harm—she sort of threatened to, at one point, if I wouldn't— and I made her get dressed and drove her back to the dorm on my way over here."

"Erin, why did you feel you had to tell me all this tonight?"

"Just so you could keep an eye on Ann. It would be—better—if I didn't."

"Especially this week."

"How so?"

"Because—well, I wasn't going to tell you this, but you've had a hard time of it—just like Saint What's-his-Face, with a lovely young nude in your chaste arms—"

"Saint Anthony, perhaps, and it's not funny, Jamie."

"It can't have been at the time," I agreed, "but you have to admit a certain farcical—okay, you don't have to. Anyway, what's happening this week is Walt says he's going to touch all the right bureaucratic bases and offer you another year here at Ebbing. It might even lead to the regular job."

"Great! with my lover back in Philadelphia."

"So you'd be another commuting couple. It's not that far."

"Have you tried to carry on a relationship between here and Philly?"

"No, my lover happens to be in Berkeley, remember?"

"And in Paris. And in a big grey house on the other side of campus. And now up in—"

"Therefore I don't feel any pain? Moreover, you don't see these pretty boys on campus coming over and peeling down to their birthday suits for *my* delectation, do you?"

"Would you want any of them to, Jamie?"

"Uh-uh, I like a man to *know* something. Though I must say, ever since the weather's warmed up, I've been nettled by all the young-in-one-another's-arms on display every time I venture onto campus."

"Me too. Which doesn't mean I'm interested in any of them, either. It just makes me long for my own youth—with the lover of my not particularly youthful choice. It doesn't mean I'm not grateful about the job, either, even if it will create some complications. Thanks, Jamie."

"It was really Walt's doing—both times. I'm only his conduit. Or something."

"Maybe it's all a courtship ritual, wooing you back by helping your friend professionally?"

"No, Walt's a genuinely nice person, more's the pity."

"I won't try to unravel *that* tonight. It's too late. But you will look after Ann?"

"Of course. Comparatively speaking, that's easy."

The nineteen-year-old lesbian to whom I turned my first attention Monday morning, though, was Helen Breckenridge, the elusive Nell. I imagined Dr. Smedley Harris's voice was like his penmanship: large, round, and plummy. But would I have relished reading about his Pacification Procedure in any hand? Or did the content affect my response to the script? Surely, small, crabbed writing would only make the work that much longer and harder. Especially since, when I finally found what I was looking for, it was only one sentence: "*As arranged, Miss Breckenridge departed for the week shortly after breakfast this morning.*"

The date was October 22, 1868. No mistaking it; although Smedley Harris didn't invariably make a daily entry, the preceding one was for October 21 and the next one for October 23. And October 23 was the night of the Breckenridge Fire. Compulsively, I checked to see if it had been the night between the 22nd and the 23rd or the 23rd and the 24th that the fire took place, but it made no difference, of course. She had been released, presumably to the custody of her family, in time for arson on either night.

"Oh Nellie, Nellie, why did you *do* it?" I cried, aware that even if the walls had ears, the walruses didn't. But I needn't call on her shade to provide an answer, I reflected, not with Smedley Harris's clinical journal still wound into my microfilm reader and the story of her lost love on the table before me. She was slated to be pacified, sanitized, and turned over as a sexual toy to the fat, complacent boy who'd already ruined her life. And her lover, whatever vows were sworn on the last page of that memoir, had unaccountably deserted her. Lizzie's marriage to Alfred Brock was around the same time, too, if memory served.

News of that might have inflamed Nell—no, scratch that verb. Anyway, somehow it had been "arranged" that she be released before the Procedure was effected. And then her family's house mysteriously burned down, and she, the unpacified one, certainly never went back for that doctor's vicious brand of treatment.

I was about to check the date of Lizzie's marriage when I was startled out of the pursuit of knowledge—not to mention my wits—by a hammering at the door of the archive. I opened it to admit Laurie and Ann. As I shifted ungently back into the twentieth century, I noticed that Ann, whom I'd agreed to keep an eye on, certainly did seem agitated. Then again, so did Laurie, who had probably spent last evening sharing a take-out pizza with her boyfriend, making love in his dorm room or hers, and, in between, working on her Emily Dickinson paper for Betsy's seminar. Nothing could be further from either of their thoughts, at present, than last night, unless it was the events of October 23, 1868.

"Just look at this—piece of crap!" Laurie expostulated, throwing what appeared to be a student essay down on my work table. An essay, to be sure, produced by the kind of student who hopes to curry favor for a feeble effort by flawless word-processing and a fancy plastic cover. This time, the dim-witted student was actually the Trustees' Select Committee on South African Investment; and the document was their promised report.

"What kind of crap?" I asked curiously.

"Stupid," Laurie began.

"No, more ignorant," Ann expanded. "And self-satisfied. And—"

Laurie picked up the thread. "And they have the nerve to call this thing a White Paper."

"Well, what could be more appropriate for something I gather doesn't go far enough in opposing apartheid? Think of all the great slogans you can get out of it."

I reached for the offending document, and Ann said they'd brought me my own copy. "It was in your cubbyhole, outside. But you'll have to read it fast: we're hoping you'll do a kind of analysis of what's wrong with it at our rally. Which, as you know, is in thirty-five minutes."

"Thirty-five minutes? What time—?" She was right, of course. I was a couple of hours, as well as 118 years, behind. "Then get out, both of you, so I can read this. But as far as your dictating my speech, how do you know? Maybe I'll just love it!"

"No way, José," Ann retorted. She actually seemed pretty much as usual. At nineteen, I would have been—in analogous circumstances, I certainly was—crushed for weeks after a real or fancied rejection. The fabled resilience of youth is something I've acquired, to the limited extent I have, only with age. What Erin called maturity.

Laurie essayed a pun in what I suspect she saw as my own style. "Come on, Annie. Can't you see the Tutu of us are Botha-ing the lady?"

"The Botha you," I corrected her. "Now, out and let me read."

The White Paper deserved its name, all right, and turned out to be easy both to summarize and hold up to ridicule. My job was to try to make the experience educational and inspiring. I wrote some quick notes and transferred them to an index card on which, at the rally, I found that a morning spent reading microfilm had rendered me unable to focus effectively.

But it was a good day for a demo, and people were drawn to this one as they crossed the campus on their way to lunch. A male student I didn't recognize was speaking as I arrived. Betsy and Bill Robards waved to me, snippets of red ribbon ("in solidarity with the ANC," I'd been told when I got my own) pinned in both their lapels. I waved back, but noting that Walt was with them, went and stood next to Lola Santiago on the other side of the platform. Erin joined us and, even so, I caught myself expecting to see Sharon's green jacket in the crowd and was once again brought up short against the realization that Sharon—whether she was feeling friendly or hostile toward me—would never turn up anywhere again.

When it was my turn to speak, I said what I suspect faculty across the country were saying to gatherings like this in the academic year 1985-1986, when the media kept insisting that our students were all yuppies in training and the jails of Middletown, Connecticut, Ithaca, New York, Berkeley, California, and dozens of college towns in between overflowed with those same student bodies. From the podium, I saw a handful of counter-demonstrators carrying placards supporting the committee's aptly titled document. Charles Rowland, I observed, was among, if not precisely of them.

After Carlos Santiago spoke about human rights, the demonstration resolved itself into a meeting, and I had to leave for my 1 o'clock class. When she got there herself, an hour or so later, Laurie announced the formation of the Front Against Racism ("FAR—because people always say we're going: too far") and the imminent construction of a shantytown on the Green. The shanties would be the focus of a continuous vigil until next week's board meeting adopted or, as was hoped, rejected the White Paper. By the time I left campus that afternoon, a couple of entirely credible shacks were being hammered into shape.

"What's that you're singing?" asked Becca, as I came in the front door.

" 'Qui a peur du grand méchant loup?' It's the Three Little Pigs' song in French. I guess it's the shanties going up that put it into my mind."

"Do you think someone's really going to huff and puff—?"

"No, in fact, I guess it means I'm in a slightly more hopeful frame of mind. Charles Rowland's the only beast on the scene, and he and his bully boys are outnumbered."

Much later I remembered the incendiary new fact that had

emerged about Nellie. "I'll have a long talk with Erin about it tomorrow," I promised myself sleepily.

But when Erin did stop by the archive, late Tuesday, it was not relationships in the last century that were exercising her. "I've got to talk to you," she told me urgently.

"Ann again? I thought she'd set up light housekeeping in the shanties for the duration. She seemed—"

"No, not Ann—*Lee.*" I realized that whatever was troubling Erin touched her more deeply than what I still privately called her Saint-Anthony episode. "I got two letters today. One had been delayed, and the other was pressing me for an answer to the first."

"An answer to what? And will you have a cup of tea?"

"Sure, thanks. Lee wrote the first time to tell me she had the chance to stay in Africa another year. The grant's been renewed, and she can get her leave extended."

"Wonderful for her, less wonderful for you and your relationship—I see *that.* So what answer was she pressing for?"

"Whether she should do it."

"What do you mean, 'should'?"

"She says she's leaving it up to me—since the separation has been so much harder on me, particularly when I was back in Philly subsisting on odd research jobs."

"Which at least you won't have to do *next* year."

"Anyway, she says she'll understand if I say I can't take another year of it. But I know how important this year could be for her."

"You were telling me she's making real breakthroughs in the way African women are studied. So—"

"So you think I should tell her 'stay.' When the one thing that's kept me going has been the knowledge—the belief, I guess I should say—that there are only so many months to go."

"Didn't you know she was applying for the renewal?"

"No, she says she didn't want to upset me prematurely—when it might not have been necessary at all."

"So instead of giving you time to get used to the idea, she springs it on you when all the other pieces of the puzzle are in place?"

"Right, and she's putting it all on me."

"When you know there's only one thing you can say. For the sake of your relationship."

"Uh-huh. A perfect lose-lose situation."

"You have to tell her she should stay there—and then come to believe it yourself. And, once you do, why don't you plan to spend Christmas vacation in Africa?"

"Jamie, I can't afford—"

"Sure you can. There are all sorts of cheap deals you can get. And if you need to make reservations before you actually have the money, I'll lend it to you. Just remember it's a three-step process. First you write a lie to Lee, then you assimilate that lie, and then you start preparing for your own trip."

"Has it occurred to you, Jameson, that you complicate everything unmercifully?"

"Because that's the only way to arrive at simple solutions." I paused, then proceeded less confidently, "Erin—?"

"What?"

"I don't exactly know how to say this, but does all this make Ann's—ah—what Ann wants—any more appealing?"

"Well, yes, of course, in a way it does—the same way a warm bath is more appealing than a cold shower. And I don't have quite the same sturdy foundation of my relationship with Lee to sustain me. But if it wasn't right last Sunday, it isn't right now."

"So you opt for the cold shower?"

"I'm afraid so."

"And I'm the one who makes things difficult?"

"Complicated, I said. It's not the same."

"Maybe. Anyway, I've got to get out to the Green. I signed up to do vigil hours at the shanty over the students' dinner time."

"And I've got to go write an enthusiastic letter to Lee—before

I start having second thoughts on *top* of my second thoughts!"

It occurred to me as I joined Carlos in the shanty that what Erin had really wanted was for me to think up a politically acceptable way to tell Lee not to stay in Africa for the extra year. I also remembered that I hadn't told Erin about the growing evidence of Nellie's guilt.

Meanwhile, Santiago and I rejoiced over the recent fall of tyrants and speculated on the future. "Marcos and Baby Doc within days of each other! Who do you think will be next?"

"That South Korean fellow, perhaps."

"What about Pinochet?"

"Well, my friends write that that's the chant—and not so far underground, either—*Y va a caer*, he is going to fall! But it will take a while longer, I'm afraid. As for these South Africans—"

"I know. I can't *remember* when that wasn't going on."

"And you are so ancient! Jamie, there is no one alive who can remember a time when things weren't awful in South Africa." We talked for awhile about the worsening conditions, heightened resistance, and increased repression. Then he changed the subject. "Speaking of fascists, I understand you slept with your husband last week."

"Nearly two weeks ago, now. The hotline must be running cool. Who told you, anyway?"

"Lola, who had it, of course, from Betsy. You are right, it is none of our business. But I warned you once before about your weakness for these reactionaries."

"Alain's not a fascist. Anyway, as I recall your argument about my supposed weakness, it was based on the 'touch-pitch' reasoning."

"Touch pitch?"

"That you can't—touch it, that is—without messing yourself up." He continued to look blank. "It's just an idiom, Santiago. 'Pitch' is another word for tar. Anyway, you have to admit that, whatever I did over vacation, I'm still carrying on the good fight—nonviolently, of course—right here in this shanty."

"Fine: next thing we know you will be back in bed with our dean."

"Sure, Carlos, and Congress will vote that hundred million bucks for the Contras after all!"

"That, too," he agreed gloomily.

By the time Erin and I actually got to talk about my latest bit of evidence against Nellie, I felt that the events of the week had helped me see the issue in a cooler, less dramatic light. It was something of a shock, therefore, to be told that I was exaggerating its significance, "blowing it," my closest colleague gently informed me, "all out of proportion."

"I think you're wrong, Erin."

"Look, Jamie, what do we really have here? The critical edition of a nice piece of nineteenth-century women's literature that will attract some nonspecialists because it's that rare thing, beautifully written erotica. Your introduction is—what?—thirty or forty pages long, and you've got to supply all sorts of context in it. Now, one small part of that context is what happened to the two girls whose sexual awakening the manuscript describes. For Lizzie—and remember, she's your real subject, because she's the author—we have quite a bit of information. For Nellie, assuming nothing else turns up, we have a lot less. What we do know is that she got out of the hospital just before an unexplained and disastrous fire that left her a very prosperous orphan. Period. What harm would it do to say something about that?"

"First of all, I think the book has more potential readers than you obviously do—readers with all kinds of motives for picking up a piece of lesbian erotica. But one of the great things about the story is the sweetness, the naturalness of the sexual relationship as it develops. That's why it's particularly good that different kinds of people may read it. And all that just goes by the boards if I also show that this sweet, natural relationship made a vicious monster out of Nellie."

"It wasn't coming out with Lizzie that made her crazy, it was how their society reacted to it."

"Erin, you know that, and I know that, and I can even try to show that in what I write. But this is an issue where our life experiences, yours and mine, are—ah—complementary. You've met a lot of prejudice head-on that I know nothing about, but I've been steeped in the assumptions and remarks the straight world makes when they're sure there isn't a homosexual for miles around. They take for granted that being gay means being deviant. They even think it's progressive—God help them!—to call it a psychological aberration instead of a sin."

"You think you've heard worse behind my back than I've heard to my face? Come on, Jamie."

"Not worse, maybe, but more. But look: don't think I haven't asked myself why I seem to be more protective of Nellie than you are. I've concluded that it's because this is not just about lesbians."

"News to me. I detect another Jamesonian complication in the offing."

"No, seriously. The history of Western culture—maybe all civilizations, but let me stick to what I know for sure—is the fear of unbridled female sexuality. Straight men, a lot of them, anyway, are afraid of lesbians because they think you can do something for 'their' women, so-called, that they can't do themselves. That you know sexual secrets—"

"Oh yeah? Then why do they say that all I need—and you too, for that matter—is a good—?"

"Bravado," I interrupted. "It doesn't mean they're sure they've got one to give. But the fear that lesbians will seduce straight women is only one part of the fear of women's sexuality in general. They're afraid because they believe that free sexuality means the crumbling of all known social values. For the past couple of decades, we've made a little progress in encouraging that freedom—infinitesimal, really, when you think about the power of the other thing. I want to make sure nothing I bring into the world moves us back one inch."

"It's like a religion with you, isn't it, Jamie?"

"What? Sexual freedom? Maybe. At least, I believe sex is the attractive force in the universe, the stuff that keeps it all together. Which is why—I've been thinking about it a lot this week—if I had been in your place the other night, I'd probably have taken Ann to bed. Knowing all the time that it was the wrong thing to do."

"No, you wouldn't. Anyway, this is taking us pretty far from the point. Which was—what?"

"That whatever shows female sexuality as an irrational and destructive force is harmful to us. Like exposing Nellie as a murderous lunatic, once she'd experienced lesbian love."

"I still think you're making too much of it."

"And I think I'm not, so this is certainly getting us nowhere." There was a pause, and I switched conversational gears. "Have you signed the FAR petition?"

"Yes, Ann passed it around the majors' seminar this morning, before we started. I was wondering when they'd get around to something that people who weren't already deeply committed could do."

"It does seem to be going in reverse: civil disobedience first, then a petition. But we took a faculty vote in the fall and held a fairly low-key vigil then, as well. That's why the trustees appointed the committee that came up with that ludicrous White Paper. So the militancy now doesn't just come out of nowhere. By the way, how was your first encounter with Ann?"

"Embarrassing. But she seems okay, and that's what counts."

"You know, when I think of the embarrassment, I'm prepared to take back what I said I'd have done in your place. I guess I'm only a sexual evangelist second."

"Second? Then what are you first and foremost?"

"A teacher. It's my legacy from Becca."

14

＊

MEANWHILE, BACK AT one of the frat houses, a STAR
was born. The Students for Treating Apartheid Rationally had
little going for them besides the acronym, but they served their purpose as an alternative focus of attention. In their ostentatiously conventional outfits, they seemed to most people on campus to have fallen
from another planet. My private reaction was less bemused, more
visceral, for I had seen their elegant fascist counterparts at the Law
Faculty on the rue d'Assas. I kept this recognition to myself, however,
as the half dozen of them, with Charles Rowland as their advisor,
simultaneously echoed official government policy and demanded
sympathy as a put-upon minority.

On Thursday, they called a late-afternoon rally of their own
to protest the College's continued tolerance of the shanties,
which, since that term had begun to acquire an honorable pat-
ina, they referred to as "that eyesore on the Green." By the time
I broke away from the last importunate poet in my writing class,
the rally was in full swing, if you can call a few guys dressed up
like their own great-uncles and picketing a couple of symbolic
shacks any kind of swing. One of their signs read STUDENTS FOR

TOPIARY AND AESTHETIC RENEWAL, and I allowed myself a quick nonpartisan smile. Walt was standing off to the side of the crowd with Dean Solow, while Ralph Ehrlich, the security chief, exchanged quips with Charles Rowland.

I've always been grateful that subsequent events never made it to a judicial setting, on campus or off, because I would have made a rotten witness. It all happened so fast—as we rotten witnesses always maintain. The student with the microphone made a sneering reference to the College's welcoming the ghetto onto the Green and gestured at the shanties with his walking stick. At least, I assumed he was gesturing, just as I'd assumed the cane itself was a strictly sartorial affectation. But the stick caught in the thin plastic window, ripping it down the middle, and its owner—assuming that first blow wasn't intentional—spun back with a new sense of possibilities. Using the jagged tear as his point of entry, he thrust his stick back in and struck the wall of the shanty sideways, shouting something about urban renewal.

Here is where it gets confused. Several FAR students rushed the kid with the stick. Laurie got there first, pulled on his arm, and then let go, positioning herself, instead, between his next blow and the shanty, as the cane followed through on its sweep. Mike Freund pushed in front of Laurie, knocking the stick out of its owner's hand, and Ralph Ehrlich stepped in and grabbed Mike, who let out a yelp of pain.

That's when I cashed in the single chip I held. Walt had moved closer to the mêlée, and I faced him across what suddenly seemed like a wide, vacuous space. "Tell him to let him go," I said, quietly but distinctly.

"Jamie, I can't—"

"Tell him to let him go, Walt." He nodded. Ehrlich released Mike, and Walt stepped in to disperse the crowd, with a particularly stern and official-sounding warning for the STAR demonstrators. In a few more minutes, it was as if nothing special had happened, except that the shanty looked considerably more dilapidated than it was supposed to.

With confused feelings, I went over to talk to Mike. "Are you all right?"

"Sure. Captain Ehrlich twisted my arm back, but it'll be okay. Thanks, Jamie."

"What happened to your vaunted nonviolence training?"

"Well, all we really did was read a pamphlet that we never got around to discussing. Laurie remembered—that's why she stopped and interposed her body instead of going for the guy. But my macho instincts took over and—"

"Not instincts, it's all conditioning," I put in mechanically.

"And I felt I had to defend Laurie."

"Who didn't want to be defended, and who, when she isn't following a non-violence handbook, happens to have a brown belt in karate."

"I know," he said sheepishly. "We've even made jokes about how weird it was to be using this handbook when the girls were all learning martial arts at the same time. The thing is, I guess inside I still believe that having the—ah male equipment means it's my job to take care of her. Even though I know it's crazy."

"Knowing better sometimes just isn't enough," I agreed ruefully. As Walt approached us, I added quickly, "Anyway, you'd better see to that arm. I would soak it, if I were you."

"Yeah. Thanks again, Jamie." He hugged me awkwardly with the other arm and loped off, as I turned to face Walt. This time, there was no protective vacuum between us.

"You may have dealt the death blow to my career as dean," he began wearily. 'Come have dinner.'

"I can't. It's my time to take over the vigil so the students can go eat."

"It so happens the FAR kids are planning to stay here to repair the shanty before it gets too dark. And no, you do not have to bring them rations, because Food Service is doing it."

"Did you arrange that?"

"No. It seems Mr. Chandler, the dining halls director, signed their petition this morning and is providing box suppers this evening. He says he does it for field trips and other educational experiences, and he's decided this counts. So you're fresh out of excuses, Jamie, and you owe me."

"If you really meant that cryptic remark about your career, we shouldn't be seen in a restaurant together."

"Then come to my place."

"Same objection. Why don't you come home with me? Between Mrs. Moyer's ideas of a sufficiency and Becca's considerably more limited capacity, we always have enough for an unexpected guest. Becca will be delighted to see you."

"But I need to talk to you alone."

"There'll be plenty of time. She goes to bed very early these days."

Becca *was* pleased to see Walt, and by the time I came down with my face freshly washed and my hair brushed, she'd made sure he fixed himself a drink and had him well launched on the saga of the afternoon's events. "I do hope I haven't missed the part where I put your whole career in jeopardy," I said.

"That's not funny!"

"You know, I'm getting awfully tired of hearing that line. But it's hard to take the ruination of your career very seriously."

"If it happened the way Walt says," Becca declared calmly, "with his asserting his authority over Ralph Ehrlich and bypassing the dean of students, it could be very serious indeed. It depends on how the political winds are blowing."

"What do you mean?"

"If the trustees vote to support the White Paper—and I understand they've never yet overturned one of their own committees' recommendations—then an administrator who broke ranks would be seen in a poor light."

"But he didn't break ranks. He just asserted his authority. I mean, like it or not—and I don't, of course—it's a hierarchical system, and Walt's above Han Solo and Ehrlich both. How could they fire him for that?"

"What Becca means—and obviously I think she's right—is that my kind of authority isn't meant to be publicly asserted that way. If I lose my subordinates' confidence—say, because I abused my authority or they perceived what I did as such—then I'd have to resign as dean. Being fired doesn't arise, Jamie."

Walt offered Becca his arm to the dining room. I felt chastened by Becca's account of matters and shamed by her disapproval. Rather more meekly, I tried another tack: "Look at it this way: what are Ralph Ehrlich's politics?"

"Pretty right-wing. At least, whatever happened, he'd see FAR as the real troublemakers, not STAR."

"And he was standing next to Charles Rowland at the demonstration. I could hear the two of them adding their own little digs about turning the campus into a ghetto. In any event, what else besides politics have those two got in common?"

"I take it that was a rhetorical question. But I happen to know the answer: Rowland's been dating Gwen Ehrlich lately."

"No kidding!" I said, momentarily diverted. "Do you suppose they're—no, they couldn't!"

"Jamie, when will you get it through your head that the people you call straight—dull, unattractive, even reactionary people—have sex lives, too?"

"I take it that is a rhetorical question? And I was trying to make a point, back there. Since you knew that Ehrlich is opposed to the divestment movement, and he was attacking a FAR student, even though the original violence came from the other side attacking a form of protected free speech, you stepped in to restore order. He did, too, Becca, in about three seconds flat. It was really impressive."

"Restoring order when a biased security chief was contributing to disorder. You're right, that's clearly the way to present it. But, Jamie, we're right, too. It will carry a lot more weight if our position wins, next week, and Walt isn't called upon to defend himself at all." Nonetheless, I felt a little less ashamed of both my words and my judgment.

"Jamie," Walt asked, "Were you particularly concerned because it was Mike that Ehrlich went for?"

"You know, I think so. What went through my mind is that, beyond Ehrlich, we have Endlich, that is, the State Police. Whose most recent line of inquiry, I happen to know, involves the students—particularly those that campus officials say are troublemakers. Well, the real trouble is Mike's getting that label pinned on him, because he was with me when we found Sharon's body."

"You don't think there's any chance Mike had something to do with the murder, do you?"

"None whatsoever. But Endlich is feeling pressured by his superiors, who are getting it from the Ebbing family. Even distant twigs on the family tree have certain privileges, it seems. They're offering a twenty-thousand-dollar reward, did you know? So the cops might find it prudent to turn around and apply the pressure to someone like Mike."

"On the other hand, not even Endlich is capable of fabricating a credible case out of nothing."

"All I was really trying to do, with my quixotic little gesture, was keep a sensitive kid from being harassed."

"Quixotic may turn out to be the least of it."

After dinner, Becca retired for the night, and Walt and I went back to the library.

"I didn't want to say this in front of her," he told me, "but the worst part of it might well be that I was moved to intervene between Ehrlich and Mike because of your influence."

"Because I'm known to be a divestment supporter?"

"And because you're also known, in certain quarters, to be my mistress."

"What a word! Anyway, I'm not, anymore. For months, all I've been is more trouble for you!"

"If you're waiting for me to contradict you, don't hold your breath. From the moment you first walked through that door"— it was conveniently situated for him to point at dramatically— "you've been interfering in one thing or another!"

I decided this was not the time to tell him about my relationship with Virginia, her Jane Austen articles, or Jenny Metz's report on her own visit last week, when Virginia had listened and seemed to agree. Yet it was my hopes for Virginia's recovery that were prompting my consternation about Walt's possible loss of the deanship. In trying to imagine their life once Virginia was released, I felt it might be better if Walt got another job. Ebbing was indeed a dead end for him as an academic, but there were a great many openings for someone with his administrative background—at institutions where no one knew Virginia's history and where there'd be a research library for her, other specialists in women's literature, perhaps a graduate seminar. But all this presupposed a successful administrative experience on Walt's part, not an obligatory resignation with political overtones and hints of a sexual scandal.

I suppressed this entire train of thought and astonished myself with what came out instead, "Walt, if you're forced to resign as dean, I'll go to bed with you again."

"Frankly, Jamie, I don't want any consolation prizes. Or maybe I'm just too tired right now for it to have much appeal."

"Well, it's been a long day. Perhaps you'd better head on home."

"But I haven't told you why I asked you to dinner in the first place."

"I reserve comment on your definition of *asking*. Wasn't it because of all this about Ehrlich and your job?"

"What I need to tell you about is another problem. It's not going to work about Erin."

"What isn't? Her job?"

"The point is, it's not her job. The history department was divided on the appointment."

"Divided how? There are only five people in History, if I'm not mistaken. Erin herself wouldn't be voting, naturally, and what's-his-name—Dick Terry—is on sabbatical this term. So that leaves three department members to be consulted."

"Well, Rice is for her. As chairman, he's heard only good reports about her teaching. And Crowder said he didn't know her very well but would be willing to go along with the appointment, at least for the year, and let her compete with other applicants for the regular line. But Rowland—"

"Is against it. Naturally. As a historian, Erin could eat him for breakfast and spit his nit-picking, racist quantitative conclusions out between her teeth."

"An attractive if confused metaphor." Walt smiled for the first time in hours.

"But surely Rowland doesn't exercise a blackball. Why can't you just go to the personnel committee and report a 2 to 1 vote? It's not as good as a unanimous one, but especially at this late date—"

"Rowland says if I pursue the appointment any further, he'll raise the lesbian issue."

"Raise it how? Erin's not in the closet or anything, and even at Ebbing College you can't just go to a committee and say 'This woman is a lesbian so we mustn't hire her.' I mean, *can* you?"

"You might. But Rowland threatened to make it a moral turpitude case. The charge is that Erin seduced a student, one of their history majors."

"She did not! The student tried to seduce her."

"Rowland says he has evidence, Jamie." A camera, I wondered, pointed through Erin's open curtains on the off chance and capturing Ann's willful striptease, Erin's holding and comforting her? Surely that was the sheerest paranoia on my part. Yet what other evidence could he have of something that had never actually taken place but whose scenario was certainly open to misinterpretation?

"Look, Walt, I'll tell you what did happen." I gave him the whole story as I knew it. "So you see," I concluded, "Rowland could have a witness, even a photograph, I guess—though I can't for the life of me see how he could get that lucky—but it would be a false picture of what actually went on."

"How could we ever convince a committee of that? Much less the president and the trustees, if it went that far? You don't know the way these people's minds work, Jamie: they think all lesbians are out to seduce straight women and that, in any case, 'lesbian' is synonymous with deviant, unstable personality." In short, all the arguments I'd made to Erin in another context were echoed back to me. "Besides, they're all men and they're sure they couldn't control themselves if a naked young girl offered herself to them. At least, they prefer to think they couldn't. You and I may know better about Erin—"

"Do you, Walt—really?"

"Of course. I know she's a fine person and probably one of the *least* crazy members of the faculty, but there's no way the whole thing can come up publicly without a whole lot of the mud sticking to her. It's a lose-lose situation."

"That's just what *she* said about—oh, God!" I told him about Lee's letter and my own advice. "I said it was the only way to keep their relationship going and growing. And it would be all right, because after all Erin would be *here* for the year, and she'd have the money to join Lee in Africa for Christmas."

"Are you sure she's already written?"

"I'm afraid so. Lee had to let them know about the grant by the first of May, next week. Anyway, I don't think Erin would want to write and say, 'Come home.' So it just makes things that much grimmer for her. And there's nothing I can do about it. Nothing!" I put my face in my hands, but I didn't cry. I was beyond that.

Walt put his arm around my shoulders. "Jamie, you shouldn't—"

"I know what you're going to say: I shouldn't have told Erin the job was hers. But I didn't even tell her when she asked what she should say to Lee. I'd already told her, you see—after the business with Ann. Then when the issue of extending the grant came up, I just used it to remind Erin that she did have a life of her own. Also that she'd be able to afford that trip. *You'd* said it was all pro forma!"

"Well, I thought it was. And you gave a friend good advice when she asked for it. Neither of us had any way of knowing the whole thing would blow up in our faces."

"So why did you say I shouldn't have told her?"

"I didn't. What I was about to say was that you shouldn't have to be the one to break the news to Erin. It's my job, but I'd be grateful if you'd be with me when I talk to her."

"Certainly."

"And maybe, if I haven't lost all my credibility after the divestment vote, the three of us could figure out some way to fight back. They haven't got anyone else for the damn job!"

I nodded my head in exhaustion and misery. Walt's arm tightened, and he held me against his rough tweed jacket. "Would you like me to stay here tonight?" he asked finally.

"If I said yes, would you say whatever it was you said before: something like 'Frankly, my dear, I don't give a damn'?"

"No, I'd take you upstairs. Though I'm not up for the other Rhett Butler bit, where he carries her."

"In fact, you told me before that you were too tired to—"

"I think I can manage."

He managed. And, although I had sworn for a range of excellent reasons never to get into bed with Walt again, I felt no deep shame over my lapse, only a familiar and abiding comfort. Our bodies came together in ways that awoke some good memories and familiar responses. It was a milder version of my reunion with Alain.

Oddly enough, this contrast, or an aspect of it, was in Walt's mind, too, the next morning. "They tell me you went to bed with your husband recently," he remarked as we were dressing.

"Honestly!" I sat back on the bed in my underwear. "Years ago, coming out of a movie theater, I saw this old guy wearing a sandwich board that said WHO KILLED JFK? Once he saw he had your attention, he flipped up that card and it said FBI AND CIA. If you didn't walk on right away, he'd keep turning over cards, and you could read all about the second assassin and the bullets and the Warren Commission whitewash and so on."

"Jamie, what has that got to do with anything?"

"Just: I've been thinking of getting a sandwich board myself. On the outer layer it would say I SAW MY HUSBAND OVER SPRING BREAK. Underneath that, I DID SLEEP WITH HIM, and then BUT I'M NOT GOING BACK TO HIM. And maybe, for those who wanted to read further, I could have separate cards, in smaller print, to explain that decision, my present emotional state, and a few sexual details, like how many times and in what positions."

"Okay, you've made your point! Now please get some clothes on before I rejoin you on that bed!"

"Now, that's not such a bad idea," I told him. So he did and we did and it was even light-hearted. It definitely did not feel like farewell.

"I'm afraid this means the Contras get their hundred million after all," I said, afterwards.

"What?"

"I told Carlos the other day that my going to bed with you was as likely as Congress turning around and voting that money."

"You told Santiago? And *you're* worried about people prying into your private affairs?"

Walt and I found Erin in her office, and we told her what

had happened to her appointment. She seemed to accept Walt's judgment about letting him fight the case if, as he repeated, he had any standing left in a week, but none of us could come up with a workable strategy.

"I'm not as afraid of the lesbian issue as you are," she told him candidly. "I haven't really got a career to ruin, after all. But I agree that it's easier to lose on that issue than to win. Legally speaking, of course, I have no claim on that job."

"Only morally," I muttered.

"The dominant ethic around here," Walt explained, "is caution: Don't Rock the Boat. That's really what's holding back divestment, not a bunch of outright racists. Because it's not even clear their investment strategy is the soundest one, it's just what they think is the safest."

"So we have to figure out a way of presenting Erin as the most conservative choice," I said.

"Well, she is already on the spot. But Rowland won't let us keep the sexuality issue out of it, and even if we prove there was no wrongdoing—what they would consider wrong-doing—they'd still rather have somebody it was absolutely impossible to raise such a question about."

"Professor Eugene Eunuch," I suggested.

"Of the University of Oregon at Eugene," added Walt.

"Except that he's in eugenics." I noted that Erin was in no mood to appreciate our game; two inveterate punsters must have seemed to her like exceptionally dubious allies, just then. "Surely all the publicity about sexual harassment—even Ebbing has its guidelines and procedures nowadays—must have made it clear that ninety-nine percent of the problem comes from straight men."

"Not ninety-nine percent, Jamie," Walt protested. "Women students do get crushes on male teachers and try the kind of thing Ann did with Erin."

"It all comes down to institutionalized male power anyway."

"Surely it's not always so ideological," he maintained. "Didn't you ever have a crush on a professor yourself?" he asked.

"Sure, but I wouldn't have made advances to him. It would have been like—taking the initiative with a denizen of Mount Olympus. And everyone knows it's up to the god to turn himself into a swan or a shower of gold and pick the girl out. Which is why we now have rules about sexual harassment—because too many of those guys were playing gods and damaging actual women."

"Well, what about the other way?" Erin asked. "Did a professor ever offer you an A in return for favors?"

"Not exactly. One of my profs did make a pass at me once, but he didn't mention any quid pro quo. So I just dropped his course."

"That's all you did about it?"

"Uh-huh. He didn't hurt me or anything, and besides it was the liberated Sixties. Fuss-making wasn't cool. Actually, though, I wondered what I'd done to provoke it, because I guess I was more shocked than anything else that this fat old man—he seemed unbelievably ancient to me, though he must have been under fifty—could think for one minute that I would—"

"I feel kind of like Mike Freund, myself," Walt announced.

"Okay, I'll bite. How come?"

"Because I find I want to punch out anyone who ever tried to mess with you—or made you doubt yourself."

"That's very lovely," said Erin, "but it just shows how this campus is seething with all kinds of heterosexual tensions right beneath the surface. Yet a case like mine would still be a losing proposition."

"Unless we can work out some way of turning it around," Walt countered. "Speaking of male professors and women students, you don't think Ann herself is Rowland's witness? That he has some kind of hold on her?"

"He *is* a professor in her major field. But I'd be prepared to swear her approach to me was genuine. If it wasn't, I give up trying to judge human motives ever after."

"I'll investigate that angle, though," I offered.

"Take it easy, Jamie," they replied in chorus.

"Meanwhile, if the two of you are through for the moment, I'd like to finish preparing my eleven o'clock class," Erin observed without rancor.

"Walt can go, but I have something else I'd like to bring up. It'll only take a minute."

As the dean left the room, Erin raised her eyebrows at me. "It's hard to follow your love life without a score card, Jamie."

"If it's that obvious, you don't need one."

"Maybe not, when the two of you come marching into my office radiant with what you just did, to tell me I'm about to lose my job for something I didn't do! Heterosexual adultery versus lesbian chastity: A lesser woman would point out the horrible irony!"

"It's worse than that," I apologized. "This business of your appointment is what brought us back together."

"Look, I'm still sane enough to realize that it's not your relationship that's my enemy here. And Walt is a good person to have in my corner. But what else did you want to talk about, Jamie?"

"I just wanted to say it's not true that you haven't got a career to destroy. When that book of yours is published—"

"If I ever get it finished—"

"—it's going to be a blockbuster. In the appropriate scholarly circles, of course."

"So you're saying I should watch my step and avoid all scandal, so that just maybe I can get a job once the book is released?"

"No! Am I? No, of course we have to fight this with every weapon at our disposal."

"Name two."

"We're smarter than they are—and we're right. Besides, we have healthier sex lives."

"I wouldn't call either of us a walking ad for the sexual revolution."

"But I also wanted to say something else: I hope you'll accept the trip to Africa as my gift. It's a guilt offering for helping get you into this mess."

"Jamie, you'll be unemployed yourself by then!"

"But I've learned one thing this year: I can always land on my feet—economically speaking, if not in other ways."

"Well, I don't see how I could—I wouldn't even take money from Lee, after all—but I'll think about it. It's incredibly generous of you, anyway."

"Think about something else, too. In your spare time, of course."

"What?"

"Whether you still think I should publish my suspicions about Nellie's role in the Breckenridge Fire."

"Requires no further thought whatsoever. Charles Rowland has convinced me where you couldn't—that and what Walt had to say about how the personnel committee would react to his accusations. There's absolutely no need to let anyone in on Nellie's evolution into the Torch of Germantown. It's just guesswork on our part, anyhow. And you've got a book—with a potentially brilliant introduction, by the way—without that."

I had won our long argument, but the reasons made me feel as if I'd lost.

Laurie and Ann were waiting for me at the archive with a new proposal. "We want to have a big thing next Tuesday night, before Wednesday's meeting of the board. Not a debate, a big forum, with lots of room for people to ask questions and get answers. Like about divestment maybe hurting the blacks more than helping them."

"Well, who do they think has asked us to work for divestment? But you're right, of course: there are a lot of honest questions like that, and if they get good answers we'll get more signatures to present on Wednesday. And maybe more people at whatever you're planning to do while the Trustees are filing in and actually meeting."

"Another vigil, with a funeral motif. But we wanted to know if you'd come and answer questions at the Tuesday thing, be one of our resource people."

"As long as you don't call me that. Or a 'facilitator.' And your 'thing' is what we used to call a teach-in." I felt very old, as I often did around these two. "Meanwhile, Laurie, are you all right—after yesterday's confrontation, I mean?"

"Oh, I'm fine. Mike's walking around looking poetic, though, with his arm in a sling."

"Captain Ehrlich must know a few tricks we never learned in self-defense class," I commented.

"Wasn't the Dean wonderful?" she went on. "He just wiped the floor with those STAR warriors."

I was about to express appreciation of the pun, when Ann interrupted. "The dean? If you weren't so busy being a heroine yourself, you'd have noticed that it was Jamie who got the dean into it."

"Oh, don't spoil it! Don't you know I've always had a terrible crush on Dean Walters? He's so cute and distinguished-looking and sort of *responsible*."

"I thought you were in love with what's-his-face." I realized this would sound more impressive if I could remember the name that went with the face. "Frog," definitely would not do.

"Roy," she supplied. "Oh, I am, I am. Roy is for real life, the dean is for my dreams!" I hoped this distinction was making the proper impression on Ann. I also wondered briefly if Mike Freund's love for Laurie was real-life or dream to him. But Ann was my assignment. I asked her to have lunch with me—ostensibly for an update on her history project.

In the event, it wasn't even so ostensible, since I approached the issue by way of my discoveries about Nellie and the problems to which they led. "The thing is," I said portentously as we waited for our lunch to arrive, "almost anything is subject to misinterpretation."

"Do you think you're misinterpreting what Nellie did when she got out of the clinic?"

"No, a crime was committed—at least, the house really burned down, and no other explanation was ever found. Nellie had an ample motive (I don't say sufficient, mind you, just ample), and I've now learned she had the opportunity, as well. You can't misinterpret arson leading to murder. Though you may have more or less sympathy for Nellie, given your understanding of the circumstances."

"Then that's the real problem, isn't it? The sympathy."

"Part of it. Only it's not so much Nellie as the rest of us—any woman who tries to experience her sexuality to the full—and particularly other lesbians. Because it sends the message that this kind of loving makes someone crazy—worse than crazy."

"But Nellie was just one woman."

"Doesn't matter—people tend to generalize." I homed in on my actual objective. "It works the other way, too: they bring all their preexisting myths and prejudices about lesbians to bear on an individual case, even when the particular person is a living contradiction of those myths. Like Erin."

"What do you mean?"

"I mean that Professor Rowland plans to use the lesbian issue as a way of making sure Erin isn't reappointed for next year. And it would probably work, because the people who make the decision already have a set of stereotypes in their minds. So all he has to do is present them with what they consider evidence of wrongdoing. In fact, the dean says it's worse than that. Even if the evidence is insufficient, they'd want to avoid the very possibility."

"So that's why he's been asking me all those questions about Erin!"

"Who? Rowland? Go on."

"Just about what kind of teacher she is and how she relates to students and all." She seemed unaware that even this might be a loaded formulation. "So I told him how great she is and how she's really shown us how to think like historians."

"That must have pleased him no end."

"And how the history majors all love her. Though the freshmen in Western Civ do, too. She makes it come alive for them. But she doesn't spoon-feed them, either," she added virtuously. "There's this girl—woman—down the hall from me who told me, 'Dr. Ni' Connor makes me feel smart.' I guess because she feels she's putting ideas and facts together."

"There was no mention of lesbianism in any of your conversations with Rowland?"

"Sure—he brought it up. Wanted to know if Erin had ever—tried anything on the students. And also if she ever proselytized. As if it's a cult or something. So I told him," her little chin rose defiantly, "I told him I'm a lesbian, too. It was the first time I came out to anyone!"

I groaned inwardly, but I had my answer. It was obvious to me—and, clearly, to Charles Rowland, as well—how that would sound to a committee deliberating Erin's reappointment. If he had any inkling of what had happened Sunday night, he didn't need any photos, because he'd also see how easy it would be to break this kid down with a few well-placed questions. To top it off, all she'd have to do is declare how much everyone loved Erin, that and admit her own sexual orientation. Relieved as I was that Ann wasn't Rowland's agent, I knew she'd be damning enough as his unwitting witness.

"It was funny, him asking whether Erin had ever hit on me. Because he's the one you hear the most stories about, himself—always the kind of thing that you're not quite sure how it was meant—much too vague to file a complaint about. So all the girls hope he'll get married soon. He's the only young—well, youngish—"

"Almost my age," I inserted wryly.

"—bachelor on the faculty."

"Hardly what you'd call an eligible bachelor, getting off on making little not-quite passes at students who have no recourse! Well, I understand he's dating Miss Ehrlich."

"What a couple!"

"So no one will be heartbroken if they get married? Nobody has fantasies about him, like Laurie with Dean Walters?" For the past hour, ever since that admission, I'd been titillating myself with the notion that one woman's unromantic comfort is another's unattainable dream.

"Fantasies about Rowland? Yuck!" she declared eloquently.

So I picked up the second half of my club sandwich and asked whether she had started making plans for law school the year after next.

I HAD NO desire to think about my new relationship with Walt—if, indeed, that was what it was. And I certainly didn't want to talk about it. I just wanted to collapse into it for as long as we both needed what it gave us. But the new circumstances that had brought us together—with Walt's job on the line and Erin's way over it—made that impossible. Besides, our problem last time had been rooted precisely in not talking about what we expected of one another. So when Walt asked if he could stay behind at the end of that Sunday's open house—he had something to say to me—I nodded my consent. It was hard to believe that it was only a week ago that Erin had stayed late, to tell me about the scene with Ann.

Walt's opening remark was more surprising than it should have been. "I was over at Hochstetter yesterday afternoon. Ginnie wants to come out of the hospital. Within the month, she thinks. And her doctor, well, he's one who worships the great god Caution, but he seems to be saying that if that's what she wants, we should go ahead."

"That's wonderful, Walt!"

"If you think so, I guess there's nothing more to discuss."

"On the contrary, there's everything to discuss, assuming you don't want to make the same mistakes all over again." I wished I'd been prepared for this conversation; it was important to avoid putting any of several possible feet in my mouth.

"Like what?"

"Like—oh do sit down if you're not really walking out—I can't think with you looming over me that way. Like what are your immediate plans if Virginia leaves the hospital at the end of May?"

"Her family has a place in Maine where we go in summer. At least, she and the kids go, and I join them for my free month. It's a good, quiet introduction to life outside the clinic: days on the beach, sailing, clambakes, and things. Just family, but it's a big family. Dozens of relatives around all the time. It's really idyllic."

"Funny: *infernal* was the adjective that leapt to my mind. Did Virginia say anything about what she wants to do with herself once she's out?"

"She did say she has some writing to do. But she can always write in Maine."

"In between clambakes?"

"You don't understand. Being at Harbor Island frees her from domestic responsibilities, all the pressures she'd face here in Jaegersville."

"What responsibilities?"

"Well, there's that big house, and the children and meals"

"Walt, you're living in that house right now and holding down a demanding full-time job. So how are you meeting *your* 'domestic responsibilities'?"

"For one thing, it's not so hard for a single person, especially with the kids away. I eat out a lot and never make anything very elaborate when I do cook. Well, you know that. Mrs. Hopkins comes in to clean once a week, and in between I sort of pick up after myself—you know, book-and-paper mess."

"I've noticed you make your bed as soon as you get out of it in the morning. And you send stuff like sheets and tablecloths to the laundry. So why can't you do all that when Virginia's in residence?"

"Because when she's here we have a regular *life*, Jamie. The kids and their friends are in and out. And we entertain a lot more. As dean, I sort of have to, and—"

"You've given a couple of parties this year, without a hostess. In fact, I think you're a superb host."

"With the help of Marian Crowder's catering service—see? another faculty wife with a thriving business—and usually an extra visit from Mrs. Hopkins."

"Well, why not? Virginia wasn't put on earth to be your hostess. Or even your wife and the children's mother. Maybe what she's supposed to do is her writing, precisely as if that were *her* business that she runs, only it's not thriving yet! As for the kids—"

"We're really only talking about the two younger ones, these days. Russ will be working at a camp up in Maine, as sailing instructor, and Craig has an internship in Washington."

"But the other two—Steve and Nicole?"

"They'll be up at the Harbor Island place, the way they are every summer."

"That's what they were going to do anyway?"

"Yes, they really love it up there."

"So let them go. Maybe each of them could spend some time here in Jaegersville—separately might be best—or you (and I mean just you) could join them up there for some of that swimming and sailing when you get your vacation. But it's not what Virginia needs."

"What makes you so sure?"

"Because I'm a writer, and I know. Look, I'm the last person to put down being free from domestic responsibilities. Mrs. Moyer doesn't let me lift a finger around here—except for the Sunday night cooking—and I love it. But I wouldn't love it if the trade-off were vegging out on the sand or in some sailboat. Not when I had a manuscript to get back to. And what about those family parties, with all the temptations they must involve for an alcoholic? Or has the whole clan taken the pledge?"

"There is that," he admitted. "They're a pretty bibulous bunch. It's been a problem, even with everyone watching Ginnie the way they do." I shuddered in heartfelt sympathy for Virginia with all those eyes on her. At least, I'd steered Walt away from the question of my special knowledge of the case. I knew I'd have to broach it with him sometime, but I couldn't imagine what time would seem like the right one—not this century.

"The point is," I went on, "Virginia mustn't return to the same life with the same old demands."

"Demands? What I'm trying to do is free her from—"

"Maybe. But you can be a very demanding man in a relationship. That's something I do know from experience, remember."

"Well, Virginia doesn't have a boyfriend on the West Coast who happens to have an additional girlfriend on the West Coast! Or a sexy husband who wants to add her to his harem in Paris!"

I restrained myself with an effort. "My point is, there's more than one kind of monogamy, and you're into all of them. You have a fixed idea of what a relationship is supposed to be, and you expect the woman to share it. Like: you talked before about how when Virginia's home you have a regular 'life.' Well, there are lots of kinds of lives, and some of them are actually death for certain people. Oh, don't sit there with that hurt-feelings look. Try to think about Virginia for a change, rather than a foreordained set of roles for her. Really think."

He looked startled. But as I had told Erin a week earlier, he was a nice person. And—most important—not stupid. So he actually thought, visibly and painfully. "Well," he began after a long pause, "maybe it wouldn't be so bad to set up, say, light housekeeping instead of heavy responsibilities, right here in Jaegersville. Live like graduate students, only with more money and comforts. But where does that leave you and me?"

"Where I guess we really belong: in the column marked friends, not lovers. I don't know: maybe it wouldn't make any real difference if we kept on seeing each other until Virginia came home, but I can't help thinking it does matter. Spiritually, I mean."

"A word I never expected to hear on those lips!"

"But you see what I mean?"

"I see. I even agree with you, dammit. But—does it have to start tonight?"

"Tomorrow will do. We've got a tough enough week ahead of us as it is."

So we began that week with a pleasure I tried not to think of as bittersweet, even though both of us knew it was the last time.

As for the week itself, we had the vigil on Monday, the teach-in on Tuesday, and a silent funeral march to open the vigil on Wednesday. There were a thousand signatures on the FAR petition by the time we turned it in.

The trustees chose to ignore all the petitioning and vigiling and marching but voted for divestment anyway, because of a last-minute coalition formed on the board itself between the most cautious savings-in-an-old-sock Pennsylvania investors and the liberal clergy. I told myself the reasons wouldn't matter in South Africa, and here on campus something had been started that might prove hard to snuff out. For the present, at least, no one was in a position to call for Walt's resignation as dean, which meant he could launch the campaign for Erin's reappointment.

15

＊

PERHAPS INEVITABLY, THERE was a letdown as the campus settled back to its routine after the unexpected divestment victory. I allowed myself to become immersed in the end-of-the-year routines of my last classes and conferences with student writers, and I got down to the business of writing the introduction to *Helen-Elizabeth*. Any eccentricities in my behavior would have been attributed to my preoccupation with Lizzie Ebbing's prose, as I rediscovered the peculiar enchantment of her love story. Erin had shown me the way to introduce readers to both the special intensity and the historical dimension of women's relationships in the nineteenth century, while my background as poet and critic helped me argue that this delicately nuanced subjectivity was the living antithesis of pornography.

Lizzie and Nell even entered my dreams, along with that other unrestful presence, Sharon Reilly. I never could remember, in these dreams, that all three of them were dead. Rather, what seemed important was that all of them knew secrets from which I was debarred.

Yet the introduction proceeded, and it was on many levels a creditable piece of work. When Richardsons sent me a contract for my first book of poems, I decided that, once the introduction was completed, I'd also approach them with the critical edition of *Helen-Elizabeth.* Meanwhile, in an act of symbolic midwifery, I got Becca to witness my signature and sent the document back to what I could now confidently call "my" publisher. I knew no comparable joy—but then, what joy is ever comparable to that one? Better, I knew no *other* joy in those weeks.

Joyful or despairing, however, I also had certain social responsibilities. In early May, as part of the long-term strategy we'd worked out, Walt gave a small dinner party and a larger cocktail reception for Erin, both on the pretext that, although she'd joined our faculty under circumstances it would have been inappropriate to celebrate, we still wanted to welcome her among us. Clutching my glass of mineral water, I circulated through both of these functions. Walt's instructions were to let no one suspect I was following a careful script as I planted subtle suggestions here and there that were to flower into a ground swell of support (mixed metaphor and all) for Erin's retention. According to my scenarist, I was to avoid the L-word, unless it came up, which it certainly had never done at any *previous* faculty party, and to maintain my serene assertion that Ebbing was unquestionably fortunate to have Erin around. Not fortunate beyond its deserts, whatever I might privately think, just fortunate. "The line is, it's a perfect match," Walt informed me sternly.

I found this playacting far more exhausting than an open struggle. Nor was I crazy about taking my orders from Walt, although he was the acknowledged expert in such maneuvers. Watching him in action, in fact, forced me to admit that there is more than one kind of courage, maybe even more than one kind of political courage.

It is some measure of my state of mind that, as Erin and I left Walt's house at the end of the cocktail party, it occurred to me that at least the dean's *wife* would get to stay on when the guests went home, assessing the party's successes and failures, indulging in mutual congratulations, and falling into bed at last with her partner in academic diplomacy.

Erin's comment dovetailed with this ephemeral longing for a life that could never be my own. "You don't have to go through this charade for *me*, you know."

"Who else are we doing it for?"

"I don't mean the party—that was lovely and I hope it works. But this business of kissing Walt on the cheek and leaving with his other guests. After all, I know you two are a couple again."

"Uh-uh. You missed a play on your scorecard. Virginia's being released from Hochstetter, and I'm trying to help him prepare for their new life." I invited Erin back to the house to say hello to Becca and see what Mrs. Moyer had made for dinner.

"Well, I sort of pigged out on those canapés, but I'll come in and say hello. Every time I see Becca, these days, I get the feeling it's really good-bye. What do the doctors say?"

"They don't expect her to make it through the summer."

The students showed up at the last few classes in scanty garments that seemed to flop or melt off their youthful bodies. "There comes a moment every spring," Bill Robards proclaimed, "when the majority of kids come to class in shorts, and when that happens we know we've blown it for the term: no way can we get through anymore." In keeping with both the spirit of this pronouncement and the official calendar, classes ended and finals began. Since there are no exams in creative writing, I was free to spend all day on *Helen-Elizabeth*. All day, that is, after my morning run.

I'd already put on my sweat suit and running shoes, the Wednesday morning of exam week, when the telephone rang. It was Edie Gold, Becca's long-time editor at Richardsons, and now mine, as well. "This isn't about your own book," she began, "but I just made the connection—Ebbing College—and I thought maybe you could help me. We got a proposal a few weeks back from a professor at Ebbing. It seems he's discovered a manuscript that sounds absolutely fascinating: a typical nineteenth-century girlhood memoir, except that the girl emerges as a lesbian."

"And what does Professor Rowland—if I'm not jumping to conclusions—"

"No, that's the name: Charles Rowland."

"Just what does he propose in his proposal?"

"He wants to do an edition for us. Well, the manuscript itself sounds wonderful, as I say, but I'm kind of shaky about him. His prospectus didn't have a lot of substance to it, and when I spoke to him on the phone just now—"

"You actually called him up about this?"

"Of course. It's potentially very interesting. Anyway, in our conversation, he sounded rather—eccentric—and he kept emphasizing what I'd frankly found to be the weakest part of what he'd sent us."

"Which was?"

"A smirking approach—scandal-mongering. I told him we were interested in the book only if that sort of thing could be kept to a minimum. Naturally, he missed the point and assured me the manuscript was what he called 'very tastefully done'— when it was *his* approach I was concerned about—and he promised to send me a copy right away so I could see for myself. He said he'd be picking it up today."

"Picking it up?"

"Apparently, it's somewhere out of town, at the author's home. Anyway—"

"Of course, Brockland. He must still think—go on."

"He hung up before I could ask him about publication

rights, guarantees of who holds the copyright, and so on, and then, before I could get back to him, I got another call, so he was gone by the time I phoned again. Then it occurred to me that in the meantime I could get in touch with our other Ebbing authors and see if you or Becca knew this guy and if he's as— well—weird as he sounds."

"Believe me, Edie, he's at least as weird as he sounds, and I can give you ample documentation. But you won't need it, because he couldn't provide the guarantees you spoke of. The manuscript is the property of the college—he didn't discover it at all—and I'm the one who's been delegated to prepare it for publication. I mean, it's my *job*."

"You're telling me he wanted to involve Richardsons in some sort of bootleg publication? I don't know if I'm more shocked by his nerve or his naïveté! I trust when you do the legitimate edition, you'll let us take a look at it."

"Of course. I was planning to. But I'm not quite finished with my introduction, and then the edition has to be approved for release by the executors of the Brock Trust. Which may take a bit of doing because the material is so sensitive. But Walt— ah—our dean is running interference for me and he's sure it'll work out okay." This reference to Walt's diplomatic activities put another idea into my head, and I asked, "Edie, you're pretty sure Rowland's off fetching the manuscript right now?"

"That's certainly what he implied."

"Okay, great! Look, I'll get back to you about *Helen-Eliza-beth*. We're going to make a beautiful book together!" I slammed down the receiver, yelled over my shoulder to Mrs. Moyer, "I'm off to Brockland," and ran for my car.

It must be confessed that, as I took the road out of Jaegersville, my motives were not the purest. Or, rather, my motives were irreproachable, but the means I proposed to use were far from it. If I could catch Charles Rowland with the manuscript in his hands, I thought, that and the letter offering it to Richardsons would give me something to trade for Erin's job: a contract for the coming year and no interference with her candidacy for a regular appointment after that. Of course, if I missed him at Brockland, I'd still have Edie's evidence, and it would be just as damning, but his being caught in the act would add a dramatic element. It was, in any event, an action in my own style: more immediate and also more productive than all Walt's behind-the-scenes maneuvering.

I understood now what Rowland had been bickering with Sharon about at the Christmas Dance. He wanted to be the one to bring *Helen-Elizabeth* into the world, although he patently had no sympathy for either the text or the relationship that informed it. Sharon, of course, would have taken a different position. But I didn't stop to think through what Sharon's position would have been.

The iron gate at Brockland was padlocked, so I had to use the key my caution had impelled me to copy back in December. This made me feel very smug about my foresight. I left the gate open behind me, in case I needed to make a quick getaway, and parked under a small clump of shade trees just around the last curve from the house—for the element of surprise. The trees were maples, I noticed, and, thinking of the long driveway behind me, I muttered, "Nothing can stand more retired from the road than Maple Grove." It's always wise to take Jane Austen along on an adventure, although as it turned out, I might have done better with *Northanger Abbey* than *Emma*.

A car—Rowland's, I realized, from the obnoxious bumper sticker—was parked at the porte-cochère and the house was unlocked. Once inside, I wondered for a moment whether I should conceal myself until Rowland came down with the manuscript or tiptoe up to the study and catch him pawing over it. There would be no need, down here, for a very elaborate hiding place, since he wasn't expecting anyone to walk in on his triumph. Behind the drapes would do or, better, the cupboard under the stairs, so I could hear his descent and pop out. But, deciding that a confrontation would be best of all, I made my way quietly upstairs, blessing my running shoes at every polished oak step.

It was hardly the moment for introspection, but I did reflect that my year in an obscure backwater had led me into some uncharacteristic adventures. Tiptoeing up these uncarpeted stairs to catch a manuscript thief and (thereby) save my friend's job was as unlikely an occupation for me as setting a trap at the college's Christmas dance, or—perhaps the strangest thing I'd *ever* done—creeping through the underground passages of an unfamiliar hospital to visit a psychiatric patient without dealing with the red tape. I have two sides to my nature, contemplative and confrontational, and neither was well served by all this literal slipping around corners. Well, my present slip would be my last, and that phase of the operation was about to be replaced by direct action.

Rowland had not shut the door to Lizzie's study. I could see him leaning over her desk, paging rapidly through the manuscript. Regretting the lost opportunity to bang the door open and cry, "Aha!" I stepped in and asked, instead, "What's that you're reading?"

He appeared unperturbed and behaved as I've noticed academics often do when interrupted at their desks. You may have dropped in to borrow a book or find out what happened after you left the faculty meeting, but they'll start off by bringing you in on whatever they were reading or writing or even just thinking when you happened by.

"Do you realize that this is only a copy?" Rowland asked rhetorically. "That stupid Sharon," and here what he had to say departed drastically from the detached tone he affected, "couldn't tell a photocopy from a nineteenth-century original!"

"Did Sharon tell you she'd stolen the original from the archive?"

"She didn't exactly volunteer the information, no, but I caught her with it when she came upstairs to have a look at it the night of that silly dance, and that's what she claimed it was. If stupid Sharon," it was becoming his standard epithet for the dead woman, who, whatever her faults, had been highly intelligent, "if she had just let me have a closer look—which she wouldn't—everything would have been different! Can you believe this? A photocopy!"

I guess it was his interrupted-academic manner that led me to what I might otherwise have suppressed as too provocative an explanation. "But it *was* the original she stole. And that was still here the night of the dance—although I'd already made a bunch of copies, so it didn't matter so much about the original, anymore."

"*You* made the copies?"

"Sure, I wasn't about to lose it a second time. But that's the point, after all: it's mine to lose or hold onto, as temporary overseer of the archive. What good would the original have done you?"

"The same it's doing you. I'd have published an edition—with introduction and notes, of course."

"But any reputable publisher—and a disreputable one would hardly serve the purpose—would have done just as Richardsons is doing—made very sure the document was what you said it was and that you had the rights to it."

"Well, you don't own the thing, either," he countered, rather like a small boy caught out in a schoolyard quarrel.

"But I do have legal access to the archive and the assignment of selecting and preparing its contents for publication. It's in my job description. I've even initiated the formal process for permission to publish my edition."

I let him assimilate this information for a moment. Once he'd done so, I planned to point out that mere frustration of his designs was not the end of it. Richardsons had his letter and prospectus on file, offering them a manuscript to which he had no shadow of a right and which he ought not to have had in his possession. His peddling of stolen goods would be made public unless Erin was assured of her job. Rowland's thoughts were running in a different channel, however.

"You sound like Sharon," he informed me. "Except that *she* didn't want to see it published at all. But of course I realized right away that publishing it was the only appropriate revenge on the whole filthy place."

"On the college? How is that?"

"For the same reason Sharon didn't want to let it out. It shows up their precious Elizabeth Ebbing as an out-and-out flaming lesbian." I understood with a shock of pedagogic recognition that Rowland must never have actually read the manuscript. All he knew was the one sensational fact. And, recalling Lizzie's accumulation of detail in the matter of fabrics and odors and slants of light, I considered how beside the point that one sensational fact really was.

It certainly explained why Edie had been so puzzled by the wishy-washy prospectus he'd written: he'd had nothing to be substantive *about*.

"I'm afraid I still don't see," I continued on the line he'd begun. "Why did you want to show up Ebbing's benefactor?"

"Because it would serve them right for the way they ruined my career. First they saddle me with a teaching load that's twice as heavy as in any decent college and then, when I manage by staying away from their stupid parties and the joys of family life"—he meant sex, I think—"to get some research done anyway, no one will publish my articles or offer me a proper job, because I come from the faculty of a place like this! This is not academic life, it's a perversion of what academic life is supposed to be, and only perverts could flourish in it. Look at Sharon and your buddy you brought in to replace her. Now it all makes sense, a perverted sense, anyhow, because it turns out the whole thing was founded on perversion from the git-go."

"I see: you wanted to blow the lid off Ebbing, the lid of hypocrisy that had damaged your professional status and opportunities? Something like that?"

"And the beautiful part is that I could do it while getting a second chance, professionally speaking. You know, this kind of scholarship, about sex and relationships and queers and so on is very big in history at the moment." I suppressed a misplaced urge to set him right about recent trends in historical scholarship. "So bringing this book out could put me right in the spotlight at the *same time* that it showed Ebbing up for what it is."

"Then you wouldn't actually be fouling your own doorstep, because it wouldn't be your doorstep much longer. You expected offers from other—better—colleges to follow publication."

"That's right. *You* don't expect to be stuck here all your life—why should I?"

Well, my job was only temporary, and I'd taken it out of loyalty to Becca. But Rowland was right, in a sense: Ebbing College wasn't where I expected to end up. "Okay," I went on, "so you had your own uses for the stolen manuscript, once you'd found out about it. But about Sharon: she wanted to keep it quiet because she also assumed it would be a—blot on the name of Ebbing?"

"I think it was more personal than that. If it was published, everyone would know about *her*, especially since she's a descendant—what a laugh, the way she always went on about The Family!—as well as a member of the faculty."

"Surely there wasn't anything like that to know about Sharon personally!"

"Look, she knew her own conscience a lot better than you do. And you're not one of them, I'll say that much for you, so how could you tell one? Besides, Sharon was also scared stiff of publication. She didn't want to dirty her little hands in real historical competition. So she certainly didn't want this real dirt published. All she wanted to do was sit on it the way she did on her own research. Sit on it and do those fancy English crossword puzzles!" He mimicked our late colleague's voice: " 'What a clever double definition: Ebbing and lesbian! And what's an anagram for homosexual?' "

And all of a sudden, I had the solution to my own puzzle. When Sharon wrote about her fear of something's "getting to Orlando," she wasn't sending me a message in a language she didn't know, she was just making an anagram, the kind I deployed every month for the Pangloss puzzle! Orlando-Rowland. It was a simple, if slightly defective anagram, with an extra *o* instead of a *w*. But she hadn't had much time—*even less than she thought*—and maybe that was why she underlined it, so I'd pay special attention. I hadn't, then, but I was certainly doing so now.

Orlando-Ro(w)land. Say she was afraid that he'd get his hands on the manuscript and wanted me to know about it. That didn't mean he killed her, did it? Maybe it depended on what she was doing in my office. "So—ah—is that what you two were arguing about at the Christmas Dance?" He nodded impatiently. "You went back and forth over the ground for all that time? It was more than three months from the Christmas Dance to— ah—the time she died." Even to him, I couldn't bring myself to say, "when she was killed."

"Well, I thought I could convince her eventually. After all, she was a historian, too. But she kept insisting that once the book came out everyone would know who stole the manuscript. She didn't seem to realize that would be small potatoes."

"Except that you couldn't *get* a stolen manuscript published."

He ignored this and pursued his original train of thought. "Anyway, she also wanted to create an obstacle for you. You wanted to see the thing published, so she *didn't* want to."

"Why'd she have it in for me?" Why was I asking him?

"She said you seemed nice enough at first, except for this obsession of yours about professional publications. But then you started having a bad influence on the dean."

"A bad influence?"

"Well, I thought that was a little crazy, myself, until the STAR rally, when I saw how you really do. Sharon said 'bewitched by sex,' but that's what she meant." What had really bothered her about this purported sorcery, though: that it was sex at all, that it was adulterous, or that the witch was someone other than herself? Even Sharon might not have been certain, and there was no way I'd ever know.

"I gather she changed her mind about me, though, about the 'bewitching'?" I asked. Not having survived to the day of the rally and seen my nefarious influence at work.

"I don't know why. Things he let fall—Walters—when they were going together gave her a higher opinion of you. She said you had 'a certain integrity.' " His voice mocked the idea as well as the tone. I sent wry thanks her way for recognizing that much. But Rowland went right on, "She actually said she wanted to give the manuscript back to you."

Had Sharon come to understand how much easier I'd be to deal with than Rowland? Did she also sense that I'd be less dangerous? Or did the threat from him appear only after she announced her decision to give back *Helen-Elizabeth*? Was there even a real threat? I decided to find out that much.

Maintaining my tone of casual inquiry, I asked, "Do you know if that was why she came to my office that day? Was it to return the manuscript?"

The answer was a lot more than I bargained for. "Well, that was what I thought, too, but it turns out she didn't have it with—" He stopped short, as he realized his admission and I realized my mistake. The last thing I felt like doing, though, was crying a triumphant "Aha!" Maybe if I pretended not to have picked up on it? Rowland gave me no opportunity to see how dumb I could play. Looking me straight in the eye, he said, "Well, yeah," and it was a complete confession.

I was silent and, for the first time, really, sensibly afraid.

"I thought she was going to leave it for you. That's why I told Gwen to alert me if Sharon let herself into the archive at any time."

"Let herself in?" I asked weakly.

"She had a key. Never gave it back after the archives were reorganized under the new Chair. You know how things are around here." It was the sanest thing he'd said so far. The more orderly the surface of bureaucratic procedures anywhere, the more chaotic the actual practices beneath. "I figured I'd have to act fast to get the manuscript if Sharon went over there when you weren't around. But after I bopped her with that little statue of yours," *bopped* almost made me retch, but I held on. The important thing was to keep him talking, whatever words he chose. "I couldn't find the manuscript. So I realized it must still be here at Brockland and I decided that was a fine place to leave it until everything cooled down, especially since I also had Sharon's keys to the gate and the house itself."

Thinking of nothing beyond a little altruistic blackmail, I had been imperceptibly drawn onto the other side of the line again, that side where the conventions and reticences called sanity cease to govern conversation. It was like my first interchange with Virginia, once I'd come through the tunnels intact, but, in this case, the retirement of the censor was by no means as harmless.

"So you didn't go over there actually intending to kill her?"

"Oh yes, we'd already had it out, over and over. I knew there was nothing left to do." The super-rationality of this explanation should perhaps have warned me off further questions.

But with all the desperate good sense I could summon, I was trying to figure out my escape plan, and it didn't seem to matter what I did meanwhile.

"Then why did you use a weapon you found on the spot?"

"It seemed like a surer thing. I had my knife, of course. Ever since I got mugged my first year in graduate school—Columbia,

you know, that neighborhood—I've carried a switchblade."
Rowland looked at me far too speculatively and I tried to direct
his attention to another aspect of the issue. Luckily, he seemed
to want to discuss the whole business. Naturally enough: I could
imagine nothing harder than keeping a thing like that secret for
months. This recognition made me wonder about his possible
accomplice.

"Was it Gwen who let you into the archive?"

"Not exactly. She'd seen Sharon go in, of course, without
signing the book, and then she called me. But when I got to the
library, she wasn't at her desk." And she'd stayed away until
well after the body was discovered. "I found the door unlocked,
though. I don't know if Gwen—"

"And you've never asked her, now that you're dating and
all?"

"No, but I thought everything would be neater if we got
married." Enough people who aren't homicidal maniacs have
crazy ideas about marriage that, by itself, this would not even
have constituted evidence. But he went on, in an increasingly
bitter tone, "And we'd have been able to get away, free of the
whole place, if it weren't for you." Did he mean my blundering
out to Brockland today, or my original discovery and copying of
the manuscript? Or even my telling him no publisher would
touch his edition anyway? By this time, probably, all three were
mixed up in his mind to make a neat motive for eliminating me.

You can never find a Brown Belt when you need one, I
reflected sententiously, recalling Laurie's confident moves
when she'd faced down the "STAR-warrior" at the shanty town.
My own self-defense class, all those years ago, had taught me
more precepts and tricks than real skills, but borrowing a little
of that confidence for the occasion might just make them work.
If you can, ran one precept, *get some object between yourself and
your assailant.* Like Lizzie's writing table, already blessedly
intervening. Then, *hit him where it hurts the most and run.*

Suiting my action to this admirable advice, I shoved the table—hard—into Rowland's groin, and missed the vital spot. The table did knock him over, though, and I made for the long hall and the stairs at the end of it.

I knew Rowland was in some pain, and I'd toppled him off his feet, but no matter how slowly he got up and started after me, I certainly couldn't make it to my car before he either caught up, switchblade at the ready, or leaped into his own vehicle and initiated a chase scene just like in the movies. Nonetheless, it was worth the attempt, because the Brockland grounds offered more places to hide and a possible access to the road beyond. Unfortunately, as I unlatched the French door I heard Rowland's rapid footsteps along the upstairs hall. Revising my plan—if "get the hell out" can be dignified as a plan—I left the door open and stepped back inside.

The long velvet curtains I'd scouted as a hiding-and-jumping-out place when he *wouldn't* be looking for me were totally inadequate now that he was. I darted across the foyer to the other location I'd considered when I first came in, concealing myself in the closet under the stairs just as Rowland began his thundering descent right over my head. The door had a latch—one of those hook and eye arrangements—on the *inside*. I could think of absolutely no good reason for this, unless Lizzie Brock had been inspired to put it in, decades before my birth, by a direct leading of providence. I fastened it with gratitude and struggled to catch my breath.

Short of a coughing fit, I'd be safe in here for the time being. As long as Rowland blustered around this end of the house, I could even stay informed of his movements. But I might not hear him go outside, and I certainly couldn't tell when to make a run for the door to the exterior world that I now saw as my one real chance. A car starting was the only outdoor sound I'd be able to hear from this dark cupboard that would soon cease to represent salvation to me. In fact, I even thought I could make out the sound of an engine off in the distance, on the road. But Rowland certainly wouldn't oblige me by driving away, not as long as he knew I was somewhere at Brockland. If he was smart, he'd just wait—unless he got the idea that I'd already managed to escape. Only the open door was likely to suggest that—faintly— and there was nothing I could do from here to further the illusion.

Rowland paced irresolutely for a moment between the door and the paneled hallway, apparently unwilling to commit to either outdoor or indoor exploration if one meant leaving the other clear for me. The imperative of pursuit would draw him to the door, but I could imagine him looking out at that green expanse and picturing me comfortably battened down in one of the old house's innumerable hiding places. So he'd turn back and consider those nooks and crannies, while recalling the un-defended acres of lawn and woods where I might even now be eluding him.

His desperate stumblings and my no less desperate efforts to track them while following his train of thought were brought to an abrupt halt by the sound of voices.

"Professor Rowland? Hi, we're looking for Jamie, Dr. Jameson. Do you know where she is?" It was Laurie and Ann, as incongruous here at Brockland at midday in mid-exam week as the latch on the inside of a cupboard, and even more wel-come—by the object of their visit, if not their present interlocutor.

"Dr. Jameson? I don't know where she is." Strictly speaking, he was telling the truth. "What makes you think she's here at Brockland?"

"This is where she said she was going," replied Ann logi-cally, "and her car's out there."

"Her car?" he repeated dully. I could imagine him looking out the French doors and seeing only his own.

"At the bend in the driveway. We thought that was where you were supposed to park, so we left the van there, too." Which

explained the engine I'd heard a few minutes back and assumed
was out on the highway. They'd taken my cue about the element
of surprise without even knowing it was one.

"A car," he said again. "Of course she'd have to have a car."
If he'd lapsed momentarily from crazy into stupid, he was now
castigating himself precisely the way any of us would for ne-
glecting an important detail.

"So she *is* here? What have you done to her?"

"Nothing," he asserted, truthfully. They were jumping to
conclusions that were off the mark, yet near enough to evoke a
denial to which those two lent no credence

Instead, they tried calling my name.

"Jamie, Jamie." I remained silent, waiting for the situation
to develop. If things worked out, not only would I be able to
escape, after all, but we might capture him.

"I tell you she's not here,' he uttered feverishly, trying to
quiet them and prevent me from hearing and responding to their
call.

"Don't give us that, you old lecher," Laurie shouted, arro-
gantly pitting her nineteen years and her exuberant sexuality
against his thirty-four and his unsavory reputation. "We know
she got a phone call and left for Brockland, and her car's there.
So where is she, Rowland?" They called again and listened for
any response, then repeated menacingly, "What have you done
to her?"

"Nothing, I—" It sounded as though he tried to push his
way past the two students or shove one of them aside and they
went for him. Like a blind person watching a karate film, I could
only hear kicks and scuffles and blood-curdling yells. These last
were in Ann's voice, following the first rule of the self-defense
class and forcing out terrible imprecations in what I took to be
Japanese or Korean, while Laurie presumably did most of the
actual fighting.

Unable to stand any more guesswork that held my own

survival in the balance, I pushed my cupboard door open a crack and flicked on the visuals. But I couldn't remain a voyeur at the scene of my own rescue. Laurie and Ann were doing very well— far better than I could manage, myself—but Rowland had a knife, they didn't know it, and I was their teacher, responsible by that fact alone for making sure they came out of this thing unharmed. Once again, though, I'd have to substitute common-sense tricks for real skills.

Watching carefully, now, for the moment he would step back toward the closet, I prepared to act. I undid the hook, cushioning it in my hand so I could work silently. As he passed the open door, I thrust my right foot out and tripped him. He fell to his knees—that part worked fine—but I lost my balance and tumbled on top of him and he made a wild, groping slash backward with his knife. I felt a sharp, jagged pain across my pelvis and thigh.

Things seemed to be happening in slow motion now as Laurie tried simultaneously to get me off Rowland and come in kicking, herself. The knife wound, awkwardly directed as it was, hadn't been very deep, but it hurt too much to move my hip. For a long moment, I rocked uselessly astride Rowland's back while he tried to break free and put his knife to more controlled and deadly use. Eventually, excruciatingly, I edged backward over his legs and feet, with new agony at each lurch. Laurie seemed to take her own sweet time selecting the perfect spot, before one neat karate chop behind the ear knocked him unconscious.

"Get the knife," I blurted. "Right side." Ann searched for it while Laurie perched warily on her victim. "Okay," I went on, quite as if I knew what I was doing, "Now use it to cut the cords off the drawing-room curtain so we can tie him up. *(Not Miz Ellen's poh-tieres,* an inner voice protested; I knew the students would have missed the *Gone With the Wind* reference.) "And be careful with that thing. It's evidence." I giggled hysterically at this belated caution and tried to pull myself to a more dignified, if no more comfortable position.

Ann returned with the rope and did a highly creditable job of tying Rowland's feet, hands, and arms. "Where on earth did you learn such workmanlike, I mean competent knots?" I asked her.

"Girl Scouts," she answered crisply. "Great organization for female bonding." It was a pun worthy of Pangloss herself.

"Good. Now we have to call the State Police and ask for Captain Endlich. You do it, Ann." I actually had a card in my wallet with the number, "while Laurie stands guard over our—prisoner." This was not a sentence I had ever envisaged myself pronouncing with a straight face. Apparently my face was none too straight now, in fact, as I grimaced in pain.

"No, first I've got to stop that bleeding." She looked around wildly for something that would work, then stripped off her tee shirt. "You make the call, Laurie, and tell them to send an ambulance, too."

"But what should I say happened, Jamie? Did Rowland—was it *rape?*" They still didn't realize they'd saved my life.

"No, murder. He's the one who killed Sharon Reilly."

By the time Laurie got back from the phone, Rowland was coming around nicely, and he began to make a number of ugly, self-incriminating remarks to the two students. The more he said, the more he seemed to need to say, so he was launched on a full-scale speech when the cops—a good dozen of them—arrived, and he spat what amounted to a confession into Endlich's broad, astonished face.

"Read him his rights, before it all goes down the tubes!" I intruded helpfully, trying to press Ann's folded tee-shirt to two places in my groin at once. I noticed the shirt's owner had covered herself with Laurie's poplin jacket, zipped up to the collar. Rowland could hardly wait for the perfunctory *Miranda* recital to conclude before he was talking again. And he was still going when the paramedics arrived to tend to my wound. They made two proper bandages and gave me a shot of something that jolted me into a manic mood before it had any effect on the actual pain. "Captain Endlich," I called, as they placed me on the stretcher. "You haven't said thank you, but I trust you won't forget about the reward!"

"Ya. Who gets the twenty thousand, you or the girls?"

"Not me. Just these two *women.*" I bit down on the word to push back my dizziness and we continued out the door, Laurie and Ann hurrying alongside.

At the porte-cochère, the procession halted, and I spoke to the two students. "Look, I don't want to be silly and overdramatic about this. It really hurts right now and there was certainly a lot of blood, but the knife probably didn't go in very far. Still—just in case something goes really wrong, I want to make sure you fix up the book, my introduction to *Helen-Elizabeth.*"

"What do you mean?"

"Something I've learned from today's experience: There's only one reason to publish, and that's to tell the truth—as much of it, at least, as we can get hold of. But that much we do have to do. So it's got to be put in about Nellie and the Breckenridge Fire, whether we like it or not. We just have to try to *explain* why a woman in her situation would—"

"Oh, no we don't!" they chorused. "That's why we chased out here in the first place—to tell you."

"Tell me what? And one at a time, it's kind of hard for me to focus."

"We've found Nellie—in the records," said Ann. "She didn't start that fire. She couldn't have, because she was *here*— in Jaegersville—all along!"

16

✳

SHE'D BEEN IN Jaegersville the whole time, the elusive
Nellie Breckenridge. That's why we couldn't find her anywhere
else.

Laurie and Ann waited with me at the emergency room and
drove me back to Jaegersville in the late afternoon, once the
staff doctor, determining that Rowland's knife had missed all
vital organs, had sewn me up and allowed himself to be convinced that I was no longer in shock and happened to have a trained
nurse's aide waiting at home. On the way, my two research assistants, first-class, told me about what they had turned up.

"It had been arranged that Nell would be Lizzie's brides-
maid," Ann explained. "God knows who dreamed that one up,
but it got her a sort of furlough from the Smedley Harris place.
So she came up here, and, for all intensive purposes, she never
left."

"Intents *and* purposes," Laurie corrected her.

"It doesn't seem to make much sense either way, does it?"
Ann countered, perplexed.

"Not much," I agreed. "But go on. Do the dates really jibe—

or could she possibly have committed the arson and then proceeded coolly on to the wedding?"

"Out of the question. She left the clinic on the 22nd; the wedding was way out here on the 23rd—late afternoon, with a reception on into the night. The night of the fire."

"You know, I was going to check Lizzie's wedding date myself, a few weeks back, but I got interrupted. Actually, I think it was you two, something to do with the South Africa business—" I caught my breath and tried to find a more comfortable position on the van's wide seat.

Nellie's story took up the rest of the trip, although we didn't fill in many of the details until later. As we pieced it together, Nellie was awakened the morning after the wedding with the news of the disaster that had overtaken her family. The Ebbings had kept her on as their guest. She was, after all, not only their daughter's closest friend—for they'd recently had reason to deplore that intimacy—but their son's all-but-official fiancée. ("Surely there must have been a big funeral back in Philly, though. Check that out, Ann.")

"And the girl was filthy rich now, too. Let's not forget that part," she put in.

Lizzie and Brock didn't take a honeymoon. It was never clear to us if one had been planned and then abandoned when tragedy struck or if they'd never intended to go anywhere. They were already in the country, after all, and he had his own place. Once it was clear that Nellie was now independent and enormously rich, she and Lizzie must have made their plans.

"But wouldn't she have had a guardian, Jamie, like the heroines in books?"

"She might have, for a time. Though you would think we'd have found some trace of him, in that case, on the Philadelphia end. But he'd mostly be looking out for her fortune, and, after all, she didn't want to do anything *outré* with the *money*. She bought herself a little house, you say?"

"Yeah, that's one of the puzzling things. The house was supposedly at the corner of Elm and College Streets in Jaegersville, but there is no such corner."

"Campuses do expand into the community, even in Jaegersville, PA, so these days it's all Ebbing College out that way. In fact," I added with sudden geographical insight, "the corner of Elm and College, if there were one, would be just about where the Campus Inn is now. Which means we've been having lunch, sometimes in order to discuss the mysterious disappearance of Nell Breckenridge, on the very spot where she lived, for—how long?"

"Well, she died there in 1928, which makes it sixty years. That much we found before we came looking for you."

"In the college van, I noticed. Does this excursion count as a field trip?"

"No, it's just that when Mrs. Moyer told us you'd gotten a phone call and then went out to Brockland—did Rowland call up and lure you out there, Jamie?"

"No, I lured myself. To save Erin's job, was my idea. Well, in a backhanded way, that much got accomplished; the dean can probably put her appointment through with no trouble now. But it's too long a story to go into in the middle of yours, which is already in the middle of Nellie's."

"Anyway, once we knew where you were, we thought we'd come out and surprise you with the good news. As a student chauffeur, I can always get the keys to the van, so we—ah—signed it out and came after you."

"Just in time to save my life, as it happens, should there be any repercussions from your—ah—borrowing the vehicle. For that matter, you're still on a mission of mercy, as far as I'm concerned. But go on about Nellie."

"Well, all we've really got so far is that she lived in her little house in Jaegersville from 1868 until her death. That was November 19, 1928, by the way. It's all in the local records. She's on the tax rolls—and the electoral ones, too, once women's suffrage came in. She was a regular person, living right there."

"Right under our noses—my nose, actually, since I'm supposed to be directing this research project—all along. I'd rather not have my nose rubbed in it, but I must say I get the willies when I think I might have gone into print with this story without knowing that the couple in *Helen-Elizabeth* stayed together for the rest of their lives! I suppose you're going to tell me next that Nellie's buried in the churchyard at St. Stephen's, down the street from my house?"

"No, back at Brockland."

"You mean, I might have stumbled over her grave playing hide-and-seek with Rowland and his switchblade if I'd ever made it out into the grounds? Of course, the way I've been screwing up, I'd probably have tripped over the tombstone, gone flying, and never noticed the name! Well, when I'm feeling better, we'll have to look for Nell's grave and take her some flowers. I bet no one's done that since Lizzie died, just a few years after she did." I was babbling on a bit to create a counter-force to another wave of pain. "Speaking of Lizzie, she was right, you realize."

"Of course she was," Ann humored me. "But about what, in particular?"

"On the last page of *Helen-Elizabeth* (and now, of course, I wonder when she wrote that page) she announces calmly that, despite what had just happened—Manley's betrayal and the forced separation—she is certain that she and her beloved will be together always. And so they were, for sixty years, 'til death did them part."

"That's one point I can't understand, Jamie. You've read a lot of Lizzie's journal, I know, and you told us Professor Parsons had been all the way through it. So how come neither of you found anything about Nell during those sixty years?"

"Well, when she first described the journal to me, Becca

did comment on the uniformity of tone Lizzie uses to tell about her daily activities, her literary work, and her emotions—especially her hatred of Brock. I've always wondered about whether I was supposed to be sensing as much irony as I did in her obsessive descriptions of household routine. But if it's all a kind of—code, where the most stable element in her life is never directly mentioned, it begins to make sense. It also explains her special preoccupation with the annual moves to the country, opening up Brockland, and so forth. That really meant going home to Nell."

"And that's another thing: what would Nellie have done with herself the rest of the year—at least while Brock was alive?"

"I won't be surprised if we check the pattern in the journals and learn that Lizzie came here regularly throughout the year, probably for weeks at a time. Otherwise, I imagine Nell traveled a lot—maybe even went to Europe to hear some music—and I bet you anything she paid good long visits to her lover in Pottsville. Anyway, even at the times when she was alone in Jaegersville, Nellie had her own music—and her freedom."

"You think she gave up just like that on her whole career?'

"It certainly looks that way. And, after all, Lizzie went on with her writing, but never published a line."

"What about Lizzie's husband?" Laurie broke in. "Wouldn't he suspect?"

"I just don't know. On the one hand, people in the last century took those intense female friendships as a matter of course. They didn't automatically assume a sexual relationship the way we might. Even the husband might not. On the other hand, these two had a history that Lizzie's family, at least, knew about. And Alfred Brock knew a thing or two about sex, himself. We know he had a semi-official string of mistresses. So perhaps they had an understanding, even a deal: she'd bear his children and be his hostess, but otherwise they were both free to pursue their own amours. Since that's a freedom he'd presumably have arrogated to himself, anyway, the only novelty would have been their talking about it, that and Lizzie's insisting on the same rights for herself. Which might have been easier, in a sense, since her lover was a woman."

"That made it easier?" asked Ann, rooted in her own times.

"Sure: it would be no scandal for them to be together so much—because of what I was just saying about women's relationships—and the material basis of patriarchy could still be preserved. Brock would have no reason to doubt that the heirs to his property were the—ah—fruit of his own loins." Rarely had I been so conscious, myself, of possessing something you could call loins.

"But what about the Breckenridge Fire?" asked Laurie. "We know now that Nellie couldn't have set it, but that doesn't bring us any closer to who did."

"Well, that's been a mystery for nearly a hundred and twenty years," I reminded her, "and no one's even sure it really was arson. Anyway, it certainly isn't our job to solve it."

When we got back to Jaegersville, Laurie and Ann helped Mrs. Moyer get me settled in the downstairs guest room. After I took one of the pills they'd given me at Hochstetter, I slept the sleep of the drugged, if not the damned, and came to, still rather feverish, at around four in the morning. In the silent house, I mulled over the new surmises about Lizzie and Nell. They had constructed the largest and most secure closet money could buy and had stayed in it—together—for sixty years. Well, for them, coming out had been both involuntary and traumatic. At the very beginning of their lifelong love affair, they'd been exposed to the harsh consequences of such a love: separation, forced marriage, incarceration, that vile Procedure, and the threat of an even uglier marriage in the offing. The Breckenridge Fire had come like a demonic deliverance, but no one could expect a second such reprieve in one lifetime.

It was not their love that was wrong—this they must have firmly believed—but its discovery. They resolved to do nothing, ever, that carried the risk of further exposure. From one point of view, Lizzie had been married a day too soon. But that marriage was also the ideal cover for her relationship with Nellie. They must have decided to pay the price of this protection: sex with a nasty man, first of all, along with the pains and possible dangers of childbirth; the demands of an upper-class Victorian household; and the need for Nellie to remain at the apparent margins of Lizzie's life. But there would be consolations and compensations, as well. Lizzie gave birth three times. That might have ended her physical relations with Brock and, as the journals reflected, the children themselves were a source of delight to their astonished mother.

Another set of trade-offs was built into the bargain. In exchange for their security, Lizzie and Nell accepted—condemned themselves to—silence. Safety, as far as they were concerned, required that there be no public recognition of their relationship. This silence was exactly what they'd sought, of course, but it must have been agony to live through all those years explicitly denying their identity, even if the right to that identity was purchased by that denial. For instance, it occurred to me, Lizzie must have been the object of both genuine and strictly formal sympathy when Brock died. People would have commiserated with her over the loss of her "life's partner," when her true life's partner was alive and well, brought even closer to her by the event. Whereas, when her real partner did die, she was forced to mourn alone.

As those 1980s women, my students, had noticed right away, embracing silence also meant abandoning any notion of a career in either literature or music. Nothing that called attention to oneself could be a desirable form of expression in the eyes of Lizzie and Nell. Not when the self who took the spotlight, however dim and modest it might have been, had something of such magnitude to conceal. So the one would continue to write and the other might keep up her music, as long as those pursuits remained as private as their love.

That's as far as I got, before falling back into confused dreams. The next thing I knew, it was broad daylight, and both Becca and Mrs. Moyer were bending over me. As Mrs. Moyer checked my stitches, I noticed that they actually looked more like staples.

"That's sort of what they are," she agreed.

"How do they put them in, then?"

"You didn't watch?"

"It's so strange: I don't remember. And later, I just assumed if they called them stitches that's what they were."

"They used to be until they came up with this new technique. It's like my family: I remember my grandmother would stuff a chicken and sew it up with a regular needle and thread. But by the time I started keeping house, there were these skewers to lace up the bird, and I don't know when those came in. They—"

"Mrs. Moyer," I requested weakly, "Could we please talk about something else? There's something about the image of that stuffing— "

From the depths of the armchair in the corner, Becca chuckled sympathetically and changed the subject. "I should tell you," she began, "that we fended off a couple of reporters yesterday afternoon, while you were still at the hospital. Well, we certainly couldn't make any statements—we had no idea what had happened—and you were in no position to. But we did give a picture of you—that soulful one they're going to use on the book jacket—to the wire services."

"With luck," I groaned, "no one will pick it up. I wish I could forget the whole thing."

"I gather," said Becca, penetratingly, "that you're not particularly proud of your role in this murder investigation, even though you did capture the killer."

"It's not so much the investigation—though Lord knows I screwed that up, too—but the whole situation, from the beginning. If it hadn't been for me, Sharon Reilly would still be alive."

"That sounds a little far-fetched, dear."

"No, it's not. If I hadn't talked so big about publishing the manuscript—"

"Which you still think is the right thing to do?"

"Absolutely. But not at the cost of someone's life!"

"Jamie, it was Sharon who made her life the stake, not you, by stealing the manuscript and keeping it hidden. And she did that, remember, before she knew you or anything about you."

"Except that I wanted to publish it. So then it got worse. She did get to know me and was apparently starting to think well enough of me to reconsider what she'd done, taking an archival document that way. Not that she'd necessarily have waltzed in and put it back, but she might have tried reasoning with me about publishing it. And, in the process, I might have been able to convince her." Mrs. Moyer made a sound somewhere between a sniff and a snort. "But then I started sleeping with Walt, and she lost what respect for me she'd been developing, and *I* lost an opportunity I didn't know I'd had. To make her see the light, I mean. Anyway, I had shown I couldn't be trusted. So, when things got even worse for her— after Rowland found out about the manuscript and wanted to publish it for his own far less worthy ends—she had nowhere to turn."

"But she did turn to you—or try to—eventually."

"That may be because Walt and I had broken up by then, or just because Rowland's actual threat had become worse than my imagined one. In any event, there's nothing to congratulate myself about there, either, since it was her decision to come to me that signed her death warrant."

"I still can't agree that any of it was your fault. How were you to guess—"

"Remember, I had more than three months between the Christmas Dance and Sharon's murder when I knew the two of them had somehow been involved in the theft of the manuscript, and I did nothing about it."

"After all, you had the original back where it belonged and you began working on the thing itself, not the murder."

"You're partially right, of course. But I got involved in the trap at the Christmas Dance because I was worried that Walt might be the thief, and then I was so relieved to find out he wasn't that I didn't think through the implications of Sharon's involvement—particularly with Rowland in on the business as some kind of side-kick or adversary." Becca nodded. "Then," I went on, "after Sharon was dead, I didn't pursue my intuition that Rowland had something to do with it."

"As I recall, it was really Walt who argued that the manuscript theft couldn't possibly be involved in the murder."

"But I was the one who dismissed the word-play about Orlando, instead of following that through." I had to stop and explain this allusion. "But, you know, on a simpler level, it was that I didn't feel I could trust my own prejudice against Rowland."

"What?"

"Well, I never liked him. The first words I ever heard out of his mouth were against divestment. Then Sharon told me he'd written a pro-slavery thesis—"

"Surely it couldn't have been that bad."

"Exactly what he said about slavery. Anyway, this term he's been more active in the anti-divestment movement, working with the STAR kids and all. And his homophobia started showing. I guess that actually began before Sharon's death, when Erin came up to lecture. But he didn't have a chance to do anything, as far as I know, until he vetoed her reappointment. I also learned—did you know this?—that the women students all consider him something of a menace."

"So, knowing he was—what?— a racist homophobic sexual harasser made you decide he couldn't be all bad, so he hadn't killed Sharon?"

"In an odd sense, yes, because I knew I'd want the murderer among us to be a racist homophobic sexual harasser. That's where we go back to something more basic—in a very real sense I never fully believed there could be a murderer among us."

"What worries me most," Becca pronounced slowly, "is your saying that if you hadn't come here, Sharon would still be alive. Well, that's assuming nothing else had happened to convince Charles Rowland that he had the same rights as God. If this affair with the manuscript drove him over the brink, I'm sure other things would have, too. And as far as what *good* you've done here—" She paused for breath.

"Becca, it's very nice that you want to make me feel better, but you certainly can't claim it's what you had in mind when you asked me to fill in for you this year. Messy love affairs, stolen manuscripts, murdered colleagues, botched investigations, campus intrigue, that's what I've brought you."

"What it adds up to is that you've brought me *life*, Jamie," she said superbly. "Don't ever forget it." She pulled herself up from the chair and marched out, Mrs. Moyer in her wake.

As I lay there mulling over the two mysteries, I saw another connection between them. Sharon had wanted to silence the manuscript for reasons that were reminiscent of those I attributed to Lizzie and Nell. It was hardly my business or my right to judge a decision two desperate young women had apparently made in 1868; the most I could do was to try to understand it. Sharon, however, was of my own time and condition. With all due compassion, I could still say unequivocally that her reasons for refusing to publish her own research were misguided. And her motives for committing theft in order to prevent *Helen-Elizabeth's* seeing the light of day were simply wrong.

On the other hand and even more simply, Charles Rowland's motives for wanting to see it published and having it appear under his aegis were also wrong. He feared and condemned the kind of relationship with which *Helen-Elizabeth* was centrally concerned. But, *for that very reason,* he wished to use it to smear the College he believed had injured him, while simultaneously resuscitating his career with this publication. He had been wrong to have those motives at all, and wrong in his estimate of what would happen either to Ebbing College or to his own professional status as a result of bringing out the book. But in the long run, none of that mattered, those errors of judgment and morality, because he'd been prepared to kill in defense of them. That was the thing: Sharon had made both kinds of mistakes, too, but Rowland had backed his up with murder.

THE POETS' HOUSE, as some colleagues had taken to calling it, was an ideal environment for an invalid, despite my power struggle with Mrs. Moyer over how long she should treat me like one. I can't say the visitors from police or the prosecutor's office were precisely what the doctor ordered, but they needed me to fill in the background on what, to them, was a baffling and esoteric tale about some old papers that had unaccountably led to a murder.

The obscure motive combined with the obscure locale made for minimal media interest in Rowland's capture and confession. My "soulful" portrait appeared in a few Pennsylvania papers and on regional television but created little stir elsewhere. At Commencement two weeks later, I was something of a celebrity to the assembled student families—after all, I'd just been on TV—but my notoriety was not sufficient to eclipse Becca's far greater deserts. I still carry in my wallet at all times my photo of Becca receiving her honorary doctorate, the sun and her impending fate bestowing a translucent quality on her slender body in its black regalia.

After Commencement, she stayed in bed pretty much fulltime. Her daughter, Ellie, moved in with us after her law school exams ended—for the summer or as much of it as we should be vouchsafed. And I set to work rewriting the introduction to *Helen-Elizabeth.*

One afternoon, Erin stopped by with a triumphant expression on her face and a book in her hand. "I've found her diary!" she announced.

"What do you mean? Lizzie's journal is in the library, all 76 volumes of it. And I can't believe you've stumbled on Nell's."

"I wish I could! That's my project for next year, though I don't suppose they'll appreciate my tearing the Campus Inn off its foundations."

"Especially since there's absolutely no evidence that Nell kept a diary."

"Anyway, this one is Sharon's. I was packing up the apartment. Did I tell you? They've found me one for next year, with a real kitchen and a study. It's Camille Morris's place—she's moving into Rowland's, which I must say I'm glad I'm not doing. Anyway, I had to pack all the books, to make sure I separated my own from Sharon's that they'd never moved out, and there, behind a bunch of them, was *this.* It's all there: the manuscript, her feelings about you and Walt, her fears of Rowland—backed up with some pretty specific threats—although of course even she had no inkling he would actually murder her."

"And?"

"Well, you were right—say, 80 percent of the time. A lot of the nuances she saw differently from the way you did, naturally enough. But on the big things—for instance, I was wrong: she did overhear your conversation with Walt at the Campus Inn that first day. She knew you were going away for a week or so and then coming back for good, so that was when she decided to—act."

"So reading it will be like going through the juicy footnotes to a study I already know."

"A true scholar's simile. Unfortunately, it would also be like looking at yourself in a distorting mirror. There's a lot about you in it: she saw you, and at the same time what she saw wasn't you. It would be painful reading and, frankly, I don't think it's what you need just now."

"Then why did you come prancing over here waving it at me?'

"Sorry about the waving. What I wanted to know is, do you think I should take it to Captain Endlich?"

"No, the prosecutor's office. Their fellow working on the case is named Pfeffer. I'll get you his number. The diary sounds like just what he needs to fill in some gaps. There are points in the story where all they've had up to now were surmises—or Rowland's version of events. I guess I don't really need to be exposed to any more half-truths about myself, either. The self-hatred level's high enough as it is."

"You're still feeling dumb and incompetent, Jamie?"

"Well, not as bad since I started rewriting my introduction. I think the whole edition looks pretty good, now."

"It's all done?"

"Not quite, but take a gander at the title page."

She read out: "*Helen-Elizabeth,* a Memoir by Elizabeth Ebbing Brock, edited by Margaret L. Jameson with the assistance of Ann Teresa Capobianco and Laurel Messer."

"There's a dedication, too. Next sheet."

"In memory of Sharon Elizabeth Ebbing Reilly, 1941-1986, Professor of History, Ebbing College. That's really nice, Jamie—dignified. And it's a good thing you decided not to peek at what her diary says about you."

"I don't know. After all, there is a sense in which we're publishing this thing literally over Sharon's dead body."

"But you—" There was a tap at the door, and Mrs. Moyer ushered Ann into the room.

"I'm leaving this afternoon, and I wanted to say good-bye—well, to both of you, of course, but I didn't know you'd be here, Erin."

"You'll be seeing me in senior seminar next year. It's Jamie who probably won't be around."

"About that senior seminar," I asked Erin, "do you really have a course schedule already? It's that definite?"

"Walt says they're doing a rush job typing my contract. With History down two regular faculty now, the position, believe it or not, is that they don't want to risk losing me!"

I turned back to Ann. "Where are you spending the summer? Not to mention your ten thousand dollars?"

"Home in Pittsburgh. And I'll be looking for a job, not throwing the reward money around."

"I thought you'd want to use it for travel, or for summer school somewhere interesting—maybe check out graduate programs that way."

"That would be very nice," she replied politely, "but my dad's still out of work and my mom doesn't make very much. So of course that money has to go to them, when I get it." Of course. My assumptions were a painfully accurate measure of how far I'd come from my own background.

"What kind of job are you planning to look for?" Erin asked, while I indulged in a moment of silent, if useless, self-castigation.

"You know: fast food, checkout, whatever I can get."

"But you have all kinds of skills," I protested. "As your former supervisor, I know."

"You may know me, but you don't know Pittsburgh," was the gloomy reply.

"True enough. I did spend a long weekend there, though, just before—wait!" I rummaged through the mass of papers on my desk, eliciting an aside from Erin about the state of the archivist's own archives, but emerged with the phone number I was after. I told them I'd be back in five minutes. "Talk to each other, you two," I added, ignoring for the moment that this might be in any way problematic.

It was actually eight minutes before I came back from the hall phone. Ann was gaping awestruck at the title page of *Helen-Elizabeth*. "Jamie, I didn't know you were putting us down as coeditors!"

"Well, you were the one who discovered the crucial piece of the puzzle. But it was *supposed* to be a surprise until I got the contract." I glowered at Erin, though I understood why she would have been eager to find an impersonal topic of conversation.

"How was I to know?" she expostulated. "Anyway, kid, it's pretty good to get your name on a publication while you're still an undergraduate."

"But what about Erin? And Mike? He was the first one to mention the Breckenridge Fire."

"They get acknowledgments. See? Here's that page. I talk about the archive itself and thank the Brock Trustees and so on, and then there's the list of individuals who helped in one way or another: Michael Freund, Erin Ni'Connor, Rebecca Parsons, Sharon Reilly, Elizabeth Singleton Robards, and Preston Walters." That list, plus the title page, pretty much summed up my life in Jaegersville.

"You both look like cats that ate canaries. Ann, I presume, is pleased about that title page, but what did you just accomplish, Jamie?"

"A summer job. You've got an interview day after tomorrow, Ann, to be assistant coordinator of the feminist arts festival in Pittsburgh. It's held the last week in August, so the culmination of your work will be just before you have to go back to Ebbing."

"They want me to help run an art show?" she was puzzled.

"It's basically a secretarial and go-fer job, lots of detail work: calling people and then calling them back to change everything, troubleshooting with the printer, scheduling space, avoiding time and personality conflicts. And it's arts, plural, not just an exhibit, but music, plays, poetry. I read there myself, right before I came here, in fact. And this year they've got State Arts Council funding—whence the startling innovation of paying the staff—so they wrote and said that since, serendipitously, I'm now a Pennsylvania writer, they'd like to have me back. That was what I was looking for, the flier they sent. Anyway, my impression from talking to Nancy Evans, who'll be interviewing you, is that you've basically got the job. Your take-home pay won't be much above the fast-food level, but you'd start Monday—no looking around—and it's pleasanter work. Besides, you'll be able to put arts administration on your resume and meet loads of terrific women right in your home city."

Ann left with the festival brochure in her hand, reiterating her thanks, with assurances that, if she got the job, my reading would be a perfect jewel of scheduling.

"I take it," said Erin when she'd gone, "that some of these terrific women are lesbians."

"You take right, as Captain Endlich once said in—believe me—a different connection. I do want to see everyone live happily ever after."

"Speaking of Endlich, there are some who didn't get the chance to. I'd better see about getting Sharon's diary to the prosecutor."

"Well, I typed up the title page and the dedication and so on this morning, just to see how they'd look, but I still have an introduction to finish. I want Lizzie and Nell to live happily ever after, too."

"They didn't manage so badly on their own," she pointed out, "closets, compromises, and all." I nodded and turned back to my typewriter.

EDIE GOLD, in New York, had the Richardsons publicity people clip all the press references to what it pleased her to call The Manuscript Murder. Even the stubby inch and a quarter the *Times* devoted to the case was grist for her mill. Naturally, she was also eager to see the memoir that had inspired the case, and her regular phone calls during my convalescence helped get me back to my desk promptly. (It also helped that the truth I now knew about Lizzie and Nell was a pleasure to write.) When I finished the introduction, she suggested I fly to New York and hand deliver the manuscript. "It sounds like you can use a couple of days off, and I'd like to get to know you a little. You're welcome to stay with my husband and me."

But when I arrived that June afternoon, Edie had bad news for me. "Elinor Parsons called from Jaegersville. Becca's going fast. They're not sure she'll make it through the night."

"Oh, my God, I don't think there's time to get back to Philly before the last commuter flight out of there. Maybe I should—"

"No, there isn't. I called around, and the fastest thing is to rent a car. So I made a reservation, and there'll be one waiting for us by the time you've had a cup of coffee and a bite to eat."

"For us? You're coming?"

"I'm driving. You're in no condition for it, and I want to—to see Becca off, too."

It was very nearly the longest day of the year, but on what felt like the longest trip of my life, the light still didn't last us all the way to Jaegersville. "I really want to get there in time," Edie told me at one point, "and we're going to give it our best shot. But if we don't make it, remember you were with her for ten whole months at the end, and that means a lot more than

these last few hours." Yet we drove on, stopping once for ham-
burgers and coffee, once to use a gas-station toilet.

On Grove Street, Jaegersville, we pulled up behind a van
with Massachusetts plates. "Jack Parsons," I explained
briefly—and I let us into the house. There was no one downstairs, but in the hall outside Becca's room, Patsy was slumped
against the wall, sobbing in great gulps. "Becca's daughter-in-
law," I told Edie, as Patsy hurled herself into my arms. "Oh
Jamie, thank God! No, you're not too late. But it's just awful!
Jack had this idea that we should—*sing* her out, and he and
Ellie have been at it for hours, but I just can't keep it going. Not
knowing that it's Becca dying!"

Jack stuck his head out of the room, saw who it was, and
joined us. "You want to hear something hilarious?" he asked
astonishingly, after a brief hug for me and a polite handshake
for Edie.

"Hilarious?" I was not so far from hysteria, myself.

"Well, we're singing to Mom—the old hymns that she loved,
the ones they put new words to for all her marches and picket
lines. I wasn't sure she knew what we were singing, but when
we tried to stop, before, she made a gesture to go on. Anyway,
the nurse—the one who's spelling Mrs. Moyer—heard us and
asked, 'What are you folks, anyway: Evangelicals?' and I told
her, perfectly straight-faced, 'No, Quakers!' "

So I was laughing, too, when I went in to say good-bye to
Becca. Professionals undoubtedly have technical names for the
stages of sinking I witnessed that night, after Edie and I joined
the Evangelical Quakers around Becca's bed. The end came in
the middle of "I'm gonna sit at the Welcome Table one of these
days." We never got to "I'm gonna tell God how you treat me,"
but it was perfectly clear that, if there was that kind of God on
the streets of that kind of heaven, Rebecca Parsons was already
giving Him an earful about the injustice growing rampant on our
troubled planet.

Accustomed since childhood to the spontaneity of Friends Meeting, Becca's kids saw no need to prepare an order of events for the funeral, much less ask anyone to speak, and we scheduled a service for the following Sunday afternoon, in Becca's own drawing room.

It had also failed to occur to them to wear—even to bring with them—the kind of clothes most people associate with a funeral. As we gathered into a silent circle, I smiled at Patsy and Ellie's flowered skirts, Jack's "Teach Peace" tee shirt, and the shining blond hair and sandals of all three. It reminded me, by the attraction of opposites, of the last funeral I'd attended, for Alain's father and brothers. That was a chilly day, and St. Nicholas-de-Chardonnet, the holdout church where they still do the Mass in Latin, had been muffled in black, as were the assembled mourners. "Well, go out and *buy* yourself a black dress, then," Alain had snapped at me. "And go to a decent house. You're a countess now, remember." Far from remembering, I hadn't fully realized it. (And, at that moment, which was the beginning of the end for us, I still had no idea what it meant.)

Jack Parsons stood, bringing me back to the present. He told about Becca's last hours, and he and Patsy sang some of the songs that had seen Becca out. If the faculty guests had been disconcerted by the informal garb of the chief mourners, the Quaker ones seemed a bit shocked at the introduction of music.

One by one, others rose to speak. Walt, representing the college officially, realized that this was no place for official platitudes, and told of Becca's magic as a teacher. Carlos Santiago, calling a truce in his ongoing debate with Becca over nonviolence, talked about her commitment to justice. Betsy told us what it meant to live literally side by side with a woman whose life centered on writing. Guests I didn't know spoke about a Becca I did not always recognize.

Finally, I felt it was my turn. "Many of you have spoken, from your own convictions, about the way Becca lives on. Well,

I don't feel that she *is* with us. Her absence is too palpable and too painful. Yet I do see Becca alive in her beautiful children, and I hear her voice in the words she wrote in the last months of life." I read her final poems for their first audience. Then I sat down, there was another silence, and the beautiful children jolted Quaker tradition again—but this was not Friends Meeting, after all, it was Becca's last open house—by asking us to sing with them. It was "The Welcome Table."

"We want to do the Movement version," Ellie said from across the room. "Where shall we say we're gonna walk the streets of, Jamie? Where's the freedom march?"

"Johannesburg. No, Cape Town, it scans better." So that was how we sang it, and I dissolved in tears.

Something about the slow choreography as we stood up, stacked the caterers' chairs, and gravitated toward the food and drink laid out in the dining room, prodded me into recalling that the last funeral I'd attended had been at Ebbing College, Jaegersville, not on the rue Saint-Victor, Paris, for Sharon Ebbing Reilly, whose murderer I had helped bring to some version of justice. On this day of the dead, I'd failed to remember Sharon.

Although the house had been my home all year, the young Parsons were the real hosts. So at a certain point I sat alone on the window seat, watching the action. Walt came by with two glasses of champagne, offered me one, and plumped down beside me, moving in a little closer than I found absolutely comfortable. "Remember the first time we drank champagne, together, Jamie?"

"At the Savage Inn, right?"

"Uh-huh. And now you're going back for the summer all alone?" Well, I was certainly *going* alone, but, as the lanky, sensuous image of Jem Morgan slipped casually into my mind, I thought, *but I sure don't plan to stay that way.* Maybe it was Walt's nostalgia for our own recent history and maybe it was just that the relationship had taught him to read my unspoken responses, but his next question certainly meshed with my sexy train of thought. "And Berkeley, that guy there?"

"Well, that's a little complicated: it would mean living with —at least relating to—both Nick and his other lover. But I do plan to move back to California sometime in the Fall, once the project at the Inn is under way." *And once I've worked through— or at least figured out—what there is between Jem and me.*

As soon as Walt left, I returned to feeling bad that I'd forgotten Sharon as a loss, while remembering her as a story, almost a "case." *As* a case, at least, the problem with her name on it had been solved, as had those of Virginia, talking composedly to Betsy across the room, Erin, making what I suspected were highly political plans for next year with the Santiagos, and Lizzie and Nell, in their graves and in press. And now Becca, too. If they weren't all happy endings, they were resolutions, and I told myself I'd done the best I could.

ACKNOWLEDGMENTS

✳

NONE OF THE people in this book ever existed off the page.
Although I hope all are credible, they are, first and last, products
of the imagination. The places are also made up. Ebbing College, its Central Pennsylvania setting and the Savage Inn are all
figments of my mind. I have taken liberties with nineteenth
century history as well. You will look in vain elsewhere for Lizzie
Ebbing, Nell Breckenridge, their families, the Breckenridge
Fire, or Dr. Smedley Harris and his Pacification Procedure. All
are fictional.

I had much encouragement and assistance with this book;
however, I take full responsibility for the flaws. The most direct
contribution was made by Richard Androne of the Albright College English Department who, one memorable spring afternoon,
suggested that I write a mystery series featuring a detective
heroine who was a professor of poetry. Other contributors were
Doris Conklin, to whose comments I owe the character of Erin
Ni' Conner, and David Gilden, who suggested the creation of
Jem Morgan. Historical novelist Meredith Tax was kind enough
to read an early draft. Her specific comments taught me much,
particularly about how to incorporate social themes into popular
genres. Many others offered invaluable support, especially

Ryan Bishop, Ellen Cantarow, the late Katya Gilden, Carolyn Korsmeyer, Jane Marcus, Michael Messing and Toni Robinson.

Among those who have given more to my novel than any claims of friendship could require, Shelley Fisher Fishkin occupies a very special place, from her first reading of the book until its present state. Finally, the wisdom, humor and generosity of Milton Fisher and Carol Plaine Fisher have made the editorial process a pleasure as well as an education.

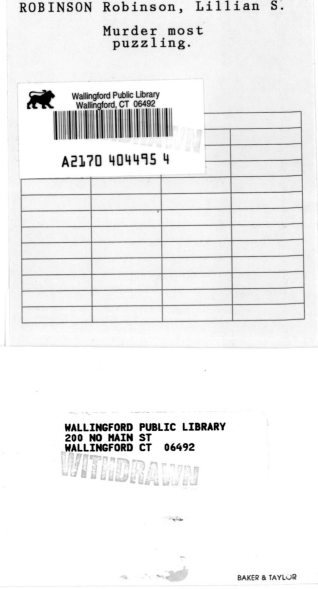